AN ESTATE
OF MEMORY

AN ESTATE OF MEMORY

ILONA KARMEL

AFTERWORD BY RUTH K. ANGRESS

THE FEMINIST PRESS
at The City University of New York
New York

© 1969 by Ilona Karmel Zucker
Afterword © 1986 by The Feminist Press
at The City University of New York
All rights reserved. Published 1986
Printed in Canada
90 89 88 87 86 6 5 4 3 2 1

Library of Congress Cataloging-in-Publication Data

Karmel, Ilona, 1925–
  An estate of memory.

  1. Holocaust, Jewish (1939–1945)—Fiction.
  2. World War, 1939–1945—Fiction.   I. Title.
PS3561.A67A83 1986   813'.54   86-25776
ISBN 0-935312-64-1 (pbk.)

Cover art: *The Past: The Great Synogogue of Danzig* (1984)
by Ruth Weisberg. Courtesy of Hebrew Union College,
Skirball Museum, Los Angeles, whose purchase of the
painting was made possible with funds provided by Sandy
Miller in honor of John and Idelle Levy.

Part One

Chapter 1

ON THAT DAY everyone in the camp was painted. Dusk was falling when the people, all fifteen thousand of them, marched out into the square of the Appellplatz and stood in rows four-deep facing a platform provided by a natural rise in the ground. There the camp authorities stood: on one side the dark blue Ukrainian guards; on the other the chief of the O.D. men — the Jewish camp police — and his aides, all in black but for the brass buttons catching the last light; the green group in the center was the SS.

The dusk deepened, blurring the mesh of barbed wires, changing the watchtowers to black squares. A shout. From the towers searchlights swooped down into the Appellplatz. And the painting began.

Buckets and brushes in hand, the painters passed by the immobile rows, splashing everyone's clothes with cross bars of red paint. All was still, only at times a bucket clinked or a blob of paint smacked to the ground. For an instant the searchlights went out. They came back on and the camp rose like a fortified city out of the dark: the flat-roofed barracks perched in rows upon the steep slope; the wires twice a man's height; and up on the hilltop the snouts of machine guns.

After an hour the SS and the Ukrainians left. The O.D. men took over now. "Quiet!" they yelled, but for once nobody took heed of them. Here a woman giggled, tickled by the brush; there, "Hello Rembrandt," a man guffawed, the painters reciprocating with "Would you rather be wall-papered, sir?" until the joking turned on him who had ordered the painting as a precaution against escape — on the German Lagerkommandant himself.

"Someone else would have wasted money on prison uniforms, but he, he paints us," they said and laughed. "What a head! A Jew he should have been, with such a head."

"A Jew." Seidmanka was laughing so hard the red mop of her hair

shook and shook. "Guess what? After the war I'll make him a partner in my business. 'Herr Lagerkommandant,' I'll say — " Pucker-
ing her long horsy face Seidmanka submitted to the brush, then
turned sharply, because the frail, graying woman to be painted
now was Rubinfeldova, her bunkmate, her inseparable friend.

"Don't splash her," Seidmanka warned the painter; then to Rubinfeldova, "Stop fidgeting. Stop it, I say."

Rubinfeldova stood stock-still. And now both of them looked at
the girl to be painted next. She was thin — not from hunger but
as some spinsters are, who defiantly, of their own will, seem to have
discarded the least roundness, the least reminder of abandoned
hopes. Yet she was young, barely over twenty, and her small tri-
angular face might have been lovely were it not for the sharp look
in her eyes, and for her mouth, full yet pursed to a deep-red line.
In another red line the paint cut across her cheek so hard she flinched
as the brush swung.

"Please, Tola," Rubinfeldova said softly.

"Princess!" Seidmanka hissed. "The only one to stand in the Appellplatz, the only one to be painted. Everybody else can talk or
laugh, but she — "

"My dear," Tola's voice was pleasant though somehow too high,
"I've just been thinking."

"About what?"

"About tomorrow, about the ovation awaiting us when we march
to work through the city."

"And who cares? The Poles never liked the Jews, the Jews never
liked the Poles, that's all." Seidmanka shrugged and the three of
them fell silent. Everywhere the joking stopped, till only the shuffle could be heard as the people shifted from foot to foot.

The painting was done. Next, those arrested on Aryan papers
were ordered to step out, mostly women who, trusting their Aryan
looks, had lived "in the Freedom" — so the camp phrase had it —
until a denunciation had brought them here. Bright yellow circles
were painted on their backs. They rejoined their columns, and at
last whistles gave the sign to disperse.

"Tola, are you coming with us?" Seidmanka's tone showed that
she could predict the answer.

"No. I don't like to push."

"The princess," Seidmanka grumbled, pulling Rubinfeldova into the crowded road. "To keep her nose up in the air, that's what she likes — to waste her last cent on sheets and such. Ah!"

"Please . . ."

"Please what?"

"You know — she is young, she is all alone."

"And who isn't?"

Rubinfeldova did not answer, so incomprehensible it still was that Tola was all alone, she who only a few years ago was a part of the huge Ohrenstein clan.

"Do you know the Ohrensteins from Joseph Street?" one would ask, and "Of course, who doesn't know them?" The answer was matter-of-fact as one would say "Who doesn't know the Kosciusko Hill?" They, the Ohrensteins had been like a landmark, generation after generation always there. First the fathers, stolid unhurried men, walking with arms folded behind their backs, and tilted backward, as if to display — this their only ostentation — the proof of piety, the magnificent full beards. Next the sons, equally unhurried, only as their piety shrank so did their beards — to small triangles, the only sharp feature in their gentle faces. Their women matched this restraint. To them the age of thirty was a boundary beyond which bright colors were forbidden, nothing but a cameo or a string of pearls adorning their dark dresses, as if being an Ohrenstein exempted them from all dictates of fashion, while imposing an obligation stricter by far — that of never venturing outdoors without a hat and gloves. Such they had been. And now only this girl was left, her sole Ohrenstein inheritance the habit of holding her arms folded behind her back.

"Stop sighing," Seidmanka muttered. But for once Rubinfeldova rebelled. And her sigh was heaved for them all: for Tola, for Seidmanka, left no less alone, and for herself, who still had a son somewhere in Russia, where, only God knew.

They had laughed, Tola thought, walking after the others up the dark street, this very morning they had laughed remembering the boy who had escaped from camp. "Herr Kapitän," he had said to the soldier guarding his detail — and "'Herr Kapitän,'" Seidmanka had sputtered, "'Herr Kapitän,' the boy said to the soldier guarding his detail — and if this yokel ever came near a captain it was to polish his boots. 'Meine Hosen, Herr Kapitän, my pants kaputt!' And off he went through a gate, then through a long passage, and into a crowded square. That was it. Ah, a genius this boy was, a genius."

True, when he had escaped, no one had called the boy "the genius," only "the criminal," able and ready to risk countless lives to save his own. There had been no retaliation. The guards had hushed up his escape for fear they would be held responsible — so the rumor claimed. And if the guards had feared the Obersturmführer then in charge, with the present Lagerkommandant they would be doubly careful.

Nothing would happen after her escape. Some anxious hours, some angry mutters, and soon, remembering her, they would laugh just as they had laughed about the boy.

But what if it was not true that the guards had concealed his escape? What if only a lucky chance had saved the camp from retaliation? She stopped, looked from the barrack windows darkened by blackout sheets to the Appellplatz where blotches of paint glistened red in the glare. Yes, even without an escape people had been shot in "selections"; whoever had the chance to save himself also had the right.

She had this chance, yet all month long, since her work unit had been assigned to scrubbing the barely guarded German houses, she had been letting it slip by. Of course there had been reasons: first the police checkups all over the city in which hundreds had been arrested; then a Jewish denouncer, expert at spotting other Jews; but after that she had been procrastinating for no reason at all. The painting showed there would be changes in the camp, and not for the better, either. If she wanted to escape she must do it tomorrow.

If only she could stop, once and for all stop weighing each possibility, each step, then everything would be simple. So that they would not be suspected of being in the know, she must march separately from Rubinfeldova and Seidmanka, then in the military barracks get herself assigned to a different group. The work would start around eight in the morning; this would give her enough time to look the street over, check where the German gendarmes were posted and where the Polish police were, forever on the hunt for escaped Jews. At noon she would slip away. From the streetcar stop she would have just a few minutes' walk; Aniela, who had served in her family for years, would not refuse her the refuge. But what if . . . Enough! She had decided. And covering the scab of paint on her cheek, she walked into the barracks.

Like a warehouse at the height of a sale the barracks looked at this hour of the evening. Crowds swarmed between the triple shelves of the bunks cluttered with pots, clothes, and bedding brought from the liquidated ghetto. Like customers fighting for a bargain the women shouted around the iron stove; more shouting at the table where bread was being dealt out. "Excuse me, may I get through?" Tola made her way through the crowd. Up on her bunk she reached into the bolster and touched the unpainted dress with the five-hundred-zloty note sewn into the hem. The Aryan papers used to cost four times as much. Still, wouldn't they be cheaper now that customers had grown so scarce?

The line at the table dispersed, the clamor at the stove subsided, and as the women settled down, as clean rags were spread under the crumbling bread, the bunks came to resemble rooms where families were gathering for the evening meal: mostly the makeshift camp families — women, young girls, whom loneliness unaccustomed and sudden had brought together — O.D. men with their curled and painted paramours, and here and there the real, prewar families, married couples and mothers to whom a daughter or son was still left.

Tola would not accept a makeshift family. Her evenings were governed by the rigid routine of loneliness. Unwilling to push, she waited till the end to get her bread; unwilling to wait in the smelly camp kitchen, she bought the acorn coffee from an old man wobbling with his kettle through the barracks. Next she spread a towel over her knees, then she ate. Usually a brief visit from Rubinfeldova was a part of this routine. But this evening when Rubinfeldova knocked on the bunk post, as at a door, Tola said something about an errand, then hastily walked outside.

Body rubbing against body, a dark mass moved through the main street to and fro, to and fro, from the O.D. men's guardhouse to the laundry barracks and back. Feet shuffled. Slashing through the dark an O.D. man's flashlight hit a yellow circle, then slid down to a smudge of gold under her feet: an inscription on one of the gravestones brought from the Jewish cemetery to pave the camp streets: "HERE LIES JOSEPH —— PIOUS, GOD-FEARING" — split where the stone had cracked, the words seemed like a stammer.

With this stammer fear stole in: at first just an apprehension disguised in the minor question about her painted coat; to hide her unpainted dress she must wear the coat until the last moment. But what if it was found right after she had escaped, what if the soldier in charge saw her take it off? She would be cautious, hide the coat well.

A new fear took shape — of a door, locked because Aniela was gone. No, Aniela couldn't stay away for long: her husband was an invalid, they hardly ever went out. And now the husband, this stranger with no obligations toward her, was shaking his withered fist. "Off with you!" he cried. "Don't you know there's the death penalty for hiding a Jew?"

She was running, faster and faster, yet there against the sky cut through by floodlights, she saw herself walking through the hostile city, dashing into a gateway each time a policeman appeared, on and on until the crowds dispersed, the gates stood locked. Across the empty square a huge gendarme was coming toward her. "Papers!" he ordered. She had no papers. And this was the end, because by now those caught in the Freedom were shot.

The crowds moved faster, boots stamped, until everywhere shouts broke out, discordant like the chorus of newsboys announcing the latest calamity, the latest hope. Here only the day's end was being announced: "Lagerschluss, all in!" O.D. men pounced upon the crowd. "Lagerschluss, all men out," they yelled in the barracks, cursing, cracking their whips though the men scrambled down as fast as they could, while from the bunks their women whispered, "Be careful as you go back."

"Tola, be careful tomorrow. If someone jeers at us just ignore it, don't talk back." In her anxiety Rubinfeldova forgot the ritual of a polite knock. "So what if some collaborators mock us? There will be others!"

"Will there?"

"Yes, I am sure, I haven't forgotten the good Polish neighbors I had when the world was still a world."

"Have they helped you, your good Polish neighbors?" Tola was about to say but did not. Rubinfeldova's "when the world was still a world" had silenced her, that statement of rebellion against the camp which Rubinfeldova tried to reduce to a nightmare, a transient freak. To say, as others did, "The O.D. men beat us to save their skin," "The Lagerkommandant shoots to stay away from the front" — to grant this nightmare any logic would have meant admitting it into the world, which, Rubinfeldova insisted, "one day will be a world again."

"I'll behave. And thank you for coming." She wanted to add something less ironical, less stiff, but instead she silently watched Rubinfeldova walk back to her bunk.

Heat lay over the barracks, heavy with the odor of fresh paint and of something sweetish, like decaying fruit. It was the bed bugs. Tola heard them drip softly from bunk to bunk. Nothing will happen if I escape—nothing, she repeated trying to soothe herself into sleep.

The thought that nothing would happen woke her up, and the rising sun. Slowly the dusty beams moved across the bunks, illuminating a long chestnut braid, an arm, a drowsy face. All was still, only from a corner whispers rose. But already feet were stamping outside, a streak of glitter cut across the window. It was the bugle. The bugler, a camp child prodigy, a boy of twelve in an oversized O.D. man's cap, puffed up his cheeks. A wheeze, then a loud shrill call.

The day began, as always, with fists banging, with boots kicking at the door, while inside the barracks elder whined her usual "Hurry ladies — oh ladies — may cholera take you all!"

Seidmanka was in no hurry. She put layers of underwear on, next two blouses, two skirts, and a coat — the contraband daily smuggled out of the camp, then sold to the Poles at work.

"Here, sell this for me." She waved a skirt at Tola. "I'll show you the customer, I'll give you half of the profit."

"Thank you, but I'd rather — "

"I'd rather not peddle. Sure, sure, we've heard that song," Seid-manka muttered, following Rubinfeldova outside.

Instead of floodlights sun glared upon the Appellplatz, but other-wise everything was as last night: the silence, the motionless rows. Only now the columns divided — one part marching up the hill to the camp workshops, the other taking the road down to the gate, flanked on one side by the SS guards, on the other by soldiers waiting to escort their details to work.

"Schneller-Schneller" the little soldier who escorted Tola's group was called, since his entire vocabulary seemed to consist of this one constantly bellowed word. Today even such vestigial speech failed him. He bent forward; he gaped, until with a rasping grunt he led them down past the Polish camp and onto the road.

Insects buzzed above the weed-grown fields; on the fences shreds of posters advertised films of years ago. And they too, marching in a long column, were like advertisements, Tola thought, like those downcast old men who, decked out with cardboard signs, used to trudge through the streets. Only here no one was downcast, here all were having fun — talking, aping Schneller-Schneller. Like those two next to her. "Stop it, stop trampling on my feet!" muttered one nicknamed the "Orphan" because of her glum home-less look, and on the other side a bosomy blonde kept whistling most cheerily.

"Beautiful," Tola said. "Like a bird rejoicing in his plumage." The blonde shrugged. "Stop pushing me," said the Orphan and stumbled on wire trailing from a wooden stump.

More such stumps, windows stuffed with cardboard, then a rem-nant of a wall once enclosing the ghetto, from which they had been brought to the camp half a year ago. "Schneller!" the soldier cried, and the column moved on, across the Vistula bridge.

Sluggishly the city was waking up. The streetcar was empty; the only passerby, an old vendor of kindling, was too heavily weighed down to notice who was marching past. In the house at the corner of Joseph Street the chintz curtains that had replaced the Ohren-steins' embroidered tulle were still drawn.

Then in the next house a window opened, a face loomed to vanish at once, and already more windows opening, more faces, some quick to take flight, some joined by other faces, other staring eyes. The aperitif, Tola thought, the foretaste of things to come; jeers, stares, and sighs heaved by those profoundly moved at being so sensitive they could pity even the Jews. There, around the corner, in the already busy street it would begin. But there Schneller-Schneller stopped; he looked at his charges, and at the street. He blinked. Until, defying all orders, he led them off into the "Planty," the broad strip of green running beside the street.

Rustling in the silence a gold-streaked leaf floated down. With the sound of stones plunging into water, chestnuts fell to the glistening sand. Here and there lay traces of yesterday — a child's trowel, a piece of skipping rope. The Orphan could not contain herself. The black mane falling into her face, she leapt across the hopscotch outlined in the sand, laughed, then was still. A red ribbon was lying in the grass. Now eying the soldier, now ducking, the Orphan made a dash for it, until in an uncontrollable reversion to childhood she plucked a white berry, and stepped on it so that it burst with a harsh smack.

"Stop it," someone cried. A cackling laugh answered.

One could tattoo their faces and they wouldn't care; Tola did care. To prepare herself for the "ovation," she was trying out poses and glances and smiles. An upright bearing was what she decided upon, a half-smile and a distant gaze. So equipped she felt calm; what awaited them did not matter any longer. Her escape would be simply the return to a place rightfully hers. Only her crooked shoes bothered her, and Schneller-Schneller flailing a branch till the leaves shed. "Los!" — the last leaf fell down, and the column marched into the street bristling with the red tongues of swastika flags.

Here it began. Here everything was turning against them, the narrow street, the old houses with their jutting walls pushing the crowds off the sidewalk and into the column, the press of horse-carts and droshkies and cars now pushing it back at the crowds, now forcing it to stop, so that the good burghers could look their fill.

Tola never looked back. Above the marchers still whistling and chuckling, an image seemed to be suspended — of one quite different, one contemptuous and proud. She tried to fit this image; head high, lips smiling thinly, she looked only at the rooftops, the coiling smoke, and the sky. But the voices pursued her. Just a whisper at first, just a gasp, they soon rose louder. "Look," they cried, "ah, look at them!" A horn tooted. *"Krakauer Zeitung!"* newsboys shrilled. *"Krakauer — "* the last voice broke off, and in a discordant chorus, "Jews!" they cried. "Jews, all painted!" Her feet slipped first, then her eyes down the glistening roofs, down the houses and on into the crowd.

It was not those staring who mattered, but the others, those not staring enough. At the streetcar stop the people turned, then turned back, a pudgy redhead went on buttoning her gloves, everyone looked only to look away, as if the entire Cracow population had always known that this September, on this day, at this hour, Jews would march through the city painted like —

"Clowns!" a loud falsetto jeered.

Next to Tola the humming rose louder. "What potato soup I made yesterday," said Seidmanka, and the splash was the Orphan spitting at the cobblestones. Then a whisper. "Perhaps," Rubinfeldova was saying, "perhaps these are different."

The old woman, her hand pressed to her eyes, was perhaps different; the grimy worker, the boy scowling from under his school cap. Perhaps. But the others left you in no doubt, certainly not the man with the falsetto voice, from his Tyrolean hat to his shining boots declaring his allegiance, in his lapel a swastika button red as a poppy.

"Red!" he screamed. "You wanted the red star and got red stripes instead."

Sir, you should order another outfit, you know, fashions may change soon, Tola would say this to him, she must. Yet she could not; she was afraid her voice would come out a screech; her shoes might slip on the muck until she lay in the horse dung, the street around her resounding with a huge laugh.

"Red stripes, lovely red stripes!"

"You . . ." Tola stammered, "you should order . . ."

A galloping droshky pushed the man away. "Zebras!" The driver swung his whip, and in the arcades the black-marketeers, chanting like an incantation their "Cigarettes, saccharin, cigarettes," grew still. They craned their necks. "Circus!" they shouted. "The circus is coming!"

Tola turned. "The funniest circus on earth!" she cried. "We could laugh ourselves to death."

"We, you — we all will laugh to death," the blonde joined in.

"All of us, all," shrieked the Orphan.

Hastily Rubinfeldova reached out. "I beg you." She pulled Tola into her group of four. "Be calm, I beg you."

The blonde was whistling. "What a soup I cooked yesterday" — so Seidmanka. And in the front of the column four boys marched upright, their heads high as if leading a parade to the din of trumpets and of kettledrums.

Only later during the day did Tola remember him, the man in the Tyrolean hat. Until then she had felt calm; the routine of the day had helped her — the soldier grumbling as usual, as usual the women bickering about who should wash the windows, who the floor. They stopped, and only the splashing of water could be heard in the white sunlit villa.

As always, Tola worked alone, on her knees, scrubbing the tiled floor in the entrance hall. At regular intervals she looked outside. The Polish policeman was merely strolling by; the streetcar stopped just paces away. And here, next to the door, was a closet perfect for hiding her coat. She looked the latch over, listened to the church bells announcing the time. Once the soldier in charge — this one long-legged and lanky — came in. Torn between his deference toward a city girl speaking meticulous Hochdeutsch and his awareness that such deference was no longer called for, he stuttered, then yelled, then left for good. Ten, said the bells. Except for a tightness in her throat she felt calm, only wished that time would move faster. But there were still things to be done: checking to make sure that the bathroom door could be locked, counting her change, then rehearsing her speech to Aniela, "Hide me, just for a day, a couple of days at the most. The moment I get Aryan papers I will leave."

Outside children were running by, and behind them a boy on a tricycle, a red balloon tied to his wrist. "Red star you wanted, got red stripes instead." And what if the man had followed them to the military barracks, then here; what if he was lurking around waiting for another circus performance?

Ten-thirty the bells struck. She would not wait any longer; she would leave right now. And now she made her body take over.

Her hands clutched the bag with the unpainted dress; her feet walked upstairs cautiously so as not to stumble on the carpet rods, and her hands again, fumbling first with the latch, then with the buttons of her blouse. She slipped the unpainted dress on. Next to see herself fully in the mirror she climbed up on the edge of the tub. I don't look too Jewish, she thought; then, I am terribly pale. And she began rubbing her cheeks.

Had she forgotten anything? Was the red-striped blouse sticking out from under the tub? No, she had left no traces. Yet at the door she stopped and ran back to see if her fingers had not smudged her cheeks. Her face was clean, only pale, terribly pale again. Clutching at the banister she walked down, took off the painted coat and threw it into the closet, turned back to make sure the closet door was locked, turned back again for no reason, then stepped outside.

Glare burst upon her, of windows, pavements, and sun. Close to the walls, ready to dash into the nearest gateway, she walked on, stopped to see if anyone was watching, took a few steps, then stopped again. She had to cross the street, with no gates, no walls to protect her. Slowly, as though about to plunge into cold water, she let her feet down and moved on, staring at one point, at the pink geraniums in the window across. Footsteps — and her breath failed; her body was enclosed within an icy crust. They passed by. She could breathe, could move again. The rapid pit-a-pat was nothing, only a child chasing after a ball; the stamping just a soldier. "Soldiers never recognize a Jew — soldiers never recognize a Jew." Walking to the rhythm of this refrain, staring at the geraniums, she crossed the street.

Bright blue in the sun the streetcar stood at the corner; it moved on. Closer, at the droshky stand, the pigeons scattered up to the roofs. A German stood there, a gendarme, and next to him a Polish policeman and a civilian fumbling in his pockets. Police check! The civilian must be looking for his papers.

Something was happening to her legs, they were swelling into huge unwieldy bales. At last those bales moved, down the curb back into the street. From an open window music blared; it stopped, and the only sound to be heard was her footsteps, the only shape stirring her shadow, black against the sun-bleached pavement. The shadow was nearing the curb, slanting across the sidewalk. She forced the bales up the curb, then closer to the wall. A gate. Something red — an apple peel, she must not slip on it. Another gate, then the white villa. The knob slid out from her clammy grip, she clutched it, walked inside, and up the stairs. In the bathroom she pulled the painted clothes from under the tub, changed, then very slowly came downstairs.

At the corner pigeons pecked in the spilled oats; the gendarme, the policeman, and the civilian were gone. Had there really been a police check? Had those three just stopped for a friendly chat? Eleven the bells struck. She knelt down and went on scrubbing the floor.

No one looked much at the column on the way back. In the streets the heat-weary crowds trudged on about their errands; in the Planty, soldiers and thick-legged wenches — numb wartime lovers with no speech but touch — sat staring at the dust. Gradually the crowds began to disperse. With the steps echoing in the hallways, with scents of cooking drifting into the warm air, dusk descended upon the city.

The column trudged on, past houses where white curtains swayed, across the bridge, then on through the ghetto. Here everyone began getting ready for the return to the camp. Money was being hidden in handkerchiefs or rolled-up gloves; food in pockets of coats slung across the arm, so that in case of a search they could be thrown aside at once. And reaching the foot of the hill everyone looked first at the slope to see if bags of discarded food lay there, then up to the gate lest the search was to begin now.

"Quiet, all seems to be quiet," those in front signaled. With a last "Schneller!" the soldier took his leave; with a loud "Achtung!" O.D. men welcomed them in, and in military formation they entered the camp.

"The Poles are inside," a crowd in front of the laundry barracks whispered excitedly, for this was the first time that the Poles, kept in a separate camp, had come here. Billows of steam rolled out of the door. And now the Polish women were coming past, in pairs; with their sacklike gray uniforms they looked like charges of a convent school demurely passing by the gaping mob. Seidmanka, the Orphan, the blonde pushed to the fore. Would they jeer, would the Poles be paid back for the ovation of the morning? But no one spoke. Only the stubbly-faced Polish foreman burst into a hoarse yell.

"Zborovska!" he yelled. "Zborovska!"

Again the door opened. A young woman, so tall that she towered high above everyone, stepped out and stood looking at the crowd with a childish curiosity, with pity and awe. Drawing closer she reached a piece of bread to the Orphan, then, noticing an old tooth-less man, hesitated and gave it to him instead.

"Zborovska, damn you!"

But the woman just stood there, whispering that she could not tell them how she felt, that there would be more bread, that she would come back, she would!

For the first time Tola was pushing, until she stood right in front of the big Pole. Then hastily she drew away. There had been no mistake. The long dark braids which this woman had worn wound round her head were gone; instead short straggly hair was falling all over her face. Yet the broad peasant face with the shining eyes and the mouth parted over the white teeth had not changed; nor the lightness with which she carried her ample body; nor the throaty voice, now still whispering, "Oh . . . I just can't tell you . . ."

"Zborovska, you Jew-lover!"

"I'd rather be a Jew-lover than the Krauts' flunky." And unhurriedly, her broad hips swaying, the woman walked on to her group.

"What a magnificent person," whispered a grotesque-looking creature, her mouth glittering with gold teeth.

"To the likes of her nothing will ever happen." The old man sighed.

And Rubinfeldova, as they walked on up the road, kept repeating that this Pole looked as though she had just come from the Freedom.

Seidmanka did not answer. "Tell me," she turned to Tola, "who is this woman? You must know, you stared and stared at her."

"She reminded me of someone, of — a maid we used to have. But I don't know her at all."

A walk around the barracks, a visit with Rubinfeldova, then another walk. All through the evening Tola did everything to keep busy. Then the lights went out. And then, lying alone on her bunk, she saw them: the woman with tired brown eyes, the shy stooped man — her parents huddling together, cowering in fear, while there at the window crimson with conflagration, the huge figure whispered, "How it burns. Oh, look how it burns!"

"No!" Everything clenched within her. "No!" Her father and her mother vanished. Only Barbara was still there, looking into the blazing night.

Barbara Grünbaum was the true name of this woman — a Jewess hiding as an Aryan in the Polish camp. At the beginning of the war Tola had met her — then a dziedziczka, a lady of the manor and of a vast estate to which Tola and her parents had come during their first flight of the war.

Chapter 2

EXCEPT FOR the electricians' detail, no one would work outside the camp any longer — the Lagerkommandant himself made this announcement a week after the painting. After that the Appell went on as ever; but when the order to disperse was given, part of the column marched up to the camp workshops, the other back into the barracks.

"What shall we do now? Tola, you tell us," Seidmanka cried, hoisting herself up the bunk.

"We'll thank God for sparing us the daily pleasure of 'Circus is coming.'"

For once Seidmanka had had enough. "You and your pride," she spouted. "Will it feed you, your pride? Or will you live off rations — half a pound of dry bread and that abomination, that glue of sago soup?"

"Haven't we had enough?" Rubinfeldova interposed, and they fell silent.

Still, things worked out better than had been expected. Prompted by his piety for the Ohrensteins and by a fat bribe, an O.D. man got the three of them into the paper workshop, where envelopes and folders for the Gestapo were made in two shifts.

A new routine began, so unchanging that soon it seemed to have gone on forever. At six in the morning the Appell, at six-thirty they came into a long narrow barracks where they folded, glued, and counted the envelopes until noon, paused for a fifteen-minute break, then again folded the envelopes, again stood at the Appell; and next day everything repeated itself — the Appell, the smell of damp paper and of glue, and the shouts of Glatt, once a waiter, now an O.D. man in charge of the shop.

"Ah, what do you know. I've got a Miss Ohrenstein here," he said, grinning, on the first day. "Well, let me tell you, times have changed, now it's all over with the Ohrensteins, now everyone's got to work," and he swished his belt across Tola's back.

"Did he hurt you?"

"No."

"Are you sure? Can we do anything?"

"No."

"Then say something."

"I've nothing to say." Tola bent down over the stack of envelopes.

This happened in the morning. And at noon, having dealt out the sago soup, Glatt stepped into the center of the barracks.

"Six!" he bellowed. "Who is going to stand six?" "Six" was the signal warning that the Lagerkommandant or the SS men were coming. "Standing six" meant watching out for them.

"So, who is going to volunteer?" Slowly, his boots stamping, Glatt strolled through the barracks. He stopped. When he looked at Tola she got up. First Rubinfeldova tried to argue with her, then Seidmanka. This was dangerous, they said. What if she had no time to run back into the shop — what if the Lagerkommandant caught her outside? She shrugged, then, making a wide circle around Glatt, stepped outside.

From then on she stood watch every morning, walking inside only when a group came back from the latrine. "Any news?" everyone whispered, as if a secret link existed between the Freedom and the camp, as if each hour, each minute could bring some great longed-for news.

"Ah — nothing much; the Allies are moving on a bit in Italy, in Africa too." The answer was always the same. But not when it came to the other news about her, the "big Pole."

"She is working again at loading the boards. She came to the kitchen, she dealt out bread, and potatoes and lumps of sugar."

"She said the Russians had taken Smolensk, the Allies are moving into Italy."

That those reports showed equally the Pole's desire to give comfort and her ignorance of geography — for, according to her, Salerno lay not far from Rome — bothered no one. With each day the Pole grew: she was no common prisoner, she was a partisan, an emissary, the special emissary of the underground to the Jews.

"Ah, for all we know she might be an agent provocateur," said the skeptics; but their skepticism was just a ruse, a means of arousing a wave of protests proving, confirming the Pole's mission.

Some claimed that Zborovska was a Jewess.

"Of course she is." Tola would grin. "And do you know why she comes to us? Out of her affection for the O.D. men."

Affection for the O.D. men? Now what did this mean?

"It's clear. The Lagerkommandant will be most pleased to learn that a Jewess is hiding in the Polish camp. Whatever pleases the Lagerkommandant warms the cockles of an O.D. man's heart." So she would mock. And yet in her a joy gathered, that now even for this woman so reckless, so unaware of danger, she was standing six.

Twice she went to the place where the Poles worked. Along the slope in pairs, joined by the heavy planks, the women were climbing up the steep slope. The one carrying a plank alone and so lightly as if she were doing it for exercise, for sport, was Barbara. Tola watched, and that she turned back without speaking to Barbara was still another way of protecting her.

How had Barbara been arrested? Why was she risking denunciation by coming to the Jewish camp? Tola wondered from her post at the door as she looked into the road. At times an O.D. man would stamp by, or a group of men with pickaxes and spades. And again the road would be empty. "All's quiet," the cries of sentries posted in front of each shop reported. "The Lagerkommandant is not in the camp; the Lagerkommandant is in his villa. All's quiet, thank God."

Days were quiet. But at night, his dog well trained to make no noise, the Lagerkommandant prowled around, stopping at every shop, looking in through a crevice, through a hole in the blackout sheets. What if suddenly at night he would come upon her? Would he once again bend down toward her — like a good-natured giant joking affectionately with a child?

Night impoverished you; during the day you had the windows and the sky, you felt the wind come in, and the feeble October sun. At night the windows changed to black squares, the air was heavy with the odor of glue, and the glare tinted with waxen pallor all

faces and hands. The womens' hands moved nimbly, the stacks of
envelopes on their tables grew fast; but the men, the bigger they
were the harder time they had of it — glue spilled, paper tore under
their touch, so that they kept throwing away the ruined envelopes,
furtively lest they be caught by Glatt.

He sat astride a chair next to the iron stove, his brilliantly polished boots tapping the floor, his bald red head turning to and fro.

"Work! Don't sleep!" he yelled, then, with a near-affectionate
intonation, "Kohnsweep!"

Kohn protested. Not that he dared to talk back — this no one
would — but the slowness with which he raised his long slouched
body, the way he dangled the broom, was an act of protest proving
to Glatt, to the onlookers, and to himself, who he had once been:
not "Kohnsweep" but Professor Doctor Kohn! Then, morose and
sallow, he would sit down, and at once it was "Kohnsweep!" again.

"What does that slob want from the poor man?" Seidmanka spread
the envelopes to be counted into a fan. "After the war I'll meet this
Glatt in some dark alley, and then even his born mother — " Breaking off, Seidmanka watched the hands being raised above the tables.
Glatt too was watching.

"Latrine?" He leapt up. "So you must go to the latrine again?"

Tola winced. Over the barracks silence spread, as at a party when
a drunken guest is about to say something shameless, while the others
wait torn between the hope that he will desist and the other ugly
hope that he will debase himself.

"Latrine, eh?" Glatt could never resist saying it — "Don't eat, then
you won't shit!" He got up. His eyes bulged with the plea for a
response, for a pittance, a shred. No response; looking at his whip
as at a comforting companion, Glatt sat down. And only now a giggle came from the children's table, where boys between six and ten
worked under the Orphan's supervision.

"Quiet!" Glatt screamed and the giggle stopped. He sat down,
and it broke forth.

The hands were still held up above the table. At last Glatt relented. Going through his complicated bookkeeping he checked
who had been to the latrine, how many times, and when; next he
chose those most deserving, then counted the orderly pairs.

A hunter stalking his prey Seidmanka became: she darted forward, hid behind a wicker basket, a table, a chair, ducked until, sneaking behind the bales of paper, she reached the doorway. Defying Glatt and the Lagerkommandant, illegal and uncounted, off she went on her fifth latrine trip.

"Seidmanka will always find a purpose in life." Tola smiled.

"Oh?" Rubinfeldova hesitated, divided between loyalty to her friend and the desire to please Tola. "Well, you know — anyhow she may bring some news."

"No news, nix," the rain-drenched Seidmanka reported, coming back. "The Allies are just standing there, twiddling their thumbs."

"Oh no," Rubinfeldova protested. "They know what they're doing, and one day . . ."

"One day! Let me tell you when this day will come: when Churchill gets sago for dinner, when Roosevelt slaves with a Glatt at his back. Then, not a moment sooner."

"Well, and what about the mystery woman, Zborovska? What is she tonight — an emissary of the underground, a secret agent, a Jewess?"

"A fool, that is what she is. She will get the Lagerkommadant after her, carrying on as she does."

"God forbid." Rubinfeldova sighed. Seidmanka answered with a huge yawn and they fell silent.

For now midnight was here, the hardest time of the nightshift, with six long hours gone by, and six that seemed even longer still left. Mouths gaped, heads lolled everywhere; and to prevent sleep the people resorted to the well-proved remedies, some to singing, others to storytelling or to washing their eyes with cold water.

"Don't sleep!" Glatt shouted, and a spoon clinked against a crockery pot: one of those still rich was beating an egg with sugar, making kogel-mogel, the camp's greatest delicacy, which to Seidmanka, who was unable to afford it, seemed not food but a salve for the hunger-bruised stomach.

"Come on," she licked her lips, "come on, let's do something. Let's tell jokes."

"Ein Witz," the albino Yekie twins — so called since they came from Germany — chimed in. "Ja, ja, ein Witz." But who could ever follow a Witz of theirs? They sputtered, they shook; then, getting no applause, stiffened, their white eyelashes blinking with insult.

"Yekie!" Seidmanka snapped. "Tola, it's your turn."

Tola was a masterful joke-teller, her voice always controlled, her mouth never cracking a smile; and while the others shook with laughter she felt a little contemptuous and very much left out — the adult among children who can be sent into peals of mirth by a mere wink.

"Enough," she said, having gone through most of her repertory, "let's leave some for tomorrow." Behind her the broom scraped, and swiftly she looked away lest Kohn — who had been her Gymnasium teacher — would with "Oh" and "Ah" and "Who would have thought it" beg her for proofs of his splendid past. She had no proofs; even in the past he had had the morose look of one destined for a better fate. But without a word Kohn passed by.

"Work!" Glatt yelled. He glanced into his pocket mirror, and off he went to a love tryst. This was a sign that the night would be quiet. Yet hardly had he left when Tola stepped outside to stand six against him, so that the people could doze off, or warm up some food on the stove.

It felt good to be alone, to breathe in the damp night air. A song came from nearby, mist drifted by in white snatches, then as a door opened, changed to shimmering fuzz. Darkness again. Blurred by the fog a group returning from the latrine came into the street. But instead of reporting the news they dashed on into the knitters' shop, and there behind the half-opened door, a hand holding a pair of knitting needles shook so hard that the gray sock slipped off and hung on the twisted thread.

Was something about to happen? Should she find out? She was running toward the knitters' shop when a shout stopped her: Glatt was back, much sooner than usual.

"Glatt!" she warned, running into her shop. "Don't sleep! Take the pots off!"

Mush oozing down her fingers, a woman grabbed her pot off the stove, but Glatt just walked on past her, past those asleep, and on to Kohn. He whispered something; Kohn jumped up. Kohn was sweeping as never before, doubled up, his eyes glued to the floor.

Both at once the Yekies got up. "Was?" they stammered. "Was ist los?"

"Selection," Glatt spoke almost gently, "a selection has been announced in reprisal for an escape."

Seidmanka picked up a fan of envelopes, put them down, picked them up again. "Tola," she cried, "Tola — what?"

"Tola, what shall we do?" Rubinfeldova finished for her.

Tola said nothing. Ten past two the clock showed. Ten minutes ago, she had listened to a song, had watched the mist drift by. That in a few minutes so much could change, she could not yet grasp; she was just remembering some past terror or dreaming an evil dream. And she waited for someone to wake her up.

"Tola, for God's sake!"

She looked up. And fear gripped her, not yet of what was to come, but of herself — impassive, letting time slip by while the others were getting ready, some hiding their money in stockings or shoes, others, the older women mostly, patting something onto their cheeks. Rouge — they were rouging themselves in order not to look so old. But this made them only more — the word escaped her, and she stared at Seidmanka, who was mumbling something about an electrician.

"Only the electricians leave the camp. One of them must have escaped. Ah, what right had he?"

"Kein Recht," the Yekies muttered. "He had no right to do that," came from everywhere. And Tola, feeling left behind only an instant ago, now felt a sense of triumph over those wasting their strength on futile anger.

"That beast!" Seidmanka hissed.

"Stop it, you won't bring him back."

Seidmanka divided herself, one part fury, one part fear; one hand clenched, the other rummaging in her bag, till it found a little tin box. Her teeth pried the lid open, she glued a dried blob on her cheek, then squashed it to red dots.

"Don't do that," Tola said. "You'll just look more — conspicuous."

"But then," Rubinfeldova said, "then, what should we do?"

They were all staring at her — Rubinfeldova, Seidmanka, and Kohn, who kept tucking the broom under his arm.

"Miss Ohrenstein," he spoke in an odd, too calm voice, "they say that only the old will be selected . . ." A pause from behind the misty glasses, his eyes looked at her, begging the reassurance that he, though balding and slouched, was not yet old.

"Miss Ohrenstein, don't you think I — "

"Leave me alone!" she cried. Kohn walked off. Rubinfeldova and Seidmanka were still staring at her. She turned away. The old, only the old, she repeated to herself like a refrain, which if recited long enough would help to recall the entire text.

The previous selections in the camp were her text. Only the old would be taken, everyone had said then. But it was never only the old; anyone could be selected; no one was ever safe except those who had managed to hide.

"We must hide," she was about to say, yet stopped short, because with the three of them to hide the gap at their table would be noticed at once. Only one could hide. Rubinfeldova — she looked weak, her hands were gnarled and old. Rubinfeldova — and what about me? Between Rubinfeldova and herself a contest seemed to be taking place, its prize the hiding place in the wicker basket with envelopes, the winner the one who could be most clearly imagined as being taken in the selection. His bloated face impassive, the Lagerkommandant seemed to be bending over her; thin legs shaking, Rubinfeldova was trotting toward him. A faint splash: the gluing brush had fallen under the table. And when Rubinfeldova ducked to pick it up her place stood empty as if she had never been there.

"Yes, you hide." Tola spoke hoarsely.

"But — what about Seidmanka?"

"She doesn't look so — I mean she looks well. You hide at once!" She helped Rubinfeldova to creep into the basket.

"That son of a bitch," Seidmanka muttered. "Oh, what he has done to us."

Walking on to fetch another basket Tola felt fear and anger rise around her like currents of heat and cold. She shared none of this anger — selections had taken place before without the pretext of an escape, whoever had a chance to save himself had also the right. Some kind of immunity seemed to lie in being different from the others: listening to the frenzied "He had no right!" she felt calmer. "Take a nap, Rubinfeldova," she joked. "Swallow," she ordered Seidmanka, who was hiccuping as she always did when afraid.

"Tola," Seidmanka stammered between her gulps, "Tola, what shall we do?" as if nothing had been done at all. "Any moment they may come."

"If — if they come now there's nothing we can do. But they won't. You remember the last selection; we'll be sent back to the barracks first; we'll hide as we did then."

"Why?"

"We must hide, because — "

"No, why should they let us go back to the barracks?"

"Because — " Nothing occurred to her.

Like someone who arriving late at the theater searches for an empty seat, the Orphan ran across the barracks, stopping at each table, looking, then running on. "Let me stay here." She pounced at Rubinfeldova's seat. "It isn't safe to sit with the children. I — " She stopped. Rapaciously, as though wanting to tear something off, she stared at Seidmanka's cheek.

Rouge she wanted. With her huge black eyes, red cheeks and red lips, her face looked beautiful yet repulsive, the face of a depraved child — and conspicuous too.

"Why?" Seidmanka demanded.

"Why what?"

"Why should they let us go back to the barracks?"

"Because — " And again Tola groped, listening to the rain outside, looking from Glatt to the windows darkened by the blackout sheets. "Because it will still be dark," the windows gave her the answer. "To select he must see everyone, and he can't in this downpour, this darkness. We'll go back. We'll hide in the barracks. Orphan, you should hide too."

"Not alone! I'm afraid," the sullen eyes told her. Tola was silent because the Orphan might scream, might give them away.

"Do you hear?" Seidmanka pointed to the door. They listened. But only a young O.D. man came in.

"The missing man may be still in the camp and hiding. The camp will be searched," he announced.

No sound could be heard, as if with such silence they were hoping to lure the fugitive out of hiding. And already another O.D. man burst in.

"An electrician has escaped," he shouted, "from work in the city."

When the selection would begin, neither of them knew.

The silence persisted; a rustle, a shuffle of a chair, and the people turned. With a glance they silenced the noise, then turned back toward the door. Behind it something clattered — nothing, just the wind shaking a loose window. Again a shuffle: an old, heavily rouged woman got up and kept tugging at her neck, stretching the skin to a sack, then letting go so that it jumped back like a piece of elastic. She sat down. Loud and even splashing came from outside.

On his tiptoes, Glatt sidled to the door and pressed his ear to the chink. No one stirred; only the old woman, tugging — at her lips now. Hastily, as though it could burn, Glatt turned the knob. He leaned outside.

"Water, just water from a drainpipe," he said, and the wind that slammed the door scattered envelopes all over the floor. Carefully Kohn picked them up.

In the basket envelopes rustled as Rubinfeldova tried to shift herself around. "Ten past four, twenty past four," Seidmanka kept track of the time. Tola was planning. They must hide only at the last moment, and on the middle tier of bunks, which was the safest.

"The waiting is always the worst." Seidmanka chewed on a strand of reddish hair.

"Tola, I can't stand it any longer" came from the basket.

"Get out, you can always hide again."

Rubinfeldova scrambled out, from her hair an envelope hanging like a large white bow. Tola removed it quickly. Again the Yekies muttered "Kein Recht," again everyone kept starting.

Soon both fear and anger began to weaken, the fear flaring up just for an instant, the anger disintegrating to a nasty irritability until they all bickered with one another. Gradually the grumbling stopped, and a torpid hush spread over the barracks.

"Strange — but I feel so calm," Seidmanka said and yawned.

"Because we've been waiting too long; because it seems as if everything has already happened," Tola fought this unwanted calm.

"Five o'clock — one more hour," Rubinfeldova said.

It was not one hour, it was at once. "Out! At once!" O.D. men yelled. As if the barracks were on fire, as if safety lay only outside, all pushed into the doorway. Only Tola was still looking around.

"Professor Kohn," she saw him at last, "you must hide!"

"I'm — I'm too high-strung. But perhaps — if I removed my glasses, see, like this." He blinked.

"Hide!" And a fist pushed her out.

In front of each shop a column stood, so immobile it looked as though another row of barracks had sprung out from the dark. A light flashed; from all sides O.D. men tore into the columns, until they broke, changed to a mêlée of groping arms, of bodies slipping on the mud. Rubinfeldova and Seidmanka were running straight at the outstretched whips. Tola pulled them away. "Together, we must stay together," she whispered as they moved on.

"Faster," the O.D. men ordered. "Don't gallop! Faster!" With each shout the odor of vodka burst upon her. They drink so that they can do it, they drink so that they can do it, Tola repeated to herself, trying to forget why Seidmanka kept clawing her hand, why, on her other side, the Orphan muttered about not being first — she wouldn't stand first in the Appellplatz, she was afraid, she wouldn't!

Tola stood in the first row. Searchlights blazed, the rain glittered, and across from her, on the platform, the figures in black leather coats glistened like steel. The rain beat against the widening puddles. Holding on to his cap an O.D. man ran to the platform. A shout. The columns turned; they were going back to the barracks, Tola realized, and she felt hollow because everything was being postponed.

O.D. men surrounded the barracks. Inside O.D. men flanked the doors. "No one is allowed out," they shouted, as if anyone were trying, as if the women were not standing in an orderly column. Tola was the first to climb up onto her bunk. Timidly at first, then more boldly the others followed, and everywhere ripped fabric swished, as everything illegal — money, jewelry, unpainted cloth — was being hidden in mattresses or pillows.

The door kept opening. Unobtrusively, as though anxious not to disturb, O.D. men came in, whispered with their women and left; soon, with the same unobtrusiveness, those women began to sneak out.

"See," Tola pointed at them, "they're going to hide in the O.D.

men's barracks. This means that we won't be counted." No one answered her.

A woman — the same who had tugged at her neck — stepped to the door, and stayed there, the ragbag in her hand, a kerchief tied neatly round her head. She stood quietly, but one by one others joined her, till a long line formed along the wall.

"See, everyone is going," Seidmanka squeaked.

"Let them, we'll hide."

"We will hide," Tola repeated looking at a ripped pillow, at the feathers, at anything but those lined up at the wall, tempting her to give in, with their quiet, everyday look.

Seidmanka stared at them. "No!" she groaned, "I won't hide. I'll hiccup, I'll go mad."

"You will not."

"And what if they count us?"

"They will not."

"Why?" Seidmanka asked, and everything was repeating itself, the bewilderment, the groping "because."

"Because last time they didn't count us."

"Last time was last time. This time they may count us. They can do anything."

"Perhaps," Rubinfeldova broke in, "if this is so hard on her . . ."

"If you prefer it, then go," Tola was about to say. "Hurry!" she screamed instead, "hurry, like those sheep, like the Yekies, running, afraid to miss something." She broke off. It had begun.

Still far away, the bugle wheezed; it drew nearer; stamping came from everywhere around. The door opened. Until suddenly the walls, the bunks were gone, only the kicking boots were left, the black arms tearing into the tangle of limbs, while above the O.D. men's yells, above the cracking of whips, the barracks elder whined her usual "Please, ladies, please."

"Tola, everyone is going."

Clutching Seidmanka's wrist, Tola watched. "No," she warned, "no, not yet. Now! Hide!" Rubinfeldova obeyed at once, but Seidmanka would not obey, she was trying to break loose. Tola held her by the scruff of her neck, feeling almost with relish how the sweaty flesh slackened, then gave in. Another push — Seidmanka was hidden. Tola piled pillows and clothing over the mattress, then crouched on the next bunk, drawing the mattress over her. "Now," she ordered, "now," because part of her became like Seidmanka, pulling her off the bunk and outside, where one could move, could breathe at least. "Now!" And all grew dark.

Boards cut into her belly, dust, horsehair clogged her breath; like stones the shouts kept smashing onto her head: "Shot — everyone found hiding will be shot!" Then a hard cracking noise; but this was nothing, just the whips hitting the bunks, and the rumble as of a train rolling above her — this too was nothing, only the O.D. men trampling on the upper tier. They could not get to her bunk, it was in the middle tier, it was too low; yet all the time out of the dark a boot seemed to swing right at her head. The bunk rocked; she pushed her fist into her mouth, gnawed on it, gnawed on the rough boards.

"Please, I'm the block elder!" the cry burst out. A whip smacked — the cry turned to a blubber. Then a loud slam.

They're gone, Tola thought, and took a small cautious breath. When again the door opened, when " 'Raus, alle 'raus" came from nearby she was not afraid, knowing almost at once it was just the O.D. man from the knitters' shop pretending to be an SS man. "The SS," he shouted, "they're coming."

They won't come, she repeated. Why not? Seidmanka seemed to ask, and suddenly she could almost see it — the gun catching the light, then the mouth, opening, unable to cry, and still opening as if to swallow what was to come from the gun.

"Your last chance to get out. They're coming!"

Fear was like an animal; it pounced upon her, clawed, choked her breath, she pounced back, clutched at it, till she forced it under her body and pressed and pressed. The door slammed. It was over. Now she would have to stay, because it was late, because even to an ordinary Appell you did not dare to come late.

The rain must have grown heavier. Through the thick padding of bolsters she could hear it drum against the roof, against the sodden ground; and here, right next to her, something dripped, on and on. The door screeched loud in the silence. Someone was lurking, was waiting for her least move, but she even forbade herself to moisten her lips, to take a deeper breath. After a while she

began to experiment, moving her hand, turning her head to get more
air through the crevice between the boards. Gradually, as only the
rain pattered, she began to trust the silence, which showed that it
was late, that no O.D. men, no SS would come anymore. And here
she had almost given up, like Seidmanka. Rubinfeldova, Seidmanka
— only now she remembered that they were right next to her. Soon
she would speak to them. "Hiding twice in a single night! Rubinfeldova, you've established a record," she would say, and to Seidmanka, "See, you didn't hiccup after all." Should she call out to
them now? It was better to wait. Still, she was preparing herself,
turning, moistening her parched lips.

From far off came a bang — just one — showing that it was only
the wind, slamming a door. Then another sound: "Ough!" choked
as though someone were drowning. "Ough!" again. It was Seidmanka hiccuping after all. But she must not, she must be quiet,
quiet!

"Ough, no!" Then a thud.

She pushed the mattress up, she turned; her eyes could see nothing at first, only the yellow glare, only a dark swaying streak, until
at last the streak became Seidmanka, groping, stumbling, running
on.

"No," Tola whispered.

"No!" Rubinfeldova cried. "Wait! Together!" Another thud and
now Rubinfeldova was running, her arm outstretched, and there at
the door Seidmanka reached out, until their hands clasped. They
waited. "Tola," they called, "Tola, together!"

"Tola!"

They were gone. She lay looking from the white puddle of sago
below the bunk to the door, then, realizing it was wide open, she
crawled under the mattresses and lay on her back, the coarse canvas
scratching her face.

"Tola, together!" they had called. Yes, she had said they must
stay together, but not when it meant dashing out at the last moment straight into the Lagerkommandant's arms. And, actually,
who had run out on whom? They had left her, they had not even
bothered to close the door, so that she would have no warning if
someone came in. If they did not worry about her, she was under no obligation to risk her neck for them, hiccuping, screaming

hysterically — now, when everything was almost over! The last selection had taken one hour, and by now half an hour at least must have passed since everyone had left.

Hysterical, absolutely hysterical, and nearby the dripping went on like the ticking of a clock. If only she had a clock, the kind with a luminous dial so that she could watch the time pass. Soon she devised a new way of tracking time: she began to count, correcting each mistake, going back whenever she had counted too fast. Around two hundred the numbers became confused. Three minutes, she thought, it takes three minutes to get to the Appellplatz. Seidmanka and Rubinfeldova must have just got there, now when it's so late — no, they must have come to their senses, must have hidden in some other barracks. And she padded the bunk with her hands so that the nails would not hurt so much.

Hurts, still hurts, her body complained, while she comforted it with promises of sleep, of water and of air, fresh, not like this hot mass that she tried to cool by sipping the breath through the corner of her mouth.

Only the wind slammed a door, only the rain splashed against the ground. Boots were splashing, the SS men were coming close. Now they were there in the next barracks and she, she had made a mistake: she was lying on her back, so that the fear could not be pressed down, so that it was pushing her up and off the bunk. The steps grew louder; but they must have gone on, she would have heard the door open had they come in.

The door had been left open; they had come in; they were pacing up and down. They stopped; bedding, pots were falling down. My dress must be showing, my hair. Then *NO! don't!* as if even thoughts could give her away. Rifle butts hit the bunks, something rattled and broke, and the rasp, which rose ever louder, which seemed to explode her head, was her own breath calling for them, begging them to come. She could not bear it anymore, she could not; she would leap down, would throw herself upon them, so that it would be over at last. But she lay there, her mouth filled with a bitter dust.

"'Raus! Alle 'raus!" Had they seen her, were they shouting at her? She did not care; she was numb, only her head hurt. Then very slowly her tongue pried a bitter blob off her palate. Horsehair, she thought, horsehair from the mattress; then, with the same apathy, They're gone.

Had they come back, had they bent down right over her, she would not have noticed, so dazed she was, as though half asleep. Still disconnected, thoughts came about the clock, about the SS and the Appellplatz, until, growing clear, they forced her up. Behind the door, left open once again, the dusk lay thick as if time had not moved on at all.

Why was it so dark still? Was it because it was raining, or because minutes, just minutes had passed since those two had dashed out, so that they had run into the SS, so that — No, they had sneaked safely into the Appellplatz, they had left long before their coming; yes, she could even check how long before: she had thought about a clock, she had counted, made herself more comfortable, and then, then the SS had come.

She was in two places at once: here wedged between the mattress and the boards and there running, always running, first to the Appellplatz, where searchlights blazed to spot out those two, late in coming, then back to the road, back to those two dashing blindly as always when she was not there to watch. Why had they done it? Why had they dashed out? "I'll hiccup," Seidmanka's voice seemed to cry; then that other voice, timid and still dearer to her, "Perhaps, if this is so hard on her . . ."

It was hard, yet she had forced them to do what was too hard, and then had left them all alone. If something happens to them I did it, I — Comfort lay in this admission, as if someone could hear it, could still save them, knowing that the guilt was hers. Recognizing this comfort she pushed it away. Her terror seemed the price of their rescue, and she paid this price, she forced herself to see them stopping, transfixed by the light. Then she saw the morning: she was standing in the doorway, crowds passed by, dwindled to groups, to isolated figures, until the road was empty . . .

At that point her fear broke down. How could she believe that they who had just been here, speaking, calling for her, would never return, only because Seidmanka had hiccuped? They would come back. And after that everything would change, she would move in with them, as Rubinfeldova had always wanted; she would be good to them. "Tola, how good you can be," Rubinfeldova had said during the last selection, when she had fetched a can so that Seidmanka could pee, then water for Rubinfeldova who was feeling faint. It was after she had brought the water that Rubinfeldova had said this about her goodness. So unbearable did her loneliness grow at this memory, that she began to listen, to jump at each sound, suddenly convinced that those two had heard the SS men come, had hidden somewhere nearby and would soon come back.

No one came. The splashing of rain softened, then stopped altogether; the sound of her breath was all she could hear. It seemed to have been with her for days, this silence, deep, as if not just in this barracks but in the entire camp she was the only one left. If someone, if anyone were here . . . And at this moment she heard it — a rustle, repeated, as though nearby someone was beginning to stir: the Orphan perhaps, whom she had told to hide.

"Orphan," she whispered, crawling out. "Orphan, are you there? Anyone there, anyone?" No answer, but the rustle went on. She crept toward it, on her belly, her arms wading through a tangle of clothes, through puddles of coffee and soup. The rustle stopped and so did she; it began, and she crept on.

A dress was rustling — Cantorova's, the barracks elder's dress flapping against the post. Pushing the dress aside, she hit against a bag, and bread began to spill out of it — slices, morsels, crumbs, all green with mold. Cantorova doesn't eat what she steals, she hoards it, she thought, absently shoving a piece of bread into her mouth.

She spat it out at once; her throat would not let a crumb through; it tightened as she looked up at the light bulb, at its glare shrunk by the daylight to a point. Why had the women not come back yet? It was late, terribly late! Everything around — the bedding heaped on the floor, the shoes lost in the shuffle, the pots — said that it was late, so long ago it seemed since the women had left. The thought that she was all alone in the camp came back, and with her eyes covered so as not to see how light it was Tola lay on Cantorova's bunk, repeating They will come back, they will. Soon even the dusk under her eyelids began to fade; then something warm touched her face.

It was the sun. Sun was flooding the barracks. The rain-streaked panes glistened; the puddle of sago shone like ice. And again she was crawling on, looking for the can used at night when going to the latrine was not safe. At last she found it, but just as she squatted her hand shook, spilling the stale urine all round. Clearly, as if this end was deserved, she saw what awaited her: crawling from bunk to bunk, scavenging for a piece of moldy bread, for a reeking can, then just as she would be squatting down, filthy and half naked, the SS would come for her — for the only one left. Because the others must have been taken away to another camp. No, this could not be. Why not? They could do anything: ghettos, camps had been dissolved within hours. And perhaps right now everyone — Rubinfeldova, Seidmanka, the Orphan, all of them — were marching down to the gate.

The stench forced her on to another bunk. A spoon lay there, and a little box smeared with something red. Rouge, she remembered, then, Oh, what he has done to us! Hatred filled her against the man who had escaped, and against herself who had mocked others for their anger. Then came hope; because no camp had ever been dissolved in reprisal for escape. And now all she could do was wait, for the least sound, the least sign that she was not all alone.

But when this sign came she ducked, she covered her face, her eyes, her ears. Another volley; the windowpanes quivered. She lay limp, her arms hanging down the side of the bunk.

For the second time this morning she was waiting for them, for the second time she was standing at the doorway, while in the distance a crowd appeared, slow-moving and hushed. Down the road, in the next row of barracks, doors opened, then silently a few women passed by her and walked into the barracks. More and more of them came in, the crowd dwindled to groups, the groups to figures — walking always in pairs, one supporting the other. Then the street was empty.

Tola walked back into the barracks. The bolster Seidmanka had thrown down was still on the floor. She picked it up, looked at the strand of red hair caught in its corner; looked over at Cantorova shoving the bread into her bag.

"Have you seen them? Rubinfeldova and Seidmanka?"

"I haven't," said Cantorova.

"No, I haven't," said the Orphan.

Tola spoke to no one else, only walked down the road; then, in case they had come through some other way, ran back and outside again. And just as sobs came from the next barracks she saw them, struggling up the road, Seidmanka all twisted, Rubinfeldova's arm supporting her.

"Be very careful, Tola." Rubinfeldova spoke in a new, steadfast voice. "Careful," at every step, "careful," as they lifted Seidmanka up onto the bunk. There she lay, on her belly, the tousled red head pressed into the pillow.

"Soon it will be better." Rubinfeldova stroked her, "I'll go get linen — I'll make a compress."

"Don't go," Seidmanka cried. "Don't leave me!"

Tola fetched the water, Tola stripped the pillowcases and sheets off her bunk, then listened to Rubinfeldova's instructions — that the compress should be wrung out well yet not too dry, left damp yet not dripping wet. Cautiously Rubinfeldova lifted Seidmanka's skirt. And to punish herself, to atone, Tola forced herself to look on. No punishment was dealt out to her: as the tear-stained face, so this bloody, bruised flesh was just another proof that Seidmanka had come back.

Water splashed, Seidmanka whined thinly like a puppy. When the whining stopped, Rubinfeldova led Tola aside.

"Twenty-five on the buttocks," she whispered. "First tables were brought into the Appellplatz, then the Lagerkommandant chose those to be flogged, mostly older women. The Ukrainians did the flogging, the O.D. men had to look on."

"And at the end? Was anyone we know shot?"

"I don't know, I couldn't look."

A pause. Then, "How many?"

"Sixty or more, so they say."

It was not what had been done to those sixty — this Tola could not grasp — only Seidmanka's groan that made her cry, "Who was it — who ran away?"

"Oh?" said Rubinfeldova. "Oh, so you don't know?"

"What don't I know?"

"No one escaped. The Lagerkommandant just used this as a pretext. But then, why should he need a pretext? What for?"

Warily, like a town struck by a hurricane, the camp was beginning to stir. Furtive figures stalked through the streets, and stopped, ready at the least warning to run for cover. In the barracks everyone moved on tiptoes, bypassing in a wide circle the bunks of those who had been flogged or who had lost someone that morning.

Gradually the streets began to fill, the voices rose louder. Soon came the coffee peddlers, dragging their kettles, soon O.D. men climbed onto their womens' bunks, and the afternoon moved on almost as on any other day.

As on any other day, a crumpled-faced woman stopped at Seidmanka's bunk.

"What is it?" Seidmanka spoke without looking up. It was about groats — a real bargain — just twenty zlotys a pound.

"Ooh!" Propelling herself with her elbows Seidmanka crawled to the edge of the bunk; another ooh and she swung down, and stood bent, hands pressed to her buttocks.

"No," Rubinfeldova cried, "you're not going anywhere."

"We've got to eat!" Seidmanka drew herself up, and grumbling that twenty zlotys was no bargain, limped off to the door.

"Wait — together!" Rubinfeldova ran after her.

"Wait, I'm coming," Tola called.

Seidmanka turned. "We waited for you once before today," she said, and the door slammed.

Tola spent the afternoon walking around — past the barracks swelling with noise, through the streets where crowds milled in the murky haze. Halfway to the place where the Poles worked, she stopped and went back to her barracks. She straightened out her bunk, got her rations, and stepped outside to check if the time for going to work was near. Another hour. She drank some acorn coffee, then walked out.

Wearing a white chef's cap and a white jacket dotted with spots, the chief cook stood by the kitchen door. "Disperse, or I'll get the O.D. men after you." He swung a huge ladle. No one budged.

Those most hungry stood there, old women, men whose flesh showed through their rags; and the grotesque gold-toothed woman too was there, holding fast to a freckled girl.

A shout inside — this was the Polish foreman; the rapid foot-steps — Barbara running out.

"For me, madam!" the crowd begged, and all but the woman with the gold teeth pushed forward. "That one got something yesterday. For me, Miss Zborovska!"

Barbara shrank away; she threw one piece of bread to the man nearest to her, glanced at the chunk she still held, then abruptly turned to Tola.

"You!" she said, and her voice was hard. "We all are hungry; but you've got decent clothes on — you look all right."

Tola would not have answered, she would have run away were it not for the fist pushing her forward until it seemed she was trying to grab the bread.

"Really," Barbara muttered.

"I'm not begging. I just wanted to greet you — Barbara."

The bread fell from Barbara's hand. Her face was ashen, her lips twisted in a cramped smile.

"A mistake — my name is Janina." And she was gone.

Slipping on the spilled sago, Tola walked on. From behind her, rapid steps came; she did not look back. "Wait!" the throaty voice called. She just walked faster, until a hand grasped her.

"Come with me." Barbara pulled her behind the kitchen bar-racks. "Hurry up, come!"

"I'm sorry, I made a mistake."

"It was no mistake. Only at first, can you imagine it, I got fright-ened." As if startled by another's foible, Barbara shook her head. "But it's over. Oh, you know me, you came to me."

"I came to warn you. You must stop coming here, it's too risky. Someone might recognize you, talk might start."

"Talk? My own people won't denounce me! But you, where do you know me from?"

"You took us into — my parents and me — your manor, when the war broke out. You wouldn't remember me; there was such a crowd of refugees."

"Oh my God! So you know my place and — but we can't talk

now. Listen, I must talk to you. Will you come back here? Or wait, I'll come to you, I know an O.D. man; he will take me to you."

"Don't come. It would be dangerous."

"I . . . must talk to someone. Where do you live? And your name — what's your name?"

"Ohrenstein. Barracks thirty-seven, the last one next to the wires."

The Appell passed quietly. In the workshop the evening began just as always. Only the children, who had hidden under the mattresses during the selection, were quiet tonight; and Seidmanka sat on a pile of coats.

"Work," Glatt shouted. "Work, Kohnsweep! Kohnsweep!" he repeated, leaping up.

At Kohn's table, a tall, dark-haired man got up and stood pointing at the place beside him. Everyone turned. The place was empty.

"Someone," Glatt shouted, "someone sweep!" And the broom began to scrape.

Chapter 3

WITH REVERENT SILENCE, with circumspect gestures those bereft would at first be treated. Then the reverence would begin to dwindle. "Work! Don't push," everyone would shout; because they, dazed and speechless only days ago, would soon try to wiggle out of work, would grab their bread or soup. And at that point the inevitable bargaining with the dead would begin.

All goodness, all grace went to the dead; for themselves the living claimed nothing but their life. Yet a debt was outstanding still. And like payments rendered on installments, so with "Ah, at least they didn't have to live through this" each moment of fear was sent to the dead, each selection, each shot. This too was not enough, the debt was still not paid off, until "Anyhow," everyone said, "anyhow they'll finish us off too."

Tola never took part in such bargaining. When asked, in the usual euphemistic manner, whether her parents had been "deported," she answered, "No, they were killed, shot last March during the liquidation of the Cracow ghetto." And she felt ashamed of this truthfulness, which in reality was nothing but a lie. They had not been killed, they had simply never existed; she had always been alone — this camp, this bunk her only home, the only greeting of her mornings the hoarse "All up!" Grief was just this: the tension between this disbelief — wanted, insisted upon — and the faith that they once had been, had smiled at her, had touched her face.

Suddenly, always against her will, this faith would come. Behind women, their glances, their startled shrugs asking where their daughters were tarrying so long, her mother stood. Together with men dragging heavy kettles and asking "Would you care for some coffee?" — not in a vendor's cry but in the tone of a courteous host — her father came into the barracks. She would start, would tighten her eyelids.

And already it was over; the ghetto streets brought no memories, the house of her childhood was just one of many houses passed as she was marched to work. Only once, when Rubinfeldova, walking in a group of four behind, began to whisper about the Ohrensteins — how beautiful their life had been, how happy — then, up there in a window, behind geraniums and tawdry chintz, her mother seemed to rise in protest against this praise that to Tola felt like a bribe.

Of happiness there had not been much in those vast, lightless rooms. Later, when everything was named and classed, even the unhappiness had become clear: the old family business was going downhill; her parents' marriage left much to be desired. But earlier in childhood, something mysterious, though heavy, rose from Mother's steps, from her sighs, and the habit she had of keeping the curtains drawn — all of them, tight — as if to barricade herself, not against the sun, for sun her mother loved, but against the dark Jewish street. In Mother's strict hierarchy, this street of gray sprawling houses, of shopkeepers tempting passersby with hooked fingers, was the lowest rung of all. Next came the airy villas around the park; next Warsaw, the Warsaw of Mother's youth, where uncles had sped in troikas; Warsaw whence you went to Italy each year. In Italy the hierarchy reached its peak; there among mimosas and sun Italians hovered like huge contented bees — and as thick grayish candles were lit for the dead, so, in memory of Italy, mimosa twigs shone in vases of Venetian glass.

Such vases, the Louis Quinze furniture and the china over which crinolined ladies strolled, Mother had brought with her as a bride. Seven days the wedding had lasted, seven dresses of embroidered silk lay in the Louis Quinze closet; yet to her it seemed Mother had come to Cracow on a civilizing mission, more as a reformer than as a bride — to convert the Ohrenstein clan from the "uniforms" of skirts and blouses, and from taking their tea in glasses "as thick as marmalade jars."

That the mission was hardly a success was clear. True, her aunts had renounced their uniforms; yet crockery kept ousting the decimated china, and the frail rococo pieces shrank from mahogany as dark and massive as Grandmother, with whom it had come. Each evening, taking stock of her defeats, Mother would look at the huge credenzas, at plush chairs and chipped glass, and then, her hand pressing her "nervous" heart, at Father, who would start and look away at once. Not a word, not a whisper fell, yet a barrier seemed to cut the room into two opposing sides. At once she rose and hurried to Father, for it was at his side that her place was in those times.

True, home was empty without Mother, nights were sleepless when she was gone. Yet Mother's white, obese body brought pity akin to disgust; no less than the sight of the old bagel peddler said to have once had both home and husband, a picture of the slender girl who her mother once had been was a portent of some vague, inescapable loss.

With Father there were no portents, no fears; nothing but exorbitant pride. For being unlike all other fathers — the villa dwellers included — for never pinching cheeks, never asking "What's heavier, a pound of iron or of down?" she admired him, and for the courtesy extended to grown-up and child alike; for his dreamy smile, his voice, his height. He was the celebrity still incognito: and she whom boys called "frog," she who stammered and blushed, was the first, the very first to have discovered him. Each sign that others were joining in this discovery was hoarded by her — the neighbors' respectful bows, a shopkeeper's saying it did not matter that she had forgotten her money, since she, Mr. Ohrenstein's daughter, could be trusted; and, above all, that day of the school parade when "Left! right!" the command fell, but right, left her feet went, all ways at once, until there in the crowd a hand waved, and "Is that your father?" a girl cried out, "Him? So young, so tall?" And her feet stumbled no more.

"So young, so tall!" everything sang in her on their walks together. Then the street, this rung that hardly counted, turned to a kaleidoscope. His least gesture and scenes full of color sprang to her eyes: from the window above Rosenblum's store with its tangles of Christmas glitter, Emperor Joseph had greeted the cheering crowds; there, where carts rumbled and horses blocked the view, insurgents of 1863, joined by rabbis with flowing beards, had marched chanting "For our freedom and yours"; when he explained to her "The earth is round," the most ordinary street curved like a fruit beneath her feet. And it seemed to her that not only shopkeepers but officers, small-waisted like young girls, mustachioed gentlemen in bushy furs, all would soon stop to greet him, knowing who he was.

The means of this revelation was the store. OHRENSTEIN & OHRENSTEIN, FOUNDED IN 1805, said the sign of tarnished gold. In its scorn for garish displays, the store would boast only of duration, of time. The visiting Emperor had read the sign; insurgents in high shakos had wondered what lay behind its door. Dusk as in a church lay inside, deepened still more by the age-blackened wood of drawers lining the walls; only in the center was an island of light — a glass cubicle where Grandmother sat knitting endless sweaters; across from her Father bent over his sacred books. And behind him shimmered sapphire streaked with crimson. The plaque. ROYAL FOUNDRY — the embossed letters said. Beneath them the enamel landscape was divided: on one side, torch still smoking, an incendiary leered at his handiwork — a house transformed into raw flesh, its roof tongues of flame, its windows scarlet wounds, and from behind the blistered scab of the door more tongues trying to scoop up the victim fleeing near-naked into the night. But succor was coming from the other side: there a house stood peaceful in the first light; the windows glimmered; not daring to transgress, a fire burned in the stove behind the door, where those hastening to help the victims stopped to look at what had saved them — the tin roof shining silver in the sun.

Father's task was to sheathe houses in such inviolable protection. Father was not just a merchant, but a man with a mission, compared to which Mother's civilizing venture shrank to very little indeed. That the mission's full disclosure was still awaited seemed not only comprehensible but proper in this world where all waited — shopkeepers for customers and better times, children for vacation and for the coming of Messiah, and all alike for the Sabbath feast.

Every Friday, on her way home from school, Tola went first to the store. It was closed; the bolted shutters and the silence a reprimand to the street, where the everyday noise still swelled, as if no one knew what was soon to come. But at home the everyday was being trapped, cunningly, like a big lumbering beast. At first, as though encouraged to take over, the everyday was omnipresent, crouching in the old newspapers, lording it over the dinner table set

so helter-skelter that Mother sighed they were dining "as if at Michalova's" (Michalova was the hard-drinking janitor's wife). With dinner over out it went — chased from room to room by fresh flowers,
by the seven-armed candelabra and the silver goblet shining on the
white damask cloth. In the vestibule, together with the scent of sacred books, a presence seemed to emerge — Grandfather, who in
his lifetime walked from shop to shop asking the owners how much
they would earn till the Sabbath, reaching into his purse, then moving on to spread silence, as the lamplighter spreads the light.

At last they remembered him, at last the shutters fell; only Rosenblum kept fiddling with his Christmas glitter, only the old woman
still brandished her bagel stick. They too were gone; wind swept
the refuse off, dusk turned the windowpanes to amethyst. And
from behind the panes, declaring the insufficiency of a clock for this
occasion, eyes looked up in search of the sign. It came, the first star
appeared, and everywhere in the street, on each floor in each house,
candle flames shone, lighted all at once. In even rhythm footsteps
sounded in the dusk; the gates swung open, and now they were
coming, Rosenblum, Jacobi, and Schwartz, dealers in alien feasts,
tempters of passersby, now transformed by coats of black satin, by
hats of velvet and of fox fur — now like courtiers walking in measured steps to an audience with a king of long ago.

Saturated, round chimes rolled into the dark; from the synagogue voices answered in a soft chant. Curled up next to Mother,
she listened; then, as the chant ended, she looked through the un-
barricaded window — to be the first to call out that Father was coming with the "poor man."

The "poor man" was a guest awkward yet indispensable. His rags
reeked of dankness, his hands so shook that he spilled the wine, but
he blessed it with an intonation that was beautiful and from far
away. And he coughed, he coughed till crumbs flew and the candles
flickered. "From," he rasped, "from the Revolution." The cough's ori-
gin stated, he rose, unfolding color upon color: across the white winter steppe "black hundreds" galloped to plunder and to kill; the sky
glowed red when the White army had passed his town; then a
pause, then the cough again, drumming in the finale for which
he produced all colors at once — darkness of a November night, red
of the army marching in, while the whiteness he himself provided

with his hands, hands that almost made the soldiers shoot him as a nobleman, so white they had been, so white . . .

Here, stretching out his gray horny hands, he embarrassed them no end, until Father came to the rescue with the Sabbath song. "We ate, we were satiated, we blessed," they all sang. The poor man had eaten, had blessed but, far from being satiated, he crammed chala and cake into his pocket; then, as though afraid those gifts might be withdrawn, took a hasty leave. Tattered and alone, he shuffled out into the dark, often to return in her dreams, the cough from the Revolution in his chest, a crumbling chala in the once white hand.

The clocks regained their power the next day. Though first on her side, saying it was early, still morning, still the beginning of noon, they turned about in a sudden switch, and already it was one, already dinner time. And after dinner, the everyday began to sneak back.

Into the streets couples swarmed; they swelled into crowds, walking up and down, peeking through the bars into the shop windows, as if they could not wait, as if this very moment they must find out what the bargain was, what its price. Later in the afternoon, when her cousins came in to play, the dresses of seven days' wedding turned into regal and knightly robes. But as Esther wooed and Roland blew his horn, she knew how out there in the street those whom Grandfather had had to bribe into holiness stamped in front of their stores, fidgeting, looking from their watches to the sky. It darkened, the first star glittered. And the shutters rose with a loud, triumphant screech.

In the next room, Father was rescuing whatever he could: he lit a candle braided of roseate strands, he filled the silver goblet with wine. "Thou who distinguishes between the holy and the everyday . . ." he sang, passing around the turquoise-studded box of spices, their sweet scent contrasting with the ordinary air to sharpen this distinction — as if this were needed, as if she did not know that outside in the noisy dark the old woman stood thrusting out her bagels that over Sabbath had turned hard as stones.

Sunday was the official holiday. Checking that all Jewish stores were closed, policemen marched through the streets, while the shopkeepers, their customers just gone out the back door, stood watching them with false, obsequious eyes. Sullen, like an unjustly scolded child, the neighborhood bristled under the enforced feast; and the rancor spread all the way home, where men with too agile hands talked of mortgages, of IOU's and payments — talk of which Father understood so little that he smiled, a cramped smile that made Tola wince.

As by outgrown dresses or discarded toys, so by Sundays could growing up be measured, by hurt turning to anger, anger to habit, and by the gradual yet steady shifting of her place till, seen from the barrier's other side, now too stooped to be tall, now young no longer, Father appeared in a new shape — a shy, ineffectual man, who kept much to himself and brightened only among his friends, men as pious and unsuccessful as he was. It was through Mother's eyes that she saw him now, but the will to see him so was her own. For what was she paying him back? Not for the revelation that never came; this, like the faith in Messiah, had been forgone long ago; but for the compliance, for the obliging ease with which he fitted into his new shape; and for breaking out of that shape, yet so ambiguously, so briefly that, to prove no remorse was called for, she forced him still harder into it. Soon the shape was neither disfiguring nor new; it was simply a part of him when the war came.

They had fled then, fled to Lublin first, because Lublin was east, because the east was safe; then, the distinction between west and east having been replaced by that between the city which might be, which was bombed, and the town that might still be spared, they moved on to Starybor, to Krasnyca, and on to the hamlet of Volka. There they stayed, in a thatched hut, in a room with an earthen floor, from which dust rose thick with every step.

Outside in the narrow passageway, the boundary between them and their hosts, smells and voices were pitted against one another: the smell of pine scent Mother kept spraying against the sour smell of pig-fodder; their own timid whispers against the peasants' mutters.

"Them!" said those mutters. "They left the door unlatched; they spilled the water, the slops." "They" meant city people, meant Jews.

"Please do something; go out, talk to them," Mother would whisper. Thus Father had become their delegate to the Polish peasantry, nominated because "he was always so good at talking to them."

This "always" referred to his one-week-long vacations in the country, when "Ho-ho, Host, what a fine gelding you've got!" he would boom — then stop short, suspecting that the gelding might turn out to be a mare. Which it did, more often than not.

"Ho-ho, Host, how are you this morning?" his carefully countri-fied basso rose over the dung-strewn yard. "Ha, Host, what is the news today?"

"Sugar is getting dear. The Germans are coming close" was the news.

Outside the village a hill rose above the wheat-covered plains, the road beneath it black with crowds fleeing eastward to Podole, to Volynia, and Russia. Tola watched them. She longed to merge with the crowd, to be carried away, not from the war — what it might bring she could not imagine yet — but away from those mut-ters, the sour smells, and the mornings when she, her parents, and grandmother lay helter-skelter on the earthen floor.

"We must leave, before it's too late," she insisted.

Her parents refused: it was better to wait, they argued; it was safer. "We can't go so far east, we don't know anyone there," Grand-mother added, implacable and black.

But when the peasant burst in shouting that Germans were in Krasnyca, that they had gathered all the Jews, had shaved off their beards — then they left in a peasant cart, Father stroking his new, his clean-shaven face.

It was to Starybor that they were to go, then on east. But hardly had the cart come into the main road when a chain of dark rounded hills rolled toward them.

"Jesus Maria!" the driver crossed himself.

"Jesus Maria!" the hills — carts piled high with bedding, with women and children — wailed back. "Jesus Maria! The Germans are everywhere; everything is on fire!"

The driver stopped his horse. "Get off," he muttered. "I'm not going anywhere. Get off."

From under the whirling wheels lumps of dirt sprang up into their faces. The road was empty. From afar the driver's shouts came, repeating something about the Jew's manor — that they should go there, that the Jewish dziedziczka was kind and would take anyone in.

Would a Jew, would someone like themselves live in these hostile wilds? Suspecting a ruse, they groped through the dark woods, stumbling on the moist moss, straying into a bog. And just when it seemed that they would have to spend the night in the woods, the thicket opened upon a winding gravel driveway. At its end stood a large white house, windows lit up, doors open as if inside a feast was going on to which all chancing by were invited.

For them such an invitation was not enough. They hesitated. "We can't simply walk in," they whispered, "we don't even know their name."

"Still — perhaps," Grandmother spoke up. And she led them inside on the strength of this "perhaps," the hope that the manor owners knew Cracow, so that the cunningly modest introduction of "Ohrenstein from Cracow, but I doubt you've ever heard the name" would be rewarded by the prompt "Of course, who hasn't heard of the Ohrensteins from Joseph Street?" which in turn would transform them from intruders into guests.

Still untransformed, they tiptoed through a dim corridor, past a long line of peasants, city people, and soldiers, and on toward a lighted doorway. "Thank you, madam. God bless you, Dziedziczka," a murmur rose from behind it.

"Thank you, dear, I mean you're welcome, I mean . . . anyhow," quite unabashed by such groping a woman's throaty voice answered.

Was this the lady of the manor, this powerfully built woman, so like a peasant with her broad sunburned face and the large hands holding the ladle? The ruby brooch proved it, pinned askew to her white linen blouse. Eyes riveted on this proof, Grandmother marched on.

"Excuse me," she began. "We just arrived — "

"Welcome, most welcome," the Dziedziczka broke in. "Now be good enough to go to the end of the line. Order — nowadays we all must keep order. " And she knitted her dark eyebrows with the earnestness of a child allowed to play with real pots and pans.

"As I mentioned, we just arrived," Grandmother began anew when their turn came. "Ohrenstein is the name, from — "

"Welcome to be sure. But now step closer so that the soup won't spill."

"And may I ask your name?" Grandmother persevered.

"Grünbaum — Barbara Grünbaum." And a pause, for what could be done with a name like Grünbaum, so common that to ask next "Grünbaum, from the textile firm perhaps?" would have sounded like mockery.

"Yes? And from where?" Grandmother made a halfhearted try.

"From where? From here, of course!" Above the murmur, above the shuffle of feet, the Dziedziczka's laughter rose, so big that her whole body shook and one dark braid unwound down her back. Then, once again she raised her ladle.

"Thank you," Grandmother said icily, "we ate just before we came."

An old mustached man came up to her. "Madam must forgive us," he said softly, "but things are not as they used to be here, and — " He broke off.

Smooth like the sound of ripped silk a hiss pierced the dark. Silence. Again a hiss; glass rattled.

"Tola, we're being shelled! Tola, where are you?" Mother cried. And while they huddled together, while orange flames burst into the sky, there at the shattered window the Dziedziczka stood, repeating in an almost festive whisper, "How it burns! Oh, look how it burns!"

She turned back. "Go down to the cellar," she ordered calmly, and saw to it that everyone went down. But she herself returned upstairs.

Crouching in a chilly corner, Tola could hear her pacing to and fro overhead, as though the Dziedziczka were hastening from window to window to watch the conflagration, whose reflection cut a pale streak through the cellar dark.

Day was breaking when the manor guests scrambled out of the cellar to lie down on the bolsters and straw sacks spread all over the floor. Only the four Ohrensteins, unable to fall asleep, sat alone around a huge mahogany table in the dining room, Grandmother staring at a plate of unfinished soup. Someone kept scampering, kept sighing behind the door. Suddenly the door opened. A frumpy-looking woman dashed in, mumbling about her jewelry: that it had been stolen, all of it, all! She stepped closer, looked at them suspiciously as though she would like to search them, then scurried out.

Grandmother pushed the plate of soup away. "No," she said, "no! I'm going back home where people know me, where I'm still somebody."

No one answered her, not even Tola. Hunger, hard work she could have taken upon herself, but not what they now seemed to see in the murky dawn — the lines in the rancid soup kitchens, the bedding spread out by indifferent hosts, and those suspicious stares that they, grown nameless and without a home, could no longer ward off. She got up. Father reached out to her, but she passed by him to the window, behind which the sky was beginning to shine a soft, silky red.

The uneasy adventure of their flight grew distant in no time. With the bolted stores, with the forbidden bread carried like a frozen puppy under the coat, the war petered out to another Sunday, the maid's endless day off, when you struggled with dishes and stoves. Only the SS, silently pushing you into the gutter just by occupying the whole pavement, were new. True, even before the war guffawing rowdies had enjoyed such tricks, yet they had faces — a glance and, "Scum," you said, "just scum." Helmets hid the faces of the newcomers; tall in their flowing coats, the booted legs supple like young tree trunks, they reminded her of those beautiful women whose cold gaze seems to see each blemish, each flaw.

Like pillars moving in the dusk, they appeared on that morning; one gone, the next replaced it at precisely the same point. The boots pounded, somewhere a candle flickered only to go out at once, and the mouselike scampering — this was her parents coming into her room. As if the street had usurped most of the room, they shrank from the window, Mother whispering that she did not like what was going on, not at all, until "Don't!" she cried at Father as he reached for the light switch. "Don't, I say!"

From outside, like a shiny water jet, light splashed into the room, moved from her parents shivering in their crumpled nightclothes, skirting her, back to helmets and glistening boots. "Get dressed, Mother," she said. "Get dressed, both of you."

They dressed hastily, as if setting out on a trip; on tiptoes they

moved through the unlit rooms, all turning to their meager experience of danger — to illness, to emergency trips — for help against
what was to come . . . "A search!" Grandmother cried, "a search
for jewelry and silver," and Mother added that she did not like it
by silently shaking her head.

"Wait!" Unexpectedly, Father took over. Awkward at first, still
uncertain in his new role, he soon played it to perfection; with each
cameo pin hidden in rolled-up socks, with each smile and wink, he
came closer to resembling Vlasta Burian, the master detective of
films he had liked so well. But for the silver even such cunning was
no match: like silver antlers the candelabra pierced the linen through,
the goblets kept clinking in the pillows; until, finding no other
way, he demoted them to the ranks of everyday things — the candelabra stuck between rusted tools, the goblets between the chipped
glass. After that there was nothing more to do, just wait, walk
around, and wait again. But Tola furtively kept hiding a dirt spot
here, a worn-out place there, until, seeing Mother doing the same,
she stopped and bent over her book. "La mienne embaumait ma
planète, mais je ne savais pas m'en réjouir . . ." she read, with a
sense of unreality, as though again watching a film, now about a
girl while the SS was conducting a search, translating . . . "embaumait" meant perfumed, "réjouir" to gladden . . .

The shame was real; it came from the window across the way:
there greasy pillows, coverlets with gray tufts were flitting by.
Clutching at something gray, Grandmother burst in. It was one of
the wigs she wore out of piety. "If . . . if . . ." Grandmother
stammered, pointing to her head; if the wig were found, they might
strip her head to the skin like a recruit's. Glass clattered as they hid
the wig among old bottles in the hall. "Tola!" Mother cried, "Tola!"
Because now they were coming.

Stairs creaked, down on the first floor doors banged, then silence
— as when the doctor comes to the gravely ill. They waited . . .
steps again, and the bell ringing without pause as if it had got stuck.
Still the perfect detective, wondering who might be ringing so hard,
Father went to the door — and drew back. Because the two helmeted men, the officer in his visored cap, did not just come in; no,
they were returning, the rightful owners taking over their home without a word, while the Ohrensteins, the trespassers caught red-

handed, shrank back to the Louis Quinze closet, its mirrors reflecting a gray spongy shape — it was a woman in the window across the way, old, stark naked, elbows pressed to her dangling breasts. A black-gloved hand pulled a shade down. A black-gloved hand pointed at the drawers beneath the mirror.

"Was — ist — da?" The officer spoke slowly, like a foreign-language teacher.

"Fetzen," said Mother. Fetzen — meant rags. Rags spilled from everywhere: after tangled silks, after clothes smelling of cleaning fluid and sweat came the spindly underclothes worn by men who dread the cold; next misshapen corsets, next brassières stretched by fat breasts; when the saggy mattress joined the pile, all was known: the days beginning with fat squashed into shape, and the nights when, fitted into hollows scooped out through years, her parents lay pale and limp in the dark.

The silver did not fit these rags, the silver seemed to disown them. Piece by piece the SS men were carrying it into the vestibule, where the heel of a boot caught on a golden thread trailing from the embroidered lion on the prayer-shawl bag. And Father, who whenever the bag fell would lift it with a kiss, just glanced at it as though to say, "Wait, my dear, I cannot now."

The officer would not wait. "Lift this!" the officer ordered. "Pray."

Father lifted the bag; Father looked like an old woman wrapped in the shawl.

"Faster!" said the officer.

"Slowly." The voice was old and cackly. "One must pray slowly." Father raised his eyes and looked at the officer as he had looked at the maids gaping when he prayed — with anger, as if he did not care who this was, as if he had foreknown that the two in helmets were to burst in, kicking the wig, with the familiar guffaws that marked them as scum.

"Ruhe," said the officer. Become statues again, the men marched out; the officer followed, picking up the turquoise-studded box on the way. And Tola waited, as if everything depended on it, she waited for him to slip the box into his pocket. But he only pressed it — hard, and when the filigree silver did not give in, he carried the box out, uplifted high in his dark, glossy hand.

"You — " Mother cried, "you and your piety — they might have

done something to you — they — they might have killed you." Her
cry faded to a whisper.

Tola was silent. To say that he had protested, that he had been
brave — this she wanted, but such talk would have mocked him
who slouched, fingers twisted to a whitish knot. Therefore, she just
touched his shoulder, and felt relieved when, as usual, instead of
helping out, he went to visit a friend across the hall.

Trucks rumbled throughout the evening, at night the glow of
conflagration lit the sky. The old synagogue had been set on fire.
Only the foundations escaped. Like a gray squarish vessel they rose
from the ground, taking in whatever came — rain, snow, and the
black city dust.

It was March — the second March of the war — when, without
Grandmother, whom nothing would budge this time, they were fleeing again, from the ghetto decreed for Cracow to Brzesko — a small
town still "close enough for the name Ohrenstein to mean something
there."

Well equipped, Mother went into her exile with hope for the ef-
ficacy of their name, with the Louis Quinze closet — its mirrors now
reflecting walls dotted by roses like an oversized rash — even with
her faith in the hierarchy that made her address as "my good man,"
"my good woman" all on the lower rung.

"This, my good woman, is crystal, this, damask cloth," she would
declare, as though converting the leather-faced peasants to such re-
finements, not bartering them for flour — the darkest kind, cheapest
of all. And because it was cheaper than buying, she baked bread
herself — up at dawn like the maids, she made the fire, soot-cov-
ered, grouching exactly as they had done. Breakfast, and she was
transformed: the graying hair pulled to a neat knot, at her collar a
silver clasp, "Please pass the saccharin," she enjoined, "please use a
saucer. We don't have to live like Michalova yet." And because one
must not live like Michalova, she starched and ironed the last table-
cloths, she polished and scrubbed, and the vases were always filled
with flowers, with leaves, or with winter berries. "For the eye must
have something to rest upon," she would say, scowling at the rash of
roses.

So it was in all the homes. The war, this endless Sunday, had restored the matriarchy. And while the women had their hands full trading, keeping the house, the men, the proverbial Jewish family men, politicked and played cards, like those once despised ne'er-do-wells.

In such diversions Father had no skill. He had become like a boy whose vacation has lasted too long, like him sent to fetch water or wood, like him looked over before stepping out, lest he forget the armband with David's star. And just as a boy clings to his sole companion — the pet dog or cat — so did he. God was his companion, God his pet. Withdrawn into the prayer shawl as into a tent, he hushhushed with Him each morning. His errands done, he pored over the holy books. Told to get up because ironing had to be set up or a wash done, he moved on, and on again, the books carried cautiously like something alive and frail.

To help with the chores, to take long solitary walks, was all that Tola had to do. Around her, the town teemed with couples — the ill-assorted couples that exile breeds: willowy, gentle girls matched to men with salesman faces; behind hefty wenches, all bosom and hips, little professorial creatures trotting on spindly legs. Peasants armed with pitchforks chased them out of the fields, children out to collect kindling stumbled on their lovemaking. But they persevered; arm in arm, branded by star-marked bands, they passed her window.

And trains passed by, bright red, the insides greening with soldiers. At times a detachment would be stationed in a nearby school. Then the yard at her window grew alive with voices, the well-crank she or Father could hardly move now whirled in strong hands, and water splashed upon young, smooth chests. She never stepped out, never glanced toward the yard. But invariably one of them would point to her window and at once they got dressed, they drew closer. "Fräulein," they called, "Fräulein, Deutsch sprechen?"

"Ja, ich spreche Deutsch. Was möchten Sie?"

"Ah," they sighed, "ah, such Deutsch, so far from home to hear such Deutsch"; and hastily, one after another, could they come in, or would she come out for a walk, just to chat, just for a little walk? She wouldn't? Did she have a sweetheart, a Schatz? No? Then why not?"

"Because I am a Jewess."

Some looked uncomprehending, some puzzled as though they were matching pieces that should yet would not fit; only at times a face, hardened with loathing, as if one reaching for a flower had touched a slimy bug instead, gave her what she wanted — that inkling into the faces helmets hid.

"Out, lights out!" they cried each night. And it seemed to her that those in helmets could search the room right through the blackout sheet to find there only the expected: the rancor, the heavy silence that comes where there is nothing more to say. She longed to take them aback — more, to dazzle them with a show of amity that would transform Father into a patriarch upon whom his family waited with devotion nothing could diminish. And she tried. Her text rehearsed as if approaching someone she hardly knew, she asked about his reading, about his preference for Joseph's story and the Psalms. But he was proud; sensing she needed him for the lead in her show, he answered as curtly as he could.

Mother did somewhat better asking about the news. "Strategy," he answered with a shadow of the old smile. "The Allies are following some special strategy, but in the spring the great offensive must begin."

June was here when it began. Each day, dressed in their best, they went to the marketplace. From lopsided houses, from blind narrow lanes, crowds streamed, slipping on feathers, on damp straw and dung, to gather around the loudspeaker. Across the way at the brick police building, the green figures stood — imperturbable, as if even the German victories on the African and Russian fronts had been foreknown. Then the crowd would turn toward them. "Wait," the eyes of the crowd said, "wait — you'll still see."

"You'll see," said Father, "this retreat means nothing. The Russians prefer not to fight on unknown, on Polish territories."

"Ah, a real Clausewitz!" Mother cried when it was Russian territory, when Kiev fell, and Charkov. The trips to the loudspeaker stopped; anyhow there was no time for them with so many guests coming in. Ohrensteins, the younger, more adventurous branch, who in thirty-nine had gone east, were now returning one by one.

Scheduled for after the war, those visits felt uneasy, like chance encounters with acquaintances between trains when neither one knows where or how to begin. What had driven them back the guests hardly mentioned. Only if asked about jewels or furs that would now come in handy, they would say matter-of-factly, "Lost when Ukrainian hordes burst in . . . lost when the SS massacred the town," as though such events were the familiar, the commonplace background to the loss of fur coat or ring.

To her they were not commonplace; to her it seemed that these guests were simply repeating the poor man's tale. Such flights, such hiding in ditches and mud could not happen to her or her parents, never. And when it was happening, when they cowered in the tall wheat, when boots crunched, when shots fell everywhere, even then it was a game, unwanted, cruel, yet a game from which she who must be shot would arise to tell how roughly she had been played with.

That the news about towns emptied into ghettos, ghettos into cattle trains — going where, no one knew — might have anything to do with her could not be imagined yet; nor that the clayish puddle from which sparrows shrank was all that was left of the fair-headed girl who used to pass her window each day. But the face of the one who had shot the girl she did imagine, and the voice saying, "Du bist zu schön um eine Jüdin zu sein."

"Du bist zu schön um eine Jüdin zu sein" — You're too beautiful to be a Jewess — a voice spoke into the dark; a giant hand pressed hard, still harder, till like a white naked kernel she was forced out. Always the same, this dream visited her ghetto nights.

By the end of August they too had had to move to the ghetto in Brzesko — now seasoned tourists who traveled light, each with just a small suitcase in hand. At the sight of the wires strung along blackened posts, Mother drew back, her eyes widening. "You know, when the train stopped, I couldn't, I just couldn't believe we were in Rome," Tola remembered her mother whisper.

Had Mother come to believe in Rome as quickly as she in her being in the ghetto? A few days, and the wires at her window seemed a most familiar landscape: the room corner, screened off by a sheet — "for," said Mother, "one must have some privacy at least" — her home of many years. And having existed so long, the ghetto, this city of four streets, must go on existing. It was too populous to vanish, too bustling with workshops springing up each day, as in a time of sudden boom.

On that afternoon, as Tola was returning home from her workshop, a silent crowd filled the streets. Announcements posted on the wall were being read: "25" — the number caught her eye. Twenty-five kilos the Jews to be deported next day could take along to Ukraine. There was no Ukraine, she knew it, but the cold, the thickening air were part of a dream from which she would wake up, if only the crowd would let her through, if she could go home.

The crowds did open up, she was home, yet no awakening came. In the rhythm of an unspoken "I don't like it," Mother's head kept shaking; the suitcases they used as a chair squeaked each time Father got up. Outside, the wires shone in the harsh sun, a fly buzzed, and "Laugh," a girl's voice was saying behind the sheet, "when I laugh, laugh, when I talk, talk back." The sheet swung. "Please come in," Mother called.

Dressed to the hilt, in gloves, high heels, on her neck a dainty cross, the girl from the next corner came in. The girl needed a tie for her brother; the girl was fleeing with him to Bochnia, yes, without Aryan papers, yes, even though the station swarmed with police. Scraping off a spot, Father handed her the tie; the cross caught the sun and glittered.

The dream broke. Envy broke it — not envy of the escape, but of such efficiency, such calm. "We," Tola steadied her voice, "we must flee, like her."

She too was efficient. She got them Aryan-looking clothes, she bribed O.D. men and the Polish police to let them out the next day; and as the preparations for the flight were shrinking to errands, what was causing the flight also shrank into something which, though terrible, could somehow be endured by the less sensitive, by the neighbors who watched her bringing in the new clothes — a green hat and coat for Mother, a blue suit for herself.

But with Father it was hard. Oh they tried on him the disguises of his salvation — sportsmen's caps and Tyrolean hats — yet his face only looked more Jewish under the jaunty brims. And as he sat there, pale hands folded on his knees, the immunity Tola imparted to those less sensitive began extending to him too, until it seemed neither impossible nor wrong to leave him behind now as in the summers when Mother had fled with her to the country, while he stayed alone in the city heat. But when he rose, when he drew closer, she felt afraid, because "Go without me" he might say, because then each day would be a gift from him, each breath a reminder of the gift's price — of his breath clogged by air like molten tallow, air that suddenly seemed to close in upon her.

"No," she started. "No!" Mother cried. Then both together, "Something — some way must be found." They found the way: a Polish trainman who, though the death penalty was threatened for such help, agreed to get him to Bochnia with a load of beer.

Everything went as planned the next day: the gate swung open, the trainman led Father away. Soon the ghetto seemed never to have been. Filled with the excitement a trip brings, she looked around the unknown country, where curtains swayed and hollyhocks bloomed round the whitewashed houses. From behind a house a long shadow fell, a rifle clanked — street, flowers, sun tottered, just decorations to be ripped off, and she was being pushed back into the ghetto, was groping for the last firm point; she gripped Mother's hand, and held it. While the gendarme walked away, Mother pulled her on toward the station where more gendarmes marched to and fro.

The crowds came to their rescue, the solid mass carrying them to the train and wedging Tola between a pimply adolescent and a smuggler wrapped with sausages like a Laocoön with snakes. The train had just started moving when Laocoön bent close to look at her. He smirked.

"Is she?" He winked at the pimply one.

"Sure she is, sure."

Woods flitted by the window, children waved with hands translucent like shells. "Is she?" — "Sure," the voices kept jeering, and a glittering needle hurt her eyes as it flashed past. It was a church spire. Heads lowered, all crossed themselves, Mother too, her arm stiff as after a stroke.

"Ah," said Laocoön, "my nose! Even if they haven't got a crooked nose, I can smell them out, even if — "

"If — " Mother spoke up, "my good man, you're practically squashing me — if Aunt Krystyna has the book on Saint Theresa she can give it to the Colonel." Uncompromising, insisting even now on

the proper milieu, Mother placed her imaginary relatives in the fin-
est surroundings, among choicest friends; and as the train stopped,
as Laocoön got off with his crony, she, expanding on the Colonel,
went on — the slightly raised eyebrows the only sign that she
was watching how he looked at a policeman, faltered, then walked
on.

Aunt Krystyna's name days were always so lovely; the Colonel
went to Mass each day; more churches, more signs of the cross made
with clammy hands, until at last the train stopped at the Bochnia
station, where they just stood, at a loss as to which way the ghetto
lay.

By the signposts of ever shabbier streets they were finding the
way, by the heavily guarded columns that marched past. Now a
column guarded only by O.D. men was coming toward them. "Refugees, from Brzesko," Mother cried, and soon the ghetto received
them, like a longed-for home.

Father had not yet reached this home. Running along the barbed
wire, they waited until he appeared — changed, a stooped, aging
man with red ears too large for his head. From the ghetto street an
SS man was walking toward the gate, and as to a friend who has almost passed unrecognized, who must be recalled before it is too late,
Hurry! she cried silently to Father, *Hurry!* until she held him tight,
mumbling something about beer, the smell of beer that hovered
oversweet around him.

That was how it began, the time of their escapes, from a ghetto
threatened with deportation to a ghetto safe because the deportation had just ended there; to and fro, to and fro, like traveling salesmen always covering the same territory. Fall was splendid that
year: past trains where talk was of Aunt Krystyna, poplars flitted in
spires of gold; in ghettos, light, summery crowds promenaded on the
streets, as on the boulevards of a spa. And the crowds never dimin-
ished. As in a spa new arrivals replace guests forced to leave, so
here refugees from towns emptied of Jews replaced those deported.

"Deported" was the only word used.

"Deported" was all that was said by those asked about their families, their closest friends. "Ten thousand deported from Tarnow,
twenty from Nowy Sacz" — so the daily bulletins came in.

And in Cracow ghetto, to which their escapes often took them back, in the jail courtyard walked prisoners sentenced to go with the next deportation, those caught "on Aryan papers," members of the underground next to girls who on their way to work had dashed into a store to buy sweets or a pound of fruit. This — that you could die for joining the underground, for a few pears, or for nothing, nothing at all — could not be grasped. Like a punishment imposed by too strict a master, death had lost all meaning. The few who, like Grandmother, had died their own deaths were praised — shrewd pupils gone before the unjust master had forced them out.

But at times, when hushed voices spoke of someone "killed, shot on the spot," for throwing himself at an SS man, for spitting right in his face, silence fell. Because this was the real, the prewar death.

With admiration akin to idolatry, Tola listened to such whispers. And often, when hurrying on some errand, she would stop, would stare at those others — the men with dark, unshaven faces, the women wrapped in lank, unbraided hair, those who when asked about their families answered not with "deported" but with some mute gesture; those who no longer cared for anything, who had given up — the minority of mourners whom she admired just as much.

They were gone. Laughter, a snatch of song would rise into sunlit air. And the ghetto, arrived at just days ago, was again like a home, stable, familiar for years.

Suddenly, it was time to flee again. Left to herself Tola would have stayed, because it was easier, because so many, trusting in their work and in their youth, did stay. But Mother would not let her. "Hurry. It doesn't look good" — a new phrase had been fitted to the habitual shaking of her head: "Hurry — and remember the cross."

No crosses, no Aryan accessories were needed for Mother. Whittled thin, with a fixed, determined gaze, she had grown anonymous — not an Ohrenstein, not a Jewess anymore, just one of the countless women who, left alone to shift for their children, give their all to this aim. It was she who organized their escapes; she who, now haughty, now begging, scrounged for the money needed to get out. And in the cities, where denouncers swarmed, she marched on, intrepid, head butting against some invisible barrier that must be pushed through. Someone would stop, someone would follow them. "You know," she would sigh, "I'd rather take the streetcar" — just an elderly lady, eager to spare her strength. On the streetcar eyes stared. "Come." Most unhurriedly she would rise. "This is our stop. This is where the Colonel lives."

It was as if they had enough strength between them for only one. When Mother led, she just followed like a frightened child. If Mother faltered, she took over. Evenings, in rooms rented to smugglers or lovers for a night by women for whom the war was an auction, a chance for bargains, Mother smiled, nodded, saying yes to everything — "Yes, they're killing the Jews off . . . yes, serves them right, those leeches . . . yes, perhaps even they are human" — and a smile, and "yes" again. At last the door closed. They were alone with a pinkish Christ. Then, like the last keepsake of the past, Mother would take out that gesture of pressing her heart; and then, for one instant she would grasp that what deportations, what police and spies could bring, or this stammering heart, were one and the same death.

Far away, in the hostile city, was Father, left with strangers like the less-loved child. Somehow they always managed to get him out — now a servant, now a customer from the old days rescuing him for the sake of old loyalty, or for money. Each time they waited for him at the ghetto entrance; each time it seemed more likely he would fail to keep their date. And the smell of beer still seemed to hover around him.

"It can't be done, madam, it just cannot," a Pole, smuggled into the Cracow ghetto to get him out, said regretfully, like a furniture-mover unable to transport too heavy a piece. The Pole left. As on that day in Brzesko, the October sun shone harshly; a fly buzzed just as then. Outside, beyond the wires, a streetcar rumbled. In its window — painted over to screen out the ghetto — a hole had been scratched, bright like a coin. Was someone looking through it? Was someone saying "The Jews will be killed off again"? Only now, seeing herself through others' eyes, she grew afraid. She got up, and so did Mother — Mother was doing something with her face, screwing it up, tightening then parting her lips as though trying on look after look. She settled at last upon a smile, the old smile saying a medicine won't taste quite so bad, while the eyes hardened, insisting, bad or not, it must be taken at once.

"Tolenka," said the smiling mouth, "this time Father and I, we'll hide. Upstairs in the dentist's office there's a bunker — but you'll go — into the city."

"No," she said — "no" to going alone, because without this voice, this firm hand, Laocoöns would smirk wherever she went. "No," she said once more — "no" to leaving them behind in a bunker to be hunted down by informers and dogs.

"I say you'll go."

Father was silent. Father just looked at them, discreetly suggesting his gift.

Somehow he must be got out. If . . . if Mother went with him, then she would be left alone; if she went with Mother, he must stay behind. Like partners in a dance she kept switching them around. If . . . if the three of them left together. This figure too was disrupted, because no matter how late they left he could not stay in the streets, someone had to find him shelter.

If again, if . . . she led him out — and she saw them, Father slouched, herself ashen, all cramped with fear; but next to them someone else loomed, now like Mother, now like that girl from Brzesko, someone who was calm and laughed and made him laugh.

"Tomorrow morning I'll lead him out." She paused, waiting for protests; when, grown meek, they did not protest, she went on, explaining how Mother must go to Aniela, to all the maids, must ask them to hide him, just for a few hours.

"And if they refuse?"

"Then — we'll take him to church." She looked at him, sitting with his arms folded on his chest, as if tied to the chair. "Father!" she whispered. "Father, tomorrow you and I — we'll go together, Father." And now he looked at her, startled, as if someone no longer expected had come in.

She clung to him after Mother had left, shyly touching his shoulder, telling him how only the vicinity of the ghetto was dangerous, how later they would just stroll, he in the straw hat, she with the flowers she would buy at the bridge to make them look casual. "Remember," she added softly, "do you remember that bridge where we used to walk?" He nodded, he even smiled. But when she brought him soup, he said stiffly, "Won't you sit down?" as to a guest too infrequent to be likely to tarry long.

It might have been a parade marching by, such crowds pressed against the wires next morning: arms waved, shrill-voiced children skittered to and fro, while O.D. men, trying to outshout the clamor, bellowed that none but those claimed would get out. Outside the gate the claimants stood — Germans, civilians, and soldiers, with all sorts of papers proving that they could take their workers out. Tola did not push with the crowd, she just watched. Now a group was marching out, now O.D. men swooped down on the crowd. She ducked. Pulling Father along, she sneaked into the group.

He had followed her she was sure, but there outside the gate a man in a leather jerkin and boots stood before her. "Come with me," the man said. "Go away!" she cried. "Go!" Yet in the instant before that cry broke from her it was as though she were rising — up and up to a high peak. To follow this man was the leap down that would crush her, would bring someone new in her place, one who could leave without one glance back.

Back behind the wires, Father was drowning in the crowd, only his arm rising above the black mass, only the tip of his hand. "Papa!" she cried, "Papa, Papinka," by this cry, by this childhood name, pulling him out until he came to her — just as a rumbling noise broke into the street.

SS trucks were rolling toward the ghetto. The crowd at the gate vanished, "Back into the ghetto! They'll shoot! Hurry back!" the O.D. men cried.

They did hurry back. They ran through the empty street, up the stairs past spilled offal, past glass, past a shrill cry, and on into rooms where clothes tripped their feet, until there at the end of a long hall the dentist's chair appeared. Above it, as though administering to an invisible patient, a hand was moving, about to block the opening into the wall.

"Wait!" Father cried. "Wa-a-ait!" And they crept in.

It was dark inside, there was no air, only dust, only cobwebs swaying over the squatting shapes. Somewhere beyond this darkness people were running, the solid clatter breaking now and then into the clicking of heels, the pitter-pat of a child's steps; and all the time, as even as clock strokes, shots sounded one by one. Then silence that could not last, that had to break with the rattle of bricks, of walls pushed in. But it stayed, swathing her, numbing all thought. And just as she could bear even such numbness, such dark, in the distance and already near, already down below, boots stamped, something crashed, something fell with a thud; then a pause, and a dog broke into loud howls.

Loudly, too, a child was crying in the dark. "Do something to it, do anything," she tried to shout. She could not, she had no lips. Now something was being done to the child, now fists were crammed into its mouth. But it was too late, they would come, light would nail her to the wall, light would make her blind. She swayed, butting against the dark, when firmly an arm gripped her; a hand — Father's hand — stroked her cheek, and she, startled, not comprehending such calm, clung to him who could do nothing, who was all she had left.

When the howl receded, she did not know. In a thin thread, sunlight came in; it faded, was gone. Far away the clock of shots kept striking, the child gasped, choking on the fist. When sobs came through the wall, they crept out.

Alone, in rooms to which no one had come back, they looked through the window, they listened at the door. "Perhaps Mother has decided to stay in the city, perhaps — " Father broke off. Hat askew, lanky strands of hair falling over her face, Mother was running toward them until she stopped halfway, then very slowly, as though not quite believing they were here, walked up to them. Outside, hammers began to pound. Wires were being moved, as the ghetto, to fit its shrunken population, was being cut to a smaller size.

To hold them fast, to stay together with them — this was all Tola had wanted. Yet, just months later they were lost to her, both within a few minutes, like coins slipped from a torn purse. Why? Had she grown too confident? Had the quiet deceived her, this long winter, when children playing "deportation" were the only reminder of what might come — "but not till spring," so everyone said. And the fear that swelling buds brought was stilled by the cold blast.

Because it was not real spring yet, because the snow of March still shone on the roofs, the SS surrounding the ghetto seemed like a memory of terror long past. "It's nothing," she said, "it must be nothing."

"All who work have nothing to fear," an O.D. man announced as he came in. "All with badges proving they're working will just go to Plaszow camp." And while she was checking to be sure they had not lost their badges — hers with a "W" for Wehrmacht, her parents' with a "Z" for Zivil — the O.D. man rapidly listed those who would not be coming along: the unemployed, children, and the old. At once the room was divided between a small group that sat on the side, left out like the sick not invited on a trip, and those who were going, who were getting ready, putting on shirt over shirt, dress over dress.

"Wait," Mother whispered, slipping on another blouse, "you wait." The empty sleeves flapping, she dashed out. She came back slowly, her lips white. "Z," she said in an odd, high-pitched voice, "Z is not going, not Z." And now Mother and Father were left out: the sick.

Letters on the white badges formed into incongruous words; crowds, knapsacks, bundles blocked her way, while she who had to find a cure, ran from O.D. man to O.D. man. They pushed her away, with clubs, with fists, forcing her into the column that stretched the entire length of the street, the men far in the front.

"Achtung! Herr Lagerkommandant!" voice echoed after voice. Spurs clinking, an SS man taller than any she had ever seen was coming toward her. He wore no helmet, his face looked kindly in the sun. Taking heart she ran to him and, "Herr," she stammered, "Herr Lagerkommandant . . . my mother works for the Wehrmacht, my mother has lost her badge." He did not push her away, he bent to hear her better. "Fräulein," he even said, "Fräulein, please —"

"Please, bring me a photostatic copy," he had said. He was joking; that jokes could be made changed what was happening into a game that could be won with the right trick. A shawl was the trick, a long shawl that would hide the "Z."

A dark-fringed shawl lay in the doorway of their room. She bent. "Men go separately," she said, still bending. "You try." Then in one huge step she moved forward and gripped Mother's hands that hung like things for anyone to take. And Father, standing at the wall, seemed a thing, a likeness made of disjointed features, a likeness that must be kept away. But he stirred, he was moving closer. "Have you seen it?" he asked. "My prayer shawl. I can't find it."

"Don't!" she cried with hatred against him for understanding nothing, for forcing her to understand what might happen to him — and to her too, unless she left at once — only not alone, but with Mother, who kept mumbling, who kept shaking her head. Tola turned, took aim. Like a net she cast the shawl on Mother, and, clutching the limp shoulder, walked out — backward, her eyes fixed on a strip of torn wallpaper, on stains, then on the embroidered lion that glimmered at the door.

The shawl had loosened while they had run to the column. She tied it fast. "Look calm," she said, "Mother, look calm." She herself did look calm; she even brought back that smile used for saying yes, as if now too agreeing with everything — the fists, the flailing clubs, and "Achtung!" resounding everywhere. Hissing, a whip swung down; it danced before her face, then gingerly moved sideways. Something fluttered, something rustled by. It was a shawl. Mother's shawl had fallen to the ground. Mother's hand had been torn away, and the cry that pierced through the loud rattle was her own. From across the street this rattle was coming, from the hospital building; there death was being brought to the sick — like breakfast to bed.

It was not her feet that marched on, not her arms that swung. She consisted only of eyes, burning, taking in each detail — a family out for a stroll, a billboard saying SUGAR STRENGTHENS, and this face next to her, the cheeks streaked black, the mouth from which dried lipstick peeled mumbling something about Tadzio, about her child. She did not want to hear about Tadzio, she did not want this woman to paw her. "Leave me," she said.

"Leave me alone!" she cried when they came into the camp barracks. But the woman followed her to the bunk, then stood, her arms outstretched, the black mascara tears dripping down her nose.

At last she was alone. She lay pressed against the boards, while around her daughters were helping their mothers up to the bunks, were fetching water for them, and soup. The clinking of spoons stopped. Sheltering his eyes from the sun, an O.D. man reported that trucks packed tight were passing by. The trucks had come back empty, the same O.D. man said at dusk. And when darkness fell, clothes were brought back to the camp, none stained — showing that those who had worn them had had to undress first.

At night a search took place. In the barracks, guards looking for gold ransacked clothes and bunks; outside, stripped to their shifts, the women stood, hands stretched out for inspection. A thin band of gold caught the flashlight beam and a woman whined that the ring would not come off — after so many years it just would not.

"Really?" said the Lagerkommandant. "Then we shall cut the finger off."

Smacking like an infant, the woman gnawed and chewed at her finger. Then, just as the ring fell jingling on the black ice, wind tore her shift up, and sallow, like a plucked hen, her body stood out in the light. Tola turned and looked only at the sky.

And again she lay on the bunk, face pressed against the bare boards.

The broom scraped; the mother of Tadzio was combing her hair. And those returning from the latrine reported the news about the bombing of Germany, the new fights in Italy, and the big Pole.

Chapter 4

Tola never went back to see Barbara; she avoided the kitchen and the place where the Poles worked. Once, when Glatt wanted to send her there on some errand, she balked and went to stand six instead. With Seidmanka still refusing to be reconciled, with Rubinfeldova timidly attempting to make peace, she preferred to keep to herself and spent most of the day at her post outside. But in the evening she hardly left her bunk. Whenever an O.D. man walked by, she would start, would wait to be called. Returning to the barracks from some brief errand, she would hover around the adjacent bunks in case there was a message for her. No message. Barbara must have understood the danger, and would not send for her. Tola was pleased: her warning, her only good deed in the camp, had worked.

There was not much talk about the big Pole any longer. Had everyone grown accustomed to her gifts of bread and inarticulate comfort? Were they disappointed that she had no more to offer? Whatever the reason, from the "mysterious emissary" Barbara had been demoted to "a generous woman" or a "kindhearted Pole," which under the circumstances was no mean praise.

Soon other events absorbed everyone's attention. Autumn, the first in the camp, was here. Until the first days of October the warm weather had stayed on and, since in the camp where nothing grew nothing could wither, it seemed as if the summer would last forever. Then overnight it was gone: the wind blew hard, a frozen drizzle made everyone shudder. "Ah, winter is almost here." The people sighed, both with bitterness that the seasons had passed bringing no change and with hope, the timid, the undeniable hope, which new air, new sky always holds out.

As if the Lagerkommandant wished to bestow a touch of autumn color upon the camp, the barracks were painted a dull yellow-brown. Next, stumpy poles spiked the boundary between the womens' and the mens' barracks. No wires were yet stretched across them, but the people sneaked by cautiously as if already defying orders. The rain fell. With the smell of fresh paint, with the barracks rising like piles of matted leaves out of the thick mist, the camp seemed so new, so strange, that a sense of expectation seized everyone, and "No news yet?" people returning from the latrine were asked.

At last the news did come. Seidmanka brought it to the paper workshop, "Eee — Eee —" she stuttered, then stood, cheeks puffed up as if she were about to dive.

"What happened? What's the matter?"

"Italy declared war on Germany. Corsica has been taken. The Allies are moving on!" Everyone looked at her. "Italy turned against them. Italy," she repeated, like the name of a long-lost friend.

Everyone was rushing toward her, as if Glatt were not there, sitting astride his chair. As a matter of fact, Glatt pretended not to be there, and when he spoke up it was softly.

"Hmm, disperse. It is not safe — hmm — to stand like this — hmm." Only with difficulty could he adjust to such civilian speech. He discarded his whip; empty hands dangling, he stepped forward. "Ah," he said, "ah, I wouldn't tell you to work, were Florence Florianska Street and Italy I — I — Idziego Street." At last he had found a Cracow street starting with an "I." Then he waited, bent, his eyes again bulging with a plea for response. An old joke, not too good even in its prime, yet this time people relented; chuckles rose, grew louder until, Glatt guffawing loudest, a wave of laughter swept the barracks. They stopped, but the children still kept up their urchins' giggle.

Soon break was announced; Tola was called back from standing six, for no one believed that the Lagerkommandant might come tonight.

"Oh, no, he is walking like a ghost through his villa. Would you like to be in his skin?" Seidmanka buttonholed everyone passing by. She hesitated: "You, Tola, would you like to be in his skin?" she brought out. "Absolutely not," Tola said, and Rubinfeldova smiled a broad relieved smile.

The tall, dark-haired man took over — he who had pointed to Kohn's empty place. He had been a teacher of history once, and though so clumsy when it came to folding envelopes, he deftly drew a map of Italy. "A fantastic map, honestly, fantastic," Seidmanka asserted in the voice of authority.

"The long boot, that's Italy," he held forth. "The ball that it tries to kick, Sicily." Then skirting the Apennines, just as the Allies would, he led them on to Rome, to Florence and Milan, until the Alps stopped him, though not for long, for if in 218 B.C. Hannibal had crossed them with his elephants, wouldn't the Allies leap over them with their planes and tanks?

No one worked, no one swept the floor. "Italy, the Allies, Hannibal," everyone repeated, all through the night.

Right after the "Italian" night a bustle of frantic preparations began in the camp. Cleanliness was the order of the day; inspection after inspection, O.D. men, guards, burst into the barracks; bunks had to be made flawlessly; no can, no pot could mar their symmetry, and for the least breach of hygiene, for a pail emptied into the street, for not making it to the latrine — which the distance and the cold considered, was bound to happen — everyone in the culprit's barracks was given an hour of "gymnastics," hopping froglike on the icy ground.

Next, every window in the camp was washed; next, white linen was issued to the infirmary, and the cooks too became snow-white, matching the gluelike sago dealt out as dinner every single day.

"A Red Cross inspection," said some. "A Commission of the neutral nations," said others.

And a Commission it was — an SS Commission from Berlin. Even the weather spruced up on the day of their arrival. The rain stopped; cold, brilliantly clear, the sun shone through the freshly washed windows. In the paper workshop, as everywhere else, preparations began at dawn: the broom scraped, the wicker baskets stood in perfectly even rows, perfectly even, too, stacks of envelopes rose on every table. And just when everything seemed arranged, "The children," an O.D. man shouted from the door, "the children must go back to the barracks." The children got up, but already "The children must stay!" another O.D. man called. "The number of people in each shop has been reported. Hurry, distribute them."

At once Glatt spaced the children far apart, and always next to someone short, so that they would appear like adults, only undersized. He scrutinized the barracks; and like a hostess before a party camouflaging the worn-out furniture, displaying those still handsome to their advantage, he now sent an old woman to a dark corner, now put a husky girl to the fore. He looked satisfied; he nodded.

O.D. men kept dashing in. "The Commission came to the laundry," gasped the first.

Had they said anything in the laundry? "Sauber," they had said, "Sehr sauber." The Commission had liked the laundry.

The kitchen, they had just left the kitchen, announced the next. They had looked at the kettles, at the stove, at every single thing.

"The bakery, in the bakery." The third O.D. man could hardly speak.

This had happened in the bakery: "Baker," the Commission had said to the crooked-mouthed Mandelbaum, "baker, how much bread per week does each prisoner get?" "Half a loaf," Mandelbaum was about to say, when Goeth, like a joker adding horns to someone while a picture is taken, raised his two fingers right above the Commission's heads. And "Two," Mandelbaum had answered, "two loaves, Herr Standartenführer."

"Goeth," the O.D. man had said, not *he*, not Lagerkommandant, just "Goeth." And "Goeth" everyone repeated, so much had this event dwarfed him who was now dreading the Commission no less than they, even asking — more, begging — favors, and of whom? Of Mandelbaum, with the crooked mouth.

Why this dread? Was the Commission on their side? This could not be; yet slowly hope began to stir, and it grew stronger with each improvement Glatt contrived: the pots hidden behind the bales of paper, the coats stacked more neatly, because for once they were doing something, not just waiting, as on the night of the selection, as on many a night before. But soon there was nothing more to be done.

"Are they coming?" everyone whispered. When soup was brought in they took heart again, for it was not sago, not even kohlrabi, but potato.

"Four — no five, I've found five potatoes!" Seidmanka triumphed, until she could not help herself — she had to say it. "The Commission," she announced, "they came to clip his wings."

"Really?" asked Rubinfeldova, her eyes round.

"Of course," Tola said. "What else would you expect from the SS, from our dear faithful friends?"

"You! Can't you grant anyone a moment of hope?"

"I . . . I'm sorry." Tola felt relieved when after the noon break Glatt sent her to a lookout point at the window.

"No, I see no one, no one," she reported. "Now," she flattened herself against the wall, "they're going to the knitters. They're coming out, they're coming!" She rushed back to her seat. A chair screeched. The clicking was Glatt practicing standing at attention. Footsteps.

"Ach — Achtung!" Glatt shouted. And they were here.

Three short bespectacled men, this was the Commission, each in spite of his field-green uniform quite civilian-looking, especially in contrast to Goeth, who towered high above them, his long overcoat swishing with each step. As he passed by Tola caught a glimpse of his face — handsome but obese — the face of a middle-aged businessman bloated by too little activity and too much food.

The others saw only the Commission: their soft-spoken ways, their smiles — for they did smile, and often — so that they resembled board members, a bit startled, a bit flattered by the stir they created, and amused equally by the ignorance their own questions showed and by the zeal of the answers. They walked through the shop, stopped at the back where the older women were tucked away, then stopped again, right at Tola's table.

How many sizes of envelopes were made in the shop, out of how many types of paper? Tola answered, her German impeccable, her voice clear and calm.

"Interessant," said the Commission, "sehr, sehr interessant." And they were gone.

Everyone looked at her. She colored and looked away. But Seidmanka would not let her be. "Oh!" she gasped, "how you spoke to them!"

"How, if I may ask?"

"So — so beautifully, and in such German, as if you were a German yourself."

"Exactly. Rolling my R's as if I were a blond Walküre."

Rubinfeldova broke in. "Why do you always have to twist everything? Is it wrong if we want to show them that we are not trash?" Tola shrugged, getting up.

Early in the afternoon the Commission left the camp. The day moved slowly. Everyone felt let down by those preparations made for a visit a few moments long.

A bordello for the Ukrainian guards to be built in the camp was the first news; sago again for the nightshift the next. Then "Mandelbaum is no longer in the bakery; he has been transferred to the hardest work in the camp — to the stone quarry."

"But — but God forbid — this will be the end of him," Rubinfeldova whispered. "Tola, he, the Lagerkommandant, stood so close to you. Did you see him? I mean really, I mean his face."

"He's fat. Otherwise he looks just like anyone else."

The Commission had declared that there was a surplus of women in the camp — this was the rumor which next evening spread over the barracks.

"What does it all mean? Don't worry, we'll find out soon enough!" Tola snápped in answer to Seidmanka's frenzied questions, patted Rubinfeldova's shoulder, then hastily went back to her bunk. More out of habit than hope, for she was sure by now that Barbara would never send for her, she watched the O.D. men passing by, each mumbling that he knew nothing, that the new rumor might be false. Another one came in, walked up to the barracks elder's bunk. The long sallow arm motioned, the O.D. man said something, and suddenly he stood before her. "Ohrenstein?" he asked. "Hurry up, she's waiting for you outside the kitchen."

"My God, I thought you'd never come." Slipping over the rank-smelling offal Barbara pulled her closer to the barracks wall. "Listen, I've decided. We . . . they, I mean — " haste made her stammer more than ever, "the Polish women will be going to Germany. I'm not going with them, I'm coming to your camp."

"No!" Tola cried. "No, you mustn't do this. You don't know what it's like here."

"I know what I'm doing. Nothing can be worse than what awaits me in Germany. Last night I thought it all over and understood this, and then . . . then I remembered how things used to be back in my place . . ." she whispered dreamily. "So. It's decided. This O.D. man says that there should be a way of sneaking me into your camp. But now I'd better go back."

A smile, a somewhat mocking "Don't look so worried," and suddenly she was gone.

"So," the O.D. man came closer, "so, someone must've found out who she is, and is about to denounce her."

"Are you sure?"

"Of course I am. Why else should she want to come here, why else?" he repeated, then turned to look at the opening door. In it Barbara stood, her face, lit by the glow of the kitchen fire, dreamy as when she had whispered "And then I remembered."

Chapter 5

THE ENORMOUS LIVING ROOM Barbara remembered first, which seemed to partake of two seasons at once. Outside one window lay green, as in spring; outside the other, August, the harvested plain yellow in the sun, empty; only sometimes a glistening crow would plummet down quickly, like a falling stone.

Only two o'clock, Barbara thought, and felt time heavy on her hands, when, just as she lay down, the telephone rang. Guests, it announced, guests are coming!

And right off, just as always, Marta, big breasts flapping like trapped fish under her blouse, fussed around the brimming larder with "Oh, what shall we feed them on, madam?" In no time carpet beaters could be heard whacking outside, while Barbara, more hindrance than help, ran from the kitchen, gray with chicken feathers, up to the guest rooms, where the sheets rose in white billows, then settled smooth and cool upon the beds.

Next day the guests began to arrive. The Herzigs came first — the rich Herzigs — came just as always, their three stork-legged girls carrying presents for everyone, the carriage sent for them to the Starybor station so piled with luggage that you hardly noticed the unusual, the famous Herzig Persian rugs rolled up in the back; just as in the midst of "Oh, how wonderful! oh, it seems like ages" you overlooked Mr. Herzig's "We plan to stay here until the situation gets clarified."

Then tea was served in the springlike part of the living room, then they all took a walk through the park, over the road cloudy with dust and gnats, and on to the stables, where "There's nothing like country life!" the Herzigs exclaimed while breathing gingerly, through the front of the nose.

Stefan came home late, this being the busy harvest time, and sat down to dinner still in his riding clothes. Looking at him among these faded city guests — taller, more powerful than ever with his copper face and the long mustache bleached by the sun — she felt an onrush of her old pride in him, then a need to shelter him from the usual Herzig jibes about his working harder than a farm hand, then also a twinge of vexation with him for answering only "Oh well, well"; and at once shame, at once remorse would set in, bringing more tenderness, more pride in turn, so that all through the five-course dinner Barbara felt as though on a roller-coaster — up with love and pride, down with vexation and remorse, then up again, only higher still. All of which was just as always. Only this was not as always: the radio speaking from the corner, its voice soft yet distinct amidst the guests' repeated "What a meal! And it could have fed twenty, at least twenty."

Exactly twenty sat down to dinner just two days later, for more and more were coming, as if to a long-awaited wedding. In order of their riches, as if the greater their wealth the more they were exposed to danger, so they came — always bringing presents for their hosts, always with the "Just until the situation gets clarified," which to her soon sounded like the name of a season fit for a country visit. The carriage rolled off to the Starybor station, brought the load of guests and went off again for more guests and for the papers. "Don't forget the papers," Mr. Herzig called from the window.

Barbara never read the papers; she often turned off the radio; the too precise voice speaking from it of negotiations, of pacts and such, somehow stood between her and those events which were drawing nearer and nearer and still like a wedding. It was to that other talk that she listened, the talk in the village where groups gathered before the thatched huts, the young people silent, the older ones talking of the last war; how from the burning distillery the spirits had streamed in a river of blue flames, and how everyone had been carried off into the heart of Russia, where people were kind — but then what could kindness avail against cold and hunger?

"Do you think you'll be called up?" she would then ask Stefan.

"Not soon," was his answer. "At least not till October, when the potato harvest is in."

Somehow October seemed only to move farther away, with so much happening. Each day there was more to be done — the new guests to be accommodated, the grown-ups on camp beds, the delighted children on beds made up from chairs; then the ladies to be kept out of Marta's way, and everyone to be entertained in some fashion. On that afternoon, a week after the Herzigs' arrival, it was dancing. "Après moi le déluge," one of the guests — a young medical student — said, with a very bad accent. "War or no war, let's dance," he added. By then everyone made the same sort of bantering apology, so that it seemed a part of everyday speech, like "thank you" or "goodbye." Soon couples were whirling on the lawn, Barbara, though an atrocious dancer, the most in demand. "It was on the Isle of Capri that I met her" came through the phonograph speaker. "Under the shade — " The singing stopped.

"Could you be quiet?" Stefan said. "The peasants are here, I must talk to them. No, please, stay here, all of you," he added, as some of the guests tried to follow him. She was no guest; she went with him to the broad driveway where the peasants stood, their patched caps in their hands.

"We have been called up, sir," the oldest one said. Then one by one they spoke, some wanting a piece of advice, some a loan, and all asking Stefan to keep an eye on their belongings, on the cattle and the women too. Barbara, not spoken to, stood on the side like a guest after all, unwanted in this world of men's affairs.

"And you?" she said to Stefan, after the peasants had left. "Will you too be called up?" When he said nothing she felt afraid.

Next morning she woke up early. Mist was still trailing over the park; here and there through the still-green thicket a maple would shoot through in a shaft of pale gold. October, Stefan's departure, and waking up alone, seemed almost upon her. She drew closer to him, and the warmth of his body pushed those thoughts away.

On this day, just as before a wedding, sewing began; only instead of sewing a frill or lace onto the gala dress, everyone was making masks out of gauze, cotton wool, and baking soda — such masks, according to the Starybor teacher, being the most assured protection against gas. The needles glistened, the ladies laughed, a trifle too loudly perhaps, while Barbara burst in with more baking soda, more gauze, then hurried to the fields back to Stefan. Because now she wanted them to be together.

And together they watched as all the sound horses were taken.

One by one the requisition officers led them out of the stables. The heavy flanks swayed, the tails swished, and as they vanished in the dust tinged blue by the evening, it seemed as if a river had carried them off.

The night, though it was the last of August, was hot. Then, heavy with heat, the morning came, the sun pouring into the room so that the breakfast table shone, like a flower bed, with the gold of honey, the garnet red of berries and the dewlike moisture upon the freshly churned butter. From outside came the sour smell of manure; she closed the windows, remembering that it displeased her guests who were settling down to breakfast, their voices blending drowsily with a bee's drone. The drone grew loud, such a stillness fell; only in the corner the radio kept talking. She sat down. From a knife placed carelessly across the bowl a drop of honey hung, elongated like a pendant. She looked at it. The radio spoke on. And when the drop fell, this was war.

No one stirred. The guests looked at one another at a loss; from the kitchen came the sound of kneading. It stopped. "So — God have mercy on us," Marta's voice said, and the sound of kneading was back, as plump and even as before.

At noon the mobilization call for Stefan came. "I see," she repeated, just because she could not see how it could have happened, not even when she had packed his things, and they sat on the veranda, Antoni and Marta opposite them.

"Well, take care of her, Antoni," Stefan said. "You know what she's like."

"Like a child," said Antoni, "if I may be so bold. Just like a foolish child."

"What? Are you both — " She broke off. Remembering the peasants' farewell from Stefan, she understood at last what was happening to her.

As if a language they had not yet learned was required, they spent the evening silently. Silently too they sat in the carriage as it rolled next morning to the Starybor station. Here a fair might have been going on, such a press of carriages, of carts and horses thronged everywhere; such crowds walked up and down the platform, where usually only a few sparrows would hop on the gravel. They too walked up and down. Barbara longed for it to be all over.

But when he got on the train, she wanted to run after him and beg his forgiveness for what she had once done to him, for the wrong never spoken of yet rankling in both of them. "Stefan," she cried, but the train moved on. From everywhere — from the station building, from the platform and the carts — the shrill peasant wail broke forth and wedged itself between them, silencing her, deafening what Stefan was calling from the train window.

"Everywhere it's like this, madam — Judgment Day! Everywhere," the coachman said, and Barbara grew afraid for Stefan passing through this wail, as through a tunnel, with no air in it, no breath.

Back at home the anxious guests were waiting for her. Someone wanted his relatives to come, someone had urgent letters to be mailed out of Starybor. Then more gauze was needed, and linen too, for little bags in which valuables would be stored and worn on the neck.

"Yes," she said. "I'll take care of everything."

Soon the sewing was resumed. And above the clicking of scissors, above the hushed whispers, hurrah upon hurrah rose in volleys from the radio as the Warsaw crowds thanked the ambassadors of England and of France for their promises. Then silence, then: "Hallo, attention, attention, it's coming, it is here." Silence again, very long now.

"Warsaw is being bombed," Mr. Herzig said. And the needles moved faster.

A bag with valuables round each neck, a "gas mask" in each hand — so when the planes came overhead they ran into the park. Barbara led the way through the thicket and into the ditch. They lay deep in nettles. Earth spattered, heads ducked into the dirt. But she looked up: like a school of winged fish, so they swam, the torsos motionless, the pointed snouts cutting through the blue sky. One came down, grew huge, and a thud of detonation shook the earth. Somewhere in the distance smoke rose. "Gas!" someone shrieked. "Gaas!" The guests scrambled out of the ditch, groping for the masks, putting them on awry, while she breathed in the clear air, and burst out laughing. And still laughing and teasing, they returned to the manor.

"A herd of cows was bombed in Volka," Antoni reported. Soon

it was not cows that were bombed; soon it was Lublin, where the government had fled. Day after day Barbara led her guests to the park, more of them each time. For they still kept coming, not in carriages sent to meet them at the railway station, since no trains were running, but in a peasant cart or on foot, and all with little bundles for luggage — all strangers until they would present some roundabout references to a mutual friend, or a party attended together with Barbara years ago.

"You're most welcome," was all she said, rushing off to put them up, some on bolsters spread on the floor, some on the frail Récamier sofas, over which Marta quickly sneaked slipcovers, muttering "Company or not, these are no ordinary times!" Every evening, clothing and the gas masks were put out in readiness, and the nights grew short as they ran to the park, then drank scalding tea and looked at the glow of conflagration, a downy red against the black sky. And throughout the days and the nights the radio kept talking.

One day, which day of the war it was Barbara no longer knew, so completely had they merged together, it was still.

"Who's been tampering with the radio again?" Mr. Herzig shouted, and he twisted the knobs, he shook the table; only a babble came, as if the radio were trying to tell him something but could not.

Yet they had news, brought in lieu of presents by the ever-arriving guests. "The Germans are moving east," they said. "They're in Lodz, in Cracow, in Kielce."

"Terrible," Barbara whispered. But soon those places — where you had gone for a winter visit, where you had bought such lovely clothes — changed into a part of "abroad," like Vienna or Paris or Rome. Only with each new guest it was harder to transform the place he named into "abroad."

When it was Kazimierz, just fifty miles away, the guests began to leave, in order according to their riches again, and yet quite differently from the manner of their coming. Barbara grew helpless. She needed Stefan. The war — for her only a richness and a breadth, only the open door and the table set each day for more — was shrinking to something meager and drab: the guests were now concealing from one another the discovery of a cart or a guide, the peasants were skinning them for an old nag, the guests in turn haggling over every copper.

At last they left. But for each one gone, more came, all name-less, a tired "We heard one can rest here a bit" their only reference. City people came; ladies asking first for hot water to wash out the plaster sifted into their hair during a bombing; portly merchants staring at their blistered feet as though they couldn't imagine how they had come by them; and a group of Communists, wearing like a decoration the gaps in their teeth — earned in prison for the Cause, they said, while Antoni muttered "You got it in a drunken brawl." And soldiers too came, hobbling on their rag-swathed feet.

"Man to man we would have fought, madam, but when it comes from the sky, then . . . then we couldn't anymore," they said, as if some explanation were still required.

Where the Germans were, those new guests hardly ever men-tioned, speaking instead of the roads, of cars, carts, and horses' carcasses piled high along the roadside, while crowds streamed on and on, where or why no one seemed quite to know.

Barbara listened. "Here, take some bread and rest," she said to those who came in, "Here, take some bread and God be with you," to those who were leaving, then watched them set out into the gray rain that fell day after day and drizzled inside, too, through win-dows that had somehow been broken. These were her only mo-ments of rest now. She rose long before dawn and, groping among the straw bags scattered everywhere, went to the kitchen, where Marta — her sole help now — was already waiting. They baked bread, heated up huge kettles of water, then made tea out of burned raw sugar and red like burgundy wine. Often in the evenings she would find her room occupied and spend the night on a straw bag among her guests. Waves of breath, footsteps rose out of the si-lence, or an abrupt chord struck by fingers groping against the piano while, wide awake, she thought of Stefan, gone on to Rumania with remnants of the army, her longing for him tinged with re-gret that he could not watch her take care of so many so well. This care of her guests she took fully upon herself. All else — hiding of their possessions, planning what to do should the Germans occupy the manor — she left to Antoni.

One morning no guests were left. She understood the reason;

she knew the Germans were almost here, right in Starybor or closer. Yet surrounded by the unaccustomed silence she felt betrayed, as if some promise given her had been broken. She stood at the window and waited.

Soldiers came as if a return had begun, westward. "Back to Warsaw," the older of the two officers said, because Warsaw was still holding out. That evening, she kept pacing up and down until midnight, when the soldiers, ready to leave, lined up outside. Standing in the open door, she handed out bread and burgundy-red tea.

When all were fed she went outside, straight to the older officer. "And so . . ." she said hoarsely, "how would it be if I came along too? I'm ready."

"At no other time could I refuse such a charming woman, but now —" The laboriously gallant voice grew tired. "Now," he repeated, "we hardly know what to do with ourselves."

"You . . . you can't take me along?"

"No, we cannot."

The other officer, a boy of eighteen or so, kept looking at her. It was only a cap he wanted, any kind of an old cap. As if this cap were an entrance fee she rummaged frantically in all the drawers, but all she found was her old school beret. She gave it to him, and looked at the infected bruise the helmet had cut on his forehead. He drew himself up and saluted, fingers stiff at the beret, too small, so that it slid to the back of his head.

Antoni and Marta were whispering as she came in.

"Hmm, madam," Antoni said, "those German scoundrels drive people out of places like this one." Places like this one meant the Jewish manors. That Antoni, whose frequent "That usurer, that Jew!" would bother no one, being a mere turn of speech, would now speak with such circumspection forced a gap between them.

"In places like this, ha!" she flared up. "And in other places? I've heard the owners are moved into — a garret or barn. Oh, you! Do you think I would ever stay under the same roof with them?"

"Neither would we." Antoni closed the gap. "Not for a single hour. And so we'd better get along, madam."

"No, we will stay till they come."

Then she and Marta looked at each other, got up, and reached for the brooms.

"Jesus Maria, they're cleaning for them!" Antoni shouted. It was Marta who answered him. "Should they say that we live like pigs, should they?"

They put the straw bags away, swept the floors, and took off the muddy slipcovers from the sofas, but only after much poring over the German dictionary was Barbara ready for them.

They came in the afternoon, the soldiers waiting outside while the two officers knocked on the door. Keys were what they asked for, with stiff, somewhat embarrassed politeness. And she gave them the keys to the barns, the larder, and the stables — empty all of them, since Antoni had given the crops to the peasants — then slowly led them to her desk.

"When you leave, put the keys here," she said in her dictionary German, "so that we'll find them when we return."

"Wie, bitte?" The Germans looked at her. "Wie?" They shook their heads, as she, stuttering with anger, kept repeating the carefully memorized phrase, for the sake of which she had stayed.

"Nein, nicht verstehen." Regretfully the Germans shrugged their shoulders.

Soon after, the cart borrowed from the village came into the driveway. Silently they climbed into it, silently they drove off, through the forest, past the Starybor station, where the last asters rose into the rain, reminding her it was October, the time when the potato harvest would be brought in.

The Poles' barracks was quiet.

"Janina," a whisper startled her, "are you asleep, Janina?"

"What is it?" Hastily, as one surprised in his nakedness, Barbara slipped back into the disguise of this name.

"What will become of us in Germany?"

"It does no good to fret, my dear. Somehow we'll manage." The woman tiptoed away; rosary beads clinked in the dark, and across from her, moonlight fell upon the gray crumpled face.

Never in her life had she so studied a face — the grain of pockmarks, the spiteful mouth and eyes; in this ugliness, in the vulgar bearing hoping to find the key to what others had told her about this woman. There was no key. Nothing could be explained: neither the ruse this woman had hit upon — sneaking through the dark to tickle the foot of that sleeping Jewish girl — nor her triumphant "You're a Jewess! A Christian when scared cries 'Jesus Maria!' not 'Oi Mama!' like you." Least of all what had happened next morning — the guards coming and leading the Jewish girl to the guns up on the hill.

Her eyes fixed upon the Tickler, she walked to the door, then outside. In thin black lines, guns cut across the wintry sky; but lower down on the hill's slope light gleamed through the opening doors: there, in the workshop-barracks, people sat and talked freely about anything they remembered and felt: there the girl was who had come to her, had called her by her real name. "Barbara . . . Barbara Grünbaum." She hungered for the sound of her name, longed to hear it spoken and to speak of herself, of Stefan, the manor and the life that had once been hers.

"Janina Zborovska — from Poznan — no, I was never married." This lay ahead of her in Germany: deception, lies, and the nights when she to whom hundreds had come for help, she whom once neither bombs had frightened nor the Krauts, would shudder each time this pockmarked woman stirred. She stood looking at the Jewish camp. Again a door opened there, letting out a broad beam of light. The light vanished, and everything was decided: she must get into the Jewish camp; she would not spend this war like a parasite, helping no one, thinking of nothing but saving her own skin.

From behind a heavy shuffle came. It was the Tickler going to the latrine. Barbara smiled. "Come here," she whispered as the Tickler returned, "I have something to tell you, come."

"What do you want, Janina?"

"Listen." Suppressing her revulsion she drew closer. "There is a Jew who's walking about free, who's lording it over the whole world."

"A Jew? How do you know?"

"He has dark eyes, dark hair, dark mustache. He's more cunning than a snake. Sounds like a Jew, doesn't it?"

"Who is he? Who?"

"Haven't you guessed yet? It's he — Hitler!"

Shaking with laughter, her feet dangling down freely, Barbara lay on her bunk. Then, very slowly she drew her legs up, and wrapped herself tight like a mummy in the coarse blanket.

Chapter 6

FAR UP ON THE SLOPE of the hill lay the camp — the black of tar-paper roofs, the Appellplatz, and the road dark with columns going to work as on any other day. Down below, the trains which were to take the women to another camp shone bright red in the sun; and there, marching next to Tola was Barbara, with her glistening eyes and her broad smile looking more than ever like one from the Freedom, among the women worn out and frightened by the previous night.

The night had begun like any other: the broom scraped; "Work! Don't sleep!" Glatt had yelled. And just as the triumphant Seidmanka had come back from the latrine, as Rubinfeldova was asking about the news and Tola about the big Pole, O.D. men in a black quadrangle blocked the door. A shout — they pounced forward, tore most of the women away from their seats, and kicking, pushing, drove them outside. Rain fell, the darkness reeked of vodka; and the huge ever-swelling crowd trudged on past the workshops, past doors opening upon isolated figures still knitting, sewing, stringing the bristle through a broom. The road climbed more steeply, leading them into the outlying parts of the camp. Boards, piles of gravestones kept blocking the way, and from the ditches gaping on both sides cries came, as those who had hidden there trying to escape were being dragged back.

At the tall wall of barbed wire they stopped. "Qua . . . qua," a woman croaked "qua . . . quarantine!" Silently, only their feet splashing through the puddles, the crowd moved on to the row of quarantine barracks, where those about to be shot were usually kept.

"I know nothing" — "It's forbidden!" the O.D. men guarding the door kept shouting. To go into the adjacent barracks, to look there for those lost in the confusion, was forbidden. At last the women climbed up on the bare bunks — none alone, even those separated from mothers, from closest friends clinging to a companion found on the way.

Tola, as always, kept to herself. "Please, I'd rather be alone," she said whenever someone tried to join her, then sat staring at the shattered pane showing from under the loosened blackout sheet.

Had one of those brought here for their last night smashed this pane? At first the thought brought the detached curiosity with which a sightseer views the dungeons where royal prisoners had once been kept. And when it struck her that she was this prisoner, she herself, her hands grew clammy, clenched, dug into her chest. The spasm passed; slowly, for her legs felt limp, she got down to look for a place where perhaps one could hide. There was no such place here; and again she cowered on her bunk, watching the zigzags of light refracted in the shattered glass.

Two buckets, one with water, one for excrement, were placed at the door. A few women gathered round, waited, then, since the O.D. man would not budge, squatted over the bucket. And the welts of sallow flesh bulging out of their torn hose followed Tola into her feverish dreams.

Footsteps woke her up. Her arms dangling loosely, an old woman was pacing up and down, stumbling always on the same board, stopping at the same spot, and pushing out her jaw with a metallic click. Again she stopped, at the door now. It opened. An O.D. man came in, raised a long sheet to the light. Names he was reading, the names of O.D. men's relatives, mistresses, and friends, who thanks to such connections would be allowed to go back to the camp. "Here, coming!" Their arms outstretched, their eyes darting, as though an imposter might grab their place, those listed ran toward him, and right behind them the others who had no such connections came, begging the O.D. man for help, sending messages to someone left behind.

Tola, having left no one behind, stayed curled up on her bunk. The O.D. man, and those he had called, were gone; soon others came, more lists were read, more groups went back to the camp, and everywhere on the bunks lonely figures cowered — those left behind not just by some casual companion but by friends with whom they had shared each morsel, each thought. Tola watched them. When an O.D. man whom she knew came in she walked up to him.

"If you see the Polish women — nothing, forget it." Hastily she turned away. Back on her bunk she wrapped herself tighter in her coat, then looked at the lining, ripped off, all the money sewn under it gone.

The lists were growing shorter, the intervals between the O.D. men's coming longer and longer, until no one came. Her fist serving her as a pillow, she dozed off; but kept starting up, awakened by the pacing, the cold, and the stench rising from the overflowing bucket.

When she looked up again the old woman was pointing at the window, at the gray rim around the blackout sheet. "Soon! They'll come for us soon." And she went on pacing, faster and faster.

The rim shone brighter. Faraway the bugle uttered its shrill wheeze. One by one the women got down from the bunks and gathered at the door. "Don't be afraid," someone shouted outside. "Don't!" an O.D. man repeated, bursting in. "You're just going to another camp." No one stirred. "You are!" he cried. "I promise you, I swear!"

Upon what was most holy to him he swore, upon his life, but only after they had come outside did Tola begin to trust him, as if the wind, the luminous mist, and the sun proved that on such a morning nothing could happen to her.

She breathed in the frosty air. And everywhere around reunions were taking place. Calling, waving, speaking brokenly as after years of parting, those separated last night were embracing each other. Tola stepped forward, ran toward Rubinfeldova and Seidmanka, then suddenly turned back. The group coming out of the last barracks, those were the Poles, the tall figure in front Barbara, stepping aside, inching her way closer and closer to the Jewish column; and now she ducked, vanished in the crush, reappeared, looking changed, wearing a painted coat. "Barbara, here!" Tola tried to cry and could not. She stood, her arm outstretched. A throaty whisper, a hand touching her shoulder. "You . . . you here?" Tola stammered.

"Sure, I said I would come."

"Has anyone noticed you? Were your women counted?"

"Oh no. Everything will be all right." As Barbara smiled Tola was filled with apprehension over an error that could not be undone. For already they were marching on, Barbara clasping her hand and still smiling, like a child delighted with its latest prank.

At the gate leading to the railroad tracks the column stopped, the silence, the downcast eyes signaling that the Lagerkommandant was here. But soon, in every four a woman turned, with barely moving lips passing on the message about a sign. Food was this sign: bread and cheese, proving that they, still worth being fed, were just going to another camp. Only Tola could hardly reach out for her bread, so hard her hand shook, when he, huge in his long cloak, raised his whip as though, as at the ghetto gate, to leave her all alone again.

Nothing had happened; they passed the gate, they marched on across a frost-whitened field, across the glitter of tracks and on into the dank chill of the cattle car. Here another sign yet was granted them: the space that allowed them to move, sit down, and breathe.

Boots stamped past the open door. They stopped; a bang, and all was dark. Calling upon God with his many Yiddish names a guttural voice cried out, loud and louder yet, as hammers pounded, nailing down door after door. "Riboyno shel Oylam, oh Gotteniu, oh Gott!" A jolt and, hurling the crouched figures against the wall, the train moved on.

Through a chink, a thread of light came in and wound itself round Barbara's fumbling arms.

"What is it?" Tola whispered. "What are you doing?"

"I'm changing, putting a painted dress on. So, done! Good riddance Zborovska!" As Barbara laughed the apprehension grew stronger.

"Barbara, you had to come here, right? You had to." Getting no answer, she insisted.

"I had to? What do you mean?"

"Someone was after you, was about to denounce you."

"Oh no, no one was after me."

"No one?"

"Not a living soul."

Tola got up, groping in the dark, bent down over Barbara trying in vain to see her face. "No one?" she repeated. "But then — why have you come here, what have you done to yourself?"

"Oh, that was no life there, no life at all."

"And here?"

"Here I can be myself again, I can do something, can help."

"Is that why you came?"

"Yes, that's why! But you, you sound as if you didn't believe me."

For a long while Tola was silent, until "No!" she cried. "I don't believe you, I can't. You couldn't have just come to play the savior; someone must have been after you, someone . . ."

"You want to cross-examine me, like the Gestapo?" hoarsely Barbara broke in. "No one was after me; when I say something, I mean it. Now remember this, once and for all."

The engine whistled. "Don't trample on me!" someone cried.

Yet Barbara heard nothing. Barbara was relishing her anger, freely, with no apprehension of remorse, knowing that soon everything would be undone by her contrite "Oh, my vile temper. Do forgive me." And she was forgiven, always.

In the nick of time this anger had come to rescue her from what felt like the corridor of some dreadful tenement, dark and filled with noise. Somewhere at the entrance Janina Zborovska had been left, somewhere at the exit Barbara Grünbaum was awaiting her. Not yet one, no longer the other, she groped on, hampered by the incomprehensible Yiddish whines, then by those questions, irritating her more and more. For in the imagined return to her own people there had been no questions, only the welcome, the joy. But the anger, this luxury prohibited until now, had set everything aright. "Ah, forgive my temper, I'm sorry," now fully herself, she whispered.

"Oh, it's all right." The girl — her name had escaped Barbara — granted the expected absolution.

"You . . . you needled me; still, I got carried away. After all, you don't know anything yet, so how can you understand why I had to come here. But I'll tell you. Ah, I feel good."

"Good!" an old voice screeched. "They herd us in here like cattle, and 'I feel good,' she says!"

"Now what is it to you?" Barbara muttered, laughed out of sudden

lightness, then moved away from the screeching voice. "I feel as if a
gag had been taken out of my mouth, as if . . . You see, there in
the Polish camp I had to watch myself."

"But then, if you had to keep watching yourself — " the girl broke
in.

"Are you beginning all over again? No one was after me, not even
that abomination the Tickler. I'll tell you about her some other
time. Still, I had to be careful. Most of the women were good souls,
but a few . . . It was Jews this, Jews that all day long. Believe me,
I couldn't even sneeze without wondering if it was a Christian or a
Jewish sneeze. And the lies I had to tell, like some embezzler, the
kind you read about in the papers: alias this, alias that. Not that
I mind lying, I'm no saint. Still, this kind of lie does something to
you; you start believing them after a while. No, you don't, not
really, but nothing else seems real either; I mean, you don't know
any longer who you really are. Ah!" She faltered, then broke off.

It was always like this with her, whenever she longed to talk, not
just to make words — empty air breathed into empty air — but to
talk, to lay her heart open, then her mind expanded into a ban-
quet hall, with guests, colors, shapes, sounds crowding into it, each
demanding to be introduced, each claiming that without him this
feast of the heart laid open would not be complete. Then she would
stutter and grope, not only because — a bungler when it came to
talking — she could not do justice to such multitudes, but also because of an almost hurt feeling that one could not simply lead one's
listener into one's mind, then with a "Look around for yourself"
withdraw.

Now she longed to lead the girl to those evenings in the Polish
camp when the women would gather together and talk. Names fell;
homes, children were being prepared for the new season; with he-
never-takes-care-of-himself husbands were being reproached. The
unslackening concern, the inviolability of their grudges conjured up
all they had left behind. Upon everything once Barbara's an inter-
diction had been passed; she shammed and lied, while within her,
like breath held too long, the truth welled up. She could not bear it
any longer, she would speak up. But nearby, pig-eyed and watchful,
the Tickler, waiting for one unwary word, could give her away.
She kept silent; yet the deception pained her, a symptom of ugly

craftiness which she knew was ascribed to Jews. At first darkness brought relief: then to a circle of imaginary listeners she would talk of Barbara, Stefan, and the manor house. Soon those talks became stale, a repetition of anecdotes about someone known casually and long ago. Soon it seemed her name had always been Janina Zborovska, her past no more than a picture postcard of Poznan that she had once seen with a red roof on it, a too green tree and an inkspot in the corner.

"Then you came," she spoke softly, "and suddenly I could remember, could feel myself once again. Until then it was like . . . wait, I know what it was like. Did you ever miss a train? No? I did, all the time. And then, as I would sit in some godforsaken hole, this weird feeling would come over me that the waiting room, the spittoon, the old posters were all I'd ever known, all I ever would know.

"That was how I felt in the Polish camp. During the day, when I was outdoors, moving around, working, it was not so bad. But in the evenings I just could not help myself. And to suffer all this misery for nothing, to be of no use to anyone — "

"Of no use? You were considered a heroine, a veritable Messiah!"

"What nonsense! And you know what, I actually got some of those harpies off my scent this way. 'If Jews weren't such cowards and misers, I would think you're one of them, the way you stick your neck out to feed them,' said one to me. 'How come you know so much about Jews? Are you perhaps a Jewess yourself?' said I. Quick, wasn't it?" She waited for a laugh.

"Grünbaum," she whispered when no laughter answered, "Barbara Grünbaum. See what I mean? An hour ago this would have meant a bullet; now I could shout it from the rooftops and not a hair would fall off my head."

"You haven't changed at all." Now the girl did laugh, in a shy unpracticed way.

"Sure, why should I have changed? But tell me, what's your name?"

"Ohrenstein. From Cracow."

"No, your first name."

"Tola."

"Tola — Tolenka." As though to tower so high above others were not enough, Barbara was very fond of diminutives. "Tolenka, when exactly were you in my place?"

"Toward the end, when the villages around were burning."

"Terrible, wasn't it? But then you should understand me, because you know what my place is like — not elegant or beautiful but large, so large. And the crowds that passed through it, do you remember?"

"Yes, I often thought about you, and it seemed so certain that you must have gone on to Rumania or Russia. The old man told us you'd go."

"Antoni, of course you did meet him!" She paused, because out of the dark his eyes seemed to look at her, ruefully somehow. "What did you say?" absently she asked.

"Why didn't you leave then?"

"I couldn't. I didn't want to . . . I . . ."

"Hush!" rose from everywhere. "Be quiet, hush." The train had stopped; wheels rumbled outside, a voice droned through the loudspeaker. Motionless, even silencing their breath, the women listened, from the confused tumult of a station hoping to extricate some hint of their whereabouts. But already the panting of a passing engine drowned out the loudspeaker. Feet shuffled by, a hammer clanked against the rails.

"Tola," Barbara whispered, "what do they think is in here?"

"Coal, wood — anything."

"And if we shouted, pounded on the walls?"

"I wouldn't advise that."

"Hush!" again, and the train moved on.

"I wish it were not so dark." Barbara sighed. "Oh, never mind, what were we talking about?"

"You said you couldn't leave?"

"I couldn't because," she was groping again, "because a war is a war."

"No doubt about that."

"Please, don't quibble." She spoke pleadingly. "Look, they smoked me out of my own home, well and good, but to keep running away like a rabbit couldn't have been right. I knew it, from the first evening when we came to Lublin. Did you see Lublin after it had been bombed? Oh, it was like a different city — now, why is she whimpering again?" The Yiddish whine was back.

"She lost her bag."

"Good Lord! Stop it my dear, stop it, you won't find your bag in the dark. Where was I? Lublin, yes; everything was changed there except the people," she snapped, irked by the whine.

There in Lublin her cousin would not change, moaning in her "oh my migraine" tone about Germans, the price of bread, and bombs. To flee from this moan she looked out of the window. A spindly acacia shook in the wind; behind it, on a gray wall a bevy of pink legs advertised some film of long ago. And at first that other poster, which she had seen all over the city, seemed to advertise a film, one of those war movies from which Barbara would return both elated and sad: a soldier lay there, gray against the gray earth, blood gushing from his chest, and lower down — blood-red too — the inscription "England, this is your work!"

The cousin moaned on and on. "Madam," Antoni cried, "madam, ah, this woman will never learn!" Brushing past him, she ran outside. And now this new city of war was rushing at her, in the rumble of soldiers' boots, the scent of smoke, and in the laughter resounding from the cavernous damp of a doorway. A woman stood there; next to her a soldier, a Kraut! "Have you no shame?" she flared up. A jeering laugh, then a rumble again as, slowly, tanks rolled into the street.

But the rain-scented park was still: the warm wind ruffled her hair, dusk fell gently as in the spring. And it seemed to her that it was in welcome of this sudden spring that the tall midtown houses had laid themselves wide open — the barriers of windows and doors gone, here and there even the roofs torn off, like hats snatched by a lusty wind, and each house breathing, each, with the least breeze, exhaling clouds of white chalk. Stepping closer she saw: the exposed walls, the gash of what had been a gate, and inside the piles of bricks, of charred wood, of glass. Something caught the light of a passing car — a doorknob, or a brass plate with a name.

"Get away! Danger!" a man cried. "Danger! Danger!" the huge signs warned, and beyond the corner, the walls were propped by poles, freshly hewn like the masts of a new ship.

A siren was wailing nearby; the passersby groping along the path
between the ruins stopped in silence, as when, ushered in by the
tinkling of a bell, a priest comes with the Last Sacraments. The am-
bulance dashed by. Only after it had vanished did she remember
what her cousin had said: that people were still being dug out from
under the ruins, some of them crazed by hunger, some blind like
moles.

Orange-red like tapered poppies, flames glimmered in the dusk,
flames of candles lit for those left dead under the ruins. Flowers
lay on the pavements, gladiolas, last asters, exuding a sweet withered scent, and around them a dark wreath of kneeling women,
shabby in their hastily assembled mourning. The passersby crossed
themselves; Barbara bowed her head, and walked on. More ruins,
more candles gleaming in the dark. And with each gutted house,
each siren and outcry of soldiers' song, a pact was being sealed between the city and herself. To break this pact, to run away — this
she could never do.

"Yes! A war is a war!" This time she spoke firmly. As though
in applause, singing rose from the dark cattle car. Timid at first,
the voices drew together, gained strength. "God knows where we're
being dragged, and they sing," the hysterical whine protested. "Let
them sing, let them!" she cried, but already the chorus was dying
out, only one voice quavering through the dark. It stopped; in a
hoarse whisper someone was pleading for water.

"My, am I parched," Barbara gasped. They shared a can of water that tasted of soot, then a piece of bread with cheese. "Do you
remember how it used to be on trains?" Barbara spoke dreamily.
"All those hard-boiled eggs crackling, and the ham pink like baby's
gums, and the bread fresh like — like oh, I don't know what. But
this bread and cheese too taste good," she defied the taste of mold.
"You know why we got it, don't you?"

"Lagerkommandant's kindness. He was worried about the deli-
cate SS digestion."

"What a quibbler you are. Listen: now, when they're losing, the
Krauts are so scared they decided to treat us better. That's why
the Commission came, everyone in the Polish camp said so." She

paused. "Everyone!" she insisted, getting no answer. "And — wait! There — do you see?" Pale blue, like a luminous eye, something gleamed in the dark. It was an opening no bigger than a coin, but by bending, by fitting your eye against it, you could catch a glimpse of outside. "Come on everybody, we've got a window," Barbara called. The women staggered up; and like theater-goers taking turns in looking through the only opera glass, so they looked one after another through this window. "Red — it must be roofs — " they reported. "Blue — a river or perhaps the sky." "Now everything's dark, we must be going through a forest." "Dark — still dark." The women dispersed. Barbara bent down once again and waited until a glimmer of light flitted by.

"This reminds me," she drew closer to Tola, "of the fence in the place where I was kept under lock and key. By whom? By Antoni and Marta, of course. Oh, I know they wanted what was best for me; still, I couldn't bear it. In the beginning it was not too bad. At dusk I would get out, see a bit of God's world, but then when it meant a bullet for walking without the Star of David they wouldn't let me stick my nose out. 'Madam must be sensible, madam must stay indoors,' they kept after me; until these times, this war seemed to me like a rainy spell, going on and on. And the place where we lived, just a shack in the middle of nowhere, and no bigger than a chicken coop! I did everything to keep my unrest down, believe me I did." Fervently she enumerated those efforts: the floor scrubbed till it shone like the freshest butter, the scales polished and polished, it was a marvel they did not melt under all that rubbing. "But how could this have been enough? Morning after morning for two years to wake up and see the same crack, the same spot on the wall. They tried to humor me like a sick child. 'Sing,' I could have said, and they would have sung, would have danced on those old legs of theirs. And each time they went around the corner it was 'Ah, what heat, madam' — 'What wicked cold.' See, I'm telling you everything, the whole truth. I screamed at them. 'Stop pretending,' I screamed. 'Is it your doing that I have to squirm like a trapped mouse?' And then I would dash outside, into the backyard, just big enough for two puddles and the fence."

Somehow it had become alive for her, this fence, and ambiguous — now the enemy barring her way, now the friend, reporting the

weather and the passing of seasons in scents of mushroomy dampness or of sun-warmed wood. Higher up there was a knothole, her
window upon God's world: the dusty country road, the processions
of barefooted peasant women, their shoes thriftily tied round their
shoulders, their baskets heaving with cackling hens and geese. They
would pass on. A feather would float in the windblown dust . . .

On the outside of the fence — this she remembered from her walks
at dusk — was the dying soldier. Rising on tiptoes she had let her
arm down across the jagged fence-top and brought up a scrap of
paper, once blood-red, now the color of caked mud. On the day
when she had stolen outside to learn how little was left of him, only
a blurred outline and the scrap of the wound, the news came of
those terrible things.

"Hot," the resinous scent of the fence had reported. "Hot,"
stretched out on her bed, she sighed. From behind the door
whispers came, stopped when she stirred; she was still and they
went on. She got up, splashed water over her face, then walked
into the kitchen. At once all of them — Marta, Antoni, and his
wart-dotted crony — fell silent, like adults caught by a child in
some obscene talk.

"So! What's going on?" she demanded.

"It's nothing, madam," Marta said hastily. "Nothing."

"Quiet, woman." Antoni got up, clenched his fists, harder and
harder, until "Tell her!" he ordered the crony. "Yes, tell her, so that
she will know what harm we're doing to her."

"In Treblinka . . ." The crony wiped the sweat of his bald pate.

"Treblinka?" Marta cried. "But I know Treblinka, I've been
there!" She seemed to be defending a person known for years and
trusted to do no evil.

"Quiet, woman, I said."

"They're bringing trainloads of Jews to Treblinka and killing them
off — with gas." A sentence had been spoken, just as any other,
each word familiar, each used before, yet when put together they
darkened, coagulating into a thing that she must pierce open to see
what it contained. Outside the sun shone; children chased through
the jungle of hollyhocks, and a dog lolled in the sparkling dust. She
turned back. Across from her at the table those three were staring
as though demanding that she speak. But without a word, and

aware of an artificiality in her subdued gestures, she walked out.

All through the day this silence stayed on, uneasy as when a dreaded illness strikes a neighbor, known yet never loved, so that one feels no grief — only the terror that such things can be. And all through the day, their home, this chicken coop twelve paces across, was expanding with ugly distances as she constantly watched to see whether unlike her they had understood Treblinka, now demanding that they should, now, as if their understanding put her to blame, resenting it. At night, when the icon light seeped ruby-red through the door, did they sigh and toss because at last they had understood?

She felt duty-bound to understand. She tried, marshaling all her meager experience of grief — the silence of a house in mourning, the peasants' wailing round the burning hut — but just as she had fitted the gesture to the hand, the cry to the gaping mouth, everything vanished in a thickening haze.

Shamefacedly, as though it were stolen, they ate their morning bread. They stared through the window, they paced around. Another day, then another, and already it was as though this dark object she had never pierced had always been there — a household thing, while you ate or talked, suddenly springing into view and being pushed away at once. Only at night, when boots would stop right outside as though about to come in any moment — now — then like a frenzied animal she had to hold back her mind, lest it pull her into an unfathomable dark. The boots stamped on. Here was the icon light, the smooth linens and her body's warmth. She was safe. She despised herself for being so safe.

"I — I was burning with shame," she said, choking. "Everyone was doing something, the Jews were fighting in the ghettos, the partisans in the woods, and here I was, just sitting with folded hands. You must understand me, to have done — to have had so much, and then nothing, nothing at all. So, I left them."

"You simply took off and left?"

"Simply — my Lord! The quarrels that went on, the yells. Then the denouncer came. 'Your Zborovska is a Jewess; either you pay me off or we go to the Gestapo,' he screamed. Some miserable drunk he was; still, when they gave him his Judas money I felt filthy, as if I were for sale. At least I put his coming to use: 'He'll keep blackmailing us, and ranting and gabbing in every bar till the Gestapo comes.' I pleaded, I argued, until they let me go. And then . . . then . . ."

She was silent, startled at how swiftly her story was nearing its end. Only the eyes, suspicious behind peepholes, the running up and down staircases was yet to come, only the doors slammed in her face. "I tried." She shook her head. "I went from Annas to Caiaphas, but I could not find them."

"Who couldn't you find?"

"The underground. All the addresses I took along, all the names. But wherever I went it was 'Arrested. Deported to Germany. Gone.' And then they nabbed me, and that was it."

"Why were you arrested? How?"

"Wait." She brightened up. "Wait, I'll tell you, it was so funny. There I was, minding my own business, sitting in the park, when a man joined me. We started talking about the weather and such, when out of the blue, exactly as in the movies, he flipped his lapel: 'Gestapo. You're arrested for stealing linen from an attic.' 'Look,' said I, 'what do I need linen for?' But he only dragged me on into a droshky; see, such a poor sleuth he was, they wouldn't even give him a car. And there in the droshky he started — his paws, you know — all over me. 'Now listen, Gestapo,' I said, 'you want to arrest me, fine; you want this, fine. But both, that just won't do.' And I gave it to him smack in the face so that he reeled back. Fool that I was. Weapons had been found in the neighborhood; he was searching me for weapons. This I found out later, in prison. Well, they certainly paid me back for smacking him."

"Were you afraid?"

She hesitated. "For a moment, just the tiniest moment I was. Then it was over; I didn't mind getting thrashed, and that they could do more to me, this I never believed. Give me some water." She moistened her parched lips. "I'm thirsty."

"We've drunk it all."

"Then let's move a bit, let's find the window to see where we are."

By now darkness had erased their window and only the sounds were left to them: "A bridge," the hollow rumble announced; the outburst of jumbled noise was a station; then "Woods," said the swishing branches, "woods — still woods." How long had they been on the way? Was it night already, were they somewhere far in Germany? "Never mind," Barbara whispered, "wherever they're taking us, we'll manage. But tell me, who are you with here?"

"I'm alone."

"Did you leave anyone back in Cracow?"

"No."

"Oh!" She touched the small, frozen hand. "Now we'll stay together, till the end. And after the war you must come to my place, Stefan will like you, I know it. Stefan — that's my husband, he's in London — army orders." Hastily she excused his safety of London, a city which to her invariably appeared as a raindrop, huge and dark with grime. Closing her eyes, she tried to recall his face, but instead Tola rose before her, reminding her of a sick child she had once visited, who out of boredom had painted her mouth so that it glowed crimson in her sharp, pale face. Even so, she liked this Tola, for her wit, her willingness to listen, and for remembering so well the manor and everyone there. Should she ask why Tola was all alone? Later — she felt tired now, she would sleep just for a little while.

Cautiously Tola got up, wrapped the coat tighter around Barbara's knees, then sat down again. It was cold, the rumble of wheels pounded against her head. Suddenly she remembered last night: the shattered window, the bunk on which she had cowered all alone. She moved closer to Barbara and, listening to her quiet breath, allowed herself to doze off — watchfully, and starting up at each unexpected sound.

Part Two

Chapter 7

THE SILENCE must have startled her: the wheels rattled no longer; from the mass huddled against the wall no sound came. Then a bang — the iron bars were being removed, and the door opened on frosty air, on darkness glimmering with snow and on oily yellow light trailing above a row of motionless shapes.

"Do you see anything? SS men, dogs?" the women whispered. Tola began sneaking toward the door but Barbara was faster. "Don't be scared," she called, leaning out. "Ah, look at all this snow."

Timidly the women drew closer to the door, but just then the train moved on and behind it in the yellow light shapes stirred, became figures reaching out as if to beckon them back. They vanished. The train rolled on past glossy darkness, past snow-laden branches, motionless, like paws of white, placid beasts. A jerk. Again the train stopped.

And before the women had time to ask about the SS and dogs, dwarfish figures appeared on the snowy plain, each waving from afar, calling, "Hob nisht moyre, vir senen Yidden!"

"Don't be afraid; we're Jews," Tola was about to translate, when those coming explained themselves by reaching up, by helping the women to scramble out. The engine whistled, steam unfurled against the black sky, and the train moved on until only the last cars were still in view, only the SS men's car, a boot swinging through the open door. It slammed shut. Red sparks burst into the dark. And when they died out the last trace of the Cracow camp was gone — of its nights, its endless Appells, its fear.

Here all was different. No one drove them on, they were allowed to rest, to stretch out their numbed limbs. They walked on, not in a column but in a leisurely crowd, like tourists stopping at whatever delighted their eyes: the full moon shining upon the vast expanse of snow, the arcades of bent bushes; and farther away woods, the impenetrable wall parting at their approach, the white straight road inviting them to come on. The air was quiet except when at times — like a hostess who, guests gone, sets her home aright and then rests — the breeze stirred, erased the footprints, restored the road to its damask smoothness, then ceased.

"Be glad. You've come to a good place," the dwarfish men — O.D. men they were — repeated. In answer the women smiled, then walked on in an almost festive silence. Throughout the years in ghettos and in camps, dirty slush was the only snow they had known, its purity bestowed only upon the world outside the wires. Now they had gained equal rights to joy in winter, to the admiring "How nice, how quiet." "Nice?" Barbara boomed. "It's splendid, the most splendid snow I've ever seen. Ah, it was worth coming here, just for this."

"Don't say such things," Tola was about to warn. Around her shone faces freshened by the frosty air. Barbara laughed, blowing clouds of white breath, until with a sudden extravagance Tola reached up to a branch and shook a flurry of snow into their outstretched arms.

That after such a walk another camp awaited them — the wires, the towers, and a screeching gate — seemed startling at first. But swift to dispel any misapprehension, here was warmth — radiators lining the large hall, blankets on the bunks, and above all, soup. And what soup, hot, thick with parsnips; and the tongue if attentive enough could taste fine strands of meat, so at least Barbara claimed, adding that not even Marta, a jewel among cooks, could have made a better soup.

The women ate in three stages: first out of hunger; next out of prudence, to store supplies; then out of exuberance, out of sheer luxury, so that "I'm full," they could sigh, "I've had enough!"

With the satiated feeling the next day began, and with the sun awakening them instead of a bugle call. The women stretched themselves, looked at the sky, blue outside the windows, then strolled to the barrels of soup, which, though turned a bit sour, was now thick like a pudding.

This was breakfast. After breakfast, as befits a holiday, came guests, the O.D. men met last night. By daylight they appeared a trifle less good-natured, a trifle more shifty-eyed; and all of them, as if this were a requirement of their rank, bandy-legged, the purple collars of their navy blue uniform shining with grease. They brought news about the camp. It was located near the town of Skarzysko-Kamienna and this section of it at least — "Werk A," they called it — was really a good place. To be sure, one was not exactly overfed here; still, with a bit of sense in your head, and with God's help, you could always do some business with the goys in the plant. Of that other section, where dim figures had stood in the yellow light, the O.D. men said little; yes, they admitted to some connection between Werk A and that place, but on the whole treated it like a poor relation of whom the less said, the better.

"Not good." They merely shrugged, and began to speak of work in their place, at the plant belonging to Hasag — to Hugo Schneider Aktiengesellschaft. "After Hermann Goering Werke the biggest ammunition plant in Germany," they added, not without a touch of proprietary pride.

"What, ammunition!" Barbara, who until now had been nodding approvingly, jumped up. "Tola, did you hear that?"

"Yes, I heard it."

"But this is terrible, just terrible!"

"You're absolutely right." A greasy blond head popped up from the lower bunk. Another "Absolutely!" and the woman with the gold teeth stood before them. Her long hooked nose too large for her face, her square torso too heavy for her wobbly legs, she looked put together from some odds and ends. "Aurelia Katz," she introduced herself briskly. "And this," she pointed to the freckled girl standing morosely on the side, "this is Alinka — my daughter."

First Tola, then Barbara mumbled something.

"I'm delighted to meet you." Mrs. Katz beamed. "And as I was saying, you are right, eminently so." She reached out, as though to offer Barbara this choice morsel of her vocabulary.

"I won't make ammunition. I'll work like a snail. I'll refuse," Barbara muttered and, brushing Mrs. Katz aside, went off.

Here and there sat the outsiders to the general gaiety, those who had left someone behind. To them Barbara tried to administer comfort, in kind and dosage always the same — an embrace, a fumbling "Oh my dear," then an equally fumbling question to find out what sorrow exactly she was trying to soothe. "Ah, you left a sister in Cracow. A daughter? Oh, my God! But things must be changing for the better, this place shows it. And the war too — it won't last much longer. Soon, in a few months, you'll be together again." Those she comforted gazed at her with half-grateful, half-compassionate looks that Tola, watching on the side, found painful.

At noon barrels of fresh soup were rolled in; and now a feast took place — an orgy of hope. Only a short line formed in front of the barrels, each woman in the line, having been commissioned by others to fetch their soup, juggling a whole cluster of cans. For the majority would not even bother to get down. They requested "Room service!" They lolled and sprawled on their bunks. Their cheerleader was Seidmanka, an inveterate optimist constantly croaking prophecies of disaster in self-defense against the assault of hope. Now faith took over — in the stomach full forever, in this "find" of a camp, in survival. It shone in her eyes; it lent high adolescent notes to her voice.

"Waiter," she piped. "Waiter, what, soup again? I ordered chicken with mushrooms in wine; and for dessert —"

"Cream puffs. Napoleons!" Barbara clapped her hands. And at last Tola too joined them with her soft, somewhat uneasy laugh.

A new idea struck Seidmanka. To extol the present she would pit it against the past.

"Someone must stand six." In mock fear she rolled her eyes. "Tola, you go."

Tired by her efforts to keep in step with Barbara, Tola stood in the narrow corridor, her cheek leaning against the cool windowpane. Laughter came from the hall. "Let's send a postcard to the Lagerkommandant," someone called. Then steps . . .

A squat, burly man stood before her, his O.D. man's jacket dotted with patches the color of the mud that caked his boots, copperstreaked hair falling upon a face so fleshy that the eyes were almost hidden by the thick folds.

"Tell me," the man gripped her arm, "are they all like you?"

"In what way?" Tola asked.

"Skinny. Flat-chested and skinny. A woman is worth as much as she weighs, Goldberg says. Goldberg, that's me." He pounded his chest, then "Ouch," he winced as she hit at his hand still clutching her arm. "Ouch, when they get skinny they get proud."

"It's the other way around. Nowadays when they're proud they get skinny." Guffawing, the man walked into the hall, but soon came back, bringing Barbara along.

"Can you imagine it, Mr. Goldberg says he knows me." Though all smiles Barbara was every inch the lady speaking of her inferior. "He used to deliver something or other to our place."

"Coal, Dziedziczka — twice a year. Yes, it's a small world! If you don't meet someone in Auschwitz you meet them here. If not here then up there." He pointed at the clouds outside the window, and went with Barbara back to the hall.

Tola stayed in the corridor. Outside a group of O.D. men were walking by the wires. Then far off, where gray slush merged with the gray afternoon sky, a tall figure appeared. It was a German, his brown military cloak blown by the wind.

"Six," Tola said coming into the hall.

"Six? What is it? Yes, sure." Barbara laughed.

"It's not a joke. I saw a German coming here."

O.D. men came in and ordered the women to form a column. The tall German who followed them looked almost pitiful — so shyly he stood in the door, so apologetically his faded blue eyes glanced around. Slouching, as though to shrink himself, he approached Goldberg, who addressed him without any excessive deference as Meister Grube.

"Ah, stop whining," Barbara flared up at Mrs. Katz, who with her daughter stood in their four, then leaning backward whispered to Tola that this Kraut looked as if he couldn't count to three.

"Hush," Tola silenced her. Nothing seemed to have changed. Yet she felt something first like a chill, then like a presence, as if a courier from the Cracow camp had brought a piece of forgotten luggage — the old familiar fear.

From the door this fear came. There a pimply O.D. man stood, next to him two women: the elder hunched up as though freezing; the other — the bosomy blonde who had whistled during the "ovation" — was slipping something to the O.D. man. Money. The blonde had ransomed herself. Why, those at the column's head must have already found out, for they grew still.

"Tola, wait, we'll go together," Barbara whispered.

"No, stay here!"

Hiding behind the column Tola stole on, then ducked. Light flashed: startled by the glare she looked to the corner where the O.D. men stood. They saw her all the time, yet nobody had bothered to stop her. And she felt afraid of this place where none of the familiar rules held: "six" taken as a joke — she, always the first to warn others, now the last to be warned, and by the Orphan.

"It's bad." The Orphan licked her livid mouth.

"What's happening?"

"We're going to that bad place."

"Everyone?"

"Some will always wriggle out. Rouge, hurry up!" The Orphan nudged the woman next to her.

"Rouge — give me rouge" rose from everywhere.

"Yellow" was what Mrs. Katz whimpered.

"Keep quiet," Tola snapped at her. In answer Mrs. Katz smiled. "You'll be sorry you didn't listen to me," this smile said.

"Well, what is it?" asked Barbara.

"Yellow," Mrs. Katz repeated, "the hair turns yellow there, the face, the eyes . . ." And she pointed at her chest, as if in the bad place even the heart turned yellow. It was the lungs she meant. "The lungs just disintegrate," she added softly, like an afterthought.

Barbara opened her mouth, but said nothing. Now everyone was silent, now the familiar rules were being restored by this silence, by the old women clinging to the young, as if their vigor could be borrowed and put on like rouge, by the young shrinking away lest those old would drag them down to the bad place. And at the window Seidmanka was gnowing at the hem of her dress. She kept her money sewn in the hem, she would ransom herself as the blonde had.

Followed by Goldberg and the O.D. men, the Meister approached the column. The blonde stood at its head; the pimply O.D. man whispered with the Meister, who nodded, then ordered the blonde to the other side of the hall. His retinue right behind, he walked on, hastily bypassing those old or no longer too strong, and choosing only the husky young women for the good camp.

"Tolenka — I don't understand. The big wenches, they're going to the bad place?"

"No, they stay here." Tola looked from Barbara's powerful arms to her own, pale, very thin.

"But, Tolenka . . ."

"Mrs. Grünbaum," the Katz woman broke in, "help us, I beg you, not for my sake, but for this child. Criticizing, always criticizing!" She scowled at her daughter, turned back to Barbara, and again it was, "Mrs. Grünbaum, my dear Mrs. Grünbaum."

"For God's sake let me think." Tola shoved her aside. Barbara knows Goldberg, she thought, he may help me to stay, he must . . . But hardly had she glanced at him, when he shook his head.

"Barbara," her mouth could barely move, "stay here, I'll be right back." And this time Barbara did not say "We go together." This time she pressed her fist to her lips.

With a moist "Pst!" and "Here!" Seidmanka was signaling to the pimply O.D. man. Then, since he still would not respond, she pointed to the money clutched in her hand.

"Seidmanka," Tola began. Only a very few could buy their way into the good camp; she must hurry or she would lose her chance. But she was no good at begging help. "Help me," she cried. "I'll pay every copper back, I'll do anything for you. I — " Tola stopped. Her shaking voice sounded exactly like the Katz woman's whine.

"I beg you," Rubinfeldova took over. "I beg you, listen to Tola." Seidmanka looked at Rubinfeldova, at Tola, then at the crumpled notes.

"Help me — I beg you — I cannot be alone anymore."

"Somehow," Rubinfeldova whispered.

"How? How would we manage? Should we starve for her? Why? What has she ever done for us?"

Discreetly the O.D. man stole toward them; he shoved Seidmanka's money into his boot, then was off.

Tola too walked away. "Ruhe," the Meister shrieked. "Quiet!" the O.D. men echoed, though everyone was quiet, though only eyes dared to beg the Meister for one moment of attention, one glance. But he, turning aside, hurried on to those fit for the good camp.

"Oh, if only you had used your pull and asked Goldberg again to help us." The Katz woman was clutching at Barbara as Tola came back. Barbara raised her fist; she would have struck had Mrs. Katz not moved away. Barbara, for all her courage, was afraid of going to the bad place; Tola saw this fear crumple Barbara's face.

"Stop worrying so much." Tola's calm changed to a bitter delight because she, always the accused, could now accuse in turn. But what for? She would rather make it easy for Barbara to stay in the good camp. "Everything is working out for the best," it seemed as if she were reciting a prepared speech, "really, Barbara."

"Really?"

"Of course. Now, don't tell me you wanted to come along with me."

"I . . ."

"You must stay here, Barbara, because — "

"Connections, Mrs Grünbaum, you've got such connections," the Katz woman whispered. "Because soon you'll form connections," Tola went on. "You'll help me to transfer back here."

"Really?"

"Of course. Don't look so downcast, Barbara."

"I — When you were gone, I asked that Goldberg for help. 'She can't stay here,' he said. Why not? I don't understand anything."

"The Mae West type is in demand here." So completely did this stale joke drain Tola's strength that she couldn't wait for Barbara to be gone. And soon she was gone. Goldberg, to bring her closer to the Meister, led her away to the center of the column, and behind them Mrs. Katz dragged her daughter along.

So, it was over; now Tola must find herself another four. "Go away, we're already four," she heard wherever she went until, alone again, she stood at the column's end. She didn't mind being alone, only she had to talk to herself, all the time: about Barbara who had learned her lesson amazingly fast, and who soon would join — yes, the "elect"; then about the pimply O.D. man smirking at Rubinfeldova and Seidmanka, like a salesman assuring his customers that they had got their money's worth. Which those two did. "My long-lost relatives," the O.D. man assured the Meister. He protested, he swore, until they were allowed to join those chosen to stay. Should she go and congratulate them? Not now; later, she decided, and

watched the Meister, who was shrinking away — as though anyone
would dare to touch a member of the Master Race.

"Aus Deutschland, wir sind aus Deutschland!" the Yekies tried
to assert their membership in this race, then, "Zusammen!" they
shrieked, clinging to each other, as if there was any reason to separate them — one the spitting image of the other. They drew aside.
Leaning forward, the Meister was looking at someone in the second
row.

"Zu — zusammen!" Barbara was shouting, was running along the
column. As someone pointed toward Tola she stopped, then ran
on, all the time shouting "Schwestern! Zusammen!" and looking
from Tola to the Meister, who was following her with Goldberg. And
behind them trotted Mrs. Katz, pulling her daughter along.

"Zusammen, Schwestern, we're sisters!" Barbara smiled the smile
of the simple-minded so delighted by their cunning that they give
themselves away at once. Never before had Tola longed so much
to stay together with Barbara, and never before had she wanted so
much to be left alone. She could not stand being compared. The
Meister and Goldberg were comparing them. They looked at Barbara, and "She deserves the good place," this look said; but her
it brushed off.

"Zusammen. Tolenka, I can't speak German. You tell them."

"Yes, I will." And in her excellent German, Tola softly began. First
Goldberg, then the Meister drew away from Barbara and closer to
her. They listened. Only Barbara, who understood nothing, kept
breaking in. "Ja," she muttered. "So! Ja!"

"Herr Meister, as I told you, we're not sisters. We barely know
each other. I ask you to use your whole authority to make this
woman stay here."

"Ja, so. Ja."

Goldberg strode toward Barbara. It looked as though he would
strike, but he laid his hand gently on her neck, and so step by step
shoved her on. "Tola!" Barbara stopped suddenly. "Why isn't she
coming? Tola, what did you tell them?"

As though to warn her, Goldberg looked at Tola.

"The truth," she spoke, avoiding his stare. "Just the truth."

"Did you hear what she said, did you? Such a slip of a girl, and
she came to me, she helped me, and now she is doing everything to

make me stay here. Ah, do you think I'd leave her alone? Herr Meister, ich — I — I want to go with her. Goldberg, you tell him. Do you hear me? Goldberg!"

Shrugging, Goldberg said something to the Meister, who looked at Barbara, then gave a slow nod.

"So I can stay with her, can I?" Barbara turned and dashed back so blindly that she collided with Mrs. Katz, who, standing in front of the column, was holding her daughter in front like a buffer.

"This Goldberg," Barbara cried, "he stands up for me, for a woman, like a stove, and here he lets a child go to that dreadful place!" And she stepped aside so that all could see who must go there — a girl of thirteen or so, the long skirt and spiked heels worn to appear more grown-up only making her look like a child dressed up for a masquerade.

"You, look."

The Meister bent over the girl. "Das Mädel bleibt," he ordered.

"The girl stays," Goldberg translated.

The girl staggered forward; she drew back. And next to her, like a ragdoll loosened at the seams, Mrs. Katz was falling apart, her arms jerking to and from her neck, her head. "No!" Her black arm raked the girl closer. "Together. Mutter, Tochter zusammen!"

The Meister mumbled something and walked on.

"You, what have you done to your daughter?" Barbara gasped.

"I . . . I . . . you're noble, but I . . ." Mrs Katz sniveled. Then, supported by the girl, she tottered back to her bunk.

Soon afterward it was over. About fifty women had been chosen to stay, while all the others were to go to the bad place, though when, no one knew. Like an adolescent relieved when the party is over, the Meister stole away. Goldberg and the O.D. men followed, but before leaving one of them had passed the word that not all work in the bad camp made you turn yellow. Was this the truth, or just a comforting lie? If the truth, how many could escape the yellow work, and in what way?

The lights went out. Barbara fell asleep at once, but Tola lay wide awake, while around her the whispers stopped, and only a bunk would squeak as someone tossed in sleep. At last she sat up. "Barbara," she whispered.

"Oh, can't you sleep?" Barbara murmured, barely awake. She herself had slept "wonderfully just like a marmot. But I'm glad you woke up, because I must explain everything."

"Quiet! Let us sleep!" someone muttered.

"I'm terribly sorry. Listen, Tolenka, when this Katz said 'Yellow — ' "

"Quiet!"

"If you're tired you can sleep anyhow," Barbara snapped back. "Now where was I? Yes, 'Yellow,' this Katz said; I must admit my heart didn't go out to her at first, and even now I'm not sure; anyhow she said it, and I . . . I could see myself yellow, all shriveled up, like a lemon gone to rot. And a fear came over me, such fear — " She was silent for a minute, then went on briskly, "Yellow, red, green — no matter what color we turn, we'll just scrub it off when the war is over. Listen," Barbara drew closer, "have you ever imagined — but really, so that you could see it — the end — the end of the war?"

"Yes. Once, I thought . . . I dreamt about it." In the Cracow camp, lying sick with influenza she had dreamed of the end; a sense of welcome had pervaded the dream as though wherever she went she was expected by the sunlit air, the pale green trees, and by the quiet — deep, yet holding the promise of voices just waiting for her call to answer.

"How was it, Tola, how did you imagine it?"

"I was in the park." Barbara's expectant tone made it harder to speak. "There was no one with me, yet I didn't feel lonely."

"And — "

"The trees were in bud, and I felt so free, somehow."

"And then?"

"That's all, Barbara. My dreams are modest."

"No, come on; that was beautiful, just beautiful. Now let me tell you how it will be.

"When the war is over," Barbara began dreamily, like a child whispering "Once upon a time." Tola listened, with the adult's envy of such faith in the world of wonders, yet soon with a twinge of disappointment, for even those wonders were secondhand, each borrowed from some other tale: the rejoicing in the streets, the Germans scurrying around like chickens — this was the Armistice of 1918; Barbara and she herself now in a ramshackle cart, now on foot, going back to the manor — transferred from the beginning of this war to its end. But what came next was new. "And there at home," Barbara said, "there, we'll go down on our knees."

"What?" Tola asked. Then, still casting around for some explanation of Barbara's fearlessness, "Are you a believer?"

"The odd thoughts you can get. To scrub, that's why we'll get down on our knees, so no trace of the Krauts will be left when he comes home, Stefan, my husband." Barbara stopped. Why, Tola did not quite dare to ask.

Yellow, red, green — all will wash off once the war is over, Barbara repeated to herself, like an incantation. The incantation failed. She saw Stefan: he was sitting at the empty table, slouched, his face buried in his hands, a tip of his mustache showing through his fingers. He was crying for her, who would never come back. And a shudder passed through her as if only in his grief lay the reality of her death.

Chapter 8

NEXT AFTERNOON they left. A thaw had stripped off the snow; black, dripping with moisture, the woods creaked in the wind, mist churned through the dark thicket, and the road was now a bog littered with heaps of pine needles, cones, and matted leaves. Mud oozing into their shoes, the women walked on into the dusk. When the dusk changed to darkness, light began to filter through the trees. In passing, one could catch a glimpse of a clearing, of a shed blackened with forest damp, next to it a cart with a broken shaft, or a barrel, the loosened hoops sliding down. No Germans were to be seen, no guard. Quiet, dimly lit, the place seemed to have been abandoned to rot in the depth of the woods.

Suddenly something changed, something was happening to the air: a bitterness — both an odor and a taste — filled it, and as it grew stronger the women moved more and more slowly. They stopped. This was the yellow place. The air declared it — so bitter that each breath hurt, the earth glittering with a phosphorescent sheen, and the trees, a yellow-green lichen eating into their trunks so that they cracked and split in half, the branches denuded but for a scorched fringe trailing through the mud. Behind the trees sprawled puddles the color of phlegm; in the brown canvas spread over squarish piles, holes gaped, their green edges jagged as though gnawed out by sharp teeth; farther off stood a brick building, the windows coated so thick by the mosslike film that no light came.

"Yellow . . . the yellow place?" Barbara stammered out.

"No, Café Royal," said Goldberg. "Picrine" was the name of this place, he explained, having ordered them on, from the picric acid which too was called "picrine" here. And what was picrine good for? For making mines, perfect in turn for blowing up bridges and such.

Was there another Picrine nearby? Wavering, fainter than before, the bitterness wedged itself into the air and with it a rustle like dried leaves shaken by the wind. Yet the wind had stopped.

The Picrine people were rustling . . .

Tola watched. At first they did not seem terrible to her, just grotesque, like a procession of dilapidated parcels somehow escaped from a cellar, the sheets of stiff brown paper wrapping their torsos, their arms, and legs, here flapping from under a torn string, there trailing through the mud. And their faces too seemed to have emerged from a cellar — not yellow, not the color of lemon gone to rot, but of potatoes stored through a long winter, and with greenish specks, like sprouts that had seen no light. Their eyes were those sprouts, the pupils blurred, the whites tinged a yellowish green.

Those eyes Tola saw only when they drew closer, when "Bread," they reached out their corroded hands, "miss, give us bread." Now they were terrible; now for an instant she believed that such a face, such eyes could be hers. "Let me go," she shrieked, "let me — "

They let her pass at last, and she ran on back to the crowd, looking for Barbara. "Your friend is there," Goldberg pointed to a dark cluster at the roadside, "getting acquainted. Look."

Rummaging in her bag, sighing "God, I have nothing, oh God," Barbara stood among the paper-clad figures. "Give me something for them," she whispered, seeing Tola. "Give me; quick."

"I have nothing." Because the small chunk of bread had been saved up for a day like this without a morsel of food. Barbara grabbed her bag. Hastily the yellow fingers were shoving Tola's bread into the gaping mouth. "You — why did you say you had nothing?" Barbara pulled her aside.

"I forgot about the bread" — how easy it would have been to go on lying. She did not lie. "Barbara, this is a hungry place," she said.

"Sure, it is! I've got eyes, too, I can see it. But look at all the flesh I've got! Of course, you — and it was your bread."

Should she tell Barbara no amount of flesh would protect her here? Goldberg tried to do it for her. "It's gone, gone," he was practically chanting.

"What? What's gone?" Barbara turned upon him.

"Your estate, Dziedziczka, your riches, your manor; all gone, not even a potato left."

"And what is it to you?"

"Nothing, absolutely nothing." Splashing through the mud he went on talking about the manor, then about that day in Lublin when somebody had first pointed Barbara out to him.

"Who?" Barbara asked sullenly.

"Everyone. The very houses made room when the Dziedziczka of Dembina came into town. But times have changed; now scum floats to the top. Like me, for instance." He struck his chest, and walked off chuckling.

Somewhere in the distance a chorus burst into song, grew fainter, then stopped. The wind blew hard. And above the trees the moon rose, no bigger than a child's fist.

"Strange." Barbara wrapped herself tighter in her coat. "God, it's strange here."

The camp too was strange. No light shone in the low stumpy watchtowers; wires hung loose on the splintery poles, and at the gate only one guard stood — an old wizened man who, shuffling like a grouchy janitor, led them into the muddy strip of the Appellplatz. Without stopping there to be counted, the women walked on, past the low barracks, all alike but for their smell: from the first one, where the glow of a fire tinged the mud red, came a cloying sweetness; next it was the odor of soiled linen and steam; next of chlorine and urine gone stale. Soon even those distinguishing marks were gone. Identical and dark as though abandoned, the barracks lined the streets; only rarely light seeped through the dirty windows, or a door would open, to let heavy air out and then an arm emptying a pail of slops into the street.

Mud splashed, rotten planks broke under foot. Once a woman wrapped in rags dashed at Barbara, and mumbling in Yiddish touched her with a mixture of reverence and greed.

"What did she say?" Barbara started.

"They still have coats!" the woman had said. This was their only welcome. In the crowd of those now returning from work hardly anyone turned to look at them. Tola understood why when they stopped at a row of barracks. Their doors swung open upon the muddy footprints, upon pails of ashes and of slops — traces of previous inhabitants whom they had come to replace. The succession of such replacements had gone on so long that no one took much heed of them by now.

"In, girls; your little nests are waiting." Goldberg again.

Was it the rumor that had crazed them, the sudden rumor claiming that those without a bunk would go to the yellow work? Was it the chance for fighting back that they had found at last? For the women grew fierce; they stormed the barracks, clawing at one another, screaming "My bunk! I was first! Mine!"

"I won't push," Barbara said. Tola did push, pummeling at the bent backs, tearing a woman away from the bunk of her choice — a good bunk on the upper tier, and with room for only two.

At last the mêlée was over. Clutching at their bunks like squatters afraid of being dispossessed, the women looked around the barracks. It was small; in the space left by the double tier of bunks a table stood, a bench and an iron stove, the ashes it spilled mingling with the gray straw that fell down from the bunks. Barbara plunged her hands into the straw; dust burst into her face and the rag that she pulled out was covered with pale specks. Those were lice.

Lagerschluss was not observed strictly here. Late into the night Tola could hear footsteps and voices rising above the heavy swishing of the woods. Then a new noise — a clanking and a rattle, coming now in a jerk, now in a regular rhythm. "What's that?" a woman cried. "Quiet — be quiet," Tola whispered, hastily walking outside.

The moon had grown; in a pale misty light it shone upon the black expanse of mud. Across it, the hoops jingling, a barrel seemed to be waltzing. A man from Picrine was waltzing with the barrel, hugging it, rolling it round and round. He stopped; his bare feet dangling, he plunged headlong inside. He was licking the leftover soup; first to unstick it, he had shaken the barrel, then crept in and licked it out.

Tola walked back, looked at Barbara, and then hastily looked away.

Chapter 9

DAYS IN A NEW PLACE began. Days of distances growing tricky, of places playing hide-and-seek, and of naming, every morning upon awakening, the bunk, the table, the stove, until Barbara knew where she was. Then came counting of the privileges won by coming to the Jewish camp: no alias of "Janina Zborovska" made her feel like an embezzler; no Tickler lurked for her in the dark. She slept quietly. "Good morning, Barbara; time to get up, Barbara," her own name welcomed her each day; and when the women addressed her as the "big Pole," "Grünbaum, Barbara Grünbaum," she insisted, relishing the sound of her name like a long untasted fruit. So, every morning she took count of her gains.

"All up!" Shouts would burst in, lights glare upon the barracks which at this hour resembled a railroad station, the women huddling under their coats like stranded passengers, waking morosely from their uneasy sleep. Barbara tried to wipe off this morose look, dashing to the door, breathing in the air to report that it felt good; because of the fine, small rain, or snow, or wind. Everything was good: the crowds outside, the goose-pimply arms brushing against her; even the washroom, where papers and rags floated like dead fish in the gray mire, but where the water felt refreshing and cold; even the beet-coffee, cloyingly sweet but hot, ah so hot!

"This tastes good," she would announce with scalded lips, then wait for Tola's meager agreement and run on breathlessly, as if she had to hurry like those others rushing to the Appellplatz. There was no need to hurry. The Cracow women, the only ones unemployed in the camp, cowered on their bunks. Outside, the thudding of feet stopped; the gate screeched as the columns marched out to work, and soon only coughing drummed in the street, a kind of local idiom heard here all the time.

"Will it be decided today? Will they send us to Picrine?" the women whispered. "Those young and strong never go to Picrine, Goldberg told me; Goldberg will help, he'll protect us." Barbara broke off, remembering the others who had no such protection. From then on she would just talk, hectically, faster and faster, about before, about after the war; both identical, for her the future being the past transplanted.

"The cakes Marta baked when guests came . . ."

"He'll like you, Stefan will, I know it."

And just when the festive table was being set, just when Tola and Stefan were about to meet, it was "Out! Out into the Appellplatz!" Each day the weather was the same, cold and windy, the straw-colored sunrays that managed to sift through the clouds soon swallowed by the clammy fog; and every day wenches with thick calves and brazen faces would push to the fore, twisting their fannies, thrusting their breasts out, as if right here, in the black mud of the Appellplatz, they would give themselves to the O.D. men in payment for not going to the yellow work.

But their unemployment went on. After freezing for an hour or more, the women were sent to some temporary chores — sweeping the dank sheds, transferring white paper-husks from one soggy carton to another. Then, long before the others returned from work, they went back to the camp.

"Good" was the word of the morning, "terrible" of those afternoons when they walked through the still-deserted streets. "Terrible — oh my God, oh Tolenka, how terrible," Barbara whispered, not unlike those hospital visitors willing to give part of their own vigor to save both the immobile shapes on the white beds and themselves from the threat of their own helplessness. The convalescents from typhus were terrible: pale balding heads shaking on spindly necks, they wobbled, purblind and half deaf, through the dusk. Yet for them there was hope: if they rested, if they got more than the beet-slops to eat, they could still get well. For the Picrine people there was no such hope; their disease pursued them in the yellow dust, poisoning their breath, poisoning whatever came near them, so that "Out with you!" the outcry rose everywhere, "You'll make my soup bitter — my bread."

"Go! Out with you!" the Cracow women were quick to learn.

Yet the Picrine people stayed; pressed into a dark lump, they stood in the corner begging a spoonful of soup.

"I have less than you, believe me, still less," Barbara whispered, because the newcomers, being unemployed, were kept on half rations. And when matching her hunger against theirs did not seem enough, she would tell herself, I may end up at Picrine just as they.

Two kinds of evil, she felt, were at work here. The first came from outside: once localized, once enclosed within huge helmeted figures, it grew ubiquitous here, lurking in hunger, in typhus and the bitter dust. The other evil was new. It came from within. It had a shape — of the "leeches," the vendors whom she loathed more and more. Wrapped, like the ancient Romans in their togas, in greasy blankets they would invade the barracks, stick their red kinky heads into the bunks, tear their black Leatherette bags open before dazzled eyes, with delicacies obscene in this place, white bread, butter and eggs tempting everyone: the rich to spend their wealth on themselves rather than to share it as they should, the poor to barter away their very last.

"Are you selling? Your blouse, your dress, your shoes. Are you selling?" they hissed.

"You, you got some gold teeth, are you selling?" one of them accosted Tola.

"Well, and how much do you pay?" Tola grinned.

"No! You must never do that, never!" Barbara cried, and with all her strength pushed the vendor away.

The fighting at the stove seemed more furious when those leeches came in, the stinking vapor exuded by clothes dried against the stovepipe more stifling. And she fled from this greed, this filth into what was pure and dear to her — into the cold, glossy dark. Clear winter stars hung above the barracks; the woods rustled. And with Tola at her side, she would walk on and on, until it was safe to go back.

Shortly before Lagerschluss a hush would spread over the barracks. Then those too shy to push came to the fore, old, gray-faced women, young girls, now at last warming up their leftover soup, or their hands at least. Watching them Barbara would feel a sudden pang. With each day she admired Tola more, for her cleverness, her pluck; yet did not those others, those neither clever nor plucky, deserve her help much more?

The day when she would help could not be far off. Through a Pole whom Goldberg knew, a letter had been sent to Antoni ordering him to sell her possessions, all of them, at once. Soon his answer would come, soon — though when exactly, Goldberg did not know — the Pole would go to Lublin. True, usurer that he was, this Pole demanded one third of the money as his reward, while Goldberg, being no better, claimed one fourth of what would be left. Still, she would have enough to help the neediest in her barracks, and above all, the people from Picrine.

Schmitz it turned out to be for her and Tola, of all the plants in Werk C the best. They went there no thanks to their youth or to Goldberg, but innocently, just by chance, just because on that day they had walked in the front of the column. Unobtrusively, so that no one took much heed of it, two thirds of the column were deflected from the road — about two hundred women sent to the Trotyl plant, where artillery shells were filled with trotyl powder that tinged your hair red, another two hundred to Picrine. And those in front walked on to a low brick building, which with its wide windows and neat shrubbery could be mistaken for a modern school. This was Schmitz. Inside, sweetish white dust hovered in the long, well-lighted hall; small tattered men dozed on piles of black packing cases, and at the two rows of tables women, young and husky, most of them, were fiddling with glittering, toylike objects. First, they strung pieces of copper wire through cylinders of pink and white chalk, next stuck the cylinders into gleaming brass husks, then screwed the peaked metal top on.

"So, what are those knickknacks for?" Barbara asked the woman introducing Tola and her to their new work.

"Antiaircraft shells."

"What!" From the tables, from the black packing crates, shells seemed to swarm up, buzzing like vicious insects around an airplane, and there among the glistening debris the pilot, a young boy, was falling — down and down through the endless air.

"Antiaircraft! My God! Well, why are you staring so at me?" In a sudden fury she turned upon Tola. "Staring and staring like — ah, how can they do this, make shells, ammunition against their own people?"

"Tsa!" The woman smacked her thick, bloodless lips. "It's all humbug. If these shells hit one plane in a thousand it's a lot."

"Are you sure?"

"Of course I am."

The buzzing stopped; unencumbered and free the plane glided on and Barbara settled down to work.

Meister Grube, who like themselves had been a transient in the good camp, was in charge of Schmitz. He came in so rarely, though, and for such brief visits that the hall was in reality run by the old Polish foreman. Vokunski was his name. His head was oblong and bald like an egg; his soldierly mustache à la Marshal Pilsudski and his tight-fitting cavalry boots were constantly at loggerheads with his civilian parts — his loose, chalk-smeared coat, and his grievous limp. Suddenly his lame leg would give way under him, he would flail like a hooked fish, grope, stumble on his coat. "Work, or off to Picrine you go!" he yelled at them. When he fell down he yelled twice as loud.

"He drinks, at times he beats, but he could be worse," the old-timers defended him almost tenderly. They all looked alike, big-boned and pasty-faced, their hair shining bright copper just from passing by the trotyl plant. They also dressed alike, in tight skirts, sweaters out of many-colored wool remnants, and too large boots; and their Yiddish accent made their rough voices sound rougher still. "Kaelanki," they called themselves — a name coined for Konzentrasionlager Majdanek, whence they had come a year ago. "A terrible camp it was; who hasn't seen it hasn't seen anything yet," they defended proudly the grim distinction of their lineage. With pride, too, they spoke of their "cousins." "A 'cousin' is the fellow who takes care of you," the Kaelanka sitting next to Barbara explained. Without a "cousin" you hardly had a chance here; hasagowka wore you out, then hunger did the rest.

"Hasagowka?"

This was a vicious dysentery rampant in the camp. "Typhusiacs," the Kaelanka went on, were the convalescents from typhus, and the yellow, paper-swathed figures were to her simply "picriniacs." Hasagowka — typhusiac — picriniac. Barbara found a peculiar comfort in those words, as if whatever could be named as easily as an everyday thing could also be mastered and coped with.

Noon was the time of soup and news; the women lined up in front of barrels brought into the clearing, while the tattered old "transport" men, who did all the heavy moving in the plant, gathered around the loudspeaker that hung among the withered leaves of an oak. They explicated the news, predicted offensives, planned battles, then led the way back to the hall. The radiators purred; when the foreman withdrew behind the glass door leading from the hall into his office, one could doze off a bit. And on the way back to the camp the Kaelanki sang; hoarsely, louder and louder, they sang of someone called Rost who was like a papa to them, of Warsaw and meeting under the cannons, Barbara singing along with gusto and very much out of tune.

Yellow puddles sprawled across the road and she was still; because suddenly her own body seemed to her like a bounty won, though through no fault of hers, at the expense of others. Another bounty awaited her in the camp — the full ration of bread. Having lost her alibi of superior poverty, she panicked, cut too thick a slice, hurled it into a tangle of yellowed hands. "What is it now?" Abruptly she turned to Tola. "Why are you eying me again?"

"They get exactly the same rations as you."

"Really? Is that so? Oh, just look at me." She stretched out her bare arms. "I have the strength of an ox; I could go hungry for months and it would do me no harm, while they — "

"They won't be saved by one slice of bread. It's a drop in the bucket."

"A drop's better than nothing. At least they know that someone cares about them."

From then on her evening acquired a contrapuntal quality. When "Kindling for sale, saltpeter paper just right to cover your bunks," the picriniacs rasped, when a part of themselves they seemed to be selling — the brown sheets an extension of their paper swathing, the kindling of their sticklike arms — then Barbara saw herself buying up all these wares so that they could rest at last. When, as a deaf-mute stares at the speaker's lips, they watched fingers peeling a potato, she was readying for them the best, the most nourishing food, and when they offered for a muddy peel the bid of greatest hunger, crying "Give it to me, I'm more hungry, miss; no, me!" then she was handing them everything she had — her ruby brooch, her sapphire bracelet, and the pearls she used to wind thrice around her neck. For it was from the sale of her jewels that Antoni's help was to come. "Soon we'll hear from him, any day now."

At last, bowing like visiting royalty, Goldberg would strut into the barracks.

"Nix, Dziedziczka," he would jibe, "the old man must have spent your fortune on women and wine." And she would dash outside, fleeing his jeers, the leeches, and her own hunger, which like everything about her, was huge.

Chapter 10

BARBARA WAS IN A GOOD MOOD. Goldberg's promise that his Pole would soon go to Lublin made her feel fine; so did the big Kaelanka who replaced Tola, working somewhere else that day; so did the weather. At last the sun was out. Brass husks, metal tops, and the Kaelanki's copper heads shone all over the hall; and when your narrowed eyes excluded the withered leaves and the ice, when outside only the pines were left bright green in the sun, then you could find yourself in the midst of summer and hope.

"Comes June and the war will be over," Barbara said dreamily.

"Was hat sie gesagt?" the albino Yekies chirped. "Was?"

"Cabbages mit kvas," muttered the Kaelanka called Magda "the Pug" on account of her broad nose and moist protruding eyes. And Barbara smiled. She harbored a host of grudges against the Kaelanki, for not caring, not sharing enough, and for "Get out, picriniacs!" sounding loudest from their barracks. But now the sun was shining, the hum of voices rose placid around her. Soothed into tolerance, Barbara allowed herself to enjoy the company of this husky wench who, with rowdy speech and raucous voice, belonged to a place not quite remembered but long ago dear to Barbara.

This voice was talking now of the first days in Skarzysko; bitter days when the Pug had longed to gnaw on her own flesh out of hunger; when she had lived more in the latrine than out of it; yes, when it had looked as if it would be the crate for her soon. Bodies were kept in the quicklime-covered crate next to the latrine.

"Hush, God forbid," Barbara whispered and moved closer to feel the warmth the Pug exuded like a large stove.

"That's how it was, my dear. And then . . ."

"Then," Barbara urged her on.

"Then I met my 'cousin.' I was sick and he nursed me; I was starved and he fed me. Oh, he's so good." A glance at the glass door to make sure the foreman was not yet back in his office, a plunge under the table. "See, from my cousin," the Pug said tenderly. Bread was from her cousin, two thick slices spread with beet-marmalade and dotted with garlic whose smell hovered around the Kaelanki like a badge of their "cousinship," a kind of wedding band.

The strong yellow teeth bit into the bread, in red blobs the marmalade oozed down. And as hunger leapt up in Barbara, the place to which the Pug belonged took shape in her memory: the workers' quarters, the slums. On every trip to a big city she would hurry there, hatless, with no gloves on, her meticulously tailored suit encumbrance enough in those streets where old, monstrously fat women crouched on the curb, huge breasts, arms — branded with sprawling vaccination scars — bulging out of their faded cottons; behind them the tenements rising huge, yet not huge enough to contain all the life which spilled over with brawls and infants' cries; the apartments, too, spilling over into the landings with carriages, cribs, and with children in singing chains winding up and down the stairs, their thin "Maple . . . maple, golden tree of maple" following her as she hurried on, past walls covered with obscene scrawls, past the stale odor of bars and past lovers embracing in the mangy grass. Stefan used to frown on those escapades, yet not for anything would she give them up.

"Listen to me," the Pug broke in. "Don't wait until you're skin and bones, by then it'll be too late. Get yourself a cousin right away, now!" Her paw maternal and heavy on Barbara's shoulder, the Pug began listing the potential cousins. The O.D. men were best, but they were all taken up; next came the "shoemakers," men who worked at Trotyl, so nicknamed because they made boots out of the leather they somehow managed to get there; next, any man. "Any man will do, if he's got a head on his shoulders. I know a good fellow, and — "

"Ah, ah." Barbara shook her head.

"Nu, and why not?"

"I have a husband."

"Here?" the Pug looked genuinely pleased.

"No."

"In Werk A, then?"

"No."

"Then what are you talking about? What can he do for you from somewhere far away? Look, God grant it, you two will meet after the war, and everything will be as it was. But now you must take care of yourself. What a woman's got isn't soap; use it, use it, it won't get used up."

"Stop it!" Barbara hated such vulgarities, finding them not shocking but touching too crudely on what must be left secret and her own. She plunged now under the table, taking out the badge of her love affair, a slice of bread which she had saved up for those in greatest need.

And just at that moment the door opened.

For Barbara people often appeared as colors. Meister Grube was the blue of his timid eyes; the red of the enraged turkey-cock the foreman; flanked by those two colors, Mrs. Katz presented herself as black — the musty black of widow's weeds, worn less in mourning than in a morose reproach against joy. A glance at Barbara and Mrs. Katz brightened up — she flashed her gold teeth, she waved, just with two fingers. Bent, those fingers seemed to Barbara, like hooks pulling her away from the Pug into some cheerless place; so once a promise given to Stefan would pull her out of the slums into airless rooms where the crystals, the plush, and the hostess oppressed her even more because of Stefan's "You're really obliged to see her." Barbara, who longed, who hankered for sacrifices, detested obligations.

Somehow Mrs. Katz, too, made her feel under an obligation, although to what Barbara couldn't tell.

"She'll try to latch on to you. Want me to send her packing?" the Pug asked.

"Yes," Barbara wanted to say. "No . . . I don't know," she faltered, looking at Mrs. Katz's wizened daughter; and for the first time she longed for Tola to be back.

Rolling her R's as though gargling, Mrs. Katz addressed the Meister, gestured, gargled some more, and suddenly both she and her daughter were sitting right across from Barbara. How-are-you's followed, accompanied by such a hearty smile that Barbara, quite unable to reciprocate, felt ashamed, then vexed. The smile broadened with expectation, with a plea for response, then narrowed to a sour smirk, the kind which in the airless rooms would usher in a "Haven't you gained a little weight, my dear?"

"Shells," it ushered in now. Had Mrs. Grünbaum ever worked at loading artillery shells?

"Never."

Mrs. Katz was silent. But so completely did her raised eyebrows deny the camp citizenship to anyone who had not loaded shells that Barbara felt almost grateful to her own hunger for proving that she was a citizen in full right.

"How fortunate that you've escaped this hell, this Gehenna." Bending over across the table, Mrs. Katz spoke of "the virtual in- ferno" of working in "subzero temperatures" with shells weighing at least forty pounds each.

"Twenty-five. I know, I used to load them," the Pug snapped.

A shrug, and Mrs. Katz went on about the miracle that had saved them from this hell. A shell had dropped, almost crushing Alinka's foot, and seeing this, the Meister — wasn't he rather humane for a German? — had ordered them to be transferred to Schmitz.

The work at loading shells was terrible, Barbara knew it, yet her pity was meager. Had Mrs. Katz's affected manners drained her of all sympathy? Was it right to be so unsympathetic just because some- one cringed and smirked? In a reminder of winter, withered leaves flitted past the window. From nearby came loud clinking: Mrs. Katz had dropped an antiaircraft shell to the floor.

"Say, you! Those things aren't candies, they explode." Indignantly the Pug moved to the adjacent table.

"What manners!" Mrs. Katz sighed. "But never mind; tell me, what's new with you, Mrs. Grünbaum? How are you accommo- dated? Do you have a comfortable bunk?"

"Yes." Then a pause, which felt like a finger poking Barbara to show that it was her turn. "And what about you?" she gave in.

"I'm not complaining. I sleep on a table — we have no bunk of our own. But Alinka — "

"Please," the girl said through her teeth. "I'm perfectly comforta- ble."

"Comfortable!" In a barely audible whisper Mrs. Katz began talking about the girl: how sensitive she was, and how she had to sleep at the foot-end of the bunk, so that last night the others lying there almost kicked her off. "Still, that wouldn't worry me too much, nor the cold and all the noise I get on my table, but — " Another pause like a poking finger. This time Barbara kept silent.

"You don't know yet what a camp is." Again Mrs. Katz raised her eyebrows. "In a camp one either stays close together, or gets separated, sent to different work, then to a different place — as recently in Cracow. Believe me, were such a separation good for Alinka, I wouldn't stand in her way. I — "

Was this woman pulling wool over her eyes? Had she forgotten what had happened in Werk A? No, Mrs. Katz had not forgotten. Her blinking showed it; her frantic blush. "Please try to understand," she whispered. "It's so important to me that you, especially you, should understand. I know why you look so surprised. Still I did not lie to you, I . . . I brought up this subject on purpose . . . to explain. In Werk A I was caught unaware; I panicked. Yet I do believe that if I had had enough time to . . . to collect myself then I could have done what's right, hard though this would be for me. Because you can't imagine how dear this girl has become to me, ever since we met."

"What?"

"Most dear."

"No. I mean you're her mother, she's your daughter, isn't she?"

"Oh no, we're not related, we only pretend to be in order to stay together. Not that this helps much, still — one tries. And in a way I feel as though she were my daughter. She," Mrs. Katz whispered, "she's such an unusual person. And then the circumstances under which we met . . . You see, we met in the grave."

"Transport!" the Pug called. The old man hoisted a black crate up onto the cart. And like someone who clings in the dark to familiar things, so Barbara's eyes clung to the Pug, the transport man, then cautiously turned to Mrs. Katz. Mrs. Katz blinked and everything was clear: this woman was mad! Longing more than ever for Tola, Barbara turned for help to Alinka.

"God, what's the use of dragging it all out?" the girl muttered.

"Dragging what out?"

"This business of the grave."

"So — you mean this really happened?"

"Of course not. Aurelia just invented it to entertain you, Mrs. Grünbaum."

"Don't," Barbara said, and to herself silently, It happened, they met in the grave. In the grave — in the grave, over and over again; then, as those words still meant nothing, she leaned forward, staring at Mrs. Katz; but all she saw was a long-nosed, ordinary woman, imaginable nowhere but in an ordinary place. "No, I don't understand," she groped. "I just can't."

"A mass execution." Mrs. Katz spoke apologetically.

"There's nothing much to understand," Alinka said sharply. "Instead of the so-called 'deportation,' they did it on the spot. Somehow we got just slightly wounded. When it was all over we crept out of the ditch — the grave I mean — and ran away."

"Yes," Barbara gasped, "yes. When did it happen, where?"

"Last June, in Radom."

Smell of tanneries — this was Radom, and the best dumplings, and the cousin who was a bore. "But I used to go there. I know Radom!" She grew still. "But I know Treblinka," Marta had cried when news had come of those terrible things.

"Tell me," she got up, "tell me, what happened then?"

Shells clinked, someone was laughing; yet she felt all alone, the sole spectator in a huge theater waiting for the curtain to go up.

What voice was suited to such events Barbara did not know, yet certainly not this mechanical drone, "The atrocities — the bestial Nazi criminals — " Mrs. Katz seemed to be reading a paper, in used-up phrases reporting something too distant to be grasped. Barbara tried to grasp it, substituting for "bestial Nazis" helmets and guns, for "the helpless victims" a young face. "The mind understood what was happening, not the heart," blurring all images, the drone went on, and the stumpy fingers stalked toward a chalk-covered crumb.

"That's how we met. I was alone; my husband . . . I lost my husband then." Mrs. Katz's hand circled round the crumb. It faltered; slowly, as though weighted down, it rose above the table; it clenched. And like another fist the purplish face clenched up, eyelids tightening, and the mouth, as though with all her strength this woman was straining to remember something. A quiver; her mouth opened in a shallow gasp.

"What did you remember, what?" Barbara was about to cry; instead she got up, bumping against the table's edge, ran to Aurelia Katz, and "Tell me," she stroked her shoulders, "tell me, what can I do for you?" The slumped shoulders stiffened. "Tell me, Aurelia. I may call you Aurelia, yes? I — wait — of course, you'll move to my bunk, you must."

A chair shuffled. Reminded that someone else still must be comforted, Barbara reached out, but her arm hit against the table, as hastily Alinka shrank away.

"Alinka," Aurelia Katz cried. "Alinka!" Then to Barbara, "I certainly thank you. Still, believe me, I didn't tell you those things to provoke an invitation."

"My God, the ideas you get," Barbara protested, wishing Aurelia Katz had not spoken.

As they did every evening, the Kaelanki sang on the way back to the camp. And just as they were passing Picrine, a new voice, ringing and clear, joined the chorus. It was Aurelia Katz.

"Sing, my dear, it'll do you good," her chagrin over, Barbara whispered. But from then on Aurelia Katz walked in silence.

The girls from the bunk below helped Barbara to get ready for her guests. One dark, one blue-eyed and fair, they bore the family resemblance that hunger brings, both willowy and translucent in their emaciation; and both in their shy, soft-spoken manners still preserved the traces of governesses and piano lessons. "Of course, Mrs. Grünbaum, gladly, Mrs. Grünbaum," they twittered, when asked to fetch water, or to shake out the saltpeter paper sheets. Smell of freshly scrubbed wood spread over the bunk, and when as a finishing touch Barbara tucked in a stray wisp, they all came in — Tola, the freckled child, and Aurelia Katz. They halted, looking at one another uneasily, like strangers suspecting they are heading for the same party.

"Come on up, everything's ready," Barbara called. Aurelia Katz first, Tola last, they got up onto the bunk, and sat as far apart as the narrow space allowed.

"So," Barbara rubbed her hands, "so," and moistened her lips. "Tolenka, you remember Aurelia and Alinka, don't you? They're at

Schmitz now; they were transferred from loading shells, dreadful work, just dreadful. And now — now they'll be staying with us."

"I see."

"They had no place of their own so I asked them to our bunk."

"I see." Then the rustle of paper under Aurelia's scampering fingers. The paper swished, ripped asunder as Barbara gripped Tola's arm. "You two stay here," she ordered the newcomers, pulling Tola down. "We must talk, you stay!"

There was no place where one could talk. Snow, sharp like glass splinters, chased them off the street, the swarm of naked bodies out of the washroom, the stench out of the latrine. And again they stood in front of the barracks, Tola flattened against the wall, Barbara pacing to work off her anger, because this time she must not flare up.

Snow fell; bobbing like a white balloon a freshly shaved head glimmered in the dark. Then Goldberg came toward them. "Good evening, ladies," he waved. "Good evening, Dziedziczka. Tell me, what's going on — who are those two Grazias on your bunk?"

"They're my friends, they're moving in with me."

"Oh! A guest brings God into the home, as the old saying goes. Frankly, I've no objection to God, at least you don't have to feed Him; but those two — "

"Keep your mouth shut! Wait, has your Pole left?"

"No. Poles have been nabbed off trains and sent to Deutschland, so he's staying put. Evening ladies, evening Dziedziczka." Sliding on the ice he took off.

"The lout!" Barbara unloaded some of her anger on him, then went on pacing, until at last she felt prepared. "I understand." This gentleness pleased her, like a newly acquired skill. "You feel that I should've asked your permission, your advice at least? But how could I? You were gone, and I . . . I couldn't put off inviting them once they told me . . . Oh!" she exclaimed. "Oh!" once again, with anger at herself, overhasty as ever, and with remorse toward Tola, who, Barbara realized, knew nothing as yet about those two. "They — " She paused to attune her voice. "They're not mother and daughter. They met — "

"In the grave. 'The mind grasped what was coming but not the heart.'"

Barbara flinched with a sense of outrage, of being cheated, duped

by Tola into remorse. Or had someone else cheated her? "Aurelia
— do you mean that Aurelia Katz made it all up?"

"She did not."

"Then — you knew and — "

"I couldn't help knowing. Twice I passed through her barracks,
twice I heard her talk about it. Not that I blame her. Everyone
here tries to peddle whatever he's got — soup, clothes, gold teeth.
Well, she peddles her past."

"She tries to ease her heart. But you, you knew and did nothing to
help her; you knew and didn't tell me a word!"

"That's right. You've never charged me with reporting every disaster story to you. Still, if that's what you want, then let's go into
the barracks, and about everyone, yes, almost everyone, I'll tell you
a story not so very different from hers. True, she's lived through a
mass execution, but standing in a selection is not so easy, either. Nor
what happened in the ghettos. I don't intend to compete with Mrs.
Katz for the crown of martyrdom. Still, everyone here has been
through something terrible. And what will you do about it, Barbara? A bunk isn't a manor house; you can't invite us all."

"Those two I can. They came to me, they begged my help. All
this misery, the very breath sticks like a bone in my throat. And
here we get a chance to do something, such a chance, and you —
you just wash your hands of it all. What are you begrudging them,
the rotten straw on the bunk?"

"Bread, Barbara, just the bread. May I tell you what happened
today, at the loading of shells?"

"I know what happened. A shell dropped down."

"Shells don't drop, they are dropped. How do I know this? I
worked there today. Mrs. Katz saw a piece of bread, muddy, hardly
bigger than a nut. She made a dash for it; of course she stumbled
and fell down, while all of us, a line of about a hundred people, each
holding a shell, had to wait for her to come back so that the shells
could be passed on. The girl couldn't take it any longer and
dropped her shell. Barbara, don't you understand? This woman
has let herself go, she can think of nothing but her stomach."

"She's starving. Is that a sin?"

"No sin whatsoever. But we too are starving, we can't just wait
for your riches. And when we get a bit of extra food, what will you

do? Will you say, 'Mrs. Katz, could you kindly turn away? I'm going to eat now.' Or will you eat with her staring at each bite you
take? Of course not. You'll share every crumb with her." A door
slammed, and nearer and nearer the head like a white balloon
bobbed through the dark. "Crumbs can't be shared, Barbara. A
crumb for her, a crumb for you — she'll be starving and so will you."
Drawing aside, Tola made room for the woman with the shaved
head. She was huge; the torn shawl trailed down her gaunt frame,
and she kept stopping, kept pulling it over something, as though to
protect a small unfledged creature. It was bread.

"Would you like to buy bread for a portion of soup? It's a nice
chunk," the woman asked softly.

"No," Barbara cried. "What are you doing to yourself? Eat your
bread, it's better for you than those slops."

"Soup is more filling," the woman said. And all the time, while the
woman displayed her bread, while she tucked it under her shawl,
then shuffled on, Barbara felt Tola's eyes darting from the sunken
face back to hers.

"Enough!" Barbara muttered. "This is enough! You're so calcu-
lating, so scheming. 'Was no one trying to denounce you, Barbara?
What you give the picriniacs is just a drop in the bucket, Barbara.'
This time you said nothing, you just stared. I got the point, though.
'Do you want to look like this woman, Barbara? Aren't you afraid?'
That's what you meant, wasn't it? Yes, I'm afraid; afraid of having
come here for nothing, only of this. Because no one was after me,
because I came here of my own will, came not to calculate, scheme,
and count crumbs, but to do something. And I will, even if you — "
She stopped. From behind spread-out fingers, Tola's eyes looked
at her, glittering and wide.

"What is it, Tola, why do you stare like that?"

"Let's not quarrel, not this way. You can ask them to stay with us,
you can do anything, only let's not talk like this, never again. I give
in. I — someone — a man who knew my family — has offered me
some money. I'll do something with it, cook soup for sale, and somehow we'll manage."

The capitulation had come too soon. "You really agree? We'll
share with them everything we have?" Barbara stammered, half
hoping for a refusal proving that she had again been tricked into

remorse. No refusal, no tricks. Tola was agreeing to everything: Aurelia Katz and the girl could stay as long as they wished, would live like one family with them.

"Ah, who can figure you out?" Barbara sighed. "You mock, you jeer, then suddenly you take pity on them. The sharper the tongue, the softer the heart, Antoni always says, and he's right. I'm sure you didn't mean half of the things you said, and I too got carried away; for some reason I always get infuriated by such cutting talk." Having equally freed Tola and herself from most of the blame, she felt calm enough to assure Tola that her anger was over, done with. "Only don't ever hide anything from me, I can't stand such secrecy. Now, who is this man? Let's go to him, at once."

"He doesn't want anyone to know who he is. A kind of anonymous benefactor, you know. Why don't you go back to them, Barbara, and I'll come soon."

Rags, torn sheets of paper — traces of the long line that had waited here for exemptions from work — littered the ground in front of the dispensary. Tola knocked. A smiling O.D. man opened the door for her, then a few minutes later let her out. And again she walked through the dark, stopping now and then to spit the blood out. Because her tooth had crumbled as he was pulling the gold crown off and the slipping prongs had lacerated her gums.

She wanted to go to the Kaelanki barracks where no one would speak to her, where she could rest; but just as she turned into her street Alinka came hastily toward her. Was the girl eager to thank her for taking pity on them? If so, she would explain that not pity had prompted her, only fear of losing Barbara, of being left alone again.

Alinka, however, showed no intention of offering thanks. Her look was sharp, her voice businesslike and dry.

"Miss Ohrenstein, I know that you don't want us," she rapped out, "and I understand you; in your place I would have felt the same. Still, it's happened, and now I'd like to know if I could be of some help."

"No. Thank you."

"I've already arranged to sleep on the bunk below." Another penetrating glance. "I — I know what you're thinking of." The girl spoke with sudden vehemence. "Of her teeth."

"What do you mean?"

"Aurelia's gold teeth. Everyone has been nagging me, 'Why doesn't she sell them, what does she need all that gold for?' Not to look like a decrepit old woman, that's why. Anyhow, the teeth which she didn't absolutely need have already been sold. We have nothing. I just wanted you to know this. And — this too: you can't possibly like her, not the way she is now," the girl whispered ardently. "Still, if you could try not to be too harsh with her . . ."

A snowflake settled on Alinka's long eyelashes, then melted to a glistening drop. Tola stepped closer. "Yes," she said, "I'll try. I promise you."

"Thank you. And anyhow the whole arrangement may not work. You see, Aurelia admires, Aurelia worships Mrs. Grünbaum, while Mrs. Grünbaum is being generous. Oh yes! This evening she even gave Aurelia her permission to sing."

Chapter 11

EXACTLY AS SHE HAD PROMISED ALINKA, Tola never said a harsh word to Aurelia. Exactly as Alinka had promised her, she disliked this woman with a cold, ever-mounting fury: for the smiles of servile admiration lavished upon Barbara and for the stilted reserve offered to her; for the way she ate, voraciously yet with her finger bent daintily; for the elegant turns of her speech and the unwashed odor of her body; for sleeping at work and waking them up at night; and for shrinking, for making herself small, the abject glances asking if such an act of "considerateness" — this her favorite word — had been duly noticed, thus becoming larger, more oppressive still. In brief, to her Aurelia Katz was a professional victim, the kind whom children scorn, whom adolescents ignore, and of whom at a party the uneasy hostess whispers, "Please, do say something to her."

Like all such victims she knew how to exploit her helplessness to the hilt. Barbara simply doted on her. A sigh — for Aurelia was a past master at sighing — and Barbara came rushing with comfort; a mishap, water spilled on the bunk below, the irreplaceable comb lost when, to show her considerateness, Aurelia tidied up the bunk, and right away Barbara pleaded "Ah, don't worry about such trifles, my dear." In the evening it was "my dear" all the time. "More salt, my dear?" "Isn't the soup wonderful, my dear?"

Tola provided the soup — her profit from peddling. At first Barbara had tried to help her. "Of course, I'm coming with you," she had insisted. "I won't sit here with folded hands, while you . . ."

"While I?" Tola prompted.

Still, Barbara did not say "while you peddle." "While you run your feet off" it was instead. Together they set out for the O.D. men's barracks. Heat and the odor of cooking burst upon them. On the bunks that still had blankets and sheets the men lolled half naked and sweaty. "Come on, Tolenka, what is it? Come on!" Barbara urged. Tola did not stir. She could not do it; some uncontrollable shriek would break out of her, she would slip, would fall down, amidst roars of laughter. But just when she wanted to give up, someone else seemed to take her place, someone who did not mind peddling, who knew how to shrill "Soup for sale, only two zlotys a cup!"

"Soup — fine soup, come on, just try it," Barbara called much too loudly, like a child delighted at playing store. Everyone stared. "Look, the big Pole is peddling soup!" Barbara winced. Now with a cramped smile, now muttering about the fine soup, she dragged herself behind Tola.

"It's pointless for both to do it," Tola said when they were done. She argued, she enumerated the chores to which Barbara should attend instead. "Perhaps you're right. I was never any good at selling and that kind of thing," Barbara admitted.

From then on Tola peddled alone. The icy kettle handle bruising her palm, she hastened, not to the O.D. men — there the competition was too great — but to the barracks of Trotyl men. It was quiet there. Homeless-looking, the men crouched on the bunks. They beckoned to her. "Did you cook the soup yourself?" they asked, for each of them put an inordinate faith in anything prepared by women's hands. Anxiously, as if it were a most rare potion, they watched the soup pour into their cans; they ate slowly, almost with piety. 'Can this be all?' their eyes asked when they had finished, just as Barbara's did after every meal. That they kept buying the soup surprised her no less than the liking many showed for her.

"You're honest, with you a cup is a full cup," said some. Others wondered about her age. When she said she was twenty, they sighed that they would have given her not a day more than sixteen — so young she looked, and refined too, a girl from a good family, one could see it at once. This fumbling compassion helped her more than she would admit.

And along with the two cups of soup which were to feed the four of them, she took this compassion back to her bunk as an antidote against what awaited her there: the silence falling at her approach, the haste with which, like a hand-shy dog, Aurelia Katz drew away. Yes, she was their guardian, so stern that this help would be much more welcome if given in absentia. So she acted like just such a guardian: she hardly ever spoke; when spoken to, she answered in monosyllables.

And all the time, while Aurelia Katz studiously looked away from the kettle, a desire rose within her, almost a lust, to draw the ladle away, to snap "Not a drop for you," then to watch this woman squirm. If she restrained herself it was for Alinka's sake; stubbornly rebuffing Barbara's advances, the girl seemed to declare herself on Tola's side and during those evening meals remained as aloof, as isolated as she.

"More salt, my dear?" "Isn't the soup just wonderful, my dear?" until at last Lagerschluss came and the dark.

Sitting close to the stove to get its meager warmth, Tola watched over the soup cooking for the next day. The sound of breathing filled the dark. Now and then, one of the Picrine women, burning with thirst day and night, would tiptoe toward the water bucket, break the sheet of ice with her can, then drink in greedy gulps. Again all was still. The soup bubbled; crackling, an ember would burst into the last flame. And gradually peace came over her. After the war — if I survive, which isn't very likely, Tola never failed to add. But she saw it: the white manor house, the door opening at her approach. Shadowy — for in Barbara's stories he consisted only of prodigious kindness, mustache, and riding boots — Stefan Grün- baum was running toward her. "I know what you've done for my wife," he exclaimed; then taking her by the hand he led her inside. She grinned at her own sentimentality. Yet invariably she would pass her tongue over her gum, which, still infected, was a reminder of a sacrifice — greater because kept secret.

Week after week passed, each day gray and so cold that what- ever you touched felt like ice. At noon only the politicking transport men stood in the clearing at Schmitz, their eyes fixed on the loud- speakers. The loudspeaker would not be coerced: "No news," the men said. "The Allies are not moving at all."

"Oh, just wait! The first warm day, the first thaw, and there will be no stopping them!" Barbara motioned in a sweeping gesture, as if the Allied armies were swarms of migrating birds sure to return with the spring. Next day, though, she was the first at the door call- ing "Anything new, anything at all?"

"Nothing, no news."

The cold persisted. On the way back to the camp the Kaelanki no longer sang; silently the sprawling column moved through the dark; only at times someone would slip, would fall on the ice with a startled cry. Silence again; the cans clinked, the sabots thudded against the frozen ground. By now many of the Cracow women wore sabots instead of shoes, blankets instead of coats — the record of disappointed hopes for help that was to come from the Freedom.

Barbara was still hoping, still writing letters to the acquaintances who were to act as liaison between herself and Antoni. Antoni, Goldberg's Pole had reported, was no longer living at his old address. "We will find him!" Barbara insisted. Still, more and more often a listlessness would come over her.

And something was spoiling between Barbara and Aurelia Katz. The gifts of comfort, of affectionate glances were being withdrawn. These days, when Aurelia spilled something on the lower bunk, Barbara would just look from her to the two girls, as though comparing their shadowy bodies with Aurelia's torso, grown even heavier, more square.

"Take a walk, Aurelia, move, do something!" she would suddenly mutter, or "For heaven's sake, come with me and wash."

No, Aurelia would not wash. Aurelia would do nothing but eat and sleep. Only when the soup was too vile for the Kaelanki's pampered palates she perked up, collected all she could get, then ate, her little finger still bent, yet scraping the can so hard that the soup darkened with rust. And she often flared up against anyone, even against Barbara. Then, retreating at once, she tried to woo Barbara back.

It was a terrible, a desperate, courtship: everything — past cultivation, present miseries, and the terrors of the grave — thrown into it, and "So fascinating . . . so inconsiderate . . . just terrible," Aurelia simpered, her nails digging into her palm, as if to scratch something, anything, to say out of it.

It was Friday, the eve of Sabbath which the old Rebbetzyn donated to the barracks by sweeping the least crumb off the floor, by lighting two tallow butts stuck into scooped-out potatoes. All looked on while, her eyes covered, the old woman blessed the can-

dles. With a jerk she drew herself up; in her face, the color of gin-
gerbread, the black eyes glittered, the withered mouth set tight.

As usual on Friday, visitors dropped in and, when to greet them
the women leaned out of their bunks, the barracks came to resemble
a quiet street, where neighbors lean out of their windows to chat
with those passing by. On the bench at the stove the blue-eyed girl
from the bunk below Tola's was humming to herself. Someone
stepped by to listen. "Sing louder," someone called. Shyly the girl
began to sing the old hits brought back from the soldiers' barracks:
about the stars in Copacabaña — about Johnny who was longing for
Hawaii.

"No, I don't remember anything else," she broke off. An elderly
man handed her a couple of potatoes. The girl made as though to
curtsy, then awkwardly walked back to her bunk.

"Ah, that was lovely. Come on girls, let's sing some more," Barbara called with a warmth rare for her by now. Next to her, Aurelia
Katz looked up, in her neck the veins swelling to thick cords. "I — "
She looked into the lower bunk to make sure that Alinka was not
there. "I — yes, I'll sing!" From her glances, from the red dots on
her face, stage fright spread like a smell over the bunk.

"Don't do it," Tola wanted to warn.

"You want to sing?" Barbara shrugged.

"Yes." And already Aurelia was waddling toward the stove.
Above her, from a shirt hung out to dry, steam coiled in a turbid
cloud.

"Celeste Aïda," this was the song which she, enveloped in the
smelly mist, had chosen. But the voice, Tola knew, was beautiful;
powerful and clear it sounded over the barracks, silencing the hub-
bub, the whispers, even the clicking of nails hunting for lice. Then,
just when granted all this space, the voice took fright, rising too
steeply, faltering, tumbling. Still, it would have recovered its balance were it not for those harassing it, not only the smirking O.D.
man but Aurelia Katz herself. Something in her did not want her to
sing, something forced her to take in each jeer, hunch up her shoulders, gesture in a grandiose, operatic style.

"Caruso," the O.D. man screamed. "He, he, our little Caruso!"

Her voice rose to a shriek, then stopped, and she stood, her mouth
gaping, between her legs a rag hanging like a gray tail. She grabbed

hold of this tail, let go, and rushed back to the bunk. No one spoke.

"Hmm, your voice is — nice," Barbara said at last.

In Aurelia's neck the veins swelled as if she were about to sing again. Yet she only spoke. "Mrs. Grünbaum, you don't really think so," she said, not whining, not accusing, just calmly stating the truth. Her face, too, was calm. Only her fingers clutched at the bunk as if this sudden dignity was a steep pinnacle to which she must hold with all her strength. But already she was slipping down into helpless anger and "Why," she whimpered, "why do you say things you don't mean? Out of pity? I — I don't want your pity. I — I — " she mumbled, climbing down. She gasped, then trotted frantically out of the barracks.

"Ee, how I need to pee," the O.D. man chanted. The old Rebbetzyn bent down toward him. "You good-for-nothing!" she cried. "Did you learn how to mock us from the Germans?"

"Tola," Barbara said, "Tola, I . . . I can't take it anymore. I've tried, but I can't. God, what a fool she made of herself, and all for a couple of potatoes."

"It wasn't for potatoes that she sang, but for you, to impress you." Tola felt bitter against the victory won much too easily over Barbara and against herself too, who could relish that victory, cheap though it was.

Chapter 12

THE SABBATH CANDLES glowed in their potato-holders; up on the bunks the women sat quietly, some resting, some mending or delousing their clothes. That it was Friday, that no quarrels, no shouts marred the rare peace seemed to Barbara like a sign of hope for the girl on whose behalf she had breathlessly run back to the barracks.

"Wait," she gasped, getting up onto the bunk, "let's not eat yet, not till I've told everything." Barbara stopped. Thin white hair falling loose on her shoulders, an old woman came in, halted to look at the candles, then moved on with a somnambulist's wavering steps. This was "old Alexandrovitch," who a moment ago, in the washroom, had told Barbara about the girl.

"Do you know what?" old Alexandrovitch had begun. Water splashed; the gray, flaccid breasts dangled above the trough; behind Barbara a woman squatted, then quickly got up. "Swine," came the outcry, "we'll get the O.D. men after you, you swine!"

To pee in the washroom was wrong; it was wrong, too, to call a "swine" someone who, with the cold and with all that coffee and soup in her, simply could not help herself. So Barbara thought, and felt how from the damp dusk a torpor was creeping over her, until nothing was clear about this place where things could be both right and wrong. "What?" A word pierced through this torpor. "I wasn't listening, what was it you said?"

Taking no offense, old Alexandrovitch began anew, with a soft moan, with an even softer "I just cannot forget this." The sight seen last Friday night in the latrine was what she could not forget. It had been pitch-dark there — the bulb must have burned out — but then an O.D. man flashed his light in, and then, "Then I saw her, a pregnant woman, quite, quite advanced. I could not see her face, only this." Old Alexandrovitch drew a steep curve above her sunken abdomen. A pause. "In Cracow pregnant women were selected. Here, I don't know — but even so, when her time comes, what else can the poor woman do?" Old Alexandrovitch murmured, her hands twisting as though to wring something out.

Barbara understood. And that she had understood so fast frightened her almost as much as what she had understood. Without drying herself, clothes clinging to her wet skin, she dashed out.

Wind burst into her face; she stopped; and suddenly what must be done was clear. Now she had learned about those terrible things before they had happened, now she would stop them from happening. She would write letter upon letter until Antoni was found. She would beg Goldberg for help, and the Poles at Trotyl. Even the peddler, passing by with a bulging bag, brought not revulsion but hope: yes, in such a bag the child would be carried out of the camp — like bread, like a loaf of bread.

"Yes, I know what to do." Barbara settled deeper into the bunk. "About what? — Aurelia, for once stop staring at the pot, then I'll tell you." And softly, solemnly, she began.

"I'm sure this pregnant woman must be young," she whispered, "and helpless — and when she remembers how such things used to be . . ." Barbara too remembered. "This girl must be slaving at Trotyl, or Picrine," she was saying, and imagined the solicitous relatives warning, "You must not lift anything heavy, you must rest." "She must be starving" called forth delicacies urged upon the one who must eat for two. And as her hands twisted in a repetition of old Alexandrovitch's gesture, as Barbara whispered "What else can the poor girl do?", "Thank God," came the relieved chorus, "thank God, everything went well."

"Yes, all will be well. I — we, we'll find her, we'll do everything we can." Each disappointment, each hurt she would forgive them; more, would take upon herself all the blame, if only they would give her what she demanded — pity and the promise of help. The bunk creaked, straw rustled as it showered down. And when she looked up all three of them looked away as though something shameful had been said. "What's going on here?" Desperately Barbara stared into their faces. "Tola, did you know about this girl?"

"No."

She didn't? Then why that shifty look? And why was Aurelia

gaping at Alinka, Alinka shaking her kinky head? "And you?" Barbara shoved herself between them. "Did you know?"

Aurelia gnawed at her thumb. Alinka blanched. "I knew." Her beady eyes stared into Barbara's face.

So! They had known, and the girls down below, who must have heard every word, and who just went on combing their hair, they too, everybody in the barracks had known, yet none of them had tried to find the pregnant woman, not to help, just to stand by her in her grief. Grief — none of them knew what grief was.

Back at home a woman had gone mad because her child had perished in a fire, one child out of a whole brood. And here each had lost her all in something a thousandfold worse than a fire, yet they just chatted and primped themselves. Where had she come to? What kind of people were they? But she must keep calm.

"Can you tell me who this woman is — or tell me how you found out?" She groped for the right question, when "Alinka!" Aurelia Katz shrilled, "A — Alinka!"

Again the girl shook her head, then turning to Barbara she said, "May I ask you what is really on your mind?"

"What? I'll help her, I'll do everything for her."

"For instance?" Alinka asked.

"For instance — Antoni will help me. In a few days I must hear from him. Then he'll come here — "

"Oh?"

"Oh?" Barbara mimicked furiously. Down below, the candles were dying out. And as she looked at them their meager flames seemed to change into the icon light falling upon the old man's face. He would not have cross-examined her as this gnome was doing. "We'll do anything for that little innocent," he would have said. Such a longing for him seized her that she could no longer grasp what ever had made her abandon him, what had brought her here.

"Very well," Alinka piped. "But even if you reach him in time, even if he comes here, what then? You can't invite him here; this is a camp, Mrs. Grünbaum."

"Enough!" Barbara drew herself up. "Enough! All of you have been treating me as if — I had been living on the Riviera till now. 'A camp is a hungry place, Barbara; you don't know yet what a camp is.' I was not on the Riviera. I know what a camp is, I won't invite him here. One of the Trotyl Poles will carry it out of the camp, like — "

"Oh?" again, but this time Barbara clenched her jaws.

"Mrs. Grünbaum," the girl went on, "do you remember how much a loaf of bread costs in the Freedom?"

"What?"

"Yes, how much? Forty zlotys at most. And how much do we pay? Eighty! The peddlers make ten zlotys or so. The rest goes to your Poles. They aren't blind, they see that we're starving. Still, what does it matter to them? And now you think they're going to help you! Will any of them risk his neck for you? What if he were searched on the way out? What if the Germans heard it?"

"Heard what?"

"It! Don't you understand? It might cry. Right? And you should think a bit before you raise so much — so much noise. Any Pole caught smuggling something like that out of here will get shot. Why should he risk it for you? You wouldn't do it for him either, would you?"

That Barbara did not grab Alinka and lay her over her knee was an act of self-sacrifice for the sake of the pregnant one. "Tola! Aurelia! Tola!" She hoped to summon not allies but adversaries other than this gnome still holding her in the double power of her past and of being, in spite of all, a child.

"I — yes, I mean no, I don't know," Aurelia mumbled.

"Alinka may not be so wrong," Tola said.

"Not so wrong? Oh you, not everyone is like — "

"Like who, Mrs. Grünbaum?"

"Not everyone in the world has become heartless. I'll go to every Pole, at Trotyl, in Werk A, I'll throw myself at their feet, I — "

"At their feet! And they will lift you right up. Why? To take you to the Gestapo, that's why. Aurelia, listen to me. By now some bunks must have become free; Mrs. Grünbaum, who is so very generous, will not turn us out into the street until I find something. And then we'll move out, because I don't trust her, I never have. You'll keep making your empty noise, Mrs. Grünbaum, you'll keep throwing yourself at the Poles' feet till everyone up to the last guard will know about — your plan. Questions will start. Who else tried to help you, who knew about it? You will wriggle out; you're a hand-

some woman, you'll always find a protector. But no one will protect us, most certainly not you. So, we're going to move out. Because I wouldn't risk a hair of Aurelia's head for — for your latest
charity."

Barbara rose. "You!" she cried. "You! All of you have forgotten
what a child is!"

"Please," Aurelia whimpered.

"Perhaps I've forgotten," Alinka hissed. "Still, some things I do
not forget, not Radom, not how we ran away from there. The face
you just made, Mrs. Grünbaum. You're tired of that story, aren't
you? You treat people like books out of a lending library: when
their story gets boring, you want to return them and move on to the
next story. But I'll tell how it was, even though you're bored. I had
to drag Aurelia like a piece of furniture on and on through the
fields, freshly plowed fields, you know, and so flat I felt even the
earth wanted to denounce us. Each time an SS truck passed by, she
tried to dash into the road. She had had enough; she wanted to
give herself up. I kept pinching, kept hitting her, till she was black
and blue. Of course, you would have been much more gentle. 'My
dear,' you would have said to her; you would have stroked her hair,
as when we first came to you. But I'm not like you. Besides, I'm not
sure that she's dear to me; I've simply got used to her, as to a cat.
But if anything happened to her, no — I couldn't bear it. To you it
wouldn't matter. None of us matters to you, neither Aurelia nor
me, not even Tola."

"Stop it!" This was Tola.

"Please," Aurelia stammered.

And to Barbara it was as if she were running through a vast plain,
on and on to a point which was, which must be there. Werk A was
that point. "We're sisters," she had cried then, had come here for
Tola's sake. Shoving the girl aside, Barbara reached out toward
Tola. Just then, ever so lightly, Tola drew aside, the pot overturned, and the soup spilled onto the bunk.

Hazily Aurelia stared at it. Her fingers waded in, and shoved a
bean into her mouth.

"You see," Barbara cried, "how can I feel anything for her, how,
when she cares for nothing but her stomach?"

"Mrs. Grünbaum." Aurelia Katz wiped off her drooling mouth.

"You are too noble, too reckless, I mean, to know what care is, you
— " She scrambled down; face hidden in her hands, she stood at
the table, as if to bless the candles, as if unaware that only the blackened stubs were left. "No!" she cried suddenly. "No!" And with
Alinka right behind her, she tottered out.

"Tola, I meant well. That little demon talked to me as no one before ever dared and I restrained myself as long as I could. But let
them move out. I can't bear it any longer. Anyhow, I can do nothing for them. Now don't you let me down."

Tola was silent.

"You won't, will you? Only tell me, how come that she, this pregnant girl, manages to keep it secret? If she is quite advanced then
you'd think everyone would notice it."

"She must be binding herself with bandages and squeezing it all
in."

"Oh? How do you know that?"

"There have been such cases before. Other than that, I know
nothing."

Chapter 13

TOLA HAD KNOWN about the pregnant woman for weeks. One day — she had been buying groats — the Kaelanki had spoken about her. "It must be one of your women," the Pug had said, while the others with their usual painless pity sighed about the poor soul. Tola had paid for her purchase and walked out.

All that mattered this evening was to conceal from Barbara what she suspected. The girl's freckled face had turned white. "Alinka!" Aurelia Katz had cried, "Alinka!" and this suspicion had struck Tola. It's all nonsense, she argued with herself, Aurelia Katz is old, fifty or more; her husband has been dead for almost a year. Yet the nonsensical thought would not let her be; at night, when Aurelia did not come back from the latrine, it forced her down off the bunk and outside.

Above the black barracks roofs the last smoke trailed; somewhere windows shone like yellow eyes, the crate loomed a grayish blue out of the dark, and at last, on the latrine steps, the loose boards creaked under feet. "Mrs. Katz," she cried. "Aurelia! Mrs. Katz!"

Only a rustle answered her; yet with an utmost certainty she knew that someone was standing inside, listening, looking at her. "Mrs. Katz! Anyone there?" And she groped on.

As in a recurrent dream everything seemed to be foreknown: the snowflakes that followed her inside, the wall damp under her fumbling hand, and the darkness which persisted though she had turned the switch on. "The poor woman loosens the bulb, then sits there in the dark," the Pug seemed to direct her. She climbed up onto the seat, screwed the light bulb back in. Impossible, wincing in the glare, she repeated Impossible, it cannot be.

It was possible. The bandages, those frayed, artfully tied rags proved it, and Aurelia Katz herself, cringing, her torso pressed against the wall. Then she turned, she clutched at her coat, but her hands got confused, they shook, they pulled the coat open. Like a drum the protruding belly pushed against her shirt; through a tear the red porous flesh showed and, veins twined into dark knots, Aurelia pulled the coat tight.

"You — " Tola could hardly speak. "So it's you. Why didn't you tell us — or Barbara at least?"

Tola could guess why. After all, the roles might have been reversed, had she herself not been — not too chaste, just too fastidious for a romance in a ghetto room. Most conducive to romances, those rooms, dark, the bodies lying close together. One night a clammy touch had wakened her; she resisted, she bit into the clammy hand. Aurelia had not bothered to resist. She had felt tired, and anyhow, such things did not matter much. Most likely her suitor had at first shrunk back from the withered flesh, then, anything better than nothing, he had rolled closer; most likely, too, someone had looked on with a smirk. And by morning what had happened meant no more to those two than a not too tasty meal. Not that Tola felt shocked. But if life could begin this way, then the crate was the perfect end.

"Out," Aurelia broke in. "I must bandage myself. You turned the light on, now turn it out." Tola obeyed. In the dark the misshappen silhouette turned round and round like a giant top.

"Are you done?"

"Not yet — not yet."

Again light flashed upon the Aurelia Katz of old, not pregnant, just bloated with too much soup, too little of all else. And how at home Aurelia seemed to feel here; she spread the saltpeter paper on the filthy seat; she settled down, the ragbag on her side, the can on her lap. Soup dripping down her lips, she began to eat.

Tola watched, hoping that her disgust at this greed would free her from the obligation of unmitigated pity. She wanted to be free, she wanted to go back and sleep, to think of nothing, just sleep. But those paper sheets forced her to stay here, the bag, the soup, taken along for the night in the latrine, like those provisions with which a young mother equips herself for the day in the park. Only a book was missing, only the knitting and a book.

She would find something to say and leave. "Should I send Alinka to you?" she rehearsed; but Aurelia concealed her latrine trips, always waiting to go there till Alinka was asleep. "Of course, now you must stay with us" — still better; half a cup of soup and two boards of the bunk as a consolation prize. Barbara would not have been at a loss. Barbara would have flown to Aurelia, comforted her, promised her anything at all. Tola had nothing to promise. All she could do was watch.

The paper sheets rustled in the draft. Aurelia rubbed her hands, sipped the gray soup, then rubbed her hands again. When the spoon slipped down to the floor Tola picked it up. When the wind pushed the door open she closed it. "It's cold — it's going to snow," she said. "You fool!" she wanted to cry. "What have you brought upon yourself, how could you have done it?" And yet what happened months ago in the ghetto room by now had nothing to do with these nights in the latrine, with cold-stiffened hands, and with the bandages pushing into the belly, so swollen it was clear that everything would happen soon. "How soon?" She stepped closer. "When will it happen? When?"

Aurelia's mouth opened, then closed. Her hand opened instead, finger after finger shooting out; then it clenched as if to hold something that must not be let go. Tola did not insist.

Time, Aurelia was clutching. Of course, she knew how much it had shrunk. On those nights in here, while sitting on her paper-covered seat, not just to rest from the bandages bruising her flesh but to soak in all the cold, all the stench she could bear so that the bunk by contrast would appear hospitable and warm, then on those nights she would budget the time, subtracting the losses, multiplying the remainder into weeks, then of late into days. Now "How soon?" Tola had asked, as Alinka had once. "It's still seven months," she had answered Alinka. "In seven months the war will be over," said the girl. So recent that moment seemed, so much like yesterday, that unable to grasp what had happened to all those months, she saw herself crouching here, her fingers standing for days . . . then for hours . . .

"No!" she forbade herself. "No! Nothing." Nothing stood for "There is no way out"; nothing was "You must not think"; nothing above all meant what was swelling within her — just a disease, a boil throbbing with pus. In due time this boil would burst open — an operation she might or might not survive. Beyond this point she had

not allowed herself to think, not until this evening when Barbara
had cried, "You've forgotten what a child is."

No. Nothing — no, but these thoughts that Barbara's cry had
brought would not be gone. She turned, stared at Tola, at the eyes
hidden under smooth lids, at the red arrogant mouth. Arrogant,
she repeated to herself, inconsiderate, arrogant, heartless! on and on
until her fury pushed what she dreaded away. She got up. "Miss
Ohrenstein," she shrieked, "you may be polite to me now, picking up
my spoon and — But I wish you to know that I do not respect you,
I never have."

This face, contracted as though with a great effort, had come between her and her grievances. Night after night she would rehearse
the ever longer list, in preparation for the moment when Mrs. Grünbaum, Miss Ohrenstein, and all of them would suddenly understand
whom they had been mistreating — and why, for what. But now
it was the soup she remembered, the half cup of good thick soup, for
which, imagining each bean, each potato, she would wait all day
long. She was hungry, Alinka was hungry, and they had no one to
help them. Had she gone too far? Should she apologize? Apologize,
for what? For having been treated with no considerateness whatsoever.

"No. I'll tell you everything. You've never said anything impolite to me, I know, but you looked at me as if I were an insect, a
mere nothing. True, you gave me soup, and I took it. But it is not
how one gives, it is what one gives. I mean the opposite —
I mean — "

She looked up to see whether the arrogant mouth was smirking,
was relieved that it was not, and felt cheated out of a fresh grudge
that would have helped her to go on. Yet she forced herself. "Oh,
I could tell you much more — and your friend Mrs. Grünbaum. At
times, when she insists, I call her by her first name, still in my
thoughts she remains Mrs. Grünbaum, and rightly so because — "

"Please, let's not talk about her."

"Why not? Is she so special? I used to believe that she was; I
used to hope she would understand that one could need help and
yet still be disinterested. Yes, I thought she would understand that
I was not a mere nothing — " She remembered the evenings when at
a loss how to make Barbara understand she would fall back upon

the story of the grave, always knowing that it was wrong, yet never able to stop herself. "Mrs. Grünbaum, she has never made me feel at ease; and you, you — now you sit here. Why? Have I got something to give you? Have I become rich? Yes, rich?" She screamed, swaying her body like a bottle to eke out the last drops of anger. Not a drop was left. Sitting down, she brushed against something hideously sleek, then with a piece of paper cleaned off her fingers.

Why was it so? She was in the right, wasn't she? Right, wrong, what did it all matter? And what did they matter to her, Mrs. Grünbaum or this girl? They could not harm her; they could not help her, either. Help, and the thought she dreaded was back, the thought that had she trusted Barbara help could have been found — and not only for her. She could not bear this thought; she must speak.

"Miss Ohren . . . Ohrenstein," she stammered, "before I might have said some things — but with all my worries — And before, still earlier I mean, you asked me why I said nothing to anyone — " She paused, suddenly hopeful that her question if only put cleverly might still bring the right answer. "Yes, I felt it would be pointless to burden you, almost pointless." Having indicated a degree of hope, she waited, her eyes closed.

Until she opened them, only an instant had passed. Yet within this instant she seemed to be lifted and carried into a room, quiet but for a voice saying, "You'll see, everything will turn out fine," and she was answering, "Oh, I never hoped for this," knowing that for this she had hoped, always.

Then she looked at Tola, at her palms upturned to show that they were empty. "We'll stay together," Tola said, "but more than that . . ."

Aurelia nodded. "Are you leaving?" she asked as Tola got up.

"No, I just thought we should sit closer in case someone came in."

"Please sit down here," Aurelia said. She smoothed down the saltpeter sheets and felt like a hostess duty-bound to entertain her guest. Or perhaps — she wondered, sensing that such duties had been canceled for the night — perhaps Tola could be asked to leave. She did not ask. She knew what would happen. As if the grudges that the camp supplied were not enough, her anger kept moving back into the past, ferreting out each least hurt, each slight, until, fleeing into the latrine from what would be, she fled back again from what had been.

Should she send for Alinka? Or for Mrs. Grünbaum? Alinka had been burdened enough, and Mrs. Grünbaum had never made her feel at ease. And already the hunger to speak seized her, not as she usually spoke, trying to bribe her listeners, hunting for the choicest word, but easily, her head tilted back, the words rising unencumbered like breath.

Alinka — Mrs. Grünbaum — "Miss Ohrenstein," it broke out of her, "Miss Ohrenstein. I know we're not intimate, I know. I have no right. But I have no one to speak to. And something is happening to me. I don't mean this." With her chin she pointed to her torso. "Please let's not talk of this anymore. Only I feel . . . I feel so resentful against everything, my past . . . my marriage.

"Still, what do I have to resent? Please, you must believe me, we were happy, we never argued, we respected each other, we — we shared so many interests." She enumerated those proofs of her happiness faster and faster, yet felt as though she were reading labels on jars, from which whatever had been stored had evaporated long ago. "Yes. We were happy," she insisted. "I know it, I know! Only somehow I can't quite believe what I know." Pausing, she touched her cheek. The feel of her wrinkled skin brought back a trace of gratitude toward him who had taken her as she was — never beautiful, no longer young, and already losing her teeth. "Yes, now for a moment I believed it, and then last night, too, when I remembered — may I tell you about it? One afternoon, on our way to a matinée we passed by a large mirror, in a millinery store. When you see yourself so suddenly, you tend to look at yourself as others do, objectively, I mean. And I recall so clearly the thought that had struck me then. You see, we were not a particularly handsome couple. I mean myself mostly; my husband was distinguished-looking but not handsome in the usual sense of the word. And then I thought, Objectively we look rather unprepossessing, yet to each other we're quite different. And then — " She broke off.

She could even remember the dress she had worn then, the wind, and the orangeade on the vendor's stand. Yet the woman in the windblown dress was unreal, just a fictional character read about long ago. What was real, what was cutting right into her, was the feeling of being reproached, not for her "he was not handsome" but for that single word *was* — for the ease with which she had acquiesced to it.

No, she had not acquiesced. "No," she whispered, "I . . . I just can't believe that this happened, this . . . in Radom. I talk about it, I talk much too much about it, I know, but I never feel that it really happened to him, to me. And I don't think about it. I cannot. Is that why my dreams are so bad? Like last night, or was it the night before? I dreamt we were sitting in a café and — " Head bowed, she stared at quicklime gray on the muck. *Faust*, she remembered, the waltz from Gounod's *Faust*, the orchestra in her dream had been playing while they, eating red sherbert out of silver cups, listened, Richard's head bent aside, his bow tie askew. And with the bow tie the dream started going wrong. Why doesn't he ever put it on right? she thought, and she looked at him seeing only how shiny, how bald his head was. "Aurelia, what shabby music this is," he said, terribly loud. The orchestra stopped playing; from every table people turned to stare, and "Ee-eeee-eee, how I need to pee," a man giggled. Then she woke up with this giggle all around her.

"Do you remember," she moved closer, "last week Friday I sang, I tried to sing, not just to get some potatoes, but because I hoped Mrs. Grünbaum and everyone might enjoy it?"

"I know, I knew it then."

"You did? You really did? And she — Mrs. Grünbaum? Oh, never mind. That O.D. man, do you remember how he jeered at me? Why would people do this? Do they think they become better if others are made ridiculous? I can't understand them, I cannot. Only sometimes it seems to me that others have done something to us — I mean my husband and me — with their mockery. They would never leave us alone, never. His relatives interfered, they didn't approve of me. And others, too, were always after us. Why? What for?" she stammered, while "Here comes a Jewess and a Jew, he has a nose like an elephant, and she like two," the janitor's drunken voice seemed to jeer; her mother-in-law simpered; and she, desperately thinking I can't hide the newspaper from him, read: "Richard Katz's first and we hope last appearance proved that his ambition soars in inverse ratio to his talent. As, with his pronounced aquiline profile, he appeared on the stage . . ."

"Why?" she shrilled. "Why can't they speak without mockery? I feel this mockery poisoned us there in the Radom ghetto. And that ghetto too was a mockery; the mockery of a place to live. Even the barbed wires were old, rusted, like those for animals that won't be kept long; and outside the wires there were streets, long streets of empty houses with only cats coming in and out of them, while we had to live ten to a room. Something happens to people when they live ten to a room. My husband could no longer play the violin — he was a music teacher, you see. Till then he had practiced. And it meant so much to me that he had not become like the other men, just sitting there, just reading the paper or staring. 'Isn't it nice to have a portable profession?' I used to joke. Even in the ghetto he had tried to practice, in the backyard, littered and smelly — we had no sanitation, no sewage system, I mean. One day from a window someone tossed him a copper, as if he were — you understand. I have no reason to suspect malice. His clothes were no longer quite what they should have been, and the violin, too, no longer sounded right, because of the dampness — dampness, Miss Ohrenstein, is bad for violins, very bad," she repeated. "Until one evening I suggested — just suggested, you know — that we should sell the violin, to buy Aryan papers with the money and to hide somewhere as Aryans. I thought we could try, at least. He refused. He was right to refuse, but — but I've never spoken about it to anyone. He said . . . he said that my . . . that our looks, yes, were too Semitic."

No, she couldn't do it, could not complain about him, no longer here to defend himself. But there was something else he had said then. They were sitting at a dinner of potato soup, close to each other upon pillows piled on the wobbly bench so they could reach their table — the top of a folding bed. The brown enamel flaked into their spoons so that the soup tasted of rust. One flake clung to his lip; he tore it off; he looked at her. "The water is gone again; that gypsy fiddler needs a full bucket to shave one cheek!" someone shouted from behind the closet that cut off their corner from the rest of the room. The loose closet door screeched. Richard's voice too screeched as he said, "Aurelia, you living as an Aryan, you with your nose!" He paused. "And I with mine," he added.

"Here comes the Jewess with her Jew." — "This aquiline profile"

— everyone who had ever mocked them seemed to crowd around her: the janitor, the relatives, the critic, and those who had put them into this mockery of a place, those who everywhere, all over the ghetto houses, had put up the posters, with the red "Jews, lice, typhoid fever," and a face — black, bearded, the nose grotesquely bent.

Suddenly it was as if someone had come into the room, had yanked them — Aurelia and Richard Katz — away, and put in ugly long-nosed puppets. She walked out of their corner into the room and onto the landing. In the dark two tall figures stood, merging in their embrace; the engineer and his wife, both young, he manly with his gaunt face, she regal, with olive skin and thick black hair. Would the engineer ever speak like that to his wife? Never! She stood watching them as she had on many a night before. With their whispers, with their slowly approaching profiles, they seemed to obliterate the stench, the trash clattering under the cat's paws, even the noise of a car, against which, on those nights, one stood watch.

"There were raids on the ghetto, night after night. The Germans came in cars, with guns, and dogs. We made a bunker in the attic; the entrance was hidden behind a sofa. No, what I wanted to say was that we all stood watch, one person for each floor. I often watched, instead of my husband; I mean, he was so susceptible to colds, and besides — " He kept falling asleep on his watch, she remembered, but she did not mention that to Tola, saying only how quiet it had become toward the end. The raids had stopped, everyone had felt a bit optimistic — perhaps also because of the weather, the sunny and warm summer weather.

"And then, that day — it was a Saturday, so calm, so sunny — we went out to look at a flower — iris, I think it was — growing outside our house. This surprised me. After all, who would have thought of planting flowers in the ghetto? 'Once planted, such flowers come back, year after year,' my husband explained; he knew so much about everything, even about gardening. And just as he said this, it began, with a bugle call — and — oh — " She nodded, now knowing where last night's dream had come from: from the way he had listened to the bugle, his head bent, his bow tie askew, as though about to say, "Aurelia, what shabby music." Through the gate of barbed wire a dark shape was rolling in, like a movie projector, only with a thicker, longer neck. A cat slipped by it, ran out. The gate closed.

They went back through the dark hallway, up the littered stairs. On the landing the engineer and his wife stood, she bent, he embracing her, holding her fast.

"We went inside; somehow the day passed." She punctuated each word with a gulp. "Somehow it must have been easier for me; it always is for a woman, a woman always has things to do. I had to fetch water from the well — it got used up, and after all we still had to eat. Then I packed. I knew it was unnecessary, still I — packed. Then we considered whether to undress. No one stood watch anymore. At times one could hear boots outside; otherwise it was so still."

So still, and yet she knew that behind the closet in the room, in the whole apartment, in the whole house, all lay sleepless. Were they, like her, kept awake not by fear but by the worry one feels before a trip that the alarm clock might not go off, that one might miss the train? Then for an instant she would grasp what it was that worried her, and she would rub her neck, to push the air down.

He lay next to her, arms folded, legs drawn tightly together, like a puppet tied and about to be shipped. From the corners of her eyes she watched him; she drew away. When the air got stuck in her throat, she thought of the engineer and his wife lying close together, he comforting her, he with his touch releasing her breath. Next to her, Richard did not stir, not once.

She did it. On their last night she, lying a hair's-breadth away from him, became unfaithful to him — she was the engineer's wife, took comfort in his lips, his touch, returning to the immobile figure only to gloat over him, who suspected nothing, who would never find out.

Then, very slowly, he began to stir, his legs twitching first, then his arms, until painfully he raised himself up. In the dark his eyes glittered. She remembered this glitter from that other night after his concert when, to know all without asking, she had put her face against his. This time she lay still; could she do it, could she just lie there, pretending not to see his eyes? Could she go back to the engineer, and leave Richard alone? Yes, she could, she understood with a mounting terror. She sat up, pressed her face against his, but unlike that other night, his eyes felt dry. His hand rose, fumbled against her cheek, then against his own.

"Aurelia," he said, "Aurelia, do you think I should shave tomorrow?"

"Richard," she said, "we've had ten years together, and tomorrow it will be just one moment, one second." Drawing closer still, she whispered of those ten years, then of their neighbor the widow — how she had said, "The first time I had to sit down to dinner alone . . ." — then of themselves, for whom there would be no dinner alone, not even once. And "Richard," she said again, "Richard!"

"Yes," he answered, "yes." And with each yes, she shuddered, because she knew that words could help no more.

She bent over him. She took his face in her hands. For the second time this night she became the engineer's wife, she grew regal and young for his sake, he who was still Richard, still mumbling, "Aurelia, should I shave tomorrow?"

"Miss Ohrenstein . . . I . . . I, then — " She faltered, staring at her hands. But the frostbitten hands were gone; gone too the muck streaked with quicklime, and the black shadows on the wall; only that night was left, and the way she had held him close, forcing into this moment their ten years together, and the promise of dinners never alone, and her lips' touch, watchful to his every shudder, every sigh, all she had, all she ever had, into this one moment, so that it would sustain itself against that other moment tomorrow.

"Then — then it happened," she whispered. Yet already the memory of that night was moving farther and farther away. "Have I told you everything? No, I — I just thought of it, I — " She got up. "Please, I want you to judge. What does it all mean — what?" she repeated over and over again, begging for what she had believed with her whole being only a moment ago, for the assurance that the rankling of her dreams did not matter, that somehow she had stood by him.

I envy you, Tola thought. I would never have thought you could be like that . . . I was wrong about you. "I" — "I" — all the time, until to silence that intruding "I" she looked into Aurelia's face.

She looked. "Aurelia, do you think I should shave tomorrow?" a voice seemed to say. Then the littered backyard rose out of the dusk: Richard Katz, the coin rolling beneath his feet, and Aurelia on her rickety legs hurrying toward him.

"What are you doing to yourself?" Tola was almost shouting. "Now you feel resentful, and this might mean something. Still, on that night you stood by him, and this must mean just as much, this too must have been growing in you through all those years." "Please don't ask me for more," she was about to say, and just then Aurelia smiled — a piecemeal smile, glitter after glitter, gold after gold coming into her face.

"Thank you. I . . . I thank you." The smile extinguished itself and, having shifted in her seat, Aurelia looked away from the can of soup. This meant that she wanted to eat but felt ashamed.

"Why don't you get ready, and I'll wait outside," Tola said, hastily walking out.

Wind burst into her face, smudges of quicklime blown off the crate whirled through the dark. If that's how life can begin, then the crate is the perfect end, Tola remembered. That was not how it began; and yet, had there been no last night in Radom, had Aurelia made up her story, the crate still would not have been the right end. Because you did not come by such a lie by chance. It too, like that night, had to grow within you. And what lie would she, Tola, have invented about herself? That she had been always loyal and brave, or so successful at peddling soup that she could have bought up the whole camp?

"I'm ready." Aurelia Katz came out the door. Tola helped her down the stairs and, cautiously supporting her, led her on.

"Excuse me, could you spare just another moment?" Aurelia faltered, standing in front of the barracks. But this moment lasted longer and longer, while Aurelia sighed small uneasy sighs. "About Mrs. Grünbaum," she began at last." Barbara, I mean. Should she be told?"

"Certainly Barbara must know the truth," Tola answered, almost with vehemence.

Part Three

Chapter 14

TOLA KNEW EXACTLY how to tell Barbara the truth by the next evening when they met in the washroom. She would explain the reasons for Aurelia's silence; she would agree with Barbara that everything must be done to rescue the child but kept secret from Aurelia. They must arouse no false hopes.

"Now come on, Tola, what is it?" Barbara grumbled.

"It is — last night, just by chance, I went into the latrine. Aurelia was there."

"Where else would she be, swilling soup as she does?"

"Barbara, do listen to me. Aurelia — It's her, she's the one who's pregnant."

"What?"

"You heard me."

"I heard you, but no, you must have dreamt it; she's at least fifty, she's too old!"

"She just looks old. It's her."

Water splashed. Craning her neck, Barbara drank in greedy gulps. "No!" She wiped her mouth. "No! My head is swimming. And last night, God Almighty, the things I said to her! But why did she hide it from me?"

"Barbara, don't shout!"

"I'm not shouting, I'm speechless. Here I wanted to do everything, everything under the sun, and she — acting as if I were a denouncer, a Judas!"

"She couldn't bear to tell you. The whole thing has been too much for her; she's afraid. And after all, what does it matter now?"

"Of course, I understand. Anyhow, you know who must have been behind this secrecy? This freckled — Alinka, I mean — who else? But to think that it's her — that Aurelia will have a child." Softer and softer, Barbara's voice seemed to come from far away.

For it seemed to Barbara as if she had gone back to a familiar place. Her longing for a child was this place, unchanged, everything in it intact: the envy of that other woman, the sense of loss, and at once the disbelief and at once the hope that such loss could not be suffered forever.

How could she abandon that hope when for years what had been a source of affectionate raillery to others had meant a fact to her — the simplest of facts. "Ah Barbara darling, you're just biding your time," they teased, "but then you'll have half a dozen splendid youngsters, more — a whole football team!" and "Sure, what else?" her own laughter rang most heartily of all.

Trusting, she waited for what was no more than her due. And with a sense of difference so strong it precluded envy and contempt alike, she watched the frumpy dziedziczki and the faded city-cousins, that other species for whom childbearing disintegrated to varicose veins, nausea — an endless succession of petty ills. Quite otherwise it would be with her soon. As if the curse cast upon Eve were to be revoked for her sake, so she felt — her childbearing only exuberance, only the growth of joy.

She waited. And she did not even notice how the teasing voices fell silent. That other talk caught her unawares. Perhaps she should consult someone, it suggested with much hemming and hawing, a doctor like that professor in Warsaw — he was known to have wrought wonders. "Wonders? Phew!" What need of wonders had a woman like her, as healthy, as strong as an ox? Another year had gone by, and she gave in.

There in Warsaw, in the white chilly room she disowned her body, hers no more when subjected to such doubt. The doubt was unfounded: "Relax my dear, and you'll have a splendid crew of youngsters," the Professor chortled, while she, irate at having been harassed for nothing, kept doggedly still.

"Yes, my husband will drop in," she muttered while buttoning her gloves. "He has no time to waste, but if you want him to come, he will."

Of that night after Stefan's return from Warsaw she remembered nothing; what had happened then was like a letter to someone else, read by mistake, to be forgotten at once.

But after that night all joy drained out of their lovemaking; after that night she had learned anger — against Stefan, his childlessness, like an infectious disease passed on to her; and envy too — her own brand of it — the instinctive conviction that passion was the prerogative of the beautiful and the strong, changing into the suspicion of those who were neither — of that other species that somehow had got hold of riches duly hers. At times she tried to reclaim those riches. Left alone with a child she would let fresh air into the overheated nursery, would devise a wild game that left both of them out of breath, the child's flushed face pressed to hers. When footsteps came she would draw away with a start.

So now she started. Like rubbish swept in by the blast a crowd of picriniacs burst in. "No water in our washroom, the pipe broke," they squealed. Naked, jelly-like bodies squirmed, shirking their touch. Barbara looked; and only at this moment did she dare to grasp how great her misery had been. But now — a warmth spread throughout her body — now everything was changed.

"Aurelia, I must go to her," Barbara whispered. "Wait. There she is — she's coming."

Slowly Aurelia was making her way through the crowd, then stopped and clutched at the edge of a trough.

"Aurelia!" Barbara dashed at her.

"Yes . . . I mean . . . Perhaps Tola has had a chance . . ." In timid inquiry Aurelia raised her face. Yet Barbara was looking only at the square torso, the house in which the child lived. She stepped closer; the dark walls seemed to part, and there he was crouching, his blurred eyes groping around. A child — the child whom she would save. And already she could feel him — his soft skin, his breath.

"Mrs. Grünbaum, has Tola . . ."

"My dear," in answer Barbara drew Aurelia closer, "my dear, everything will be well, you'll see. Only tell me, does he stir?"

"Please . . ."

"Just tell me."

"Please . . . no! I mean . . . I mean yes."

"Everything will be well. Antoni, if only you could see him just for a twinkling then you would understand."

"Barbara, not so loud," Tola warned.

"I'm sorry. But everyone is willing to go through fire for him. 'Help me, good people,' he'll say, and they will. And I — I'll do my all, Aurelia — Aurelia — " Barbara called as to someone walking away, for Aurelia stood with her eyes downcast, her lips pursed tight.

"Aurelia, don't act so strange. I know, last night I said some abominable things to you. But then I didn't know. And you — you treated me like a Judas. And am I holding it against you? Not at all."

Aurelia was silent.

"I beg you," Barbara whispered, "I beg you, try to understand. You have reasons to be angry with me, I admit it, I've not behaved rightly toward you. Still, I haven't been myself. Everything here has been so hard on me — the bickering, the counting of each crumb, the filth. I've been in a fury, not against you, God forbid; only against this accursed place. But remember when you first came to Schmitz, my heart went out to you right away, Aurelia, you, in spite of everything — you've always been dear to me."

And at last Aurelia looked up with a shy smile.

"Perhaps, Mrs. — perhaps, Barbara, if you really think something could be done —" Aurelia stopped. Her sabots clattering, Alinka came toward them and pulled Aurelia away, as if she were a child caught playing in the company she had been ordered to avoid.

"Barbara, you mustn't do this," Tola began. "You mustn't start promising her too much."

"Don't you set yourself up against me. I know what I'm doing."

Tola did not answer. She was thinking of Aurelia, of that smile for which she, Tola, had had to struggle through the whole night and which Barbara had won almost at once, not with her promises, but with her "You've always been dear to me!" Well, Aurelia is old enough to take care of herself, she told herself. Anyway I'm tired of being the eternal guardian.

"Have it your own way," Tola said. Then, moving closer, she began telling Barbara about that last night in Radom.

Barbara listened. Barbara sighed, shook her head, and sighed again. "How terrible," she brought out when Tola had finished. "But now that is over. Now we must think only of him, of the child."

On the same evening, a letter went out through Goldberg to Antoni — Barbara dictating it, Tola translating her pleas, her pity and
hope into an elaborate code of caution.

From then on a new era began for Barbara, the era of hope. The
hope was always within her, a nucleus of warmth that restored the
old brightness to her eyes, lent deep caressing notes to her voice.
"Now Aurelia, rest a bit," she would murmur, "now have a bite, now
try to work just for a tiny while." She herself worked all the time,
for the two of them — more, for three, as if the quota were demanded even of him, of the child squatting within Aurelia's
womb.

But only back in the camp did her real working day begin. First
she fetched the bread for the entire barracks, in order to watch lest
bread pasty or speckled with mold would be foisted upon them.
Next she got the rations for her own bunk, pushing and vociferating
even against an injustice the size of a missing crumb. The women
felt hurt. They had loved her with the love that the aging and subdued feel for a madcap youngest sister — her unworldliness, her
wild generosity, a token of what they might have been. Now, how
changed she was. "Ah, it took you no time to learn how to be
grabby!" They grieved to see such unworldliness gone.

"Sure, I learn fast," Barbara grumbled back. That they thought
it was her own hunger which made her grabby occurred to her no
more than to a highborn lady the suspicion that the charity she
promotes might be mistaken for vulgar begging.

And again it was "Eat, Aurelia, here is a lovely piece, Aurelia,"
and off she went to bring more food. The liking the Kaelanki had
for her paid off now; this big sensual woman they felt to be one of
their own, foolish though she was to be saving herself up for that
husband of hers, so faraway he might as well be dead and buried.
Still, who could argue with a fool? And so they helped her loyally,
and gave her their linen to wash — the sheets and the prayer shawls
they got from the clothes-depot to curtain their bunks.

"Thanks, girls. Hoopla!" Barbara would hoist the bundle up onto
her shoulder. As if hope could nourish her, the process of wasting
away had been arrested; and when, stripped naked, she knelt on

the washroom floor, rubbing a sheet with a stone, her breasts, her broad hips swaying rhythmically, all, even the picriniacs, looked at her — not with lust, for what could they lust after but food, but with delight as if it were a comfort to find such a big white woman still in their midst.

Late in the evening, when "Lagerschluss!" resounded through the winter dark, she would return to the barracks, frozen, drenched through, yet full of smiles.

"For you!" and she would hand Aurelia a few potatoes or a chunk of bread. When Aurelia ate the food she had brought, the child too ate, smacking with relish. When Aurelia with her help took off the tight bandages, the child was stretching, was resting at last. With every day he needed her more; needed her bread, her care, her hope that was like air to him, like the very breath. How he would have fared without this hope, Barbara dreaded to think.

Somewhere in the distance beyond the child were the others partaking in his secret existence, softened, like figures seen in the last sunrays, by the afterglow of her tenderness. Now and then one of them would step out into prominence: Tola, who had changed for the better; Alinka, still unchanged; and at times Aurelia Katz. Aurelia too had changed for the better. True, sometimes Barbara wished she would not show her gratitude with such mechanical regularity. Even so, Aurelia took better care of herself; she hardly ever grumbled or whined. Yet now and then a listlessness would come over her; she would sit there, face vacant, snapping her fingers on and on. "Come on, Aurelia," Barbara would pat her shoulder. "Now, be good. Now, what has got into you?" Nothing helped, until at last Barbara mobilized a forgotten talent of hers, mimicry.

When being herself she groped for the simplest word, but never faltered when mimicking others. She limped like Vokunski, strutted like Goldberg, she turned into Meister Grube, all blushes and dangly limbs. "Bravo, Barbara!" The women laughed, leaning out of their bunks. "Wonderful, bravo!" Always a bit out of step, Tola's laughter would come next, and then, at last, she for whom the performance had taken place would give a laborious smile.

Tola let herself be carried along by the peace that emanated from Barbara; she vied with her in watching over Aurelia; she too said "Now, don't sleep, now you should eat something," not as before in a strict guardian's tone but gently. When Barbara praised her for having changed, her sharp face colored with pleasure.

She was changing. She was trying to be good; goodness seemed to her like a foreign language, which once practiced is not half so difficult as it was rumored to be. True, like all beginners, she made her mistakes: a glance from her would spread silence on the bunk, or the old cutting note would sneak back into her voice. But at work she waited for the chance to snatch a heavy crate away from Aurelia; back in the barracks she brought her coffee, or warmed her soup. Only Alinka's reproachful glance troubled her in such moments. But soon the girl began absenting herself from the bunk and also from Schmitz, whenever possible volunteering for some work outside.

The other language Tola was trying to learn was that of a peddler. She was no longer selling soup — the competition had become too great — but old clothes, coats from which the lining had been ripped out to make a dress, dresses reeking of sweat, and crooked shoes. Remembering the proverbial Ohrenstein honesty, the Cracow women gave her such wares on commission. She took them. At times a woman would break into an apologetic whisper; how she had tried not to leave herself in rags, how she had fought against hunger, but now could not, just could not anymore. "Keep these clothes; you'll be hungry anyhow in a few days!" Tola longed to shout, to throw the clothes back on the bunk, to dash out. Instead she took the clothes to the barracks of Trotyl women, who would try selling them to their Poles. Here in those barracks she bargained with a skill of which Seidmanka would have been proud.

Seidmanka — Rubinfeldova — how far away they seemed. She wished one of them would reappear and tell Barbara that turning into a peddler was not exactly easy for her. All her sacrifices were bound to pass unnoticed; even her first sacrifice, her lacerated gums still a reminder of it, had remained secret; saved up for too long, it had lost its value in the inflation which Barbara's generosity had brought about.

Yet Tola's nights were troubled. When no clothes had to be sold, when no one had to be shown how good she was becoming, she felt formless and at a loss. Often the creaking of the bunk would waken her from uneasy sleep. It would be Aurelia, against

Barbara's strictest orders, stealing out to the latrine. Tola never followed Aurelia there; and during the day she was much too busy to spend any time alone with her.

One evening — two weeks had passed since the last letter to Antoni had been sent, and Barbara had gone off to Goldberg to see if the answer had come — Aurelia made Tola stay. "Don't go, please, not yet," she said, nervously plucking at the saltpeter paper sheet.

"Aurelia, stop it please." The harsh rustle made Tola edgy.

"I'm sorry." Aurelia drew back, but soon her fingers shot out and scrounged around, bringing her whatever they could find — a crumb, a tuft of dust.

"I . . ." Aurelia spat the tuft of dust out. "I'm so grateful you stayed." Then, having drawn herself up primly, she thanked Tola for her kindness. "I appreciate all you're doing for me — and —" She broke off like a pupil who has forgotten his lesson.

> "All the animals I knew and you
> Live in my broth like in a zoo . . ."

A teen-age girl sang down below, tap-dancing as she sang.

That's a Shirley Temple song, Aurelia remembered. Looking at the girl's face, withdrawn into some indolently sensual dream, she tried to recall her name, then, just as hazily, wondered why she had asked Tola to stay. The shoes clicked once more, then stopped.

"Do listen to me," the pleading whimper seemed to burst out of itself. "It's so hard to explain what I want to tell you. Still, I must talk to someone. You see, Barbara wants me to be optimistic, and you too want it, don't you?" Aurelia paused. "But somehow," as Tola said nothing she went on, "somehow I find this so difficult. Is it because of all that has happened? You understand what I mean, don't you? Or because I feel tired, though Barbara, and you too, of course, are doing everything to let me rest. Or perhaps . . . it is that I can't help remembering the way this thing used to happen to other women. Not that I compare myself with them, not that I can ever forget where I am."

She faltered, unable to prove how hard she fought against those memories. But they returned: "Just look at this place," they mocked. "Can it end well in such a place?" And Aurelia could not but agree.

After all, of birth she knew only the ceremony: only the palms, stiff in the hospital foyer, and the crimson cascade of plush rolling down the staircase, then on into the hushed corridor, where the nurse floated like a white bird. "Please do not stay too long — it is for *her* sake," the nurse would whisper as the door opened upon flowers, flowers everywhere, and glistening among them a glass of milk. Luxury — this was birth; flowers, and the conspiracy of protectiveness toward the young mother, the silk gown open on the breast. Such license too was birth, and admiration, and praise — the easy birth admired, for wasn't it just like her? so energetic, so brave! The protracted labor praised no less, as no one else could have emerged from such an ordeal so radiant and oh, so lovely. "How lovely you look" was what one had to say. "A bit pale of course, but absolutely lovely!" And "Lovely!" again at the window, a nurse holding up a white bundle. Then the crimson cascade again, the stiff green palms . . .

Those were the attributes of childbirth. Was it possible without them? Aurelia tried to convince herself that it was. Anything that could be salvaged from that other, that real birth, she did salvage: the solicitous glances; the extra slices of bread; even the sense of luxury to be extracted from the least comfort now granted: from leaning her aching back against the radiator at Schmitz; from the relieved feeling when in the evening weariness drained into her swollen feet. So it would be soon, a weariness, greater by far, ebbing away from her body, the burden lifted from her at last; and praise too, if not of her loveliness then of her endurance at least.

"Work!" the foreman would yell. The air would turn bitter or throb with coughs. And at once, this moment which she had just constructed with such care was tumbling down; she was falling down and down into an icy dark where something huge like a train, something ablaze with light, was coming upon her, closer and closer, while she, petrified, stared waiting to be crushed.

"No." She shook her head. "No. I try not to think about it, but I'm afraid, terribly afraid. Believe me, I try to keep calm; and I feel calm, for hours, at times for a whole day. Then suddenly this — this terror comes upon me and then I don't care about anything, then I just want everything to be over, in what way, I don't care, as long as it's over. You see what I mean, don't you? Only don't tell this to Barbara. No, do tell her!" Something wild broke into her voice. "Barbara, yes . . . That time in the washroom, the first, the only thing she asked me — " Aurelia stopped. "Does it stir, tell me, does it?" Barbara seemed to whisper, and the anger was back, the burning anger against the ease with which this question had been asked, against the way it had hurt her then, and still was hurting because, in spite of all the promises of the extra bread, the rest, the hope was still in her, the hateful, the ever-present hope that perhaps it was stirring no more.

"Tell me," she spoke in chokes, "tell me, am I a monster, an unnatural moth — person? I don't know, I'm losing my grip on myself. 'Tola is clever; Barbara's good,' I keep telling myself. 'If they believe that all will end well, why can't I?' And I try. But for you it's easy to believe this; if everything goes wrong, you'll wash your hands of it and leave. I cannot leave. Oh, no, I'm not a monster! Even if I don't care, I'm not. I never wanted this to happen; it was an accident, do you understand? Can one care for an accident? Should one? No . . ." She shrank away. "No, I didn't mean it quite that way. I . . . Please tell me, are you really optimistic?"

Tola said nothing. Hardly had Aurelia began to speak when a wariness stole upon her such as might be felt at the approach of a friend whose talk leads up to a request for money, for a sum much too large to be granted.

"Am I a monster?" Aurelia had cried; now she sat like an old, toothless woman with her mouth sucked in. And looking at her, Tola longed to grant this request, even if it might mean losing Barbara, yes, even if it meant that she would be left alone with Aurelia when her time came.

"I've been trying to believe that all will end well, but I can't." No, she couldn't bring herself to say it. "Go and talk to Barbara," she wanted to cry. "I don't want always to be the Cassandra. I've had enough."

"Yes, I believe everything will work out," she said, and even managed a smile.

Aurelia sat plucking at the saltpeter paper. When she looked up, Barbara was sitting next to her, Tola was standing at the door, her face small and tired within the gray kerchief. Why had she sought out Tola again? Why hadn't she spoken to Barbara? Was it because, in spite of everything, she liked Barbara better? Was it liking when you felt somebody to be so oppressive, so far above you?

"Aurelia, is anything wrong?" Barbara drew closer.

"No. And — you — I know what you're thinking." Her own daring took her aback. "You think that I'm indulging myself, that I'm self-pitying. Yes, I am self-pitying, and you — leave me!" And pushing Barbara away, Aurelia understood at last what she wanted: not to be comforted. Comfort was a burden; it made you feel obliged to the one who had offered it. To cry and not to be comforted was what she wanted. But this no one would give.

"Tola, why was Aurelia so upset yesterday?" Barbara asked next evening as they were walking toward the barracks.

"Perhaps you should talk to her, because I — " Tola broke off as Alinka suddenly stepped out of the dark. From her head, turbaned in a faded rag, rose the smell of beet-coffee with which, for lack of hot water, she had washed her hair.

"Excuse me, may I have a word with you?" she asked.

"Sure," Barbara muttered uneasily. "Only you'll catch your death standing with your wet head in this cold."

"Don't worry about me, Mrs. Grünbaum. After all, you have others to worry about. Anyway, since you two have taken over so completely, I'd better give you the money — a hundred and fifty zlotys. I didn't mention it to you the day when we moved in," she turned to Tola, "because we've kept this money for emergencies, for the doctor, I mean. Here, Mrs. Grünbaum, take it." Barbara, to whom money always seemed something unclean, drew back, and it was Tola who took it.

"Don't lose it," Alinka warned, and made as though to walk away. Suddenly she turned back. "You must be pleased with yourselves, very pleased." She tried to speak calmly, yet her voice was breaking. "Well, I'm not pleased; I wish we had never met, Mrs. Grünbaum. I should have seen through you, right there in Cracow. Aurelia used to take me to the place where you worked, to look at you, as if you were a work of art in a museum. 'Alinka,' she would say, 'this person has restored my faith in human beings.' You know Aurelia and her nonsense. And then I too thought that you — What idiocy. But you," the turbaned head pointed at Tola, "once I respected you, for being honest, for not pretending that you love us.

And now you're aping your — your generous friend. How can you?
We, Aurelia and I, never even mentioned what was to come, never!
Tola, you know why, you couldn't have forgotten what was done
to women like her in Cracow, even after — after birth. It's different
here — is that what you think? But it isn't. We don't know what
might happen to her. In a camp one never knows. And you — God,
I've had enough of you two." Alinka glowered, then was gone.

"Barbara," Tola said. "Barbara, she's right."

"Right? How? We'll hear from Antoni. I swear that we will. And
the moment his letter comes we'll find someone, some Pole, to take
the child to him. So. And as for you, don't you start anything."

Chapter 15

GOD, WON'T THEY EVER stop laughing? Oh, God, Alinka repeated to herself. The jokes of a German soldier, leading a group of women to scrub the military barracks on the outskirts of Skarzysko, across the woods, were being rewarded with this laughter. Alinka, a black spot on the general merriment, marched in silent disapproval. A scrub-woman for the Germans since the age of thirteen, she had had her fill of such laughter; it was shameless, she felt, obscene, the ever-present laws against "Rassenschande," the pollution of the race through contact with Jews, lending it the licentiousness of what might, what would have been, had this chaperon ever absented itself.

Finally she had had enough. "Have you no shame left?" she had flared up. Shrugs were her answer, then arguments: these simple soldiers were no Nazis, just decent boys; and showing her proof of this decency — a piece of candy or bread — "Sour grapes!" the women leered, "sour grapes, because no one would give a kind glance to a gloom-owl like you!"

Of such kindness Alinka certainly had no need; still, how could she prove it when, kindly or not, no one had ever glanced at her.

Wincing at the volleys of laughter, Alinka walked on. And a dream came back to her, the old dream about the proof. A soldier was one of the dream's protagonists, an officer of rank; she the other, yet somehow transformed, so that, although the crossbars of paint on her clothes warned him who she was, he could not help feeling drawn to her. He struck up a conversation, she answered curtly, just to prove that the silence, which was about to fall, was due not to her ignorance of German but to choice.

He praised her German. "Excellent!" he exclaimed. "Where has Fräulein learned such excellent German?"

"As a child I had a German governess." This too was a proof of how cultivated a Jewish girl could be.

And after that — the dream grew rather hazy at this point — after that he would offer her something, perhaps a special delicacy, perhaps a chance to rest, and to chat with him.

"No, thanks."

"Why not, Fräulein, why?"

"Because I am a Jewess," and she would look straight into his eyes. He would leave without a word; but later on he would tell his Kameraden of his meeting with a Jewish girl — how proud she was, how different from what he had imagined Jewesses to be. In silence the German soldiers would hear him out and the doubt she had sown within him, would be transplanted to all of them.

"Hey, you! Stop trampling on my feet," Magda the Pug shouted at her. The dream was gone. It seemed to have come only to measure the distance separating her from those days when the worry about Aurelia had not yet pushed such idle fancies away.

The barracks they soon reached took her aback. Warmth, the scent of milk, to Alinka, who had usually worked in private houses, these had meant a German place. Like a dog she used to snoop around, sneaking through the rooms with doors you could close to be alone, peeping into closets filled with warm woolen clothes. Longest she would linger over the photographs in some stubborn hope that those looking back at her could give her an explanation. Yet they, the girls in windblown summer dresses, the young men with straight open faces, explained nothing. Did they know what was being done in their name?

Convinced those smiles were merely shrewd disguises, she would look down at herself instead, always frozen, always in the same rags. "Even with Stalingrad, with all the bombings, the Germans are still pretty well off," she would decide with the supercilious smile of one finding his worst suspicions invariably confirmed.

This smile did not seem quite appropriate as she walked past the drab shacks huddling low against the ground, then on into one such shack, furnished with nothing but cots. On the windowsill where she climbed to wash the panes something rustled in the draft — candy wrappings piled in an ashtray. The smell of peppermints wafted from them, so tempting that at last she gave in, stuck the wrapping into her mouth, and sucked and sucked till the last trace of sweetness was gone.

Something crashed, the ashtray which she had pushed down. And just as she was kneeling to pick up the shards, steps came from outside. Hastily she swept the broken glass under the bed and jumped back on the sill. The steps grew louder. Clutching the rag, she remembered how once in Cracow a shrew of a German nurse had berated her for breaking a vase and how she had longed to snap back "Well, why don't you take its price off my wages," yet had been afraid and had hated herself for this fear.

Across from her the door began to open, the widening crevice turning green, then pink higher up. The door opened to its full width; and Alinka smiled, a relieved, even amused smile.

How strange it felt not to be afraid of a German. Yet who could fear him? — this overblown infant, the stiff collar cutting into his pink baby neck, the misty glasses making his round pink face still rounder.

"Hmm," turning even pinker with embarrassment, "hmm." What followed upon this *hmm* was clearly given him on loan: his jaunty gait borrowed from some debonair comrade, also the expansive "Guten Tag, kleines Fräulein," next the broken Polish of "Panienka, dzien dobry," and last the uneasy laugh of a civilized man half amused, half startled by his plunge into such a barbaric tongue. As though feeling ashamed of accepting this last loan, the soldier fell silent. His glance, humble yet somehow making her blush, was his very own, and so was the awkwardness with which he proffered her a crumpled cigarette.

"Danke, I don't smoke." Her curt refusal seemed familiar.

"Oh, ja," he exclaimed. "Ja — so Fräulein speaks German."

The sense of familiarity was clear. It was the dream, granted to her at last, but how differently — the officer transformed into this simpleton, this laughingstock, now tugging at his tobacco-specked lips.

"Where — ja — where has Fräulein learned such fine German?" he managed to bring out.

"I used to have a German governess." She could not but accept her role as faithfully as he was performing his.

"So educated," he marveled, "so highly educated and so — so winzig."

"Winzig," Alinka knew meant "tiny"; winzig was what his gaze had been calling her from the start. "Ah, Aurelia you should have seen what a conquest I made," she would have said in the old days, before those two had come between them. "Aurelia, he must have weighed a hundred kilos, yet was as shy as a mouse." And Aurelia would have laughed and laughed, and later on — her thoughts drifted away from the soldier — they would have gone for a walk or, how Aurelia used to love such talk, she would have told stories about the shoes lined up before the bunks, sending the boots up the mountains, the crooked pumps into museums and lecture halls. Now there would be no talk with Aurelia.

Yes, I made a conquest, perfect for a "gloom-owl," she thought. Yet within her something warm and pleasant insisted she was no scrawny owl, just "winzig." Arms pressed to her body to hide the holes under her sleeves, she went on washing the window. The water dripped; the soldier sighed, puffed moistly on his cigarette, sighed again. "How old is Fräulein?" he asked at last.

Alinka hesitated, having three ages to choose from: her true age of fifteen, the thirteen Aurelia would claim, hoping to squeeze out some "considerateness" toward them, and seventeen, the official age given the camp authorities.

"Seventeen," she said, not quite knowing why since he bore no hint of authority.

"Oh," he mumbled, "oh, ja. So young, and so educated. And I — I am from Stuttgart, a big city," he blurted out as if coming from a big city could compensate for his being neither educated nor too young. A pause, a laborious gulp. "I mean from Plochingen," he confessed, "from a village nearby."

Alinka felt uneasy. Was it because his outburst of honesty injected a needless personal note, or because, with the window-washing finished, a reversal of position would now take place, with herself no longer perched above him, but scrubbing the floor at his feet?

Somehow, this very reversal made her more winzig for him. She sensed it from his sighs blowing warmly down her neck, and from the way he would jump forward trying to lift the water pail for her. She stopped him each time, each time wondering if "because I am a Jewess" would be in place should he ask why.

"Where are you from, Fräulein, I mean — where is your home?" he asked instead.

"My home?" She felt a vague unrest. "I have no home."

"Then — why — then where do you live?"

"In the camp."

"In the — what?"

"In the concentration camp." Unsteadily she touched her sweater, felt her face turn white: the red crossbars, the sign that was to warn him who she was, had worn off. Was it possible he had not guessed the truth? No, this just could not be.

"Impossible," he echoed. "A con — con — a concentration camp is for criminals. And Fräulein could not have done anything wrong, of course not," he pleaded for her innocence. "Then, why, Fräulein, why?"

"Because I am a Jewess." How wrongly the moment had come.

"A Jewess." And he jumped back.

"Ja, because I'm Jewish."

Not for an instant had he suspected the truth, how could he — his stare now showing he must never have known a Jew in this Plochingen of his; but she, she had known Germans before, only too well, and yet she had flirted with him. Why else had she simpered and blushed, why else had she pretended to be seventeen? "Ah, those Jewesses," he, no longer despicable, having gained the right to despise her, would jeer. "I met one today, not knowing who she was, and you should have seen her making up to me!" How they would laugh, all of them! But she no longer cared, she only longed for him to leave. Hearing his steps, she drew aside to let him pass.

Instead he bent over her, which meant — she realized with relief and a faint touch of contempt — that he had not seen through her.

"I cannot believe it," he began, "just because Fräulein is a — a — Still," he bent down lower, "ja, still, ja." With every "ja" his voice sounded softer, more resigned. For he had to believe her, was forced to see what she, now doing her utmost to deny being winzig, displayed freely — the bare, frostbitten legs showing from under the tattered skirt, the tears in her sweater, the ribs sticking sharply from under it. A sunray came in the window and glided over her head. She winced. Her hair was all coated with lice eggs.

"We . . . we get no soap," Alinko stammered, "and we are sixty to a barracks hardly bigger than this." She blushed with shame, then with anger at herself — begging pity of a German! — and with a different shame again, sensing that such blushes made her winzig once more, as if she could not free herself from this role. It was safest to keep scrubbing. Suddenly she looked up.

"Der Führer," he was whispering ardently. "Fräulein — der Führer, I know it — I've seen him at a rally, he never meant someone like you — only the others."

"What others?"

"The capitalists, the big Jews."

"Really?" She raised her eyebrows.

"Really."

She got up and stood before him, her face, her tiny body weighed down by the water pail asking "Really, am I so big?" And a new kind of joy came over her, joy over the absolute right she had to hurt him, this Nazi, this Führer-lover!

"You, Fräulein, with you it must have been a mistake. Mistakes are made in a war, in a war we all suffer," he went on, frantically groping in his pockets, as if he were taking out his words like coins scrambled together to settle some urgent debt.

Their miseries were those coins and he was piling them before her, one by one: first the bombing, its victims counted out carefully; he listed the cities, next the number of casualties, and then a piano, lovely, almost new, lost by his cousin in an incendiary raid.

He stopped. "Enough?" his eyes asked. "Enough?"

"No, not enough!" her smile answered.

The German hunger he offered next, then glancing at her sticklike arms, turned to the dead instead, so many of them fallen, and far away from home.

Another pause, another thin smile. "I, I've been for three years in the Wehrmacht, hardly a day of furlough," he muttered, while she went on scrubbing. And again the ardent whisper rose over the scraping of the brush.

"Der Führer," he was whispering, "der Führer, Fräulein, can do no wrong. I know it, I've seen him. But even near him, there are people, who . . . who are not so good." Even this he offered, the painful admission that error could exist near him whom he had seen, and having seen, had loved.

No, this was not enough, not by far. Her eyes narrowed, she

watched him. Then, catching a longing glance he cast at the door, she got up and walked, almost danced, across the room.

"You really should not stay so long with someone like me." She pushed the door open, she waited, but he stood as if nailed to the floor. He stayed because she wanted him to stay, just as he would soon learn the whole truth because she wanted it.

"It's so cold, Fräulein, please close the door," he said softly, then smiled, as though struck by a pleasant thought. Her parents made him smile; he hoped they were well and healthy and together with her.

"Who? My parents?" She feigned not to have quite heard him.

"Ja," he nodded eagerly, "ja."

"I have no parents." Her mother had died long before the war, her father was in Russia; but she did not falter, feeling herself the spokesman for those left all alone. "None of us have parents anymore." She spoke looking aside, seeing instead of him, a German soldier shouting himself hoarse under the crimson swastika flags.

"No parents? Why, Fräulein?" Pushing this substitute away, his sorrowful voice made her wish he would not lay himself so bare. "Why, for God's sake, what happened to them?"

"You know," she hardened herself, "you must know!"

"I . . . I?" His vague half-smile disclaimed all knowledge, admitted that such ignorance might be culpable, begged forgiveness. "I . . . really, I know nothing."

"They were killed."

"Killed? By whom?"

"By the SS." To say by you, by the Germans, she could not. His face checked her, crumpled with helplessness and beet-red.

Then his mouth hardened, his eyes glared. And once again her face turned white. "Greuelpropaganda, this is Greuelpropaganda," he was muttering. "I met a Jewess spreading Greuelpropaganda," he would denounce her; "Greuelpropaganda," the guards seemed to shout, "the prisoner who spreads Greuelpropaganda must report himself!"

God, why had she come here, what had she done?

"Fräulein has been poisoned by Greuelpropaganda." His shout

made her shrink into a black bundle. "Don't ever dare to repeat such stories; they are not true, they cannot be!" Taking pity on her, he spoke more softly. "Ja, Fräulein is refined and educated, but just a girl, just a child. Fräulein cannot know what evil people there are in the world. How can you? The British, they're evil, they're guilty of everything, they must have spread such rumors. They, the perfidious Al — Al — "

Albion — in her boundless relief she almost helped him out.

"Because such things just cannot be! And now Fräulein," he spoke in a fatherly bass, "now you must tell me everything."

"Everything about what?"

"About — about the parents. Yes, I believe that they are not with you. But they must be somewhere, working or — the authorities must have told you something about them. They — they always do."

She was silent.

"Fräulein!" he admonished her.

"When the whole thing started," she rambled, hardly knowing what she was saying, "there were posters announcing they would go to work in the Ukraine. But — "

He allowed no but's. "Ukraine, of course Ukraine," he exclaimed, then went on so rapidly she could barely follow. Ja, he himself had been in the Ukraine, and there one day his train had passed through a town called — called, the name he no longer remembered, yet there he had seen — He gulped, showing, what she had known anyhow, that as before with Stuttgart he had been tampering with distances: he had never even glimpsed the unnamed town; anything he claimed to have seen there was no more than a rumor.

"I saw a camp there," he assured her, "and with people in it, looking like . . . like Jews but otherwise — in general — quite well. They were the parents, of course. Ja, Fräulein, ja, they are well, working in the Ukraine." And having convinced himself, he was silent.

She did not protest. For now it was granted her to trace pity to its very source, and to see how much timid compassion, how much cowardice and frantic self-defense went into comfort, into the giving and the receiving alike. Once they all had believed such rumors.

Suddenly they would sprout in a ghetto, a presence, a transient guest, bringing hope into the crowded rooms, bringing strangers together in the street. "A soldier came with greetings from them," this rumor said; "an officer, an important man." And the rank grew higher, the greetings more tangible. There was a letter that a neighbor's friend had read, then the neighbor himself. But no one ever managed to see this letter, and soon the rumors stopped, silenced by events such as those in Radom.

Radom — should she tell him about it? No, she would not, ever. Even if she could force herself into believing that the last day there had not just been a nightmare; even if she could tell him every detail, he would not believe her; and for the effort this disbelief would cost him, he would come to hate her.

Was she simply afraid again? Yes, she was afraid; if she talked about Radom to him, he might denounce her — he would.

A narrow strip of the floor remained still to be washed and, kneeling down, she began to scrub, while from behind her his stamping came. It stopped, and something rustled. She looked up. He was coming slowly toward her, his hands filled with peppermint candy. "Please, Fräulein, take — do you like peppermints, Fräulein?" He corrected himself in the belated make-believe that she was a fastidious young lady, accepting gifts out of fancy, never out of need.

She nodded. Stooping down he poured the candy into her hands, then picked up the few that fell to the floor; she, feeling he deserved this concession, put one into her mouth. "They're good," she said, rising from her knees.

They stood facing each other, their shadows elongated and dark upon the floor gleaming in the afternoon sun. She watched his shadow draw closer. "The war, Fräulein, makes everything so hard." He sighed, the cold air giving his compassion the shape of a white cloud. "But perhaps, perhaps this war won't last much longer." Another sigh, another white cloud, this one fainter and swifter to disappear. He turned away, then, pivoting on his foot, turned back. "Fräulein," he said softly, "you must remember, der Führer never meant children. Never."

And at last he was going, walking backward, as if still at a loss how to leave her.

"Hey, Freckles, what you got in this bag?" the Pug nudged Alinka as they were marching back through the weeds.

"Nothing much," she shrugged. Yet how to resist such a temptation? She stopped; slowly she opened the bag.

"Oh, look at that," the Pug marveled, "where did you get all that candy from?"

"From a soldier; he was a decent fellow — and — " The traditional, almost obligatory "he wasn't a Nazi" would not pass Alinka's throat; but then, he was decent, wasn't he? Could one be both decent and a Nazi? Angered by her confusion, she pulled the bag away.

"Sell them to me," the Pug urged her with each step. "For two chunks of bread, for a quarter. For half a loaf, you sell them to me."

"Half a loaf of white bread." A pause. "Hancia, white bread, half a loaf." The word was sent to a vendor in front.

And just as, regretfully, as though parting with a souvenir, Alinka was handing the Pug the peppermints, a motorcycle forced them off the road. In the red sunrays woven through the pines, Alinka caught a glimpse of glasses shining beneath the steel helmet. Her soldier had a motorcycle. By motorcycle the town should be at most fifteen minutes away. "Der Führer had not meant children!" he had said. And if she turned to him for help? If he agreed? Then all could still be well; then Aurelia would know who really cared about her. No! It had been decided long ago that not a hair of Aurelia's head must be risked. And then, she herself was afraid of such a risk; she had no desire to play the heroine like Barbara.

Alinka came into the barracks only to leave at once. For just as she was putting the bread on the bunk Goldberg shoved her aside and handed Barbara a closely written sheet of paper, a letter from that Pole of hers, Antoni or whatever his name was.

Chapter 16

BARBARA WAS NOT YET reading the letter. Wedged between Goldberg and Tola she sat on the bunk, motionless at first, until slowly, carefully, she smoothed down the crumpled sheet. The clumsy scrawls told her everything: how, gnawing on the gray mustache, Antoni had paced up and down; how he fumbled with his spectacles, wiping them, putting them on askew, only to take them off again; and how at last he had started writing, his sinewy old man's hand shaking harder with each word; and behind him Marta, with sighs awaiting her turn, then sitting down shyly, as though she were in church. The barracks glare blurred in Barbara's eyes. "Yes," she turned away when Goldberg nudged her, "yes, I'll start reading at once."

They would do everything for the little innocent, the letter said. They would beg help everywhere, and then would come to Skarzysko within a fortnight, well in time. Next came words crossed out — a sign that the old man was fighting hard, until, unable to restrain himself, "Madam," he wrote, "Madam, what misery your willfulness has brought on you and all who hold you dear." After that the words shrank as though in shame, for now they spoke of money: grown scarce, not wasted — God forbid — only robbed by those godless —— Again thick lines crossing out his anger, then his quavering signature; then Marta's postscript, "May God keep you in His care."

"Thank God," Barbara sighed. Bypassing Tola, she handed the letter to Aurelia and watched her lips part in a deep relieved sigh. Only Goldberg marred this joy, with his deceptively childlike smile. "Of course. Tola, give him something." Barbara remembered why he was still hanging around. But though a fifty-zloty note passed from the little bag on Tola's neck into his mud-crusted boot, Goldberg showed no desire to leave. "Well, Dziedziczka," he moved closer, "well, mazel-tov to you."

This much Yiddish Barbara understood: you said "mazel-tov" when someone got married or when . . . when a child was born.

"You brute," she could hardly speak for anger, "you good-for-nothing! Did you read it? Did you?"

"Sure, Dziedziczka. I read every single word. I studied it." Abruptly his smile vanished. "Is it you?" he muttered, and so fast that she could not draw away, his hairy paw pounced at her body. "No. I can tell it isn't you. And it can't be this skinny rail, nor this ancient scarecrow. So who is it? Why are you doing this? Do you want to bring disaster on yourself and that poor whore?"

"Go! At once!" She tried to push him off the bunk, but he, clutching at its edge, settled down more firmly. Again he was smiling. "Oh, my darling, I've greetings for you . . . such nice, hearty greetings . . ."

She said nothing. Shoving Tola aside she moved closer to Aurelia to protect her from those jeers, those red hairy paws. Suddenly, next to them another hand appeared — yellow, its fingers grubby and thick and sneaking along cautiously like the hand of a boy hoping to catch a fly. This hand was hoping to catch a chunk of bread; it drew closer, then closer yet. Her eyes narrowed, Barbara waited. The fingers closed round the bread, she took aim; she struck — then winced, for the flesh under her fist felt mushy, like an overripe fruit. Wiping her fist, she looked down. There stood a picriniac, a big hulk of a man, his head shaved to the skin, his face round and sleepy, like an Oriental's.

"You," she choked, "you're still fat. You thief!"

"Oh, no, madam." The man spoke with mild instructiveness. "I'm not fat. I'm just swollen — from hunger." He nodded, then walked away, backward as though afraid she might sneak upon him to strike again.

"Oi, oi," Goldberg chuckled. "You've a lot to learn, Dziedziczka. And you will, you will. But I mustn't forget — the greetings."

"What are you gabbing about?"

"About the greetings from Rost, from Herr Doktor Rost. Don't you know who he is? He runs the whole show, by remote control from Werk A. What a man! Not half as handsome as me — just a scrawny, bespectacled fellow — but," he raised his forefingers, "how tenderhearted he is! They say he cries bitter tears when he's got to have someone shot. A bullet costs two Reichsmarks, a lot of money, considering that a few weeks at Picrine can do the trick for nothing, even with profit."

No longer trying to defend herself she just stared at him. He sat quietly; yet it semed to her as if once again he had pounced upon her and was tearing her hope to shreds, was kneading it, just as on her other side Aurelia was kneading shreds of the saltpeter paper into tiny, hard balls.

"Stop it!" Barbara cried. Aurelia jerked and was still.

"Sometimes," Goldberg went on, "even Rost can be most generous. Like last year when that boy from Trotyl took off. A hundred marks Rost spent then, and two liters of vodka — the reward for the Pole who brought that poor devil back. Fine lads our Poles; each night they comb the woods — two liters of vodka is nothing to spit at. Still, I don't like it. 'Franek,' the other day I told one of them, 'where is your proletarian conscience, Franek? Do something, go on strike; three liters of vodka or no Jews delivered. Now, thanks to you . . ."

Once again trying to push him off, she gripped him by his collar. He freed himself. "Thanks to you," he whispered, "they will get lots of vodka — for you, for the bastard, and for that poor little whore. Well, so long everybody." And he jumped down with the agility of a squirrel.

"Aurelia," Barbara moaned softly, "oh, my God, Aurelia." In answer Aurelia flashed her mechanical smile, as though to say "How considerate you are, thank you!"

"Aurelia — wait for me — wait!" Barbara cried from the doorway, then ran on.

In the place where a square, pale shape gleamed in the dark — the stove on which one cooked in the warm weather — she stopped. This was her favorite spot in the camp. Behind the wires tall pines stood, their overhanging branches smuggling in the contraband scent of pine needles and of cones. She stepped closer to the wires. Rising to her toes she pulled a branch down, then passed the damp tassel over her mouth.

"Hey, get away from the wires."

The branch snapped back. Her mouth, absently sucking her scratched hand, tasted of resin and of blood.

And at this moment a sense of revelation came over her: she knew what to do as clearly as if someone had spoken to her. She would carry the child out, she herself, and no one would harm her, neither the Krauts, nor those with whom that brute had tried to frighten her. In confirmation faces seemed to flash out of the dark — Tola, Aurelia, and Alinka — till they formed a single face, bloodless under the black kinky hair, the eyes too black, the nose bent into a hook. Such as they had to be afraid; she was different. In her no one would discover a Jewess.

"Barbara, are you there?"

"What is it, Tola?" She was angry at being disturbed.

"It's almost Lagerschluss."

"You and your worries. Tell me, how is Aurelia?"

In answer Tola's fingers made the familiar snapping sound.

"We must go back to her. No — wait! I'll show you." The idea struck suddenly. "If I just tell you, you will start caviling. So, stand still." Barbara gripped Tola's shoulder. "Now, you're a denouncer," she muttered, holding Tola at arm's length.

Tola jerked away. Yet Barbara noticed nothing. "A denouncer!" she exclaimed. "The kind Goldberg spoke of; now talk like them, pretend you're after a Jew."

No answer. "You see!" Barbara triumphed. "You don't know how they talk, what they're like. While I . . . wait, you'll see."

A frenzy of make-believe seized her. "Yoo-hoo!" she uttered a clear hunter's call, "yoo-hoo! Here it comes, boys, a stag. After him, after the Jew!"

A pause. "That's how they talk," she gasped. "Wait." Noiselessly she moved aside. "Hush," she whispered. And now it was no longer make-believe; now she felt herself become what she should have been — a peasant woman, a mother of one flesh with her child.

"Jesus Maria," she lamented, "you take me for a Jewess, me? Ah, you — you're worse than a Jew, frightening a poor woman out of her wits. A beast would've taken pity on me, but not you; you have no God in your hearts!

"Where am I going? It's nothing to you. What am I carrying? Something I wouldn't even let you touch. Hush, stop that noise or you'll wake him up. I'm taking my baby to Skarzysko, to the priest.

Look, he turned all blue this morning. I ran to the parsonage. 'The Reverend Father is gone to Skarzysko,' his housekeeper says — and so I'm running there to have the child baptized. And you, had you anything but vodka on your minds, you would take me there. For I'm all distraught with fright."

The end had come too soon. Not yet ready to return to herself, Barbara was rocking her folded arms. "Do you see what I mean?" she whispered at last. "Do you?"

"Wait, please Barbara, wait," Tola said, then stood looking into the distance. Frayed to a blurred thread by the mist, a searchlight moved in the dark, swerved and pointed to a slow-moving line of picriniacs going off to load shells. Behind them, a dim figure ran, staggered, slipped and fell into the frozen slush. A shout; the figure reappeared, tottering along behind the others. Soon she would be like the one who had fallen — always apart from others, always alone. Because once gone, Barbara must never return.

"Tola, why don't you say something?"

"Don't leave me, I'll go under without you" — if only she could force herself to say this, if only she could speak to Barbara about herself, and about the child too. "I know what you feel for him," she would say, "yet, whatever happened to him, he wouldn't know it; and I will know what's going on with me all the time, until the end!" But Barbara had a chance to be free, to be safe and free.

"Well, have you got no tongue?"

It was decided. "Barbara, your performance was perfect," Tola began. "You almost fooled me."

"Really, Tolenka?"

"Yes, of course. And do you know, I too have been considering that possibility; still, it seemed wiser to wait. Now everything is clear. And I . . . and we will manage."

"What do you mean?"

"We. Aurelia, Alinka, and me. We'll manage without you."

"No, I don't understand."

"Barbara, don't tell me you were thinking of coming back here?" In need not so much of support as of something tangible close to her, Tola leaned against the stove; fumbling over the icy iron plate, she touched something brittle and smooth — a piece of charred wood. She clutched it. "Of course, you won't come back." She watched the ashes sift through her fingers. "A concentration camp isn't a hotel where you return after a little trip. Once you leave, you leave for good."

"But I haven't been thinking such thoughts, really. And something terrible might happen here if I escaped. People might be shot in . . . in . . ." Barbara groped.

"In retaliation," Tola helped her out. "This isn't the Cracow camp. Here something could be done to cover up your escape . . . and we, and I . . . I will manage." She grew still. When this silence, offered like space to Barbara, remained empty, Tola felt as though the cold outside had moved into her and solidified until it seemed to have become a creature — a thin-lipped scribe who had come to help her settle all accounts.

He now dictated her words, each naming what Barbara was feeling. "Do you remember," Tola whispered, "once you said to me — yes, I remember exactly — 'I'm afraid of having come here for nothing, only of this.' But it will not be for nothing. You will have the child, the child you saved. He will need you, you'll take care of him. And I think . . . I'm quite sure that the hunt for Jews is over. It must be, with the few Jews left locked up safely in camps, and those who could have been caught on their Aryan papers caught long ago. Antoni won't keep you under lock and key any longer. Why should he, now? You will take walks, Barbara; just think, Barbara, you will simply go anywhere you please. And in the spring you will take the child to the park, as if nothing had happened, as if there were no war."

Tola waited. Far off a train rumbled, pulling out with its load of shells.

"Do you hear?" she said softly. The shrill whistle seemed to cut right through her.

For a long time Barbara said nothing. "No!" All of a sudden she flared up. "No, let me be. You started this talk. I've never thought of running away from here, not really. I've no right to leave that poor woman, Aurelia, I mean . . . or you . . . and . . ."

"Me?"

"Yes, you. Enough of all that talk. Let's go back to Aurelia. I can't bear the thought of her, sitting there with not a scrap of hope. Wait — we must tell her something. Not that I'll do it, because she might not believe it, because that pipsqueak might start poisoning her mind against me — she always does. 'Someone has been found,' you tell her this, I'm no good at lying. No, you'll ruin everything with that lukewarm way of yours. I'll tell her tomorrow, after I've figured everything out."

"As you wish," Tola said. And they went back.

Obligingly the swollen picriniac opened the barracks door for them, and kept it ajar while staring from under his heavy lids at Barbara.

Tola too was staring at her. Why had she noticed nothing until now? She had never looked at Barbara's face, only at her clothes, which since they weren't hanging too loosely showed that Barbara was not yet wasting away. But her face was wasted, thin, the nose protruding sharply, the eyes dark — sunken and very dark.

"Tola, why are you staring at me so? Come, let's go in!"

"Please listen to me." She touched Barbara's shoulder. "We'll do everything, we . . . I'll stand by Aurelia, no matter what. Only forget what you told me before, you must; now I'm telling the truth."

"What are you talking about?"

"You . . . you can't escape, you cannot."

"Why? What has changed?"

"Nothing. Only I was wrong before. You will be caught."

"How?"

"Because . . . you'll be recognized."

"I won't be. Why?"

"Because . . . because you look Jewish."

That Barbara would flinch she had expected, but not so violently, not with such a frenzied shout.

"No, I don't!" she was shouting. "It's only these rags, the accursed louse-ridden rags."

All evening Barbara kept silent. And long after lights went out, Tola saw her pass her forefinger down her nose, her cheeks — like a Picrine woman, trying to assure herself that what lay under the yellow film was still her own face.

"Tola, I talked to Aurelia," Barbara announced the next evening. "At first I was worried she might ask too much — how we could have found that Pole, who he was. Then I swore to her, on my life, on everything I hold dear, that it was true. And she believed me. Oh, if only you could have seen her at that moment." Barbara stopped. "I know you want what's best for me," when Tola said nothing, she went on. "Still, what you told me yesterday, about my looks, I mean, is just not true. I know this. I do."

"Look, Barbara, we still have a month. Let's stop planning so much and —"

Goldberg came to her aid. "Death to the lice!" he shouted, bursting into the barracks. This was his way of announcing that on Sunday the Schmitz women would go to the Entlausung in Werk A.

Chapter 17

How BARBARA RELISHED that Sunday morning. Even to walk through the woods, free from the pang Picrine brought, or from the remorse at having forgotten this pang, would have been enough. And more had been granted her: the warm sunny weather; the thought of Aurelia, who, exempted by the doctor from the Ent-lausung, was resting quietly; and of Antoni's letter. Constantly re-read, this letter seemed to promise more and more hope.

"When he writes he will come here in a fortnight he will, on the dot," Barbara said to Tola, who for all the new warmth looked as frozen as ever.

"Perhaps we'll see Rubinfeldova," Tola answered. "If we make it by the noon break the Werk A people might be expecting us."

They were expected. Under the billows of black smoke uncoiling from the huge chimney, a crowd milled, calling, waving from be-hind the barbed wires. As in a home tables for refreshments are set out at the guests' arrival, so here stones, here bricks and planks were being piled, and the Werk A people climbed upon them so that the food they had brought could be reached over the wires. It was soup, the thick never-forgotten Werk A soup.

Tatters flapped, sooty arms dangled down the barbed wires, while on the other side, the women reached up, groped, reached up still higher trying to get hold of the cans from which the soup splashed down.

"I don't like it here, Tola, let's move," Barbara insisted. Tola would not give in. "There! Barbara, do you see her?" she called; and there was Rubinfeldova, her face black as a chimney sweep's.

"You look well, Rubinfeldova," Tola said hastily.

"And you too." Rubinfeldova brought her lips closer to the wires. "Yes, both of you." And Tola again, asking about Seidmanka, who was well, Rubinfeldova said, just resting after the nightshift.

Perched on a pile of bricks, Rubinfeldova tried to hand them a can of soup, but her arms were too short to reach over the wires. A scrawny man who had been watching helped her out. "Thank you kindly." Rubinfeldova smiled, then, clearly mindful of being in a way the hostess, she asked if the people in Werk C were of good hope, if they believed —

A siren whistled, drowning her voice. The crowd dispersed. "Goodbye Tola, goodbye Miss Zborovska!" came already from afar. Zborovska. How strange that name seemed to Barbara, as though years had passed since it had been hers; sadness came over her, grew heavier as they marched on, past more chimneys, more wires, then past grimy sheds shaking with pounding noise. Once a door opened: with the precision of ballet dancers, a row of figures was moving through the dusk; they stretched out their arms; they caught a giant prong. A deafening din. Again they moved forward, again they stretched out their arms.

"God," Barbara whispered, "what a hellish place."

"Hellish?" an O.D. man piped up. "Not at all; I know it; I used to work there before the war."

Had such places existed even before the war? She sighed. And the war seemed to change into an octopus extending its tentacles farther and farther back.

The stench of heated urine and of sweat burst out from the Entlausung barracks, stifling as if piles of poorly washed clothing were being dried against a stovepipe. The stench grew stronger as the door opened. "In, ladies," a prissy voice called. "Only fifty at a time — in, ladies."

Group after group went in, while those still awaiting their turn stamped in the granular gray slush.

"Next group, please." Two Polish women were ordering them around; hateful creatures, Barbara decided — their bleached hair hateful, their smiles, and above all the way they simpered "Ladies, ladies," as if to mock the women swarming through this narrow muddy place.

"Undress, ladies!" Bending over a low counter the Poles clapped their hands.

"Undress, shoes must be left in here."

"Left here?" There was an outcry, because by now no shoes were safe from thieves, not even the wooden sabots which were often stolen to be chopped for kindling wood.

"The devil take them. I'm keeping my shoes on," Barbara muttered, fumbling with a button. It snapped off; instead of looking for it, she stood still. Mostly old women were around her, and now as they undressed it seemed to her that they were taking off layers of skin, so exact a record those rags bore of what had been plaguing their bodies; of a scabby itch, of lice, and of hasagowka that made the latrine too far to reach.

What emerged from under these rags were not bodies but dough: gray, flaccid dough. She tried to ward it off. She stiffened, she shrank back, yet the dough clung on; smacking, rubbing against her, it carried her on to the counter where the Poles sat.

"Your shoes!" one of them — she wore her hair in bangs — ordered. Barbara could not answer; her very bigness had turned against her; it made her the most exposed, the most naked of all.

"Your shoes, I said."

"So you did," she bellowed, "you — flunkies! I wouldn't even have kept you as charwomen in my manor." The Pole who wore bangs raised her eyebrows; the other one smirked. "Look!" they giggled, "look at the lady of the manor!"

"Barbara, give them the shoes." This was Tola, staring right into her face, to remind her — of what Barbara knew exactly — of that evening when she, acting a peasant woman, had said "You don't know how to talk to them. I do."

"Barbara!"

"Go away. I — I hate you!" Furiously she kicked her shoes off, and already the doughlike mass pushed her on into the shower room.

Inside, streaks of brown water dripped through holes in the ceiling. The mass swayed, broke up; and now it was not dough anymore; now sagging breasts, bellies like crumpled sacks shook everywhere; turning purple in the steam the sticky bodies gyrated; they pushed, they squirmed, trying to catch some water, or at least the used-up drops oozing down others' backs, dotted by black wisps of dirt and large reddish scabs.

"I'm getting sick, I must get out." Barbara raised both hands to her mouth. Her fingers moved up to her cheeks, then on to her nose. "Jewish . . . you look Jewish," Tola had said, and her nausea turned to fear that those writhing around her had done something to her face, and would do it to her body unless she got out at once. Stumbling on the tangled feet, she ran toward the corner, toward the window blue with the sky, and there she clasped her arms to protect her body, and the memories of all that had touched it, air, sun, and the hands of men praising the pleasure it could give.

A stare forced her to turn. It was Goldberg; his eyes darted straight to her belly; then reassured, they moved on, to her neck, her still large breasts. She submitted; she was craving this comfort, this proof.

"Hurry, girls, hurry my little Eves," Goldberg called.

Barbara started. "Out with you!" she yelled, for Alinka's, not her own sake. Something about the girl's pale little body touched her to the quick — the innocence, the stubborn faith with which it was going about its work of ripening, the hips barely widening, the breasts barely beginning to swell. He must not look at Alinka, he must not! "Off with you!" she yelled again.

No towels were given out. Puddles forming round their feet, the women scurried naked through the barracks. Someone was feeling faint in the stench; "My shoes have been stolen," someone was crying. At last the Poles brought back the deloused clothes; they were scorched, and the lice, merely quickened by the heat, were creeping all over the seams.

Barbara marched back to the camp with the Kaelanki, not with Tola. The pines swayed, rivulets gurgled past the bright patches of moss, and soon Barbara felt so much better that she could smile at the Kaelanki's rowdy talk. It was the soldier who turned her smile to laughter. Herding a group going to load shells, he waddled by, his glasses glistening, his face redder than a cock's crest. Suddenly her laughter stopped. Screaming, the soldier swung a branch over a picriniac, and there, across from him, Alinka stood petrified, her face white.

What happened? What frightened her? Barbara wondered. But at once the Kaelanki linked arms with her, a song burst forth, and thinking of Antoni and the day they would meet again she, singing at the top of her voice, was filled with a dizzy lightness as if a love affair were about to begin, or a trip to some new, distant place.

Chapter 18

LURED OUT BY THE SUN, the guards were standing at the gate, six wizened men with guns dangling down their shoulders.

"A search?" The Cracow women were hastily forming fours. "A search, is it?"

"Fools! What would they search us for — for lice?" Magda the Pug gibed. "They're just warming their old bones."

The Pug was right. "I know this place inside out; we'll just be taken to load shells, or, more likely, we'll be counted," she explained as they were marching into the Appellplatz. Here the whole camp had gathered. On one side the Trotyl people stood, to their right the picriniacs, while the space opposite Trotyl had been reserved for the Schmitz column. This delighted the Kaelanki, eager to greet their "cousins," many of whom were standing there. Shoemakers, they were called, though they worked at Trotyl — why, Barbara could not remember.

"My cousin," the Pug pointed at a husky fellow, his mouth moistred in the swarthy face. She waved, and a dialogue began, wordless yet clear to Barbara. The Pug touching her cheek meant "You should have shaved, dear"; the cousin's shrug, "Who cares?"; and the Pug pointing at herself, then around, this was "Certainly not me, but what about the others?"

"A fine fellow," Barbara declared, and "Oh," the Pug sighed, to show there were no words to say how fine he was.

The sun shone, icicles dove from the roofs into the blue puddles, and everyone, even the picriniacs, seemed cleansed by the soft light. Then came wind, bringing the scent of thawing earth, a reminder that March was near. Barbara sniffed the warm air. "Pug," she nudged the girl, "spring is just around the corner."

The Pug did not answer. "Shut up!" she yelled instead at old

Alexandrovitch, who seemed to be playing blindman's buff, crossing and uncrossing her arms to catch the O.D. men who kept dashing by. "A — a selection?" she wailed. "Tell me, a selection?"

"Keep quiet!" Barbara cried.

"Mrs. Grünbaum," old Alexandrovitch began slowly, "you've become so impolite. Today in the Entlausung, you pushed me, Mrs.
Grünbaum."

Of the Entlausung Barbara refused to think. "Who will count
us?" "Oh, someone from Werk A," she repeated after the Pug, then
asked the names of the various cousins, and their girls. Her own
questions, the Pug's amusement at her knowing no Yiddish, above
all the carefree mood as of one who, suitcases packed, ticket in
pocket, would soon be on the go — all this made her feel like a spectator invited to watch a strange performance.

In this performance the O.D. men were playing the servants
aghast at their master's unexpected return. They counted and re-
counted the people, picked up sheets of saltpeter paper from the
ground, while others rushed through the barracks, yelling, "Out!
All out!"

All had to be out, all had to be counted. Slamming the door a
woman dashed out from the kitchen; next the washroom keeper
came; next a group of picriniacs brought back from loading shells.
The picriniacs, Barbara sensed, were afraid. None of them stirred;
only in the first row, the one not fat but swollen with hunger —
"the Chinaman," she had learned, was his nickname — kept tightening the rope round his waist, so that the can tied to it would stop
jingling. And the Cracow women too were acting oddly, primping,
even rouging themselves.

"Pug," Barbara whispered, "are you sure we're just going to be
counted?"

"Quite sure."

Again a door banged. Two more women were running toward
the Appellplatz — Alinka, Barbara realized, and Aurelia, to whom
she had given not a single thought. "Here, come here!" she called to
make up for this omission, but it was to Tola, beckoning from the
column's end, that they ran, as they had to, Barbara assured herself,
since in her own four no place was left. Yet Barbara felt angry.

From this anger, for which on one could be blamed, from the Pug's tensing face, anxiety sneaked upon her and grew as silence fell, as all looked toward the gate.

"Pug," once again Barbara whispered.

"Quiet!" the Pug snapped, and Barbara's anxiety turned to fear. God, let it be over. God, let nothing happen to Aurelia, she prayed to the One who for her was a guarantee that the ultimate helplessness could not exist, God, I beg you. Behind the gate, drab birds rose up from a pile of dried leaves. They vanished; far off a motor whirred.

A small car came into the road. It stopped, the window rolled down, and a gloved hand waved out of it. Stiffly, as though trying to run at attention, two O.D. men dashed to the car, then back. Meister Grube got out of the car, and behind him a stranger — a spare little man in brown uniform with a red swastika armband. What made Barbara flinch were the spats he wore and his sharply creased trousers, which gave him the look of those meticulously efficient clerks whose very approach had made her freeze. Or perhaps she had seen this man before? Somehow he seemed familiar.

The six wizened guards drew themselves up. The O.D. men clicked their heels, and halting to look around the little man entered the Appellplatz. When he stopped, so did Meister Grube; when he walked on, Grube checked his feet, lest they should overtake the stranger who was clearly higher in rank. Now they were approaching Picrine; now they stopped, their shadows trailing on the ground. It was those shadows Barbara watched, as if they and not this insignificant little man, made the picriniacs petrify into a yellow wall, their paper wrappings like posters flapping in the wind. A furtive cough. "Don't — don't cough," Barbara signaled to them in her thoughts, but already more coughs, and more, until all shook, gargling with phlegm they feared to spit out. A desire seized her to become his fear, to pounce upon his back, and dig her fingers into his neck, right between the stiff white collar and the hair. But all she dared was to repeat, God let nothing go wrong.

Now the Trotyl men stood bolt upright; now the Trotyl women held their breath; now those from Schmitz. The man turned; poised exactly in the center of the Appellplatz he began to speak, softly as though to spare his voice. What he was saying, Barbara, who understood almost no German, did not know; and as once in the movies, when the subtitles had flitted by too fast she would watch Stefan's face to learn if it was time for hope or fear, so now she watched Goldberg standing among the O.D. men. He shook his head to show she had nothing to fear; but she, wanting more from him, kept drawing a curve over her body until by shaking his head again he told her Aurelia too was safe. And now he was glancing at his feet, at his sturdy boots. "Schuhe," the man was saying. "Schuhe" meant shoes. Had he come because shoes had been stolen in the Entlausung? What was it to him? Why should he meddle in business that was not his?

"Schuhe" once again. Glancing at his watch, the man bent his wrist, and the pale flesh glimmered, too naked, almost indecent for him who seemed to be made only of those meticulous clothes. He raised his gloved hand, motioned, just with two fingers. In answer there was a splash — loud, as if hundreds of divers had plunged into water. To her it seemed that only the O.D. men were left here, only the two figures in brown and herself, grown too big, exposed again. The others had fallen to their knees, all of them at once.

A puddle splashed under her knees. Ducking, she crept on to the firmer mud near the Pug, then turned toward the column's end. Tola and Alinka were helping Aurelia down. But it was not Aurelia who was meant. This was not a selection, the calm look of old Alexandrovitch reassured her, and the Chinaman, his eyes impassive, his can allowed to jingle a bit.

Then with something like resentment, as if a promise given her had been broken, she understood where the fear had moved to: right here, to the Kaelanki, rigid, the Pug panting as she stared at her cousin. He knelt slouched; his mouth was red no more, and trembled.

Barbara was afraid, not for herself but for the Pug, who, tongue lolling out, clutched at her wrist so hard Barbara almost shrieked with pain. "Help me, do something," the Pug's hand begged, gripping Barbara's. And she tried, holding it fast, stroking it when the Pug blinked as if she wanted to, yet could not cry.

"Where are you . . . do something," the Pug's fingers said as they clawed her flesh, then loosened; they seemed to be listening. Rattling loudly, the soup cart was being pulled into the Appellplatz.

Behind the cart the six guards were marching as if to watch over it, though only a rusted hoop lay inside. They halted, unhitched their rifles.

Something enormous was about to happen, something far beyond her grasp. Yet along with her dread grew her sense of distance, as if this were only a film and she were free to escape its terrors by closing her eyes, by remembering how at the start the actors' faces had been flashed on the screen, not torn by pain but smiling; and the last one to appear — a proof justice existed — the one who in the world of make-believe wielded such powers, was in reality a minor actor fitted only for the stock villain's role.

Suddenly the Pug's hand turned limp, and all her strength seemed to go into a single motion, into the quiver of eyeballs under the tightened eyelids. "I cannot look, you watch!" this quiver ordered, and Barbara did watch him, the dapper little man, as he passed through the Trotyl ranks. He stepped out, and What's his name? she wondered, as if to know that he, like anyone else, had a name could help. But she could not remember.

The arm with the swastika band pointed at a man in the first row; the black slush scattered as the man staggered up. "He . . . my cousin?" the Pug's trembling fingers were asking. And soon, when it was the cousin, Barbara wanted to lie yet could not, because of the way he struggled up, clutching at the mud until at last he stood, and tottered with a thin, childlike gasp.

She, too, could not look anymore, she only listened to the splashing of the mud, each splash indicating that another man was getting up. Then silence that went on and on. A cough; the Pug's hand tore out of her grip and then returned to stroke her gently.

The worst had not happened, the Pug's face told her at once, transfigured, tears streaming down her muddy cheeks. And there in the center of the Appellplatz five Trotyl men stood, intact; only the Pug's cousin looked shrunken with his legs bent into bows. "Picrine," the man from Werk A said and Barbara gasped in boundless relief, because the men would just go to Picrine, in punishment for whatever they had done to shoes.

Now an O.D. man was counting the picriniacs; now he was reporting their number. In exchange for the new men five picriniacs would go to Trotyl; of this Barbara felt certain, for the man stopped right in front of the Chinaman, believing as she once had that he was fat, was strong, and worthy of good work.

"Don't cough, don't," she was signaling again. The Chinaman was doing well: he jumped up nimbly, he pressed the can to his hip. Blown upward by the wind, a sheet of paper rose above his shoulders, as if to hide the one behind him — a young boy with a shadow of yellow mustache above his mouth. The boy was struggling up; the boy was forced down by those around, arms pushed down, his mouth gagged by a fist.

From under the paper sheet, the Chinaman's hand crept out, the palm held outward, the bent fingers shaking harder and harder.

She ducked. As if her lover's life were in danger, she closed her eyes, clawed at the Pug's arm. From the dark came the thumping of boots and the splashing of picriniacs getting up. Again a splash. "Me too! Together!" a boyish voice sobbed; then a jingle; then no sound. Until the silence, the air itself, was crushed; rattling, rumbling it fell upon her. And again all was still.

Somewhere, farther and farther away, the motor whirred, stopped, and a clatter pierced her head. "You can look up," the Pug's touch said. "Now you can."

Perhaps nothing had happened. Perhaps the shots had been fired into the air. Perhaps, because the center of the Appellplatz where she had dreaded the picriniacs would lie, was empty. But where were they? She searched for them, in the Picrine column, where the former Trotyl men formed a black path; in the Trotyl column, where empty spaces gaped; then at the gate, where the guards were now standing, the rifles back on their shoulders.

The clatter was back: a cart was clattering — a soup cart passing by, piled up high with a dark mass, a paper sheet hanging to one side, and an arm bumping against the boards. Something fell into the mud, a potato with its greenish stalk still dangling down. She knew where the cart was going, yet understood nothing. And when a bang of the lid hitting against the crate came from afar, she felt sickened, as if an obscene joke were being played upon them, and they, dazed by a drug, would soon wake up, in the crate, and would be too frightened, too weak to push up the lid.

Another bang. She knelt staring at the mud.

Bouncing lightly, the empty cart rolled through the street. At the gate the guards drew aside and from behind them, gingerly skirting a puddle, he, the man, stepped forth. Him! And the car? Grube must have left in the car. The man's name is Rost, she remembered. But now it no longer mattered.

Ice was breaking under the shifting knees. Rost spoke again, of what, she did not try to understand. After what seemed like a long time, Aurelia, she began repeating in her mind, feeling as though someone were dictating this name to her, Aurelia . . . a woman . . . woman . . . Frau.

"Frau," Rost was saying, then again, "Frau." Which Frau?

It can't be Aurelia, only not Aurelia, she begged. Then, Not me, merciful God, let it not be me. But it was she Rost meant. She!

A chunk of flesh seemed to be torn out of her, icy slime oozing in through the breach, flooding her, clogging her throat, only a segment of her brain left free, thoughts milling there, each startlingly clear. "Frau," Rost was saying, then "ein Pole." The Pole had read the letters. The Pole had denounced her. "Pole," Rost repeated. And now he was walking — straight toward her.

She must do something, must hide, run, ask help. "Pug, you help me; he means me; help me!" she tried to say, but her lips were locked. And the Pug understood nothing. None of them did. All of them were calm, knowing it was not they who had sent such letters; not they were meant, but she, all alone, with him drawing closer and closer. From this loneliness she grasped what was coming, from the hate and envy of those who had abandoned her, who would go on kneeling right here, when nothing of her was left. Nothing. No, she could not bear seeing those faces. But the moment her eyes closed she tried to force them open, so that he would not sneak upon her out of this dark, so that she could see him at least. Yet now her eyelids would not rise, and her groping fingers found nothing to clutch at, even the earth gone, only icy water running through them. The fear snapped; a lassitude numbed her, a conviction that this was a nightmare, that she could wake up soon, if only her eyes would open.

They opened of themselves. And at once she wanted them to close, but now they would not, she had to stare — at the spats, only at the spats. Was she screaming, was she struggling up? She did not know anymore; but her head kept swelling, and inside something kept strumming very loud. The strumming stopped. She was a torso, a blind legless torso. "Carry me," was what her blubbering meant as someone touched her, "you carry me . . . I can't . . ."

Who was touching her, was stroking her shoulder? This touch was warm, she began to understand, this touch seemed to mean no harm. Yet she still would not dare to look up. She only groped for the voice seeking her through the slimy dark. The voice was familiar, it was Goldberg's. "Girl," he was saying, "my girl, he is gone!"

"Gone?" And she longed to take his hand, to hold it against her face, her mouth; but her arms would not move, only her mouth opened slowly. Again the strumming — her chattering teeth.

"Pug . . . is he gone?" she tried to say, and instead choked on the air, too much of it all at once, hard racking coughs that brought tears to her eyes. They helped; they unglued her lids.

Cautiously she looked around, with difficulty matching color to shape, shape to name: the pale blotch a face, the Pug's face; the gray, a stone; and here, still plunged into the puddle, a hand, her own. It rose, wiped her eyes. With amazed gratitude she looked at its motion, at this big kneeling body not yet fully hers; rather, a faithful animal that had waited for her while she had been gone.

"Ah," she gasped, "ah." As her lungs drew in the air, the muddy strip of the Appellplatz seemed to expand into a farmyard, all its creatures rushing out in welcome. Smells nuzzled her — thawed earth, resin, the bitterness of picrine, and another she had no time to name, for already sounds were fluttering round her: a call, a faint rustle, while she listened and looked up higher and higher, at the darkening woods, at the brighter green of firs, so tall that they seemed to prop up the oily red ball of sun, up and up, till her eyes hurt, till they could take no more. Then again the stone, the puddle, and a glistening lump of mud.

"Pug," she said, "Pug," just so she could hear her own voice, then looked to the column's end, where in the fading light three heads glimmered — brown, greasy blond, and black. "Tola, Aurelia, Alinka," she repeated with longing, as if since their parting years had passed. Soon they would be together. It seemed only right that all kinds of stratagems had to be found to effect this reunion, that she had to clench her fists, use her arms as levers. She got up. "Down!" A shout forced her back to her knees.

But here someone was allowed to leave the Appellplatz — the boy with the yellow mustache, an O.D. man clumsily supporting him. They halted. Fumbling, the O.D. man reached out a chunk of bread, the boy pushed the bread away and they moved on.

The wind blew colder, the dusk deepened. And as the kneeling rows turned to thick irregular furrows, as in the woods only a few treetops rose from the inundating dark, a heaviness overcame her, never marring her joy, yet becoming more oppressive — a memory of an obligation too heavy to be carried out.

Later, she told herself, later, and watched Tola lead Aurelia to a corner well hidden from the watchtowers. Aurelia squatted; now she would feel better; to thank Tola for getting the O.D. man's permission to get up, she must have smiled her slow, glistening smile. So Aurelia had once smiled at her. "Mrs. Grünbaum," she had said, "Barbara, I'm sorry, of course, Barbara. I can't tell you how I feel about what you just said." "The child will be carried out of here safely," this she had said.

Again she got up; again a shout pushed her down. But she had to be with them, she had to tell them that she could not do it, could not carry the child out, not after this day. "I cannot let go." As "Don't cough!" before, so now she sent this message through the dark. "I didn't understand. I can't do it."

Still bent awkwardly, the O.D. man who had taken the boy to his barracks passed by her. "Me too! Together!" the boy had cried. The boy had been ready to go with the Chinaman. What had given him such strength? She could not understand this, ever. It was not fear itself that would have stopped her, but what had made her afraid: her greed for all she had once had, and even more — greed to walk again without O.D. men, without guards, and to eat her fill of bread, warm white bread, so much of it, till she could eat no more; to be with a man again, with Stefan as on those first nights when she would start out of her sleep for joy at finding him near. She wanted all this, and more, more still.

Was she a coward? If not wanting to let go meant being a coward, then she was one. She could not help herself, nor did she want to. But a coward, so she had thought, was one who feared misery. And of misery she had no dread. She would have taken anything upon herself, even the clogging fear, even the final pain, if only she could be certain it did not mean the end.

Believe me, I wasn't lying then, only I did not understand, she signaled once more, and when Tola waved to her it seemed that they understood. But the child . . . and I without it? Later, she said again, later. Now she could think no more.

"Cold — oh so cold," the black rows complained. "Cold, cold," she too moaned. Her moan grew hoarse, her knees dug harder into the ground. And it seemed to her that this ground, this very earth was a living creature, a beast of burden, huge yet very mild, upon its ever-moving body patiently carrying thousands and thousands of beings, some made to kneel in the bitter cold, others warm, others free to walk or rest, yet all clinging hard to this creature, all afraid to let go. High above, like figures rising from a cathedral dome into the dark sky, were these two, each apart, neither to be comprehended, the man in spats and the boy with the shadow of a yellow mustache.

"Cold — so cold — and dark," the straggly chorus sang. But lights seemed to flit by, like windows glimpsed from trains, of villages and of towns where those free to rest were now getting ready for the night. Somewhere among such places was London. Was it morning there now? she puzzled. No, it must be evening still in London where Stefan was. Stefan. How rarely she remembered him; his name when recalled was now hardly more than the address of a place where at times she had been happy. Now she thought of him, the big, taciturn man, so ill fitted to being alone, stumbling as he carried the decanter of water which she had always brought and shuffling on to the bed that, if she knew him at all, was left unmade day in and out. Or perhaps . . . perhaps he had a woman with him?

A pang of jealousy shot through her, then dissolved in the pain that cramped her body. She looked up: darkness had taken over, making earth and sky alike black glossy surfaces dotted with the sprawling shapes of puddles below, of clouds above. Now and then a faded half-moon broke through the clouds to form a wavering smudge upon the dark ice.

"Oh, we can't kneel anymore, we cannot." a chorus shouted, then faded, until only a tremulous solo was left. "Oh, Mr. Goldberg, dear Lord, Mr. O.D. man, I cannot. I'm cold." Old Alexandrovitch was reporting her ills to all the authorities she could think of.

"Goldberg, when will you let us go?" Barbara whispered as he passed by her. And when he shrugged in answer, she tried all sorts of remedies, made a cushion under her knees from her coat hem, then from her hands. Nothing helped. Motionless again, she thought of old Alexandrovitch whom she had rudely pushed some time long ago, then of her shriveled body. Old, Alexandrovitch was old. To be old meant that this, which Barbara dreaded even to think of, could happen to you of itself at any time; and so many were old here, everywhere, always. Yet somehow they went on, with courage, with such courage.

On the watchtowers the pacing was done now; as if in alternate rhythm, grown lonely, those perched there were conversing with each other in this way. The pacing slowed, and listening to it, she fell into a half-sleep, woke up whenever the pain tore at her muscles, then dozed off again.

"Cold — you — I'm cold." The Pug's sniffling startled her. They tried to warm each other, first by huddling together, then by kneeling back to back, but it was just pressing cold against cold, and soon they drew apart, each doubled up, Barbara nestling her fists within the drenched sleeves. From the dark lump in the center a smacking sound came. As once old Alexandrovitch, so now the O.D. men crossed and uncrossed their arms, trying to catch a bit of warmth. They gave up, and the only sounds left were the steps, the slow shuffle of old men.

It stopped. Was everything going to happen all over again? The silence was back, hanging over the forest now, not a twig stirring there, as if judgment were to be passed over the woods, over each tree, each bush. The silence grew; the wind swished, just once. And slowly, in large damp flakes, the snow came down, came in sheets, in drifts, thicker and thicker until it buried those kneeling, until they turned to white mounds.

"No!" a ringing voice called out. "No!" Aurelia was standing in front of the mounds, her legs spread apart, her arms lifted up, as if single-handed she hoped to push the blizzard away. "No! Let us go, no!" Her voice stronger with each "No!" led an ever-swelling chorus; "No!" Barbara was crying against the white blindness, the cold, the pain. The ringing voice stopped. Deprived of its leadership, the chorus grew fainter and fainter.

The snow kept falling. After the Appellplatz, the barracks and the woods had merged into one undulating sheet. Wind blew, twirled funnels in the snow and to the kneeling ranks white drifts were added, companions sent to them for such a night. The drifts rose higher, thin animal moans trailed through the dark, and when they broke off, from the watchtower a shout came. No one answered, no one stirred when the stairs creaked.

The only dark point in a white world, a guard stood in the Appellplatz and shouted.

"Disperse!" an O.D. man echoed his shout. But only after a long time the mounds began to move, turned into a white chain, turned into white figures wobbling on and on, like a procession of puppets marshaled to some great marriage feast. From the watchtowers the shout came again. A few more mounds scrambled up, but when another call came no one answered in the Appellplatz, only the drifts were left there, and in the center a squashed can caught the light that swooped down, wavered, then went out.

Chapter 19

ONE BY ONE lights flashed on in the barracks. But hardly had the women come in when "Lights out!" the shouts ordered. "It's after ten o'clock." The O.D. men scolded them like children up past their usual bedtime. "Lights out!" and all grew dark.

The darkness fell too soon for Barbara. "I . . . I didn't know what was coming. Aurelia, Tola, had I known, I would have stayed with you," she stammered, putting her arms around them. At first they would not relent; then with a soft moan Aurelia huddled against her, and after a while Tola too drew near.

The smell of damp wool lay over the barracks. From clothing spread out to dry, mud splashed down to the floor while they lay shivering in the cold. And when they huddled tighter, when their bodies, though each was frozen, lent a bit of warmth to one another, peace came over Barbara, as if this — to be still here, still together — was enough.

"Excuse me," Aurelia murmured. "Could you move, a bit? I feel —"

"Aurelia, is something wrong?" Tola started.

"No, just my leg got cramped. You know, for me to kneel . . ."

The peace was gone.

"Aurelia!" Barbara began.

"Yes, my dear?"

"No. It's nothing. Only sleep well, and you too, Tola, and you, Alinka," she called down to the lower bunk. To tell Aurelia now would be wrong. Aurelia was tired, she must sleep.

In Barbara's sleep snow fell. An arm, it was Stefan's, groped over the white rows. "No!" a ringing voice cried, "oh no!" and she woke up. A loose board squeaked. "Quiet. Can't you let people sleep at least?" someone whimpered; and the slow shuffle was Aurelia, stealing out to the latrine.

Should she follow Aurelia, should she talk to her right away?
"No!" Aurelia would cry when told, as in the dream, as in the Appellplatz when the snow had come. She would hold Aurelia fast;
then, "I too am unhappy," she would say. "I too, just like you." But,
what should be said until this cry came; how could she explain that
no ordinary fear had forced her to break her promise? Or perhaps
Tola could speak to Aurelia. Tola had never set her whole heart on
this hope. For Tola it would be easier.

As though guessing her thoughts Tola sat up.

"I . . . I just woke up, Tolenka." Barbara drew away.

"Listen," Tola moved closer, "are you still thinking about doing
it?"

"A dreadful day this was, just dreadful!"

"Are you?"

"No! Didn't I say as much?" Barbara rapped out, climbing down.
Something rattled. "Thieves, they stole my bread, the thieves!" a
whine followed her as she ran outside.

The night was clear. In the damp snow shone tracks, of boots,
and of something which had left long wavering traces as though
someone had swum through the snow. A bang. And she stopped,
she huddled against the wall, hard, as if a huge object were coming
toward her and not the tattered paper sheet. It was not a door that
had banged, but a lid, the lid of the crate. And now she was running.

"Aurelia!" she called, bursting into the latrine. "Aurelia, are you
here?" Of course Aurelia was here, eating soup, as on any other
night.

"Oh, it's you, Mrs. — Barbara." She scrambled up. "Did you just
come, I mean come just to the latrine, or — "

"I came to you, to see you!"

"Then please sit down." Aurelia fussed with the paper spread on
the filthy seat. "Cold, isn't it?" as Barbara remained standing, she
went on. "Such a damp chill is most penetrating." She sniffled and
a drop fell onto her lips dotted with red crumbs. Hastily Aurelia
wiped it off.

"Don't," Barbara said softly. "Don't fidget so . . . I . . . you
know . . ." She stopped. With an enormous surprise it dawned
upon her that Aurelia knew nothing, that she still believed a Pole

was to carry the child out. "The least trouble in your camp and I won't help you — not for a king's ransom," a drunken voice seemed to boom, as if such a Pole had existed, had really spoken those words. And if, if she just said, "After what happened today, the Pole won't help us . . ." No, the truth would come out. And she had no fear of the truth, she was no liar.

"The truth," she blurted out. "Aurelia, I'll hide nothing from you, I'll tell you the whole truth. There never has been any Pole. But I haven't been lying to you. I believed it, with my whole heart I believed that I could do it. After today — forgive me, I cannot." It was over. Her eyes closed, she waited for the cry.

A faint scraping sound, then, "Of course," Aurelia said briskly, much too loud. "Of course, I understand. Fully," Aurelia added even louder. Her short legs dangled over a quicklime-covered pile, her teeth glittered. Only the frayed bandage showing from under her coat proved to Barbara she had not misaddressed her confession.

"Aurelia," she whispered, "I . . . I wanted it so much."

"Of course. And do you know, I'd often thought you planned to do it yourself."

"Who told you? Tola?"

"Oh no. It was just a suspi — a premonition, yes. Then today Alinka dropped some hints." Aurelia's mud-streaked face turned purple. "She said . . . that you were most courageous; still . . . after a day like this no one could expect — "

"Wait," Barbara broke in, "you know nothing yet. He, Rost, spoke of the Poles and of a Frau who had dealings with them — you knew this, but not that it was me he meant. He was after me, he still is, I'm sure. Because he came up to me and stared, you understand, stared right at me. Some miracle saved me. And only then this fear came over, no, not an ordinary fear, but such a dread I thought I would never breathe again."

"How terrible!"

"Yes, it was terrible, it was!"

"No. I meant how terrible that you don't know German."

"That what?"

"That you don't know German, that you got frightened for noth-

ing at the Strafappell — the punishment Appell, you know. Some
Poles, women too, were implicated in the affair about shoes; that
was all he said. And he looked at many like you, strong, still able
to work. What a terrible misunderstanding. Now, really, you must
calm down."

Barbara felt cheated, not calm: the great dread, the great joy had
been a farce. Yet the dread persisted. "No," she whispered.
"No, even if he isn't after me, I can't do it."

"Oh, I never meant you should. And now," Aurelia glanced at her
timidly, "hadn't we better go back? You must be simply exhausted.
And it's so cold here; such a damp chill."

"You want to go? But — you don't understand. 'It's cold — let's
go,' you say as if nothing were the matter. But I know what misery
I've brought upon you, I feel it myself. Oh, it's terrible for you — "
She waited. "Aurelia . . . don't tell the others . . . but I will
never have any children, so I know how terrible this must be for
you, just terrible." She stopped. With each "Terrible!" Aurelia
pushed harder against the wall, her eyes narrowing, her mouth
sucked in.

"Aurelia, don't be like that," she pleaded. "Shout at me, cry, do
anything, don't sit like that. For God's sake, move, say something
— move!" Aurelia did move. She got up, she bent forward.

"Hoopla!" She clapped her hands. "Be happy, Aurelia Katz, be
full of hope! Hoopla!" and a clap again, "be miserable, be full of •
despair. No, I cannot switch so fast, Mrs. Grünbaum, I am not like
you. You . . . you used to be so solicitous toward me . . . it was
too much, your solicitude, much too much. But today, when I
waited for you to come, to tell me if it was me they were after . . .
then you didn't come. A child had to take care of me."

"A child?"

"Alinka! Isn't she a child? But if you had needed me I would
have come to you, even though I'm a monster. A monster, yes! Because I don't feel terrible, I don't care what happens to . . . to it. I
don't!" she shrieked, then slumped down.

"I don't care!" The cry seemed to echo on and on. "I don't care,"
Aurelia had said, about the child, her own child. A child . . . the
child . . . this child, Barbara repeated, yet felt empty, all spent.

Had this woman infected her? No, with her it was different, she was merely worn out by the dreadful day. Dreadful . . . how dreadful, the door squeaked in the draft, monotonously, like a clock.

She felt no anger, just the rankling unrest that comes when an occasion ends abruptly and chores must be remembered sooner than expected. What her chores were she could not think yet; she stared at the puddle, at the quicklime dust. At last she got up and walked to the door. She couldn't bear going back to Tola's needling, back to those screams about thieves. "Thieves — they stole my shoes, my comb, my bread!" would waken her tomorrow. Tomorrow was what she must think of, and the next day, and the next. How would she get through those days with nothing to wait for but soup? She would get the soup, would look away from the rotten beets, then would wait for the bread, for the evening to come; in the evening she would again look away — from the marks of squashed lice on the sheets. And she would wash those sheets, evening after evening, for three potatoes apiece.

Potatoes were all she had to give — potatoes all anyone ever wanted from her.

I'm cold, she thought; then with no transition, I came here for nothing. She shuddered. But instead of unloading itself in this shudder, the cold stayed in her, thickening to a slimy mass, rising up and up, till she could not breathe, till she had to clutch at her throat. This helped. She could move, could think again. For nothing, she thought, and, I've got gravel in my shoe.

She took off the shoe. The gravel splashed into a puddle. "For nothing," with each splash said voices, now Antoni's, now Marta's: "Once they shut you in with those Jews you'll perish — like them — for nothing."

"No," she shook herself, "no." Then softer, so that no one would hear, "Get me out of here, get me out!"

Somehow in her bewildered mind this new hope grew distinct from the other, just abandoned hope, as if those who forbade all sacrifice would not begrudge her the concession of letting her go back where she had come from. Antoni must help her; he must get money for her, and he would; not everyone had forgotten the Dziedziczka of Dembina. True, he had not scraped up much till now, yet what did he know of her misery when for herself she had never complained? Now he would gather thousands, with thousands you could buy anyone: any Pole from Trotyl. "The least trouble in your camp, and I won't help you — not for a king's ransom," the Pole's drunken grumble was back. And again she clutched at her throat.

But there was, there had to be some way out. In a fortnight, no, in ten days, Antoni and Marta would be in Skarzysko. From Skarzysko to the camp was only a two-hour walk. What were two hours? Going to Schmitz and back took as long. They would hear in what a hell she lived, they would find help, would come for her. And she stood motionless, even holding her breath, so that the longing for them would fill her up, so that they would feel it, would come and get her out.

"Mrs. Grünbaum — Barbara, is anything wrong?" Across the floor a shadow swayed with its nose bent into a sickle. This was the Jewish nose, the Jewish face. Had she too come to look like this? Was Tola to be trusted, or that cracked mirror on the washroom pipe, into which the Picrine women kept peeking, until these yellow blobs seemed like her own face?

If only she had a mirror, large, without a flaw, then she could see herself fully, then she would know how much she had changed, if at all. She looked at her hands, then away at once. She had never had those bony knobs at her wrists, nor those knotty fingers, the skin reddish as though eaten through with rust. Trotyl was eating into her hands; they were rusted just from passing by the Trotyl works. Chlorine, she thought, I could scrub them — with chlorine. The cramped smile hurt her lips.

Outside feet shuffled. "Three o'clock, first Picrine shift up," a drowsy voice called.

"Three o'clock — you must sleep." It somehow helped her to split into two beings, a frightened one and a comforting one.

"How can I sleep?" asked the frightened one.

"Then go back to Tola. No? Then to Alinka. Or to Goldberg." Yes, she would go to him, he was good, his touch felt soothing and warm. But halfway to the door eyes stopped her — the Chinaman's eyes insisting that one capable of going to a man on a night like this was no better than those who cared only for soup.

Sleep, she thought, go to sleep; perhaps by tomorrow you'll figure

something out. Tomorrow? How would she get through tomorrow
and the next day and the next?

A wire seemed to push through her head. It twirled, it made her
twirl along. To stare at one point, at the spoon gray with soup,
stopped this dizziness. Only now the spoon seemed glued to her
eyes. It grew, it was not a spoon anymore but the underbelly of a
huge snail swaying above her, sucking her in. The snail had sucked
in her hands, her face, and she had known nothing. Again the snail
would sway, again she would know nothing, until one night she
would see herself — barefoot, in rags, her shoes, her clothes gone
for bread, and the bread too gone, only barrels left that she would
lick out, like the Chinaman who had swollen from hunger, then was
shot. And then . . .

She bent down, she bit into her fist. The pain did not help, she
saw it: the O.D. men pulling at the mud-caked feet — then the crate
— then the long wavering tracks.

"God Almighty . . . good God Almighty . . ."

It was over. She felt quiet, though drained as after a bout of fever. Pursing her lips she sipped in some air, then, very slowly, swallowed. Another breath. Then another. I must do something, she
told herself. I know what to do, I'll sit down.

Across from her on the wall, her shadow sat. It slumped, so did
she; it grew smaller, and she too shrank. To shrink helped. When
she shrank, the cold mass in her seemed to ebb away. And perhaps
this was the way — to shrink, never to think or speak, just to sit
quietly, as now. A gray haze was rising around her, and her head
felt like an apple with its crown pared off; upon the exposed nerves
dust was sifting like sugar into the hollow where the core had been.

Apples. When had she eaten such apples, sweet with sugar, with
cinnamon and cloves? On the eve of her going away, Marta had
baked them for her. "I can't eat," she had said. "I'm too excited."
Marta scooped the apples into the slop pail. "Excited!" Antoni
cried, "our madam is beside herself with joy; our madam can't wait
to get away." She smiled. Behind him on the console lay the hat
chosen for going away, a toque of royal blue; next to it, Antoni's
prayerbook, which with its cross thin and sallow upon the black
cover always made her think of getting old and of small, inconspicuous dying.

And it was then that they had said those things about Jews, about perishing like them for nothing.

She started. Grown large again, the shadow was spilling from the wall onto the ceiling. And knowing she could never shrink, What shall I do? she asked herself. What?

"Barbara, what is it? Have I upset you so?"

"No," she said. But she kept her eyes closed, because the light hurt them, and the long-nosed face.

"Have I done it to her?" Aurelia was asking. How could it have been when — but for the final outburst — all she had wanted was to end this talk, expected, though not so soon. When Alinka had whispered "Aurelia, things don't look good," just as in Cracow — as if they had found no powerful protectress, and the caked rouge was again her only defense — then this hope had left her. She had never trusted it much. Soon, even to hope that the O.D. men's clamor did not mean her was hard enough.

But what was the spell Barbara cast over her? A glimpse of her, flushed, snow glistening in her windblown hair, and the hope was back — only to vanish again. Yet Aurelia tried to be considerate. But when Barbara's stare tore into her, demanding all the grief she might own, then something within her refused. She screamed; Barbara ducked. Through the dusk her scream slashed, like a blow aimed at someone else.

Even so, she had been right, at least in part. Yet this part kept dwindling, her anxiety kept mounting with the silence. Now looking at Barbara's mouth, gaping as if it lacked the strength to close, Aurelia remembered her huge resounding laugh.

"What's wrong?" Her legs shook as she bent over Barbara. "Tell me, has that dreadful misunderstanding about Rost upset you so? Or is it that nothing can be done anymore?" She waited. "No, it isn't that," just by tightening her eyelids Barbara said, and Aurelia allowed herself to sit down. She craned her neck to keep the gray face in sight, yet with each moment Barbara drifted farther and farther away, until to hold her somehow Aurelia began anew, asking did something hurt? did she feel feverish, did she — "No, it isn't that. No, not that," said the impassive face.

Outside, wind blew; rustling, snow slid from the roof. Barbara started, then with a shudder reached out her hand. Timidly, just with her fingertips, Aurelia touched it, and Barbara gripped her hand at once. When the grip slackened Aurelia felt afraid; it regained its strength and she nodded "Yes? Yes?" so eagerly that she almost missed the moment when Barbara looked up. But already, like a peddler forcing his way through the least chink, she pushed her face under Barbara's eyes. "What is it," she smiled, "what can I do for you?"

"Have you got a mirror?" Barbara said slowly.

"I beg your pardon?"

"Nothing." Turning, Barbara listened to the steps outside.

"O.D. men," Aurelia explained promptly, "if you'll excuse me, I'd better turn off the light for a moment until they are gone." Having gently extricated her hand, she tiptoed away, backward, to watch over Barbara, who had slumped down again.

"Where are they going?" Barbara whispered.

"Walking, just walking by."

"Are you sure?"

"Quite sure." And "Don't be afraid," she signaled with her eyes only, for wouldn't it be a breach of order if she, always afraid, tried to encourage Barbara, of whom once everyone had said, "Nothing will ever happen to the likes of her." This she must repeat to Barbara — this, right away.

"You, you must feel optimistic" was all she could bring out, because of Barbara's hand, at once fumbling toward her. And offering Barbara the comfort of her clammy fingers, Aurelia felt ashamed.

To hold on to that hand, Barbara felt, was not helping much. She clutched it, as a child would anything familiar — a blanket, an old toy. But the ingratiating voice annoyed her. "A mirror, didn't you ask for a mirror?" it insisted.

She had asked for it to deal once and for all with the thought of escape.

"Unfortunately I don't have a mirror on me," Aurelia went on hastily, "but you look quite . . . quite well. A bit tired, of course, a bit pale, still amazingly — "

"Jewish," Barbara broke in morosely. "I want to know if I look Jewish."

Aurelia stepped back. And as she tilted her head to gain a proper perspective, Barbara felt a twinge of hope that her face would be restored to her by the startled "You, Jewish-looking? Of course not."

"Slightly . . . somewhat . . ." Aurelia faltered. "But why do you ask?"

"Because I want to get out of here." With a vindictive pleasure she watched Aurelia wince.

"Oh. I understand; anyone would, if there were the least chance."

She was not anyone. Trying not to listen to Aurelia's explanation about the Strafappell, Barbara looked up at the crevice in the roof, the sky shining through it like black glass. Abruptly "Sabotage?" she echoed. "Did you say that sabotage is going on here?"

"No. Not exactly. I just meant that the fact so few people were shot was exceptional, in a sense, because stealing belts could be considered — "

"Belts? You said shoes before."

"Yes, the shoes are soled with conveyor belts stolen from the Trotyl machines. And in wartime — "

"What does that mean?" Barbara muttered. "How could they work at Picrine and steal at Trotyl?"

"Those shoemakers who made the shoes stole," Aurelia said apologetically, "the men from Trotyl. But this is a work camp. And in a work camp nothing happens to those still strong."

"Strong?" Barbara felt her old anger, against those explanations which explained nothing, against that shameful way out Aurelia was suggesting to her. "Why shouldn't they be strong? They steal, they can eat their fill, while the Chinaman, the others, oh God!" She even waited for tears, but her eyes burned dryly.

And Aurelia's eyes burdened her, doglike, constantly asking "What can I do?" as if she knew. "Why don't you go?" Barbara shrugged wearily. "In your own way you mean well; still, I'd rather be alone."

Hardly had Aurelia turned away when Barbara cried, "Don't go! I cannot be alone, it is back, filling me all up — I thought it was better, but it isn't. I must do something, I must talk. Talk," she repeated. Her words felt like the Picrine cough that must go on till that cold mass was forced out. "In one day this has happened to me," she whispered, fearful of the least pause. "Or perhaps, not in

one day, perhaps before too, I was afraid. Only then I had this
hope. You don't want to talk about it, but I must and anyhow to you
it's nothing; didn't you say so yourself? And I . . . I didn't mind
the filth, or the noise — you people are as noisy as magpies — not
even the hunger. At night, my hunger would get so great all of me
would feel like one big mouth. But then, then," she repeated softly,
"I would just tell myself how I would go back soon, after the war, I
mean — we, all of us. 'Just look at this child,' I would say to Antoni,
'and tell me if I went off for nothing.' And now — " she lowered
her head, "what is there for me to think of now?"

"Somehow a person like you — "

"No, don't say anything yet. 'Anyone,' you said before, 'anyone
this, anyone that.' I am not like anyone, I came here — three times,
in a way! First I left my old people, then I ran away from the Polish
camp, and then when I volunteered in Werk A to come here, that
was the third time. I came here for Tola's sake, not that I hold it
against her, God forbid. Still . . . 'Green, red, yellow, no matter
what color they make me, I'll manage,' I told myself. And now —
I've not gone to Picrine, I've not turned yellow here, but I . . . I'm
afraid." She sat up. "I'm afraid something terrible will happen to
me here," she whispered.

She had coughed it out. Then unhurriedly, steadily, the cold mass
began to gather again within her. "Talk to me," she commanded,
"you talk."

Aurelia was pinching her neck till it was dotted with red spots.
"No," she said shrilly. "No," in a nasal mumble this time. The third
"No" rang so clear that Barbara had to listen.

"You must never allow such thoughts." Aurelia spoke almost
sternly. "You must have faith in yourself, just because you came
here, you must. Who else would have dared to take such a step?
Only you! Only you had the courage, no, I don't mean simply courage, I mean something more essential. I mean — vitality!" Her tone
was both solemn and wistful, as if pronouncing the name of a place,
a place too exotic, too far away for her ever to see. "Everyone," she
went on, "everyone senses this in you. Oh, you don't know what you
meant to me, to us all, there in Cracow. It wasn't the bread you gave
away, really not. 'What's the news, has anyone seen her, the big
Pole?' in a single breath people would ask. I . . . I still remember

the day we met, or rather I met you. There was such a crowd. You came out to give us bread, when your foreman — a dangerous man, positively a criminal type — yelled, 'You Jew-lover, you!' Anyone else would've been petrified, but you. 'I'd rather be a Jew-lover than the Krauts' flunky,' you laughed. And then you brushed him off, like dust — like a speck of dust! 'Nothing will ever happen to the likes of her,' everyone whispered. Do you see now what I mean, do you?"

Did she? Barbara was not sure but, impatient to hear more, looked at the sign showing that Aurelia was about to go on — at the vein quivering in her neck. "Hope." Aurelia plucked at it. "Please, don't misunderstand me, I don't feel jealous or — anything, still sometimes it's hard to believe how much you've got to hope for — your husband, your estate, your friends. Soon you'll go back, and there they'll be, waiting for you, as if nothing had ever happened, nothing at all!"

Her face hardened. "Those like Rost can't do it . . . this . . . to everyone. Some will survive. And if anyone does, it will be such as you, it will be you." She spoke fast, as though suddenly in a hurry. "Yes, it must be."

"Do you believe it?"

"Yes. Yes."

"Really?"

"Really. Only excuse me — I must adjust something. My bandages." Aurelia stepped aside.

Barbara sat very still. She had listened to Aurelia's speech as once to stories about her childhood — how, having fallen off a tree, she had picked herself up laughing; how, lost in the woods, she curled up and slept. Stories of courage so out of the ordinary that they were a voucher of glory, vague, yet certain to come. And like these tales, Aurelia's story had ended much too soon.

Yet it seemed to her as though she, carried on by a relentless river, had caught a glimpse of the true Barbara, from a distant shore beckoning at her as a sign that they would draw together, if only she fought hard enough.

"Do you know, I feel a bit better," she reported when Aurelia came back.

"I'm so pleased." Aurelia coughed, her lips pursed; suddenly they began to tremble, then her chin, her neck, until all of her was shaking with sobs.

"Aurelia, what is it? Here I tell you I feel better, and you — "

"Nervousness. It all piles up," Aurelia stammered. "Everything just came back to me."

"Everything?" Barbara began to understand. "Are you crying because of what I told you, when I first came in?"

"I . . . yes!" Aurelia gulped.

"Oh, my God, and I like a fool," Barbara whispered. "No, don't cry, don't, I can't bear it." Clumsily she stroked Aurelia's head. But the sobs went on.

Barbara groped for something to say, when suddenly she remembered: Aurelia's eyes! While O.D. men had stamped by those eyes had comforted her, shining steadfast out of the dark. Now, in turn, she tried to help Aurelia with such a look, but found it hard, since her own eyes kept blinking; her thoughts, too, refused to be still. How strange that Aurelia should cry only now. Everything was strange, the secrecy, the fear, as if she were not an old woman but a burly servant girl, jumping off tables to rid herself of her trouble.

Pity filled her for this woman, for her ill-fitting fate, and for the tears dripping from the porous nose down to the crimson-specked lips.

Rouge, Barbara understood with a start. "My dear, my dear, why on earth did you rouge yourself?"

"To look younger. It's not safe to look old."

And the pity grew: for hoping that stale rouge would make her younger, for those hours of kneeling in the cold, and for the cold that now made her shiver all over. "Such a damp chill," she remembered; and in such a chill Aurelia had stayed, for her.

"For me, hour upon hour you stayed here." She could barely speak for surprise, for tenderness and vague remorse. Squatting down, Barbara clasped Aurelia's knees. "Oh, do you know what strikes me at times? That I am a fool, a big hulk of a fool. Fool or not, I know when someone is good to me. And you were so good, you had such patience — like my old people, just like them." She felt a warm speck within, as if part of them had come over to stay with her from now on.

"Thank you, I'm so glad. Thank you." Aurelia dried her eyes.

Taking the route of her lined cheeks, two more tears rolled down, reminding Barbara that another sorrow must still be pitied. She did not want to remember it now. "Come," she said, "let's go back."

The wind had erased all the tracks. Smooth, and glinting more sharply where ice had formed, snow stretched before them. They walked rapidly. But as they were approaching the barracks Barbara drew back so abruptly that Aurelia slipped and fell headlong into the snow. "Watch out!" Barbara cried. And when she lifted Aurelia, when she held her fast, her tenderness rose to a frenzy; she wanted to help Aurelia, to give her something, to keep her safe from all harm. What the harm might be the long wavering traces showed her, cutting through the snow where Aurelia had fallen.

The child has been like my own to me, she thought. And yet — and yet, what if I did what must be done? Because it had been like her own she must do it, because she would do it not as the others would, from indifference, from fear — only for Aurelia, to save her from something no mother could bear.

"Aurelia," she had to speak at once, before other thoughts broke through, "when your time comes I . . . I'll do everything for you, you understand?" She waited for the prolonged shiny look, but Aurelia turned away and walked silently into the barracks.

Morning was near when Aurelia sat up, carefully, so as not to disturb Barbara, who lay fast asleep. Yes. Barbara seemed to feel better, Barbara had not guessed why she had cried. "If anyone survives it will be you," she had said to Barbara, and just then she had remembered the engineer and his wife. That was why she had cried — because what she still believed with her whole heart was not true.

No more tears came; she sighed, and another sigh answered from the dark. The Rebbetzyn, Aurelia thought. For her, awake night after night, each sound by now had a name. The breath too soft to show whether she was asleep was Tola; Alinka, the brisk gasps; and farther away old Alexandrovitch smacking her lips.

She listened. And a sadness came to her, went from bunk to bunk, then having finished its round returned to her, and even to the child — as if she cared after all, though neither as Barbara had demanded nor in a way she herself could grasp.

Part Four

Chapter 20

LIKE ROYALTY IN DISGUISE, so since that night Barbara had come to treat Aurelia. A word lacking the propriety she deemed due, a glance cast askance at Aurelia, and "How dare you!" she would boom. "Do you know who this woman is?" Something like triumph vibrated in those shouts; because she, only she knew. And at times when Aurelia broke into a cantankerous whine, a look of gentle reproach would come into Barbara's eyes, as though Aurelia herself could fail to understand the true Aurelia Katz.

For this Aurelia Barbara felt ready to do everything. The idea of sacrifice took possession of her; never imagined clearly yet ever present, it lent her days the sense of ascent toward a towering peak. Upon this peak a transformation would occur. She, her whole being, would be suspended, someone else would take her place for that instant, and at once she would be brought back to kneel at Aurelia's side, to whisper, "I for you — everything." And later, later all would end: the hunger, the camp, the war.

This she believed; because the news, Aurelia, and the approaching spring held the promise of such an end; because otherwise it simply could not be. The peak was the furthermost point on her journey. Once reached, what else but return could be left? Soon she would go home, with her Aurelia like a precious souvenir brought along from her travels.

Night after night Barbara imagined their return. For nights had changed; they lingered on into the day like the memory of a task left unfinished, rankling stronger as outside Schmitz the pines began to darken, as she walked through the windswept woods. Evening granted a deferment which she tried to prolong — by restlessly moving from one end of the bunk to the other, by talking more rapidly while the street emptied and over the barracks a hush began to spread.

"Lagerschluss!" And hastily, to outrun other thoughts, she would begin, "The news is good, the war can't last much longer."

Not once did she return to the vast panorama painted for Tola on that night in Werk A, to the singing crowds, to Germans fleeing in mortal fear. She came to prefer what was small but her own: the gold-rimmed cups jingling as a carriage rolled into the driveway; the lace that sun wove upon the velvety surface of the piano; or the credenza, smooth, a bit sticky under her touch, like the loaves of honey-cake with which it was scented.

The cups were jingling, everyone — Stefan, Antoni, Marta — running to the door, for a carriage was coming, bringing Aurelia. "This is Aurelia Katz — my friend!" Then, having made sure that their smiles were proper for such a welcome, she dashed upstairs to smooth a wrinkle from the satin bedspread, to brush off the least speck of dust. The door opened upon the gleaming floors, upon the flowers and the Persian rugs.

"Do you like it, Aurelia?"

"Oh, Barbara, it's wonderful!"

"Do you like Aurelia, Stefan?"

"Oh, she's quite wonderful." His mustache quivered with a little smile, for at first he found Aurelia "a bit fantastic." But he would come to love her in his slow patient way, which she would allow him this time; because Aurelia would stay with them forever.

If sleep came at this point the night was overcome. But often what she feared came instead: thoughts of what, even with herself doing everything, might soon happen to Aurelia; thoughts of Tola, grown a stranger somehow, even though Barbara, trying her best, always remembered to call "You come too, Tola" when she took Aurelia for a walk. Hardest in a way were the thoughts of food. Even to remember the larder back home was not safe. At once scents swarmed upon her, steaming plates floated through the dark, came closer, and vanished, as though snatched away by a rapacious creature. Hunger was this creature. Hunger stole through the barracks, from bunk to bunk.

"I'm hungry," whispers started, "I'll eat my bread now."

"You can't work on an empty stomach. You touch the bread and I'll do such things to you — I'll pinch you."

"I'm hungry now, I'll eat now."

It happened — only once — yet it did happen, that Barbara reached up to the bag with tomorrow's food: one soggy beet, two potatoes for Aurelia, bread. Under the cover of darkness the bread expanded, promised to grow into a loaf so big it would quiet her hunger forever if only she ate all of it, this once. Tola stirred, and she drew away.

Since then she would deafen those whispers about food by counting to a hundred, by remembering names of her maids, her flowers, her beaux. And at last sleep came.

Between sleep and awakening a threshold stood. She did not want to cross this threshold; she wanted to lie there, curled up, without a thought. "It's time, Barbara." Aurelia would stroke her head. Then she would get up. Aurelia Katz understood everything, Aurelia was good to her. When those thoughts she feared sneaked up on her, a sigh was enough to arouse Aurelia from her daze.

"And what do you say to the news, Barbara?" she would ask. "Oh, it's so hopeful." Then, in the chalky dust coating the table, Aurelia would draw for her the map of hope: the Allied advances in Italy, and above all the Russian victories, each day bringing them closer to the borders of Poland.

Or again, "Amazing," Aurelia would smile, "you lift those heavy crates like feathers." From her smile "vitality" was rising — this patron saint whose protection, once revealed, could never be withdrawn from Barbara. Whenever Barbara lapsed — soon by design — into the camp phrase "If I ever live through this," Aurelia would interpose " 'When,' you meant to say," as though correcting a minor grammatical error. Such comforts helped. Reasserting the value of Barbara's discovery, they brought an onrush of tenderness — and if with it came the thought of the sacrifice, so did the faith in the end which would be granted soon.

Perhaps — perhaps no sacrifice would be called for. Were it not for this hope, Aurelia Katz could never have watched over Barbara so well. A superstitious dread that the hope if even hinted at would be denied her made her keep it secret. And the hope grew stronger. Within her was peace. What had stirred in her body, with kicks like cries protesting against being "just an illness, a boil," had become still.

And as the sun shone more brightly each day, as she, always

frozen, could now have her fill of warmth, Aurelia came to feel she had been carrying no more than a chunk of winter, which now at last was dissolving into the mild spring air. Soon the last vestige of this winter would be expelled, soon she would become like everyone else.

At times it happened that a quiver would disturb her peace. "It will be nothing, it must be nothing," she repeated like a magic spell. If the spell proved potent and the quiver stopped, she calmed down. If it returned, even for an instant, terror seized her, until, reaching the point beyond endurance, the terror turned to anger against those three — working as usual, as if nothing was the matter.

How, though, could she give vent to her anger? Suddenly it was only children who surrounded her: Alinka, a child and neglected for the sake of Barbara, whose face, like that of another more sensitive child, fell at Aurelia's least harsh glance. True, Tola was not a child; but when once, in an uncontrollable attack of fear, Aurelia took to nagging at her, Tola smiled so wistfully that she could not go on. At times Aurelia felt worried about this aloof, strangely aged girl. But preoccupied with Alinka, Barbara, and the tremors within herself, she could do no more than to interpret for Tola — the news, and also Barbara.

"Do you know, my dear, in spite of her inner strength, Barbara is most sensitive," she would say in an all-embracing apology.

The new "sensitive" Barbara Tola treated with the guilty helplessness with which someone suddenly crippled is treated by those who had loved him for his inexhaustible vigor. She pitied this woman with big bony hands, yet shrank away afraid lest comfort from her would only appear patronizing. Or she would long to say, "Barbara, I've seen too many Strafappells — can you understand me better now?" The words were less a reproach than a statement of balance: on one side what she had seen, what she had become on the other.

It was at her last Strafappell that Tola had begun watching Meister Grube. Slouched more than ever, he trudged behind Rost, his face blank as if, like someone too young to witness such a spectacle, he had left a part of himself behind.

"I cannot do it," Barbara had said the night after the Strafappell, and his face reappeared to Tola, bringing a new hope. What if she went to him? What if she said, "A child will be born here, you can save it"? He would not denounce her; when told how simple it was, how close those who would take the child were, he might agree to help.

And more faces came, filled with gratitude, with remorse and startled affection. "Who would have thought you'd save it?" voices said, Barbara's the loudest. "Frankly, I didn't think so either," she answered. Even her laughter she could imagine, even the sense of liberation — as if at last she could stretch out and rest.

They spent the evenings together — she and the approving faces — as, bent under her peddler's pack, she canvassed the barracks. "Herr Meister, may I speak to you?" she would rehearse. "Herr Meister, as you must know, there is a pregnant woman among us." He certainly must know — from the Kaelanki sighing in Yiddish over "the poor soul whose time must be coming near," from the lame fore-man heard muttering about "the big bellies." That the Meister had not reported this knowledge proved he could be trusted.

The Kaelanki gave her more proofs. "Tsta, tsa, what a fine man he is," they smacked, "and a liberal too." Why? Let her just see the other Meisters and she would know why. The other Meisters beat you up black-and-blue, but he, not once had he touched anyone. He was so softhearted that long ago when women from Schmitz had been taken to Picrine, he could not bear to select them; the foreman did it instead. And even before that, when all of them had first come here — they from the camp of Majdanek, he from Germany — he had chatted with them so kindly, had given them bread or soup; and once — they only had water for dinner then — he had whispered, "Girls, you're drinking Hitler wine." Who had heard him say this Tola could never find out.

She gathered, she weighed those stories; added to them what had happened in Werk A: the pity he had then shown for Alinka; the attentive, almost respectful glance he had granted to her, Tola, when she had asked him to order Barbara to stay in the good camp.

Yes, he would help her. After all, what had he to fear? He would simply drive into Skarzysko, would walk into the inn — just another German dropping in for a solitary beer. That he had left a parcel in some dark entry, that an old man grabbed it, this no one would see. And the day was not far off when it would help him to have proof that he, Rost's aide, had been kind to his Jews.

It was on those lonely evenings that she learned the brittleness of logic. Her own eyes destroyed it, just by looking around: identical in the glare, faces swarmed in the barracks; out in the streets more swarms were turning black as dusk thickened into night. Whether one such face, one dark lump was added or subtracted — what could it matter to him? At once dangers mounted: his car could be searched; someone might overhear them talking; he, in his fear of being denounced, might denounce her to Rost.

There was a pattern to those evenings, as if, hurrying through the windy streets, she was keeping a series of appointments: with hope, with fear, and with the thoughts that made her mouth taste of rust. What if Aurelia doted on Barbara just for the sake of the money Barbara might get? What if Barbara were already getting the money and sharing it only with Aurelia, or with no one, at night stealing outside to eat and eat and eat?

Then the last appointment with Barbara's bony hands groping toward the bag with next day's bread, and at once Tola longed to run back, to beg their forgiveness for such thoughts. It was to her dreams about the Meister that she ran instead. Yet in such moments he failed her, the rumors of his great kindness fitting him as little as stories of youthful exploits fit an aged, balding man.

She came upon those other rumors among the "natives" — the women from Skarzysko, like all old-timers fond of recalling their pioneer days: how, knee-deep in snow, they had felled trees in the Appellplatz, how they had built the barracks with hardly a tool but their frozen hands.

"In those days, too, a pregnant woman was discovered," a girl said one evening.

"No, it was just talk, there was no pregnant woman in the camp then," said the others. Everything was a legend among them, the eyewitnesses gone, the stories they had left behind blurred by much repeating.

"That woman was here," the girl insisted. "She's dead now, but when she gave birth nothing was done to her." To her — nothing.

But for days everyone felt like creeping under the earth, because of the child's cry. It had gone on and on, so it was said.

Tola listened, then walked outside. The days had grown longer. In the woods the last sun wove a luminous nest in the thicket. And to her it seemed that a wail was piercing the descending dusk; not a child's — she, who had not seen a child for years, had forgotten its sound — but the mechanical moan of a siren that makes the passersby start, then walk on faster.

A murmur of tired voices came from the barracks while she sat on the threshold, her face buried in her hands. Often the pack of musty clothes on her back would seem to change into a being so weak that it had to be carried; and then fear would strike her — of this cry, of what soon might be demanded of her, who was neither sensitive nor good. "Clever," they called her. "How enterprising you are, how clever!" they exclaimed when she gave them her peddler's bread.

Darkness had fallen by the time she got up. Where the glowing nest had hung, moonlight trailed. She felt calmer. Soon, without telling anyone, she would ask the Meister for help.

Chapter 21

THE NEXT NOON, smiling like a girl displaying her engagement ring, Barbara was showing her hand around, to Aurelia, to Alinka, then to the group of Kaelanki who sat nearby. And what she at last came to show Tola was a green ring woven out of the new grass.

"Ah, look what I found, Tolenka," she beamed, "there along the bushes everything is getting green."

"Spring is coming," Tola said; Barbara said that the wind felt fine; and silence fell, as always when they were alone. At last, merely to break this silence and regretting it at once, Tola began talking of the Meister.

"Tomorrow is Sunday. I'll get ready tomorrow, and the day after I'll speak to him."

"To him, to a German?" Since the Strafappell, Barbara no longer said "the Krauts"; Germans, it was now, the Germans or *they*. From then on only her eyes spoke: the bewildered look meant fear, the measuring — doubt that Tola could have such daring; and the sharp startled glance was envy. "Together," Barbara said fervently. "Were it not for me, you'd never have thought of going to him, of going into such danger, I mean. Now I won't leave you in the lurch. We'll go to him together."

"A delegation?" A delegation, Tola explained, would never do. The fewer there were who knew what she was asking, the safer the Meister would feel. Anyhow, how could Barbara help her, when she hardly knew a word of German?

"Perhaps you're right. Oh, Tolenka, how well you've figured everything out! And what pluck you have!"

"What pluck," Barbara's glances said the next day. But in the evening, when Tola was preparing herself — washing her clothes, ironing them by passing each piece against the stovepipe, Barbara looked nonplused. "Tola, what are you doing this for?" Clearly she could not contain herself any longer. "How can you even think of such trifles?"

"Because I'm a Cinderella, off to a ball without the help of a good fairy. Tomorrow I must get away from the ashes. Tomorrow he must see in me someone like himself. You still don't understand? Then look around."

And Barbara looked: at the fingers hunting for lice, the mouths gaping in shouts.

"No . . ." she stammered. "No, I don't believe in it."

"You don't believe that I'll speak to him?"

"No! Why do you say such things? I mean — I don't quite know what I mean. Only, he's seen too much; he must have gotten used to what he has seen."

"I've decided," Tola said.

The door had closed behind the Meister, the corridor was empty, yet Tola still could not understand what had happened. Just another rehearsal had taken place; since it had gone wrong she would rehearse again, then would speak to him.

But it was over. She had failed — though not through fear only. At night the fear had come. "He's seen too much," she remembered, and what he had seen stood before her like a dark shapeless mound, from under which she must lift the child, must hold it up to him so that it would be the first, the only one he had ever seen here. In her dreams the mound fell upon her; she could not breathe, she awoke and lay staring at the sparks dying out in the stove. In the morning the fear was gone. Instead, a sense of expectation filled her, so lighthearted that she talked and jested till all but Barbara laughed.

Here in the narrow corridor joining the Meister's office to the hall the joy began to ebb away. She felt calm, only very tired. And the waiting was hard. Blurred to a shadow by the door of opaque glass, the Meister would rise toward her. He was coming, she must tear herself away from the wall. The shadow vanished. He had sat down again. And again she stared at the gleaming glass.

Behind it, the telephone rang. Listening intently she caught isolated phrases: the shells — the supplies that had not come on time, which caused — what, she could not hear.

The receiver clicked, a chair scraped against the floor. Now — he was coming. She moistened her lips, then, arms glued to her side, walked toward the door. It opened. And just as the Meister halted, to straighten out the red swastika armband, she felt it — the speck creeping down her wrist.

She clenched her fist, hid it, and felt maimed with one arm cramped behind her back. Under her sleeve the louse moved on, up to her armpit, and there it seemed to multiply, the gray specks dotting her collar, her neck and hair. She must not think about it; she must be calm.

Her voice did sound calm. "Herr Meister," she heard it saying, "may I take just a few minutes of your time?" That he, not used to being so accosted, would shrink away she had expected; but not this look, blank and at once turning toward the cracked wall. "Herr Meister, once you were most kind to us." Her voice — she felt contempt, almost hatred, for its pedantic clarity — delivered the carefully memorized phrases. "It was in Werk A, Herr Meister, when we first arrived here from the Cracow camp." At that point it began. Not fear yet, just a grotesque sensation as if her mouth were moving with no sound, as if like the lice earlier the red spots on her face now multiplied, covering her with a rash. Somewhere a voice — it no longer seemed hers — was talking of kindness: she had always remembered his kindness; his kindness had encouraged her to turn to him in her helplessness.

Had it only seemed so, or was he flushed with anger? She could not look. Her whole strength was needed to move her mouth. "As you may know," said that mouth, "there is a woman here . . . this woman . . ."

His blush darkened. He glanced at her, as at a beggar presuming to be familiar — not angrily, just with great surprise that one so irrelevant and so revolting could bar his way. And at once the child to be born was coming to resemble her, as though those distant eyes had passed on to her their knowledge of what it was bound to become — insignificant, always hungry, always cold. With this sense of utmost futility came the conviction that someone like herself must be crushed, not in punishment but because this might be safer, because it could not matter less.

"Excuse me," she said hoarsely. "I . . . it's nothing . . . I don't feel quite well."

Only now when it was over did he really look at her, with resentment, with something like pity and shame. But she was already moving away, hastily first, then stopping, afraid to stumble upon a quavering line on the floor. It was only a ray of sun. She crossed it. Turning toward the wall she stared at the crack that he had watched before. And again she was waiting — now for his shout, for blows, for any sign that he might denounce her, so that she would not return to Barbara with nothing.

But the Meister was walking back toward his office; and with every step, he — who had centered in himself now all the benevolence she knew, now all the dread — shrank into just another German, stooped, with cuffs showing frayed edges from under the brown uniform. And at last he was gone.

The damp speck was creeping down into her palm. Her nails clicked. She flipped her finger. And just then Barbara came in.

"Will he denounce us?" Barbara could hardly speak. "Will he?"

"Don't worry. He has nothing to denounce." She would have gone on — about the louse, about the sense of her own grotesqueness — but Barbara interrupted her.

"Still, what courage you had," she exclaimed. And Tola said nothing.

"Hardly had I begun when he muttered something and walked away," Tola said to Barbara at noon when they came into the clearing. "Please, forget the entire incident," she added, then turned to leave.

"Stay, do stay, Tolenka," Barbara said. "I can't even remember when we talked last, really talked."

When Tola had said "You look Jewish, Barbara" — that was the last time; Tola did remember.

Now Barbara talked of Aurelia. Aurelia was good, so good there were no words for her; without Aurelia she would have gone under; Aurelia understood her, saw right into her heart. "And she needs me, too," Barbara whispered. "I know what she is like, ever since I saw her cry that night after the Strafappell, I do. And now I'll take care of her, I," her voice deepened, "I'll do everything for her, you understand? Everything — even what is most terrible."

"Don't," Tola flinched, "don't say such things."

"But then, what else is there to be done?"

"Nothing. There has never been anything."

"Then why did you give me that odd look when I said — ?"

"Because of the way you said it, so solemnly, with such awe."

"Go on." Barbara came closer. "You've begun. Now go on."

"I will. 'Terrible,' you said to me; terrible to you means tragic, and noble, ever so noble. And why? Because you will do it, you, as a self-sacrifice, for Aurelia's sake. And when this thing happens it will be terrible, not in your sense but in mine — terribly ugly and meaningless, to everyone, even to Aurelia."

"Go on, I'm listening."

Tola was silent. "Barbara," she said at last, "I don't know why I said that. Only when the time comes — when this thing happens — then — you mustn't come to me."

Distant, like the Meister's, Barbara's eyes looked at her. "I wonder," she said dreamily, "I really wonder what you get out of putting such thoughts into my head?"

"Less than you know, Barbara." Tola grinned, then watched how Barbara ran on to Aurelia, and how, bending down her heavy body, Aurelia began drawing in the dirt — a map of Russian victories most likely, because Barbara gave an approving nod. Tola too was drawing: first a bunk, then a figure, just one, upon it. She was this figure. Moving to another barracks, changing to another shift here meant separation, complete, like emigrating to another country. Perhaps she would emigrate, perhaps. Seeing Alinka approach, she rubbed out the drawing with her foot.

"There is something I must talk over with you. Come this evening to the washroom and bring Barbara along," the girl ordered, then walked away with stiff heavy steps. For the second Sunday in a row Alinka had been nabbed and sent to load shells, from which she returned so worn out that she could barely move.

"It wasn't accidental that I went to load shells," Alinka announced as the three of them stood round the rusted trough. "Each time I volunteered so that I could see him."

"See whom?" Barbara broke in.

"Stop interrupting, then you'll find out. The soldier, the fat soldier who passed us when we were marching back from the Entlausung. No, I'd better tell you everything from the start." To protect herself from eavesdroppers, Alinka turned on the faucet. "I met him

about a month ago. I cleaned for him, he gave me peppermints. This
will sound senseless to you. I knew he was a Nazi, he said so himself;
more, when he spoke about 'der Führer' he was practically melting.
And yet, I don't understand how this is possible but it seemed possible then, I felt he was a decent man, stupid, abysmally so, yet decent. He has been supervising the loading of shells. I went to see
him, and I . . . I understand nothing. Has he been poisoned with
propaganda? He isn't the same. He beats — not to draw blood
like the Picrine Meister — yet he beats, I saw it myself. This Sunday he noticed me; and then, you know what happened? He
couldn't disappear fast enough, as if he were ashamed. And what
of? Of what he is now? Of what he was when we met? Because
then he was good to me; then he said, 'Der Führer hat die Kinder
nicht gemeint.' "

"What about der Führer?" Barbara blurted out.

"The Führer never meant children," Alinka said very softly.

"Oh!" Barbara looked at Tola. "I . . . don't know," Barbara
wailed faintly when Tola kept silent. "I haven't been in the camp
long enough, I don't know."

"Well," Tola said, "I do know."

"I just wanted to tell you about him." Alinka stopped. No one
spoke. From paper sticking to the pipe yellowed scrubbing powder
sifted into the trough.

"This filth!" Barbara said through her teeth. "No, Alinka, don't
go yet. How soon will it be?"

"How can one tell exactly?"

"I don't mean exactly. I mean . . . you know, when exactly did
it happen; you know . . . this thing . . . in Radom?"

Alinka counted, bending her fingers. "In two weeks it will be exactly nine months," she said.

A clock seemed to have been put on the bunk that evening: "Two
weeks," it ticked, "ten days — eight — " And when Barbara tried to
run away into her dreams about "after the war," the ticking only
got louder. Then she would move close to Aurelia. "Are you cold?"
she would whisper. "Should I rub your feet?"

"Yes, I feel rather cold," Aurelia always answered; and as the
frozen feet grew warm within Barbara's palms, a peace would fill

her, the same peace felt the night after the Strafappell, as if only touch was pure enough to bring it back.

"Tola," some obscure remorse would seize her, "you too must be tired, Tolenka, you — sleep well."

"Keep quiet, and let Aurelia get some rest." This was Alinka calling from the bunk below. Even at night she spoke in her business-like manner, only more sharply, like one vexed at having to keep such late working hours.

"Five days," the clock ticked on the night when Barbara started out of sleep. Something — a sound — had stopped the moment she looked up. But the barracks was quiet, Aurelia lay breathing evenly. "Why do you wake me up?" she complained when Barbara bent over her.

"I don't know. I thought I heard something."

"What is it? Has it begun?" Tola sat up at once.

"Has it?" came from the bunk below.

"Nothing has begun. Nothing hurts," Aurelia answered. "Please, I feel so tired, let me sleep." They too were tired; one by one they fell asleep.

Only then Aurelia scrambled down from the bunk.

Clasping her belly like an overfilled basket she ran outside, then stopped, and pressed it against the damp barracks wall and pushed and squirmed. Nothing helped. Powerful, refreshed by the long rest, the kicking within her went on. Now she knew what was inside her: no disease, no boil, but a tormentor who sucked her strength, snatched every crumb away, then hid to make her believe the persecution was over, and now came back for good. Rhythmical and hard, the kicking went on.

Rhythmical and loud, thumping came from a distant watchtower. Aurelia listened. She tore her coat open. Slowly, like someone taking part in a procession, she walked on, her white shift puffed by the wind, her coat flapping, and behind her the bandage in a thin long train. Someone squatting in front of a barracks saw her and ran away, someone started and cried out, while she walked on, closer and closer to the tower. She stopped. High up in the tower silence fell, as if even the guard were amazed by what he saw: a misshapen woman, with wide glittering eyes and shoulders drawn back to display fully the big pale ball of her body.

The thumping resumed; she waited. Then heavily, as if after a long journey to pay a visit she had found no one at home, she began walking back. And above hovered the light that tied together her, the tower, and the guard.

Chapter 22

THE FOLLOWING day a frenzy of reorganization swept over Schmitz. All but two of the transport men were sent to Trotyl; new methods of packing shells were introduced; and the two shifts were to work alternately, one week in daytime, the other at night.

Night came to Tola like a gift. At night she was indispensable — the "six" once again, on the alert against the permanently drunken foreman, against sleep, and against what could begin any moment.

There was something else still to guard against — the mood that had come over Aurelia. She hardly ever spoke; spoken to, she answered with a vague gesture, then sat absently fiddling with a shell. Suddenly she would start and would cling to Alinka, or would stare at Barbara with a pained, helpless look. "Don't stare like that!" Barbara cried back. And "Don't touch me — it hurts!" she pleaded whenever anyone came near, with her cupped hands protecting the boil that had sprouted on her shoulder.

"Together, Mr. Foreman, let us stay together," all of them except Aurelia pleaded every night, because the sudden reorganization was just a cover-up for a shortage of work, and all the time women were being sent to chores outside Schmitz.

On the third night of the new shift, the foreman would not relent. He shouted, he shook his rubber truncheon. "I'll go," Tola said at last. "I won't be far away. If it begins, send for me at once."

If it began tonight everything was prepared, she thought, walking with a group of women through the clearing. Goldberg, who came each midnight with the soup, would take them back to the camp; Goldberg when told the whole truth had found a safe place for Aurelia, the clothing depot which stood far away from the towers. Still, it's unlikely that anything could begin so soon. With older women such things always take longer, she reassured herself, walking into the shed.

Squatting low on the packing crates, the women transferred the cardboard husks from carton to carton. Tola worked rapidly. But all the time, while arranging the husks in rows, bringing empty cartons, pulling the full ones away, she kept looking toward the door. A sudden rustle and she dashed outside; no one was coming, the steps she heard were just the transport men unloading their cart in the clearing. And again she crouched on a crate, the husks flitting past her tired eyes.

"I must rest for a moment. If anyone's looking for me I'm there." She pointed to the pile of husks.

She could not rest. "Herr Meister, may I speak to you?" the rehearsal went on. "Tola, who would have thought you would save it!" Barbara seemed to exclaim. Then the Meister again, looking at her as at a beggar. She burrowed deeper into the husk and lay listening to the song drifting over the shed.

The singing had stopped when she woke up. Instead a girl was retelling *Gone with the Wind,* an all-time favorite in the camp. "Scarlett, Rhett Butler," dreamily the girl dwelt on the outlandish names. Then a pause. Someone was panting, someone — not Barbara or Alinka — was calling her name. By the time she had climbed out, whoever had come in was gone.

"An old woman was here. She said you must come at once to the hall. She said you must be careful."

"Careful — be careful!" the woman called after her, as she ran through the clearing. Suddenly she halted. What if everything would be as always, Barbara and Alinka comforting Aurelia, she left alone with the child — with what must be done to it? She turned around, then walked on back to the shed.

"I couldn't come," in the morning — and by then everything would have to be over — she would say. "A guard stopped me. I almost got shot." Once again she stood still. And now she was running back to the hall.

Tears glistening on her ashen face, old Alexandrovitch was groping through the corridor. "Have you heard?" She clutched at Tola. "Have you?"

"What's happened?"

"Bread. They stole my bread — they stole it!" The wail followed Tola as she ran on.

A lassitude such as heat might bring had settled over the hall. Slumped to dark heaps, the two transport men dozed on a pile of crates; at the tables the women swayed drowsily; and the few still groping for a shell stopped midway, as if they gasped "Hot, ah, much too hot to stir." Only it was cold, bitterly so.

Loaded high with crates, a cart was blocking Tola's way. She could not push it away. "Transport!" she called, "transport, help me!"

"Shh, the foreman!" a whisper warned her. It stopped; from the front of the hall came a moan, soft, almost tuneful like a chant. Aurelia was moaning. Why were they allowing it? Why hadn't they taken her away to the latrine?

"Transport!" The cart moved on and Tola flinched. No one was left to take Aurelia away; Aurelia was alone; the one bending over her was not Barbara, but an old woman with a shaved head.

"Aurelia, where are they? Where have they gone?" Everyone was gone. A stranger bearing an incidental resemblance to Aurelia Katz had taken her place, a tightlipped woman who seemed not to know her, whose rapt, glittering eyes looked only at one point — at the glass door opposite. Behind it, on a bed made out of two chairs the foreman lay, a large white pillow under his head.

"Aurelia! Where are they?"

Reluctantly Aurelia turned. "They left," she said with an unconcerned shrug.

"They left!"

"What else could they do?" the old woman protested, "O.D. men kept coming. First they took the freckled girl away, then the Pole. She begged them to let her stay, she begged me to call you at once. But I couldn't get out. The foreman is in a state, he's drunk."

"And she, how long has she been so — "

"So strange? Since the Pole left. I asked her what's wrong, but — " The woman broke off.

Heavily, Aurelia got up. "There," she pointed at the carton with the cardboard husks, "I want to lie down there. I'm in pain." Detached, utterly toneless, her voice seemed to come from some far-off heights.

Aurelia was in pain, Aurelia must not stay in the hall — Tola knew this, yet she did nothing. Next to her Aurelia began to rock gently;

everywhere the women were rocking; pain and lack of sleep were the same; Aurelia just needed sleep, Aurelia should lie down like the foreman, with a pillow under her head.

Above the pillow an arm rose. Aurelia bent forward, and now she was stretching out her arms, as though trying to swim toward the foreman across the hall.

"No! Don't!"

The arms moved down. From the bag Aurelia pushed across the table, Alinka's comb fell out, a strand of kinky hair still caught in its teeth. Hazily Aurelia stared at it, then at her own hand with the same strained look, as if that too were something left behind by one gone away. This hand shook.

"Tola, help me!" Aurelia whispered. "I don't know what I'm doing, help me."

"I'll help you, I will." She supported Aurelia under the damp armpits and held her with all her strength, not only to help but to feel this staggering body, this sweat, so that she would grasp at last what was happening. "I'll help you, just come with me," then to the women at each table, "Tell Goldberg we're in the latrine. Remember, tell him!" The steep threshold, the corridor and the tear-stained face; then at last the latrine.

At the doorway Aurelia stopped. Thoughtfully, as though weighing something, she looked from the women dozing in the stench to her belly; suddenly her fist clenched, she jerked, and shoved Tola aside. The stranger was back; the stranger had to be pushed into the cubicle, and down onto the seat.

"Go to the other cubicle; someone is sick in there." The shaved woman kept watch over them. She left and others took over. Yet Tola kept clutching at the knob. She was afraid, not of the foreman — he was still asleep — but of this woman with the pursed mouth and the fixed stare in her eyes.

At times their look softened. "Aurelia, how bad is it? Aurelia, do answer me," she pleaded, and at once the fixed stare came back, as though the two of them were playing hide-and-seek, Aurelia sneaking closer, then as Tola was about to catch her, disappearing behind the stranger, who sat there inimical and still.

"Goldberg." She was trying again. "He will come soon, will take us back." Aurelia kept staring at the wall.

"It must be almost eleven. In one hour you'll be able to lie down, just one hour."

A shrug, showing the length of an hour to one who was in such pain.

"Time will pass. And now, tell me, can I do anything?"

"Nothing."

"It's cold in here, let me wrap you in your coat."

"No."

"Your mouth is parched. Do you want some water?"

"No."

Scissors seemed to snap, cutting every thread with which she was trying to draw this woman closer. And outside feet shuffled, the door creaked as the women were going back to the hall.

"Back! He's up! He's in a fury!" someone shouted. Again a creak, sabots clattered away. And now only water dripped, loud in the silence.

"Aurelia," her voice shook, "Aurelia, how is it now? Say something, say anything to me."

No answer.

Clutching harder at the knob, Tola pressed her ear to the door. A rattle, probably of the transport cart, came from the hall, then a thud and a hoarse yell. "Work!" the foreman was yelling, "work, or I'll give it to you!"

"He won't come in here," Tola whispered. "I'm certain he won't. Only we can't just sit like this. I . . . I cannot. Do it for me, let's talk about something."

It was only Tola who talked. Frantically, in a strange rasping voice, she talked of Barbara and Alinka — that they had been forced to leave, that they would come back, any moment, soon. She waited. "Barbara," she began anew, "Barbara needs you more than ever. Yes, you always tell me how . . . how sensitive she is. And she, 'Without Aurelia I would have gone under,' she said to me. And if . . ." "If anything happened to you," she had almost said; but nothing would happen, Goldberg would come soon, would take them back. "And," she groped, "and . . . you . . . you must take hold of yourself. Think how good the news is."

Though aware how poor was her imitation of Aurelia comforting Barbara, she went on and on — about the news now. "The

Allies are advancing," she said. "Who knows, in months, even in weeks — " She stopped. Aurelia was smiling a thin, twisted smile. "You don't believe a word of it," the smile said.

She did not believe it, she could not. And it seemed that this woman with the fixed stare knew everything she had ever tried to hide: that her "all will end well" had been just an aping of Barbara — this Aurelia knew; that tonight in the clearing she had almost run away; and that her going to the Meister had been a hoax; this too.

"Aurelia, was the Meister in the hall tonight? Was he?" A drop of spittle oozed down the pursing mouth. "You!" Tola was almost shouting. "What are you paying me back for, what have I done to you?"

"Nothing."

She gave in. She squatted there, staring at the black streaks oozing from under the partition wall. They widened. The slops seeped into her shoes, and each time she stirred, a squeal came, as though something was being squashed.

"Aurelia, it must be close to twelve." She spoke just so as not to hear the squeal.

"Women, what time is it? Women — anyone there?"

"Anyone there?" Once before she had called like this — in Cracow, when she had hidden under the mattress during the selection. Now selection aimed at the two of them was taking place. As then the dust, so now the stench was clogging her breath; as then Seidmanka, so now this woman would break out, screaming so loudly that the foreman would come, the O.D. men, and at last the guards.

If this scream came she would hide somewhere — yes, under the barracks that stood on stilts. She would leave the camp with the dayshift, would come back to a different barracks, in which no one knew her, so that Barbara would never hear she was there. She would never see Barbara again if this scream came.

No! Aurelia would not do this. She seemed hardly in pain, her breath was quiet, and now, now at last she was about to speak.

"I think I'd better go back," Aurelia said casually, as though they were sitting here just to while the time away.

"Back? To the hall? The pains may start again, you'll moan, and if the foreman hears you — "

"So what? This thing is not like shoes."

"Like what?"

"Like shoes. This thing is not sabotage, like stealing conveyor belts to make shoes."

Somewhere a door slammed. The bulb swung, and a chunk of plaster fell into the puddle.

"In Cracow." Aurelia regarded the puddle. "Yes, in Cracow this thing was considered illegal, but not here. Nothing will happen to me if I lie down."

"Illegal — not illegal — nothing will happen," the casual voice went on and on. Soon more voices seemed to join it, speaking of that other woman, who was dead by now, but to whom nothing had been done when she had given birth.

If Aurelia went back to lie down nothing might happen to her; if Aurelia went back everything that had to happen after the birth would be out of their hands.

"I'm going back — let me pass."

"Stop it!" Tola shrieked. "Nothing is legal here, they may do anything to you, understand me? Anything!"

Did she imagine it, or did Aurelia give her an odd, a haughtily mocking glance? She could not tell. And Aurelia's immobile face told her nothing. Trying to flee this face she looked from the cracks on the wall to the specks of plaster floating upon the puddle. But the face pursued her. Swaying to and fro, it moved between the two walls. After a while the swaying stopped; blank, the sunken eyes closed, this was a face of a statue or of one dead.

"Aurelia, are you in pain?" Had she spoken, had she just meant to? She did not know, she knew nothing anymore. She and this motionless woman were merging together till they were no longer separate, till she could not tell which of them imposed, which accepted, this stony calm. Water dripped, plaster crumbled through the gray air. Slowly, painlessly, her body too seemed to crumble away; she felt no cold, no fear; she was gone, only her eyes were left her.

Those eyes saw a hand — huge, yet not cruel, just systematic about its task. She and Aurelia were this task: the hand was molding them — gave her a caved-in belly and a chest with no breasts, Aurelia the bloated belly and the swollen legs. Once more the hand would press, the fingers would flip to discard the squashed specks. If Aurelia screamed, her turn would come tonight; if not, then on another night not far off. Others had passed through this hand — their names just items in the long catalogue of losses.

This loss too, it seemed to her, had happened long ago. Long ago Aurelia had broken out screaming; long ago she herself had hidden under a barracks. Now, while awaiting her own turn, she was just remembering — the night, the frenzied cry. And when to prove that they were still here, still together, she stroked Aurelia's forehead, this touch had given her no proof; what she had stroked felt cold and slightly damp, like the knob she was clutching still.

It was at the knob that Aurelia was staring. She was listening to something — to the door opening in the corridor. The foreman was coming; Aurelia would make him come with her cry.

Someone else was crying, was wailing as once before tonight. "Bread. They stole my bread — " old Alexandrovitch had wailed, clutching at her. "Aurelia — they killed Aurelia," and Barbara would clutch at those passing by, as if to be killed were like being stolen, as if those capable of such a theft could repent and bring back what they had taken.

"No," she whispered, "no!" then listened. A bang. This was the latrine door; the thumps, the foreman hobbling in; and the gasps that came from behind her — this was Aurelia, struggling up, her mouth wide open.

She gripped this mouth, wrung and twisted it, till the cry throbbed within her palm. But he had heard the cry, he was banging, was rattling the knob.

"Keep quiet!" Tola let go of the knob. "Quiet!" She flung the door open and stood, her legs astraddle, her arms spread out so that she would hide the bloated body behind her. But the face must not be hidden. Flushed, the lips parted as in a cramped smile, this was the face of one who was sick — just old and very sick.

"Mr. Foreman, I beg you — look at her." She herself was looking only at this face, and when the dazed eyes glanced at her the foreman was not fearful anymore; he too was old, he too had eyes dazed with lack of sleep.

"Mr. Foreman" — she must pierce through this daze — "you see how sick she is. It's typhus, I'm sure. How could I leave her alone, when she's in fever, and something hurts her. Now did you hear it, did you hear her moan? For God's sake let her have some rest. An old woman like her — " breaking off she reached out, because his lame leg bent under him, he staggered, hit against the wall.

"To Picrine — off to Picrine you go," he blubbered, and was gone.

Only now came fear, then relief, then a choking fury. "You," Tola muttered, "you wanted to scream, didn't you? Stop looking so innocent; it wasn't I who wanted you to do this, you tried to make an end of it — you! I won't let you, I — " She broke off. Something soft was brushing against her — the bandage hanging from under Aurelia's coat.

"The bandages . . . I forgot about them . . . they must be hurting you." She was hurrying to remove at least this hurt, but her stiffened fingers fumbled with each strip, each tangled knot. "It's almost done, almost," she repeated, crouching lower and lower yet, until she was kneeling in the puddle. Another bandage, another knot. Reddish and bruised, the enormous belly pushed against her, like a knoll of clay earth over which wheels had rolled.

"Aurelia, do you think I should shave tomorrow?" Tola remembered, and it was as if the gratitude of the dead man had been passed onto her, until it was she who had been comforted in her terror, she who now must give this comfort back. Carefully, lest an abrupt gesture would impair what had gathered in her, she got up. "Soon it will be over," she said, "soon you'll lie down." Even the place where Aurelia should have lain down she saw: a white bed, a white, quiet room. Somewhere there were still such places, somehow it should be possible to carry Aurelia on and on until a door would open upon this safety, this peace.

"I'll carry you." Tola drew closer. "If there's no place on the cart I'll carry you all the way back."

The crumpled eyelids rose. "I'll carry you," Tola repeated whenever the dazed glance brushed past her. And then she grew still, because Aurelia was about to speak.

"It hurts," Aurelia said sternly. "It hurts" came softer and softer. And it was as if Aurelia were descending a long flight of stairs, stopping to look at the heights left behind, yet coming closer and closer, until in an apologetic whisper she stammered, "Oh —

Tolenka — how it hurts!" and a spasm thrust her into Tola's arms.

Together, with their joined hands, they gagged the cry, but soon more cries came, rattling, pushing against the trembling mouth. Then a moment of respite. Brushing off a sweaty strand of hair, Aurelia drew away. When she nodded, "Now it's better," Tola said; her motioning arm meant "The pain comes in waves." But what her pointing at Tola was saying Aurelia had to translate: "You're good," she said softly. "Yes, you are." And more cries had to be gagged.

The spasms grew more prolonged, the gasps harsher, and when they ceased Aurelia's mouth went on moving without a sound. "I — it's not the pain." She licked a drop of blood off. "Only I'm afraid to be left alone with it, to see it, and — "

"You won't see it, I promise." Tola spoke calmly but had to look away to hide her suspicion: the ugly unwanted suspicion that everything up to now — the stony calm, the cry, even the soft "You're good" — had been a desperate pretense aimed at extorting this promise out of her. Yet the joy was still here, because for once she had been called not "enterprising," not "clever," but simply "good."

Soon afterward Goldberg came in. Without a word he walked out, without a word he came back, then led them outside where the O.D. men stood around the cart. They loaded up, the soup barrels first, Aurelia next, and the small procession moved on into the woods. And just when the darkness turned bitter with picrine Aurelia rose and stood with her arms flung forward, like a charioteer driving on his horses with thin, high-pitched cries.

"No!"

Aurelia slumped down. Motionless and squat, she seemed to be one of the barrels jingling with their torn hoops.

Chapter 23

IN THE CLOTHING DEPOT that smelled like a trunk opened after a long time, Aurelia lay on a real bed, a few prayer shawls for her pillow, a man's coat for her coverlet. Another coat screened the window, its sleeves flapping as the doctor came in. The doctor was a small man, with a disproportionately large, graying head, and a sallow face that looked angry at first then startled, as though something desperately needed had been lost to him. He had lost the right to anger: anger against the young wench he had hoped to find here, her body so fattened up that seeing how well she had been paid for what had caused her present misery, "You fool!" he could have flared up. "Can't you watch out when you whore around?"

Instead, Aurelia lifted to him her withered face. So he just mumbled something, then, stumbling on the clothes piled everywhere, he began pacing up and down.

He halted. He was only lifting up the coat covering Aurelia, yet it seemed to Tola that everything was already happening: the doctor was holding up something squirming and damp, he was forcing that damp thing upon her.

"You," the doctor turned to her, "where are you off to?"

"To stand six — to watch. Aurelia, I'm not leaving you, I'll be right there at the door." But as she was walking out Aurelia rolled to her side and watched her every step.

And outside everything was in flight. Swept by the wind, bits of offal floated past; from above a barracks roof smoke drifted to the green moonlit sky; while Tola crouched on the threshold, her arms clasped round her knees. The wind ceased; the cold immobile air lay like a crust of ice upon her. Whenever her face felt too icy she would walk inside, would say "I'm not leaving. I'm right here"; then, Aurelia's gaze following her, she would walk outside.

Once the doctor came out to her. "Last time, when a birth occurred, Dr. Rost was informed at once," he rapped out. "The woman was not punished, but Dr. Rost gave orders — " He spoke faster and faster, until a moan called him back.

"Dr. Rost — Dr. Rost — " she repeated after he had left. And the bespectacled man in spats seemed to her like another physician supervising each birth from afar with his orders: the child should be laid in cotton wool — he had ordered — the child should not be fed anything, not even water. Only last time those orders had not been followed; it had been fed, water with sugar. That was why everything had taken so long. Tola knew who had disobeyed Rost; she must run to the doctor, must beg him not to do it again. Instead she clasped her knees tighter. Soft, as at the night's beginning, the moans came from inside, and in the dark a shape seemed to loom, bedded in cotton wool, like a trinket wrapped carefully before it is mailed off. She shook herself; the white spot drifted away.

Her dreams were like waking. In dreams fear took a precise shape: now of Rost's gloved hand, now of the Lagerkommandant bending down toward her. But when she woke up, when from behind the door no sound could be heard, then the fear grew vague, like a dread that dreams bring.

The wind was blowing again; again she ran inside, bent down over the bed. Aurelia lay with her knees drawn up, her mouth now pushing the breath out, now snapping as if to snatch the rag that the doctor held.

Through a street crimson with flags the Lagerkommandant was walking toward her. The stamping rose louder: she started awake. "Someone's coming," she called, knocking on the door, "don't let her cry!" Only an O.D. man staggered by. "Picrine up!" he droned. "Three o'clock shift up!" Lights flashed, behind the grimy windows shadows swayed and swelled as if those getting up could inflate themselves. The paper swathings that made them swell swished as the picriniacs passed by. "Lights out!" All was dark, all still again. But no longer did she allow herself to doze off. Walking up and down she waited, until suddenly the scream burst upon her, piercing, as if Aurelia had won at last, had broken out into the dark. Silence again. When a light came through the opened door she recoiled.

"No, nothing yet." The doctor pressed a bucket and a squashed can into her hand. "Go! Get me some coffee and water."

"Water? What for? Why?"

"Because she's thirsty, that's why." And he pushed her with unexpected strength.

It was quiet in the kitchen. "Work, girls, work!" the Kaelanka in charge called, and beets splashed into the barrel, round which a group of women sat. The one who wasn't working — the one whom the Kaelanka was poking now — this was Barbara, sitting fast asleep.

"Barbara!" Tola called.

"You here? Has it begun?" Barbara jumped to her feet and already she was running to the Kaelanka, was stammering something, then ran on, to the door and out.

"Wait," Tola called. "I'm carrying something heavy, I can't run." But the street was empty, even the sound of footsteps had gone.

She walked on, the cold water dripping down her legs, the pail feeling lighter and lighter. Then a few meager tears moved down her face; because the water had run out from the leaky pail she was crying, because in the darkness she did not know her way. And when the tears stopped, she pressed her eyes tight, to bring more tears, for the child now being born. If only she could cry — a second, even one second would be enough — then she would know it was not she, really, who would do what must be done; then she would believe it was done for Aurelia, and for the child above all; and the fear would be gone — the sickening fear that she had grown used even to this. If only she could cry. If the others, if Barbara could believe that she had cried.

The light was out in the clothing depot. "Barbara!" she called walking in, "Barbara! Doctor!" But only the coat flapped against the window.

Then a cry — an infant's cry. She ran outside, held the door fast. The cry grew louder; it changed to a wail, as if the child had guessed she was standing there, her face pressed to the rough wood; as if it were begging her to come back in the only speech it knew. The cry bound her, it twined round her neck. And when it stopped, she still could not tear herself away, not until the wind pushed air down her tightened throat.

The blast forced the door open. The cry was back, rising over the creaking of hinges, over the loud, repeated bangs. Her eyes closed, she kicked the door shut, then walked away.

Where the cry could not reach her anymore, there she sat down, on a threshold again, again listening to the sounds coming from inside — the quiet breath of those asleep. And nothing seemed strange any longer, neither the cry's sudden return, nor the thought that the child had got up and was looking for her. Carrying a small shape in his arms, the doctor passed by; the cry broke out once more, and from inside the barracks a sigh rose, crumbled to a cough, then died out.

Back in the barracks where Barbara had brought Aurelia, the night went on as usual: "God, oh my God," the Rebbetzyn called out in her sleep. "Don't dare to touch the bread," someone muttered, just as on any other night. And for a moment it seemed to Barbara that nothing had happened. There had been no red wrinkled face, she had never dragged Aurelia on and on through the mud. Only the cold frightened her, the lifeless cold of the hands and feet that she must make warm again. Aurelia did not want to be warm; Barbara drew closer and Aurelia turned away. "Does it hurt still?" she asked, and Aurelia would not answer, even her breath she withheld. Barbara needed to hear her breath, she chased after it, leaning down till their faces touched. Then Aurelia lay still, pretending not to be there.

At the least noise, a screak, a rattling door, Barbara, too, pretended not to be there, lest they were coming for her, lest they would drag her back to the wrinkled face. That this face would never be she had promised Aurelia, but that was long ago, before she had seen it, before she had come to hate it — because she could not bear to look at it, because it was there.

The whispers around them, going on as usual, helped no more, everything was back: "This isn't right!" Aurelia was crying; the doctor running behind them, she was dragging Aurelia through the piles of clothes and on through the mud. And the splash — this was Aurelia falling down and lying, a black motionless heap, in the mud.

"But it's over now," she said to herself. "Aurelia, it's over," she pleaded. "They won't know who it was. They'll do nothing to you." At last Aurelia did respond. As if to embrace Barbara she raised her arms, they stiffened, the fists stuck out in black lumps. "Enough!" Aurelia said firmly. "I've had enough!" And she pushed Barbara away.

"Don't!" Barbara cried. "Don't! I'm so afraid . . . " And for the first time Aurelia would not comfort her. She lay there, her glittering eyes staring into the dark.

Barbara climbed down from the bunk and stood at the door, breathing in small careful gulps. When the familiar footsteps came from outside she gave a slow nod; when Tola walked in, she pushed her back to the door, then outside.

"You," her own voice seemed to come from far away, "you do it. It's easier for you."

"It's easier for me. Perhaps you're right, Barbara, perhaps . . . most likely so . . ." Tola fell silent. Tola was smiling a strange, almost jubilant smile. And now she was walking away, unhurriedy, her hand passing to and fro over her face.

At daybreak the doctor came. Aurelia would get well, he mumbled, she must just get some sleep, must eat, and she would be well. Later — though it was he who had ordered Barbara outside — he stood silent. "Well?" he snapped at last. "Well?" he repeated. And when she still would not answer he gripped her shoulder. Shaking her harder and harder, he muttered that this time would not be like the last — he would see to it — he would.

"Last time?"

"It lasted for days! Now . . . do you understand what I mean?"

Barbara understood him, yet said nothing. Above the woods the sun rose, the windows glittered, and a picriniac who was passing by stopped to pick up a rooted beet; from under his tightened fingers the black mush oozed into the mud. For money he would do it, Barbara thought, and felt sick.

"So, this must end," the doctor said. "For her sake, for everyone's sake it must. If it happens today, of itself — and I doubt this — you must send them a message."

"A message? To whom?"

To Tola and Alinka; they were going to load shells. "Why? Because some soldier is there." The doctor was already walking off.

She dragged herself back into the barracks. "Aurelia," she spoke

without coming near the bunk, "Aurelia, I'll be back — I'll — I — "
With each "I" she was stepping farther away. In the doorway she
halted and ran back. "Sell it!" She threw her coat on the Rebbetzyn's bunk. "Sell my coat and get her bread! You're going to
work? Then tell Goldberg to do it." And she dashed out into the
road.

At the corner, behind the Kaelanki's barracks, Alinka and Tola
stood. Bending down, Barbara stalked on, then stopped, out of their
sight yet close enough to hear them.

"I've had enough," Tola was saying. "Aurelia wanted to scream,
wanted to give herself up, and I didn't let her. So, I'm not going
anywhere. I've had enough."

Now Alinka was talking, about the child and the dispensary,
where it was, about the soldier, the Führer and the child. Then suddenly they were gone.

Ducking whenever they looked back, Barbara ran after them, lost
them in the crowd, ran on, until at last she saw them in the Appellplatz, in the column forming next to the gate.

"I can't stay — I cannot," standing before them she whispered.
Tola turned away. "Go back!" Alinka shouted. "I order you — go
back, you fool!"

"No, I can't bear it — I can't," Barbara begged; then seeing
Goldberg, waved at him, so that he would help her, would force
them to take her along. He only glowered at her. "So you left her,
Dziedziczka," he muttered, "all three of you left her, without anyone to give her a drink of water. And she is calling for you."

"For me?" Barbara started.

"No, for her," he pointed at Alinka, and already he was dragging
her out of the column, then away.

"A message — if anything happens, I'll send you a message,"
Alinka's call came from afar.

The column moved on. "Tola, if it happens of itself, she'll let us
know, will send us a message," Barbara fumbled. Tola walked on
with her eyes glued to the ground.

Chapter 24

IT WAS THE GLARE that Barbara could not bear: the glare of the vast yellow stubble, of the tracks running below the embankment, and of hills shining like green ice. Shells formed those hills. At the other end of the line that had just stretched out along the embankment more shells lay trapped in cages. Cautiously, as if the glare were sharpest next to her, Barbara glanced at Tola. And at last, though in an odd, toneless voice, Tola was speaking to her. "Here, your share." She handed Barbara a slice of bread.

"I, oh, I can't eat," with boundless surprise Barbara brought forth. "Tolenka, you want it?"

"No."

"I want it, madam," said an old picriniac who grabbed the bread, then carefully broke it in half. "His share," he pointed to the boy running over the tracks, "him and me are together."

In spite of all, Tola and she were together, too. "I — I left my coat behind." To show how frozen they were, Barbara raised her arms. "I left it to be sold, so that Aurelia can get something to eat." Her arms dropped down. She waited. "Tola," she cried, "Tola can't you understand?" Not she herself had said "It's easier for you" — Tola must understand — but someone else who had replaced her so completely that the suspension of her whole being, once hoped for, now seemed to have happened, and if wrongly, the fault was not hers. "Tola," she whispered, "later I'll explain everything to you, now tell me — is it true that Aurelia tried to give herself up? Is it?"

"Yes."

"No! I mean — why?"

"I don't know."

"You must know. Aurelia must have said something."

A train rumbled. "My butt, Professor." The boy was wrangling with a bald picriniac down on the tracks. And Barbara shuddered because in answer Tola had shaken her head. Yet she went on try-ing. The pain had driven Aurelia mad, she insisted, the pain and the fear. "But now it's over; the doctor said that Aurelia will get well, that — "

The rattle of a motorcycle broke in, and with it a new fear of a mission never believed in, yet to be undertaken soon. The motor-cycle stopped; yells came out from the tracks. He, Alinka's soldier was yelling, was chasing with a stick after the picriniacs. The rum-ble drew closer and suddenly everything — soldier, picriniacs, and tracks vanished in the billows of steam.

Slowly a freight train rolled in and stopped at the pile of caged shells. "Ah, look at this — Paris!" the old man marveled at the names on the cars, "and here, Co — Copenhagen, and Oslo. Ah, did he ever whack them!" he added, with the same mild surprise.

"The soldier," Barbara caught up with him, "the soldier beats, doesn't he?"

"Ah, and who doesn't beat?"

If he beat, he could not be trusted, she decided, and the mission was over before it began.

"If anything changes, I'll send you a message," Alinka had prom-ised. The message must come, there was no other way out. The message meant that she herself could rest, could sleep at last. Some-thing clanked, like chains bolting doors for the night; somewhere a voice was talking of sleep.

"Don't sleep! Take it!" the boy was shouting. Starting, Barbara reached out her hands. Ice scalded her palms, it was too heavy, that icy thing — she could not — she would let go. "Don't you dare!" Tola cried and, panting, Barbara passed the shell on. It was done, but now she needed time to catch her breath, to do something about the boil throbbing on her shoulder. There was no time. "Take it!" the boy kept shouting; more cold was thrust into her hands, more weight pulling her down, while the soldier's yells pounded against her head.

"Take it!" and the stare warning "Don't dare drop it!" Arms wrapped in paper — and Tola's arms, quick like gadgets fashioned just for such work. Between them she, consisting only of her hands, and the boil, throbbing like a second heart.

One green hill had been razed; the shells felt warmer, and even

her exhaustion began to bring comfort; it was too great to be all in
vain. Soon an exchange, invisible yet just, seemed to be taking place
— each throb of pain, each burden of a shell was accounted for,
then exchanged for rest for Aurelia. Sweat, burning her cracked
lips, she next added to this barter, then the peculiar sensation of
growing transparent, quite light. Hunger made her so light; but
Aurelia was not hungry. "Potatoes," Aurelia ordered, and a steaming pot stood before her, "bread," and Alinka gave her bread spread
thick with beet-marmalade. Suddenly, as on Barbara's sleepless
nights, the pots, the bread seemed to be snatched away, as if Aurelia
had to stay hungry, as if the coat Barbara had left behind could
provide no food.

"Watch it! You'll smash my foot!" The boy scowled. "I'll watch,"
she promised him, and herself, "I'll think of nothing — not till noon
when the O.D. men come from the camp."

It was hard to keep this promise. Having reached its peak, the exhaustion began to ebb away. Clear in the sunny air each detail
stood out before her: two crows strutting across the stubble, green
points of buds on the distant clump of birches, their trunks striped
dark like something seen last night — like the prayer shawls in the
clothing depot.

And with the birches it began. Nothing was safe, everything became a reminder of last night: the heap of earth of the one who had
fallen into the mud; the red wrinkled leaf of the face they had fled.
Even behind the boy with the shadow of a first mustache over his
lips a memory stood obscure, and better left so. Only Aurelia's
face she could not remember, no matter how hard she tried.

"Los! Arbeiten!" the soldier gasped, dashing by.

Oh, how she hated him, not just for those shouts and the swishing
stick, but for the gasps, affected to show that he, too, worked hard,
and for the barely smoked cigarette, which — why, if not just to
flaunt his German riches — he threw into the grass. Everyone
watched him, even Tola, as if she also were hankering for his butts.
The soldier whistled, the shells stopped coming. And shoving the
boy aside, the bald picriniac dashed for the butt.

"He — he, Professor," the old man snorted. "Was it grabbing you
taught to those goys in the university?" Laughter answered. And

when the breeze came, when a cloud muted the glare, everyone began talking, exchanging looks or at least sighs. Only Barbara was alone, Tola's eyes turning to glass under her least glance.

She tried talking to herself. "The message will come; everything must be over by the time we go back." The message seemed to her like a comforting being: "It's over," this being would whisper to Aurelia, "it happened of itself." And at last Aurelia would rest; for now what rest could she have?

"Take it!" Barbara stared at the boy, she nodded: "Me too! Together!" the boy had begged at the Strafappell, when Rost had ordered the Chinaman shot. "Rost — Rost's order's," and "Tola!" she cried, "does Aurelia know what Rost ordered last time? Tola, don't punish me now, speak to me."

"Does it matter whether she knows?"

"Of course it does."

"And what can she hope to feed it — soup?"

Soup — soup, kept buzzing in Barbara's head. Milk they needed, lots of fresh milk. Had Rost given no orders, had she, had all of them been rich like the O.D. men, the richest in the camp, they could never have had enough milk. "I did not understand," she said to no one in particular. That the child would come and vanish was all she had ever understood; but that it would come to stay and grow till it became like those picriniacs who got nothing because they could no longer get down from their bunks, of this she had never thought. Stop, stop thinking about it, she ordered herself. She even tried counting the shells — One, two, three. Yet the child would not be gone; hunger made him present, hunger joined them together, until above the boy's wheezing she could hear its cry demanding what she did not have to give.

Anyhow — it knows nothing else, she thought and for the second time this morning felt sick.

The nausea was over. But from then on she was looking only at the shells, as if except for them the world around her had changed to bread that she — what other loyalty was left — must refuse.

"And Aurelia," without knowing it she spoke out loud. "Can she eat, even a morsel, can she get any rest? Tola, listen to me. On that night after the Strafappell she got so angry at me. 'I don't care what happens to it!' she screamed. I — I believed her, even though later on she cried for it, I did. And now — Tola, what does it all mean to her now?"

"I don't know." Tola's eyes were no longer glassy, only immensely tired.

"But you used to know."

"It's different now."

"Different, why?" It hurt Barbara to speak, but as though to win someone over she went on, about the message again — that it must come, because . . . because it must, because it was best for Aurelia and for him too, for him above all. Even the train passing by confirmed that hope: a traveler had got off at the wrong station; realizing his error, the traveler could do nothing but leave.

Enveloped in the steam, the soldier ran past. Now, with Rost always there, he seemed not hateful, just foolish — a coarse foolish dolt, his sudden power gone to his head. He whistled. Instead of a shell the boy passed a can of water on to her. "Nine o'clock break, you can rest, lady," the old man said.

But she stood there, dazzled in the sun. It had been winter, she was freezing when she had left the barracks; now the heat of summer burned, as though seasons had gone by with no news from those left behind. Around her everyone was resting. Humming, the old man was unwinding the rags from his feet; the boy lay stretched out in the dry grass. If only for a moment, just one moment, she could be like the others: free to talk of the news, the Russians, and of the wild-strawberry plants — a girl was pointing out their bronze tendrils in the stubble.

"Aurelia, what a feast we'll have in June," Barbara heard herself say.

"My dear," this was Aurelia, "In June you'll have strawberries served to you, with sugar and cream."

Later, that's how it would be; later was time together, and sleep, and rest; later was the plenty that her coat, her shoes, and chores she must find would provide, now even its foretaste to be shunned, yet all there, like full bags waiting to be unpacked. Remorse too must be postponed till later; remorse for the wooden "I don't care what happens to it" she had forced out of Aurelia, and for more, much more. But now work was beginning again; she must watch out against the soldier running toward her.

He stopped next to the old man who, pointing at his toes, swollen, the skin a rubbery red, winked slyly as though to ask "Well, what do you say to this?"

"Schrecklich!" said the soldier, his face as red as the toe.

"Schrecklich, Herr Soldat, terrible," the old man whimpered secretively, but already those around pushed toward the soldier, shrieking, shoving under his eyes whatever they had — boils, sores, fingers no thicker than pencils, as if they were for sale, and cheaper than the old man's toes.

"Los! Weg!" Flailing at the air the soldier ran on.

"That dolt" Barbara muttered. "He could have let you rest, somehow — he could have."

"Really?" Tola asked sharply.

"Nu, it cost nothing to try." The old man smiled. "Anyhow, things will get easier soon. See, he's sending our O.D. men to get reinforcements."

"From camp?"

"Yes. Are you waiting, lady, for news from your cousin?"

"From my friend." Something overflowed in her, had to be spoken. "My friend is sick, very sick."

"Ah!" the old man heaved a dutiful sigh. "In about half an hour they'll be back."

She put that half-hour to use, trying to bribe some malicious powers: first, the manor went in exchange for the message; let it burn to ashes, what did she care? Next a more costly bribe, a year with Stefan, two, whatever might be demanded, as long as they would still be together. Could this be all she had to give?

"I'll be good to Tola." And that was her all.

White flakes, skin torn off the blistered hands, clung to the shells. Ready for another load, a train rolled in. She read the names on the cars, drank some bitter water. And now only the waiting was left.

"What did he expect — Samsons?" The old man chuckled as the soldier shouted at a group of old women. The "reinforcements" had come from the camp. Behind the women one of the O.D. men was sneaking along the line. He was stopping, was asking for someone. "Here," she called, and the boy helped her, waving at the O.D. man each time after he had passed a shell. A whistle stopped their flow. The O.D. man was standing between the boy and her.

"Talk louder!" she cried at him. "I can't understand you. Louder!"

"Quiet," the boy nudged her. The O.D. man was talking to the boy, was selling him bread — bread for cigarette butts. "And for me . . . no message?" she stammered out, then hazily watched the boy raking through his rags. "Professor, you stole my butts, you thief!" he screamed. The O.D. man walked on. The boy's hands were shaking as hard as her own.

She was the first to calm down. If the child had to vanish, why it had once mattered what would bring this about she no longer knew. Everything else was clear; the soldier was no Rost; the soldier, when he saw her boil, would let her go back to the camp at noon. By noon a line would have formed in front of the dispensary; she would not need to wait in the line, the doctor would take her right in. "It's over, it happened by itself," he would then tell Aurelia, while she herself must hide so that Aurelia would not hear of her return. In the evening she would go back to Aurelia. "I just heard that it's over," she would say and then — then Aurelia —

"You! Hurry!" the boy wheezed. She was hurrying, was trying to steady her arms, when with a choked gasp he thrust the shell into her hands. She lost her grip. Barely missing her feet, the shell rolled down the slope.

"Barbara!"

"It'll explode, it will hit the tracks and explode!"

"Barbara!" again; but she saw neither those fleeing nor the shell, stopped by a bush; saw only what had made her go all limp — Aurelia, though it was over, pushing her away with another "I've had enough!"

"What . . . what is it?" she muttered to Tola, then looked at the boy on his knees picking up the butts spilled where the Professor had stood, and then at the soldier bearing down upon her.

"Grosse Frau," he brandished his stick at her, "grosse Frau, los!"

"Brush him off like a speck of dust," Aurelia's voice seemed to order. "I cannot," she said. "I'm afraid." Then a frenzied bellow.

"Nix," she herself was bellowing. "Nix — too much." The pain was too much, she could not bear it, she would give it to him, to this yokel, this dolt.

"Hurts, nix beat!" she grabbed the stick. "Nix, Soldat, nix!" she snapped it in half, then stood looking away and afraid.

No one was shouting at her. The soldier must have gone away. But when she looked up, he was standing before her, his gaze straining as though to decipher something on her shoulder. From it pus was trickling, mingled with blood.

"Schrecklich," the soldier shuddered, "schrecklich!" And breaking into some gibberish he stepped close to her.

Ask him. Now I could ask him.

Somewhere a motorcycle seemed to rattle. The day was beginning all over again — with the mission never believed in, with the fear.

"He's gone, now go and lie down," Tola said hoarsely. "He ordered you to lie down and rest."

"Because he beat me?" Because he beats — even if he beats, Barbara repeated, sitting down on the slope. Did it really matter that he beat? She too had struck the Chinaman; she too longed to beat — not only the grabbers, the thieves, but even the picriniacs begging bread of her who had not a crumb to spare. Still, how he strutted, how he yelled! Tola understood those yells; Tola must tell her what to do. Getting up she tore out the tufts of dry grass, so hard did her fingers grip them.

Tola had a mouth black with grime, and a look warding her off.

"I don't know." Barbara disregarded that look. "He, the soldier isn't worse than the Meister. The Meister didn't denounce you. And perhaps the soldier too would keep quiet if I spoke to him. I don't know. You decide."

" 'Child' is 'Kind,' " Tola said gently, " 'woman' is 'Frau.' "

"What?"

"I'm teaching you what to say. You want to ask him for help, don't you?"

Barbara flinched.

"Yes, you have my permission, Barbara. Will you go to him?"

One by one the dry wisps slipped out of her grip.

"You see," Tola smiled, "it has been always like this, always. Of course, it would have been easier to say 'I was ready to ask him, when

Tola forbade me,' much, much easier. But everything that's easy is reserved for me; for you I'll make it hard. He beats because he's crazed by what he sees; he scatters cigarettes around for the picriniacs; he begged your forgiveness. Must I put even such thoughts into your head? You saw his face when he looked at you, and at the old man. You know that he's better than the Meister. Wait, I'll tell you something that will please you: I never spoke to the Meisster, I never even came near him. I lied to you, I did. But today, after the soldier hit you, I almost asked him for help, just out of vanity, Barbara, what else? You won't ever blame me openly, but your every glance will be like fingers pointing at me — the evil one, the coward! And I'm even more cowardly than vain; I won't take the risk, I won't ask him. Aurelia doesn't have to do it herself, that must be enough for her. Because the soldier might talk, out of stupidity, out of fear; because there are four of us, while the child is just one. Such calculations are also easy for me, everything is so easy that I should be thriving. But even I can't thrive here. And now . . . go!"

Barbara did not go yet. "Enough? No, not enough," she whispered, then slowly walked away.

"Enough . . . I've had enough" Aurelia's glittering eyes seemed to look at her. She had seen women with such eyes. "Get up," one said to them, and they just lay there and stared. "Get up, Aurelia," she would say, and Aurelia would not even push her away. Then they would dress her, would carry her to work, and with each day Aurelia would get thinner, yet heavier to carry, until one day they would leave her lying on the bunk and staring, would come back to find her staring at the same point, would leave her again and then —

"No!" she whispered. "No!" But wherever she looked she saw them — Aurelia's torn shoes, all that was left of her on the empty bunk.

Away at the tracks' other end two long lines were forming in front of the barrels. As through a haze Barbara saw Tola speak to an O.D. man who merely shook his head. And across from the O.D. man, the soldier disappeared behind the pile of gravel.

The haze thickened as Barbara walked on. But at the top of the gravel pile it lifted; she wanted to run back, to call Tola, to think over what must be done. It was too late: sliding, the gravel pulled her down, until she landed right in front of the soldier. He started with a thick grunt, then, having recognized her by the bloody scab on her shoulder, he sighed oddly, as though blowing at something hot.

"Soldat," she said, "soldat, nix talk," and finger pressed to her mouth she looked at what seemed least German about him, at his thick lips. Those lips parted in a smile, and "Frau," she whispered, "Frau hat Kind." With those words she entered a new, safe place, where what appeared strange was not such talk but fear of this man with the fat, troubled face; and the ease with which she, at a loss in any language, could speak to him showed how much at home she should feel there.

"Kind," she said, "Kind klein." How "klein" her hands explained, no bigger then their joined span. Aurelia was Schwester — long ago Tola had taught her the word — then stroking the motorcycle like a docile horse, she tried to show him she was asking for a ride, just for a ride to Skarzysko.

"Ska — Ska — lzysko." The trouble the word gave him made him even less frightening.

"Skarzysko," she corrected him. "Skarzysko. Familie — mine!"

But though he looked most pleased at her having "Familie," she could not go on; for now she must speak of Rost, and his very name was a blow pushing her out from that newly found place. "Hunger," she said instead. "Kind klein, hunger gross." And the gravel slid down, pushed by her arm spread to show the hunger's size.

The gravel rustled; she waited. Then her heart sank, not because he answered "Nix verstehen" but because the glance he cast at his watch made him again a German soldier caring for nothing but shells. Putting all her trust into her mimicking talent, she tried again. She cried a thin helpless cry, she stood stony-faced, her eyes staring at one distant point.

"Schwester so." She groped. "Schwester nix gut. Schrecklich!"

"Frau," he cried, "Frau, nix verstehen!"

No longer caring what language she spoke, "Stay here!" she ordered, then climbed up. "Tola!" she shouted. "Tola! Quick, come here!"

At once — was she hiding nearby all that time? — Tola came. Gripping her shoulders, Barbara shoved her on. "Don't," Tola shrank back, "don't push me, I'm going."

What was Tola saying? Why was she talking about the Führer? Why did the soldier turn beet-red, what was he mumbling, what did his nod mean? He was gone. Only the dust his boots had raised was left, and a white candy wrapper fluttering on the ground.

"Tola, will he denounce us? Will he?"

"I don't know. 'Bring it,' he said. 'Bring it this evening before six.' And you should go back to the camp, he said."

"Alone? No," Barbara cried, "oh no!"

And they were going back together. An O.D. man had sneaked Tola out for the price of a hundred zlotys that Barbara, in the presence of witnesses, had had to promise him.

"How will you pay him?" Tola asked as they walked into the woods.

"Somehow. With my coat; no, it must have been sold; then with my shoes. Come on, how can you think of such trifles?" Barbara paused. Very cautiously she took Tola's hand, on it round bruises shining like red metal coins. "Tola, I have never been good to you," she said. And from then on they walked in silence.

The first fly was buzzing in the barracks. A beam of sunlit dust trailed over the bunks where the women lay still asleep. Aurelia was not asleep. Aurelia lay exactly as Barbara had left her, arms folded on her chest, eyes fixed on one point far above Alinka, who sat bent over her. And when they climbed up on the bunk Aurelia did not stir; only her gaze moved from Barbara to Tola.

"No." Barbara drew back. "No, it's not — it's not what you think. He, he agreed."

"He did?" Alinka cried.

"Who?" Aurelia asked in a wooden voice. "Who agreed? To what?"

"The soldier," Alinka began. "I, you see, once I cleaned for him . . . He gave me peppermints, he said . . ."

"We went to him," Barbara broke in. "We . . . but you know me. It was Tola, really. She spoke to him." Tola looked at her and she stopped.

"The doctor has been doing everything," Alinka took over. "The doctor has been feeding her; water, water with sugar."

"Her?" Aurelia asked.

"Yes, her."

Propping herself up slowly with her elbows, Aurelia sat up. "Excuse me," she said, "I mean, forgive me, I . . . I feel. I don't know how I feel."

And silence again.

Alinka broke it. It was high time Aurelia ate something! The doctor had pleaded with her, then Goldberg, then she herself, but Aurelia would not touch anything, not even kogel-mogel. "Now you must eat." Carefully Alinka unwrapped an egg. "Barbara, you beat it; you have the strongest hand."

"Me? God forbid. Two left hands and both made out of clay, that's me."

"I'll do it," Tola said. And the spoon began to clink.

As if the fear stored up for that day had not yet been fully spent, so anxiously did they watch the spoon. Barbara muttered that Tola was beating much too slowly. "Too fast — don't hurry so," Alinka warned, and again they moved closer, again they watched. The cream was thickening, the spoon could hardly move. Yet they would not be satisfied. "Go on, let it get thicker," they insisted, until the cup was almost overflowing.

Alinka supported Aurelia's head while Barbara fed her, leading the least trickle back to her lips. They pursed. "Really," Aurelia said, "really, I've had enough."

"What?" Barbara started.

"Oh no!" Alinka snapped, "you will finish it — to the last drop." And at once Aurelia opened her mouth.

A woman knelt down at the stove, put some kindling in, and a swarm of red sparks drifted toward the open door. Aurelia watched them. "I think," she began, "yes, I think I would like to go to . . . I would like to go outside."

"You've gone mad."

"The wild ideas you get."

"Perhaps she could get up," Tola said. "Let's ask the doctor."

The doctor had nothing against a short walk. They dressed Aurelia, helped her down from the bunk, then across the threshold.

And as, leaning on Barbara, she walked on — very slowly, the distended belly rising steep under her coat, and the coat trailing like a robe around her ankles — she looked like all the other women after childbirth, as they stroll through the hospital corridor, the strongest visitor lending his arm in support, the others following, a hushed, watchful retinue.

So they walked on; past the barracks, past benches on which women sat, their faces uplifted to the sun, under their feet the puddles blue with the mirrored sky. Where they were going, only Aurelia knew. Silently she led them on across the Appellplatz, where guards stamped on their towers, past the washroom and the clothing depot, its window still screened with a coat. Beside the line standing in front of the dispensary Aurelia halted, made a step forward, a step back.

"For the first time, you've walked enough," Alinka said, and they turned back. Once again they carried her — across the threshold, up onto the bunk, and there they moved aside as if Aurelia were growing big again, as if she needed all the room they could give. But she lay there very small and black. From under her crumpled eyelids tears came, then moved down to her lips, still coated with kogel-mogel so that they glimmered a pale faded gold.

Part Five

Chapter 25

ON THE SAME AFTERNOON the child left the camp. To silence its cry, the doctor dosed it with a potion, and the bag in which Goldberg carried it to the soldier was wrapped tight, so that no bitter scent would show where it had come from.

"We shall take care of this poor crumb, madam. Now we must leave," a note from Antoni said, which like a delivery slip was brought to them next day. Barbara read this message, Aurelia managed a pale smile — and that was how "later" began.

True, the plenty Barbara had dreamt of never came — for no one would buy her torn coat, and most of what they owned Goldberg and the O.D. man took in payment — but if hunger was great, so was hope. Because at last the Russians were in Poland.

"Have you heard?" now Barbara, now Aurelia would exclaim. "Dubno has fallen, have you heard?" "They've taken Rowne, they are moving on, toward Tarnopol and Lvov." At once all distances were shrinking: to show the speed of the new offensive Aurelia's fingers galloped across the bunk — airplanes were thrown into the battle, paratroopers joined in. "You'll see," Barbara whispered. "They will be here soon!" A pause followed, and "Tola, what do you think?" they asked. "Tola, what do you say to this?"

So it was now. No event, be it a great victory or a camp gossip, was complete without her verdict, which in turn became an occasion for approving smiles, for the intent, almost solemn looks thanking her for what she had given them, for this peace.

Was such gratitude deserved? Of this, Tola, unable to forget how grudgingly her gift had been offered, was not at all sure. But what if everything had happened differently, if she had never wavered, if she and she only had saved Aurelia and the child? Unmarred by the least flaw, such a deed appeared to her as a trophy, always within her reach, to prove what she really was. And on the con-

trary, had she run out on Aurelia, had she left her alone in the latrine stench, this too would have been a trophy of sorts.

Why such thoughts came she did not know. Yet they kept coming, and she fled from them to those too grateful faces, to those whispers that the war must soon end. "Perhaps." Her assent was cautious. But at that moment — and always against her will — what to
the others was a dream and a hope stood before her as an accomplished fact. "One day," softly she would begin, "we'll walk
out of the barracks, and all will be still — no guards on the
towers, no guards at the gate. And the earth will shake as in the
beginning, do you remember, Barbara?"

"Oh, do I remember! And then . . . ?"

At those expectant stares something would snap in her. "I . . .
oh, I was getting carried away," she would shrug and look at her
faithful ally, at Alinka.

For the girl's skepticism was not to be overcome. "Nonsense! The
offensive might stop as suddenly as it began," Alinka would retort,
glancing up from her sewing. She was making clothes for Aurelia
out of Barbara's coat.

On the eve of the day on which Aurelia — till then granted an
exemption from work by the doctor — was to return to Schmitz, the
new clothes were ready. Alinka helped her to put them on, gave a
tug here, a pull there. "Well, how do you like them?" she asked in
a high, tense voice.

No one answered her; for now they could see just how much of
Aurelia had been the child: the blouse made out of the shiny lining
clung to the sunken breasts, in sharp angles the bony hips stuck out
from under her skirt. Only her legs were still swollen huge, as if
unaware by how much their burden had shrunk.

"Well?" Alinka said. Aurelia answered her: "Alinka," she said
softly, "Alinka, you have hands of gold."

Next day, supported now by those hands, now by Barbara's and
Tola's, Aurelia Katz marched back to work: to Schmitz only for a
moment, then on to the loading of "baskets," as the light crates used
for transporting shells were called.

High on the slope the shed in which the baskets were stored
shone gently like tarnished silver. Down below, ties left from the
abandoned railroad tracks stretched along a narrow brook. The

brook babbled, the scent of sun-warmed wood filled the air. And the women sang, all the time, because to pass the baskets was such light work, because strong glossy grass was pushing through the stubble, and winter was over — its only trace a shriveled mole that a careless foot would uncover, or a bird, pressed flat, its wings outstretched as though hoping for one more flight.

And down below spring blossomed. Round the trucks bushes tangled. "Raspberry bushes, blackberries," Barbara exclaimed, "and see those tiny leaves — blueberries they are, what else, and the smell — ah, what mushrooms will be growing here!" As from a menu so from the shape of bush or leaf she read to them the list of delicacies the woods were preparing. Soon her eyes would move uphill; like children's impatient feet taking two or three steps at once, they skipped over the sunlit heads, and stopped, right at the door of the shed. There, hands folded on her lap, sat Aurelia on a chair which Barbara had made out of the baskets.

The rest, the warm sun, and her own hunger, proving she had tricked Aurelia into eating an extra slice of bread, all mingled and tasted sweet, as though she were relishing a mellow fruit. But let Aurelia gasp for breath, or clutch at her heart, or let her simply bring into full view the small sunken face, and the sweetness was gone; fear came, and turned into a fury of anger, even into hatred against that face, against those spindly arms, and she longed to force — as long ago crumbs into a fledgling's beak — her own strength, her own breath, into that gasping mouth.

"Aurelia!" Her shout echoed over the hill, and at once she was running up to berate Aurelia, always at fault because she sat baking in the sun, because she froze in the shade, because . . .

"Really, Mrs. Grünbaum," the women intervened, "you should control yourself a little." Many of them had somehow found out about the child. "Is it true, Mrs. Katz, that the underground organized the rescue?" they asked, or "My dear Mrs. Katz, I heard a partisan came for it, all the way to the camp; is that right, is it?"

So the child, carried like a parcel out of the camp, kept growing, until it was big enough to take upon itself the burden of their longing for a proof, for the least sign that out "in the Freedom" they still mattered.

"Please, I . . . I'd rather not discuss such things," Aurelia

pleaded. "Please, leave me, all of you!" she would shriek if they persisted. And the women obeyed, paying homage not so much to her
as to her election to good fortune. They enthroned her on the seat
of baskets. "Rest, Mrs. Katz," they said, "just you rest." And they
warded off Barbara's wrath.

"Ah, you don't know what she's like," Barbara muttered back.
"She . . . she would never take care of herself."

Of the remorse she had promised to Aurelia on that day of loading shells not a trace ever came. How could it, when to believe she
had ever demanded more of this woman than to eat, to rest, and to
take care, good care, of herself was simply not possible?

With Tola it was different. "Tola, I have never been good to you";
Barbara could not forget those words. Eagerly, almost with greed,
she took all the blame upon herself. The least inkling that the blame
could have been divided more equally she pushed away; her every
harsh word, every glance she recalled with meticulous care. Yet
how those words, which fear or worry or just her "wicked temper"
could explain, how they added up to what she sensed was her guilt,
to the frozen loneliness that hovered around Tola, this Barbara
could understand no better than why Tola, now that Barbara was
trying to be good, shrank under her praise — like a plant that once
trodden upon would not straighten up.

At night this small frozen figure rose before her, and always, as
though some secret tie existed between them, to usher Stefan in.
Ever since the child had left, she had worried about Stefan. Was he
still safe in London? What if London were bombed again? What if
he were lying sick and alone in his room?

How clearly she saw this room — the tousled bed, the overflowing ashtrays, and the chair in which he sat slouched forward,
face hidden in his hands. She did not want him to be all alone.
"Stefan, try to be happy. I don't mind, really I don't," she told
him. She even found him a mistress, a woman not quite in her
first youth, an exile whose husband had stayed behind in Poland, so
that those they longed for formed the link between them. Somehow
this link grew too strong; "the sweet young thing" who replaced the
melancholy exile presumed so much that she too was sent packing,
and a couple from Poland were what Barbara settled on. They
thought the world of him, he dined with them each evening. But

soon those evenings grew too long. Hiding their pity and their yawns, the hosts cast meaningful glances at the clock and afterwards, standing in the window, watched him shuffle off alone through the dark.

When she could bear it no more, she plucked him away from London, put him on a train heading for the little station ablaze with zinnias and phlox. There she stood waiting for him. Lights flashed, with a shrill ringing the barrier came down. The train was coming, there he was, leaning out of the window. "Stefan," she cried, "Stefan!" and held his face in her hands.

Yet next night he was back in London, slouched, face pressed against his fingers as against bars. Barbara knew clearly when she had seen this imprisoned face — on that night which had always seemed to her like a letter opened by mistake and closed right away. Now the letter was being reopened. Above the Orphan's gasps harsh with fever of typhus, above the Rebbetzyn's moans, monotonously, as if paging someone, repeating "God — my God," Stefan's voice rose, reading parts out loud to her.

And yet, when remembering the letter's opening lines, she took heart. Her very disbelief that the mornings of which those lines spoke ever existed helped her. Because if such mornings did exist she would have known how much had been given her: the miniature rainbows shining around the mirror, the scent of fresh hay that made the room open and vast like a field, and above all Stefan's touch on her face.

"Stefan," she had said on that morning, "today I'll come into the fields with you."

But he had to go away that day, to settle some affairs in Warsaw. "And while I'm there," he added, "I'll drop in once more on the doctor."

"Ah, that old babbler," so she invariably called the professor who had guaranteed her a dozen splendid children. "I tell you, it's just a waste of time." And it was at this moment that the sense of artificiality came upon her, as if the nonchalance of such remarks had been rehearsed separately by each of them.

Should I go with Stefan? she wondered. But then, what for? And soon afterward he was gone.

Like a huge bee the yellow carriage dissolved into the morning glow, hoofs rang, a whip cracked once again, then silence settled over the big white house. Slowly she walked around: here irises had to be arranged, there the first roses; the new carpet clashed with everything, but the bunch of cornflowers was lovely, sapphire, almost black, against the ecru curtains. At the window she paused for a rest. It was haymaking time; in even rows rakes swung over the fields, pitchforks glittered, and when suddenly they clashed, hay showered upon the sunburned faces like pale green rain. The hoarse thirsty shouts followed her on the way upstairs.

Of late she had been spending time in these rooms. Plain, sparsely furnished, they were a reminder of those days when she and Stefan, homeless lovers then, would find a refuge in some cunningly borrowed flat. And it was in just such a whitewashed room that he had proposed to her, or rather — as they were fond of saying — they had proposed to each other. June had just begun then; then, too, she had awakened at Stefan's touch. "It's late," he was saying, "your friend may come in any moment, it's late."

"If she comes," Barbara's voice grew dreamy, "if she comes . . . just say you'll marry me."

And if he said it, should she marry him? Should she, should she not? He was taller than her previous men, so that to kiss him she had to stand on her toes — this she loved about him; and his strength, and the way he looked at her, his eyes widening as if startled ever anew at finding her near. Then, there was the estate, vast, far enough away for all her relatives to worry "how one could ever live in such wilds." "Yet," each of them was prompt to add, "what a brilliant match it would be." This "brilliance" spoke against him, the wealth he, as the son of a great lawyer, had to offer. Should she — should she not?

"Barbara," he spoke almost harshly, "Barbara, I want to marry you, and you know it. Still, you could have anyone, just anyone, while I am nobody special." He was smiling, yet his face looked changed — furrowed, almost old. "Many times before I tried to tell you about it, but somehow you never quite listened. Look here, Barbara, you should understand: everything I've ever done has been a waste, a complete failure — my years at the university, my studies in medicine. I felt at loose ends, I didn't know what to do. The estate is the first place where I have ever felt sure of myself. But until now I've never mentioned it, to anyone . . . but . . . until now I haven't been very happy." His smile broadened. "Not very happy at all," he added, and suddenly only the furrows were left.

She understood. Oh, it was not those troubles at the university, of which everyone knew, that made his face look old, but the unhappiness confided only to her, some sorrow secret and profound. To the conventional good match a new element was added. Marrying him was an elopement with suffering, a mission only she could fulfill. True, at times it seemed to her that the mission had ended right there and then: successful in his work, held in high regard by landowners and peasants alike, he was happy. So was she — though on days like this the silence weighed oppressively upon her.

And now when weighed down by this silence, she remembered Stefan's errand. She saw him in the professor's office — white, all unmanned, lying on the narrow bed. The incongruous image was gone; but now, more than ever, she did not want him to go there. What for? What need had they of professors and their help?

A calendar on which it was still winter hung on the wall. She tore off page after page, then bending her fingers, counted over and over again. She was late, by one day; one day meant little, and yet how changed her body felt — heavy, the breasts hurting under her touch.

"You see, Stefan, I was right, I was!" everything in her kept exclaiming as she ran downstairs. And there an exodus seemed to begin — the heavy furniture was leaving first, next the mirrors she could never abide, and the knickknacks, and the scatter rugs, until only space was left, space for those who would be coming from now on.

So it would be soon. And now she was waiting for Stefan, looking at the clock, at the window, at the clock again. Afternoon was here at last. In the hall the door opened, but it was just the "agronom" coming in. Like the new carpet the agronom was her contribution to their lives, like the carpet he clashed with everything. He had been brought in to free them from the payday squabbles, from the talk of prices and such, but he somehow only made such affairs more oppressive by his visit, by his constant "Unnecessary, madam, quite unnecessary" in answer to her least suggestion.

"Unnecessary," his bright darting eyes declared as he surveyed the carpets, the Sèvres china, and herself — as if she too were a knickknack, costly, yet of no use. Then, probably to show that to such waste more waste was the answer, he proceeded to roll bread-balls out of the canapés the maid had brought in. Gray and sleety like wet mice they scurried under his fingers.

"Please," she began, and just then Stefan's steps came from the hall. "How was your day?" was all she could ask with the agronom next to her. He smiled yet he looked at her cautiously, as if without knowing it she had been taken ill.

At dinner only the agronom ate, trying to slow himself down by punctuating the huge bites with equally huge gulps of water. Something was "unnecessary" to him, something had gone up in price or perhaps down, and the faint crackling sound was the pale enamel she kept peeling off her nails.

"They will fleece us, sir, they will."

Heavily she walked to the window. Like a brown placid river a freshly plowed field rippled in the last sun, over the darkening plain haystacks rose in a chain of tawny hills. And a sadness stole over her about this day spent on dreaming and waiting. "It's getting dark," she said hoarsely. "It's late." And at last the agronom took himself off.

As if uncertain of his proper place Stefan kept looking around. "There," he pointed to the blue Récamier, "let us sit there together."

They sat down, awkwardly somehow. Like a black leaf carried on a current of air, a late swallow flitted through the dusk. When a branch swayed under its touch she could be a mother still; when the swaying stopped — no more.

"We can't have children," he had said. "I cannot." And she understood nothing. But the breeze grew cold; everywhere around, the furniture was settling to a triumphant rest, and, as a governess rebukes her ill-mannered charges, so someone seemed to admonish her that a good wife should not just sit there and stare.

Obediently she stroked his damp hand, wondered if one such touch were enough, stroked the hand once again; he, still unsatisfied, kept looking at her.

"I see," she said. "I can't believe it," she added, and at that moment the belief came, like a weight swinging right at her. "No, it cannot be true," she cried. "You shouldn't have gone there, I mean

. . . I mean we'll go to someone else." She paused, drew herself up. "We'll go to no one," she said. "We'll simply wait."

They had nothing to wait for, his silence answered. Then at last he began to explain. A childhood disease, he was saying, "a rare yet possible consequence," and she longed for him to stop, so that nothing would ever be known, so that like Antoni they could just say, "The Lord has granted us no child."

"Examination" — "microscopic tests," each word was prying their life wide open, until what had been only theirs and secret was laid bare, like wares exposed to a grimy touch.

"No!" she said. "No, don't talk, it's all so . . . oh, I don't know."

"Of course, of course. You deserved better than to marry a sterile man," and his voice grew shrill, as during his arguments with some too clever city guests.

"Don't say such things," she whispered. They fell silent. When the telephone rang they both got up, equally prompt, equally hiding their relief.

Stefan's aunt, to whom Barbara would rather not talk, was calling. "We're fine, thank you," his voice came muffled through the door. "Yes, Barbara received the silver basket, she will write soon to thank you. Yes, we too enjoyed your visit . . ."

Anger seized her, against the net of petty obligations cast around her, the unwanted visits, the thanks for gifts just as unwanted, and it grew, because all right to anger was denied her from now on. He — no, not he, something inscrutable had hurt them, her more than him. He had the estate, he had his work at least. Yet this hurt gave him a new power over her — because from now on her every outburst would be read as payment for what had happened.

"Regards to you," Stefan said, and again they sat silent, waiting for the clock to announce the day's end. But when the clock struck she shrank deeper into her chair, longing to spend the night alone, right here, or in the plain rooms upstairs, in the bed at the window shaded by a huge maple, so that she would wake up as in a nest amidst nothing but green. Yet this right, too, was no longer hers; even the time she spent that evening on brushing and braiding her hair seemed like a transgression. She bent toward Stefan, she touched his face, then lay down at the other side of the bed.

A smell of jasmine invaded the room, crickets made their fine drilling sound, as on all the other nights when she had lain motionless so as not to disturb the child whose home she might have just become. And it seemed to her someone had been watching her on those nights, someone who looked like the professor and said "quite unnecessary" in a high squeaky voice.

Other voices were quick to come — they whispered behind her back; they said it was to the women who looked like Mother Earth that such things often happened. "Yes, it's my fault," she would tell them, "only mine!" The sacrifice was meager, as was the comfort it brought. And the whispers went on, wondering how, with nothing at all to do, she spent her days, just as once she had wondered about others.

Now they were paying her back. Now they all gathered around her, sallow-faced women who spoke of their ailments as of love affairs, and those in hats like fruit or flower stands shuttling grimly between hairdresser and modiste; and at last those whom she found most obnoxious, since they had appropriated what might have been hers — women who, as if their reproachfully modest clothes did not needle one enough, still had to add, "In our times one must be socially conscious!"

Was she to become like them? She must go somewhere, she must do something, but what? Should she take a child which was not her own? Later perhaps she could do it. Now all within her shrank from those orphanage children, strange to her with their dark faces and large pained eyes.

But then, as if to reciprocate her lifelong loyalty, the slums appeared to her — a dingy square, old men walking dogs as mangy as they, old women with faces like maps charted by years of hard work. She too was there, dressed simply, her hands like theirs leathery from work. "That is a woman for you — working her hands to the bone to help her husband finish his doctor's schooling," their toothless mouths said.

"Stefan." It hurt her to see him rise. Perhaps, perhaps I should wait? she wondered, recalling the smile that had made him look old. How could she wait, though, with all these unanswered questions before her? "Stefan," she repeated. "Listen, I have everything figured out. We will go away from here. I'll work, you know I can do it — you must know. In a way we are rich, but everything we

have came from your parents; we should take nothing from them
any longer," thus she clung to her newly found poverty. "And
I . . . I won't act like a fool anymore, I . . ." She fumbled, at a
loss how to explain that she indulged her costly whims just because
they meant nothing, because she could take or leave such frippery.
"You will see, I'll change," she said meekly. "I'll work like an
ox."

"And what about me?" She had turned away but she could sense
he was smiling.

"You will finish your schooling, your studies, I mean." He said
nothing, he only kept looking at her.

"You could have waited with your . . . your suggestion," he said
at last. "Still, one mustn't ask for too much. To answer you, Barbara: I cannot do this, and you know it; you've always known."

"Of course you can. You have me to help you now. Everything
has changed."

"Everything except me. I haven't changed, I'm no more talented
now than I used to be."

"Oh God, why can't you understand? You don't have to be a
genius; hundreds of people study, thousands . . ." The argument,
bringing back the memory of wizened provincial doctors, turned
against her. "Stefan, it is so empty here," she longed to cry yet silenced herself. "We must get out of here" was what she said. "Here
we have no life at all, no life! You come home, and 'Ah, you must
have worked hard!' you say to me, when all I did was to bake bread
or to move furniture around, as if this were work, as if this could be
enough. And you — " She hesitated. But already she was resolved,
not for her own sake, only for his, to hold up to him the image of his
life — in warning, before it was too late. "And what about you?"
she whispered. "You don't even work with your own hands, you
just count — how many acres have been seeded, how much money
you will get out of them. You sit and count — like the agronom,
worse — like some smalltown grocer."

"Is that how you see me?"

"Yes!" she said, and she felt afraid.

His brooding silence meant anger, and she longed for the outburst to begin, for the shouts, the banging of doors, so that reconcili-
ation would follow when cautiously they would approach each

other, would flare up, until, holding each other close, they would burst out laughing.

But when at last he spoke, it was very quietly. "Since you seem to forget things rather easily, let me explain once more why I cannot do what you want." This unfamiliar, too careful voice went on . . . and to her it was as though she were looking into her Italian phrase book; as there the lovely mellifluous words shrank on the opposite side to some paltry talk of shopping or food, so here, in his translation, the profound and secret sorrow that had been her betrothal gift, her mission and her hope, kept shrinking to something tawdry and small; to nights spent over books, nights kept secret like a shameful vice lest others mock those futile efforts, to the clammy fear of examinations, and to failure.

"Failure . . . I failed." He seemed to be conjugating a verb. "I failed . . . I asked for another chance, I failed again," he was saying, and over him a musty odor seemed to rise as over those other failures, the poor relations taken out of storage on some inescapable family occasion. Had he, when begging for another chance, smiled like them, a loose, patched-up smile?

"Enough," she broke in. "Enough, it's all so, so — "

"Ugly," he finished for her. "Of course it was ugly!" And suddenly he was gone.

Outside the window beyond the black bushes a light glinted and went out, a dog barked, then silence so deep, as if the manor house, the barns, and the village had grown empty. She ran toward the next room, hesitated, then stopped. His feet were shuffling like those of an old man. Should I call him? she thought. Should I go in?

The wind helped her, by flinging the door wide open. There he sat slouched, face hidden in his hands, from behind the bent fingers his eyes staring at the floor. And now she understood. This man was Stefan, her husband, he to whom she ran for help when distressed, when hurt or when she had hurt others, and she wanted to free his face from those limp hands, to say something. But what?

He started, the smile that had not been enough to stop her still on his face; but at once he rose, drew himself up, then, powerful and erect, walked toward the door.

Just as the door was closing right in her face, a cramp gripped her, and another and yet another. Trustfully, aware of nothing, her body was preparing itself for what would never come. She shuddered. One by one her children were drifting away from her like leaves from a fall-stricken tree.

Scattered in glimmering crumbs the moon shone in the water bucket. "Hot, oh I'm hot," the Orphan kept moaning, while Barbara lay there wide awake. What had come over her then, what fear had pushed her on? "Barbara isn't afraid of the devil itself!" people used to say. "Fear has big eyes," she used to joke; and yet she had been afraid of so much — of the empty days, of people's idle talk, of small things. Small things, and what were they anyhow? Once nothing had been big enough for her, now she would creep on all fours to get Aurelia a piece of bread, now she would do it — yet how long it was since Aurelia had cried "You're too reckless, Mrs. Grünbaum, to know what care is."

If only she could waken Aurelia, not to ask forgiveness — how could you be forgiven for something you had not understood? — but to tell her about that night, and to find out what had once made her so reckless, why it had taken her so long to change. Yet nowhere, at no station, would Aurelia wait for her husband, no wrong between them could be set aright anymore. That was why Aurelia could not be told of that night; but perhaps — Tola. Tola, Barbara repeated, and felt afraid, as if Tola would reward her with a clarity for which she did not yet feel ready.

Chapter 26

ONLY WHEN THE TYPHUS epidemic broke out did one begin to notice the mothers. "Always. You've always been a mean, spiteful daughter," in the seclusion of their bunks they used to hiss, reciting some immemorial motherly grudges of their own. Now those grudges came into the open: calling everyone around to witness, they cried out against those daughters who lay uncovered, who would not touch the soup, who did nothing right, now just as always! And as the typhus cases multiplied so did they . . .

The epidemic, though it swept over the barracks within days, took no one by surprise — had there ever been a camp without typhus? The epidemic was bound to come, everyone said, until typhus dwindled to a sort of childhood disease, inevitable yet posing no threat. And every single one of them believed herself safe because that other belief — that your body, loyal through all those war years, could now, at the last moment, turn against you — was just not possible.

"The sooner we get typhus the better," Alinka said at the start of the epidemic, by "we" meaning herself and Aurelia, since the others had been through typhus as children.

And soon it was as if the sweetish smell of diarrhea had always filled the barracks; soon no other news but that of typhus crises was remembered; and the waiting for typhus to arrive merged in Barbara's mind with the waiting for the child's arrival. But deep within her there was hope that somehow this first illness would be counted to Aurelia's credit.

It was not counted. "Typhus" the doctor said. Yet Barbara still tried to bargain, mumbling that this could not be, because Aurelia did not feel hot, because not one purplish spot could be seen on her. The doctor said something about the spleen being swollen. "Oh, I understand," she said, and understood nothing. Only, familiar from long ago, came the bewilderment that a word, a single moment could change so much.

"Don't you worry, Aurelia. You won't go to the hospital," she said, vaguely recalling that all the sick should be comforted in this way. Then following the others, she got down off the bunk.

"We must separate," Alinka said dryly. "Nights I shall take care of her; during the day you two. We'll have to work on different shifts."

"Yes." Barbara stared at gray rain behind the window. "No, no," she stammered out, because something was wrong: Alinka — she was much too frail to take over such care. "I'll stay here at night," Barbara began, "because you — "

"Don't you know yourself yet?" Alinka in sudden fury broke in. "If anything happens, a selection, or a Strafappell, you'll just run around and howl."

"Then Tola!" Barbara looked at Tola and stopped.

"Don't leave Tola alone again," Aurelia's order came sullenly from the bunk. "Tola has had enough."

They separated according to Alinka's plan. Yet at first there was hardly need for such constant care; faintly flushed, a soft, almost joyous luster in her eyes, Aurelia appeared not sick but rather preoccupied, so that only a whisper would answer them, then something like a smile, then just a flutter of her eyelids. After a while even such an answer came no more — Aurelia was gone far beyond their reach. The bunk, so narrow that when one of them turned all had to turn, too, seemed to expand, till it was vast enough to contain two lands, so distant that no contact was possible between them. Even their climates differed; the sun of noon blazed, smoke and heat drifted up from the stove and Aurelia froze, her teeth would not stop chattering, her feet felt cold as stone. But when the fire died out, and the sun, she began to burn.

Someone was haunting her in her delirium, was insisting on something. "What do you want of me?" her eyes pleaded; "No, not again," she shook her head. But already she had to give in, she thrashed around and gasped; then just as suddenly grew still, sweat running down her strange, bemused face all the way to the chapped mouth dotted with scabs like crumbs of rouge.

The doctor should have interpreted those looks. Yet he had

changed; he, once never tired of singing Aurelia's praise — "My favorite patient," he would call her, "my only successful case!" — now hardly looked at her, while Tola and Barbara he treated like hysterical relatives pestering him with their whims. "What do you want of me?" he muttered. "Hurry up, undress her!" Tola — no matter how heavy the heat she always warmed her hands with her breath — took off the blouse that now served as a nightgown; together they propped up the sick woman. Impassive, like a lover whose desire is long gone, the doctor pressed his head to Aurelia's breast, flaccid, the nipple wrinkled and black like an old raisin.

"Have you got any money?" came next.

"Yes, we have money," Tola answered. The money was needed for Aurelia's heart, for camphor, which was smuggled into the camp at a dear price.

Motionless, Barbara watched the watery fluid oozing into the syringe, the sudden glitter of the needle — her stare like a peasant's now suspicious of being robbed by some strange trick, now convinced that this trick, just by taking his all, must perform wonders. She even spoke to the doctor like a peasant to his betters, obsequiously, ever mindful of his title. "Doctor, you know everything. You can do so much, Doctor," she bestowed upon him omniscience and power. But he would have none of it; he glowered and was gone.

With eyes new for her — the eyes of a child, dumb yet most eager to learn — she soon came to observe Tola. "Like this?" she whispered when taught how to remove the sweat-drenched blouse or to wring a compress out. "Yes, I see. Like this." They hardly spoke to each other, yet it seemed to her as if they had merged, so that Tola was the voice giving the orders, she the hands, clumsy yet doing their utmost to obey. When Tola was near, her haggard face brightened with gratitude; when it was gone, such desolation would come upon her that, trying to sound just like Tola, she would talk to herself. "Now, be more gentle," she whispered, or "watch out when you give Aurelia the pan."

The scalding urine ran down her fingers. Intent, stiff, she carried the pan to the slop barrel and ran back to warm the freezing feet, to fan the burning face, or again to force between the clenched teeth a spoonful of some mush that to her was not just food and medicine but a message telling the one faraway of all that would await her if only she would come back.

Somewhere beyond the sick woman was the barracks, distant, as all the other hospital rooms are to those inside them keeping their anxious watch. At times, though, a moan brought the barracks nearer: "Mama, you will not die on me!" nasal, like the honking of a goose, it would cry. When it stopped the barracks receded. For Barbara had learned well how to defend herself against the silence. It fell and she turned away, she saw nothing but Aurelia: the sunken eyes, the mouth that looked rouged — and the face rose before her like a mountan, immutable, bound to exist forever.

Someone had died, this silence said. "The Rebbetzyn has died, and old Alexandrovitch and Zosia from the bunk below." "Goldberg has died, have you heard? Goldberg!" She started. "Like this," she admonished herself, and spread a compress over Aurelia's head.

But once she had turned around too soon. The door stood wide open. Along the sunny road two picriniacs were carrying a stretcher covered with a dark sheet, and right outside the barracks an O.D. man was handing something to Tola. It was a girl's blouse; the small buttons shone bright like pebbles. For the first time Barbara fully understood where the money for Aurelia's heart came from. "Tola!" she cried, "Tola, come here." But Tola only glanced at her and ran off. Now I don't know how to help her — I should have started long ago, Barbara thought, and the old omissions lay heavy upon her.

Tola was trading in the clothes of the sick, who were ready to barter whatever they owned for a bit of cornmeal or bread, and mostly in the clothes of the dead, which the O.D. men grabbed as if they were the rightful heirs. With Aurelia's typhus this trading had begun.

"Don't ask too much of me. Don't leave me alone with her, not till after crisis," silently she had pleaded then. "Tola has had enough," Aurelia had cried, and Tola felt at a loss, as if the grudge against them was a possession which she could not do without. Yet the demand was there. Hardly had a stretcher passed by outside than someone seemed to bear down upon her, a creature, an insatiable mouth that she must do everything to glut. She saw an O.D. man walk by carrying clothes stripped from someone just dead, and she ran toward him. "I'll do anything," she whispered. "I'll get you the best price." That was how it all began. Since then her days were divided between her bunk and the barracks.

Typhus had illuminated most of the barracks. Once gray and murky, now it glowed with fevered faces, with shiny black flies, and with flames leaping bright orange from the stove. This ramshackle iron contraption was the barracks' heart — kitchen, laundry, dispensary all in one. The healthy, the recovering, and the sick lined up before it, many of them dressed only in soiled shirts, most so wobbly-legged they swayed like passengers in a swiftly moving bus. Shouts came from everywhere, everyone was fighting for something — the O.D. men for their inheritance, the women for a turn at the stove, for water, for a splinter of kindling wood.

Only the sick were quiet. Intent on the burning within themselves, they panted on their bunks, shirts twisted to grayish ropes over their chests, the inflamed bodies pressed so tight together they melted into a broad crimson stripe. Some secret loyalty bound them together. "Stolen!" one moaned, and at once they all sat up. Straw, paper, stale crumbs flaking from their heads, they leaned over the edges of their bunks, and "Give it back!" the parched voices called, "give . . . give me something . . ." Forgetful of all but their own hunger, they begged, softer and softer, until only a muffled whisper was left, and arms groping through the smoky air.

Those arms, Tola felt, lay in wait for her — they tugged, they pulled at her, and she, so as not to tear them off like brambles, had to learn a special way of looking. She truncated the sick. A baked mouth was all that those asking for water were, those who had dropped a piece of bread nothing but fingers, inept like the fingers of very small children who have not yet learned how to grasp. Often those hands would force upon her, like a thank-you gift, clothes worn to a thin mesh. "I cannot sell this," she would refuse, turning away in order not to see how their eyes grew wide with reproach.

In each barracks it was the same: the parched moans, the bedsores, shiny like patches of silk, and the stench that picrine made bitter. For the picriniacs were everywhere. Immune to typhus, since lice did not savor their blood, they rolled the soup barrels in, the barrels of excrement out; and they even tended the sick — the rich, who to keep their riches had stayed alone and now relied upon hired nursing.

"Anything to sell? Anything?" Tola whispered at the bunks of the rich. But no matter how furtive her question, other peddlers came running at once, opening their scaly black bags, showed with what they could pay — with cornmeal and beet-marmalade, and fine, fresh bread. From the bunk no answer came. She had been outbid; she must move on.

"Anything to sell?" Up and down the barracks she trudged, displaying herself, so that those with something for sale could get a thorough look at her.

"Miss Ohrenstein, come here, closer!" the signal would come at last. Like a lantern gleaming in a tunnel, the inflamed face shone from the bunk's dusk, fingers raked through the straw where shoes or a dress lay buried.

"Miss Ohrenstein," dry, like the rustle of straw, a voice would whisper, "I know you won't cheat me like those typhus profiteers, Miss Ohrenstein; you are not a harpy, you come from such an excellent family." On and on the woman would rasp, remembering the Ohrensteins' dinners in their home, the bridge played with some Ohrenstein aunt or other. "You would never take advantage of a sick woman, you are an honest person." This always came last.

Tola understood. A true Ohrenstein would never have sullied himself with such bartering. Their suspicious looks said she was nothing better than a harpy, recklessly abusing her old, respectable name. If they turned to her, it was only because her prices were better. And what if those looks were right? Could she not have turned into a harpy for her own sake, just to eat well, to get better clothes like the Kaelanki — each, thanks to typhus, a fashion plate? Perhaps. If others could do it why not she?

Something was forcing her to become what those eyes saw in her. She haggled loudly with her clients so that all could hear; so that all could see, she slowly counted the money that was her profit. And she took the clothes the O.D. men gave her, not stealthily as the other peddlers did, but openly, lifting each piece up to the light.

When she looked at the O.D. men, at the peddlers, and at those on whose bunk someone had just died and who sat there gulping

their soup, a frenzy would come over her. She would buy bread
with the money for camphor, she would gobble it up to the last
crumb. A cry, a burning touch, and without knowing why or how,
she would find herself up on a bunk washing a sick woman, dressing
an infected sore — and unaware of the pus on her hands, she would
dash out to rest on the bench outside.

Then came visions. A piece of broken glass that caught the sun
was a brooch; they sold it and lacked for nothing. "Go on, bring
more money, it's easy for you!" Barbara was showing her the
door; or the typhus she had had in childhood did not count — she
was sick, no one could blame her if she lay down to rest. This vision
came most often.

At times it happened that the stretcher would be carried out of
her barracks and she just sat looking at the glossy mud; at times a
glance hardly had to touch her and fear came; that glance meant
something, something must have happened on her bunk. And she
ran on, repeating "I did all I could," adding each copper, each
crumb to the balance of her innocence. But she never came into the
barracks without first stopping and listening.

Lived through again and again, the event seemed to have already
happened, so that only what she was listening for — Barbara's cry
— was still needed to make it final. And she, would she cry then, or
would she go on eating her soup?

"Barbara, how is Aurelia?" she would call, bursting in. "No change
Tolenka. How I've been waiting for you . . ."

So meekly that it almost hurt, Barbara would touch her shoulder;
a flicker of recognition would come into Aurelia's eyes, and at once
those thoughts which had dogged her in the other barracks were
gone. It was not she who had thought them. They came from outside, like an impure mist.

"You sleep," Barbara murmured. "I'll watch over her; you lie down
and rest." And curled up at Aurelia's feet Tola would fall asleep.

Sleep helped. Sleep was a long dark passage that led her away
from all she had seen before. Upon awakening she felt peaceful;
gently, as though carried by a calm ebbing sea, the sick, the dying and the dead drew away. She was new to grief. Those
sunken eyes, this heart burrowing like an animal in fear, signaled
the threat of her first loss. Of her past only what could now be put

to use remained: her sickly childhood stood by, helping her to read the signs of thirst or pain, and her mother, showing what comfort there was still to give.

When she washed Aurelia, her hands just glided over the wasted body. When she combed her hair, each finger guarded against the tangled knots. "Barbara, now we must turn her" came next. And quickly, as though translating for a foreign guest a remark in a language unknown to him, "Now, Aurelia, we must turn you," Barbara would whisper. Together they turned the sick woman, they bent over her back — marked by the stiff paper sheets, by straw and boards, "but not a trace of a bedsore!" Barbara exclaimed in triumph; because, though worn out by childbirth yet with no such sore to sap her strength, Aurelia was at last the equal of the other sick.

Everywhere around such washing and turning went on. Water splashed, flour, gray as dust, was sprinkled to powder the bruised backs. "Let me comb you, it won't hurt, you'll see," the women whispered. One by one they grew still, and when the late sun came into the barracks only a faint rustle was left — exemption slips, freeing the sick from work, were being pressed into their hands.

Then, withdrawing deep into her bunk, Tola would put on the clothes to be smuggled out of the camp. Often, as she was hurrying to the Appellplatz, a woman would stop and stare at her — the woman who had nursed the wearer of those clothes and to whom they should now have belonged.

Each evening the column that marched out to Schmitz grew smaller, and the road it walked along shrank, too, as the woods pushed into it with new grass and the croziers of folded ferns. The air was clear; from pale early-flowering bushes sweet scents rose, gave way to the bitterness of picrine, then returned to follow the women all the way to Schmitz.

Here, furtive, like lovers hurrying to a forbidden tryst, figures stole through the thicket. They waved, softly they called — for Tola and other peddlers. Of late Poles from Trotyl had ventured all the way to Schmitz, where the prices for clothes were cheaper.

"Many dying, miss?" they asked.

"Yes," she said, "many."

They looked over her wares, and they sighed how poor they were, and how she haggled, though soon, for the likes of her, money would be of no use. She smiled. "Jews always haggle — it's a national trait," she answered. And she waited, more eagerly each day, for the proof that would change their hints to a certainty. Because then nothing more would be demanded of her, then she could just wait for the end.

"Getting rich at last?" The old foreman smirked, waiting for the bribe he got for letting her dash outside.

"Yes, Mr. Foreman." Tola grinned back. "Yes, I'm getting exceedingly rich."

"After the crisis — this stops" was all Barbara ever said.

Of crises, talk went on all through the nights: of those who had passed it, and of those who had failed, though such failure was always explainable — because the old never fought hard enough, because the young had fought too hard. And all through the night, tiptoeing like guests careful not to disturb others by their early departure, those just struck with typhus kept sneaking out for a rest — more and more of them, till the long line reached as far as the Meister's office. Pretending not to notice them, he would rush by, and those asking for help he pushed away with one blank look. Yet he did give Tola the bottle of valerian drops she had asked him for.

"You'll peddle only till the crisis," Barbara muttered incongruously as she lifted the bottle up to the light.

But Aurelia kept them waiting. Others were done with crisis in a week, in ten days at the most; yet almost a fortnight had passed, and in the morning, when the two shifts were passing each other, "No change," Alinka reported, her lips tight, as if to ration even such comfort.

"No change," in the evening Barbara and Tola called to her.

But on a morning when rain was beating hard against their faces, "Cold!" Alinka cried, "Aurelia feels cold."

The rain kept falling. "Cold," Aurelia Katz moaned, "oh, how cold." For the first time in weeks she was sharing their climate. Her crisis was over. And all through the day her teeth chattered, clinking like beads twisted by an anxious hand.

Chapter 27

IT WAS A QUIET and sheltered street. Even in the least clement weather wind was barred from it by the embankment on which an occasional train rolled, and when the sun grew harsh, coolness wafted in from the nearby Planty. In a long green strip the Planty — the gardens that replaced the old fortifications — ran along the adjacent street, acting both as a place of shaded rest and a filter for heavy traffic, for their narrow crossings would let no trolley or truck through. And the street reciprocated; for the Planty was not two-faced, like those city parks, during daytime alluring with the vast expanses of lawns but growing desolate, even fearful, at the first sign of dusk. Here you always felt safe. All the night long, light sifted in through the bushes, reassuring sounds of footsteps came from the street, and if pale figures startled a passerby, they were just statues, gathered in a silent conclave within a circle of willows.

Such give and take pervaded the entire neighborhood all the way to the bank, which with its darkly barred windows might have resembled a prison were it not for the children twittering within each niche. Toward noon, when the weather had declared itself, a migration into the Planty began: tricycles and scooters led the way, a while later the toddlers came, tugging at their reins, and last, baby carriages, and old ladies tripping along to the jingle of the needles in their knitting bags.

With succulent sounds balls jumped against the ground; bangs, ribbons, and braids twirled in the sun, and often a chase would begin as a fugitive balloon sailed into the street, a child behind it and behind the child mothers and nurses tripping over the cobblestones. Like beds of unwithering flowers, roseate, purple, and red, these cobblestones adorned the street, vying in their colors with mosaics of fruit outside the stores: the plums as dark as ink, pink watermelons covered by stiff green nets; and cherries out of which little girls·fashioned themselves earrings as they dashed past the turbaned Moor who sat among the aroma of coffee and spices and tea, rolling his bluish plaster eyes.

And farther on, trays of pastry balanced upon their heads, bakery boys hurried along, the floury dust trailing after them — and a scent — the homelike scent of bread. Where this scent lingered round the bakery, the quiet side street branched off. Droshkies stood at the corner. Inside, battered derbies pulled down over their noses, the drivers snored, until suddenly a horse would shy, whinnying into its burlap nosebag, would rock the droshky, sleeper and all, and send from under its hoofs a cooing pigeon cloud.

The least commotion was promptly recognized here, each new sight. A stranger could be spotted at once. He would ask for a house number in the twenties and the truth was out — he needed assistance, he was lost — for the street had never grown beyond its teens. Not that there was anything intrusive about such familiarity. The inhabitants greeted each other with a nod, the gray solid houses with their swaying curtains, while the black iron gates vouched for privacy.

Dusk, cool and soothing, lay over the entrance hall; on the checkered tiles heels clicked with the high-pitched sound of the upper piano keys; and together with the smooth banister, seats placed on each landing aided those tired in their ascent toward home.

This was the street Aurelia had found, this was where she moved in — after heat had lashed at her and cold, after something crying was pushed into her arms, after "Ask, go and ask," a voice had insisted, after the crisis — this was the street. She did not find it at once. At first fog had spun around her, she was washed ashore, seashells rustled against her ears. Slowly the fog began to lift, the rustle ebbed. And suddenly everything hurt, noises crushed against her head, hands tore into her eyes and, most painful of all, hurt faces bent toward her, each disfigured by the overlarge eyes. She wanted the fog to come back, she lay down and cried.

But after a while — though not without effort — she developed a *modus vivendi*. "I was sick, I'm weak still," in a vague, half-understood apology she said to those faces; when noises came crashing she ran for cover to her hands. And as for the barracks, she simply moved out: her glance was forbidden ever to stray into it. For all her needs, for air, for light or news of the weather, she depended on the bunk — equipped even with a window, which doubled as a clock.

At night, when her mouth tasted so bitter she feared that picriniacs were lying next to her, she would stare at this clock, at this narrow crevice, a star shining in it like a speck of gold. At last the star vanished, the crevice faded to a pale gray. Soon morning would come and she would ask for water to rinse her mouth.

During the day the crevice entertained her; raindrops hung there, streaks of fresh air sneaked in or — and this she loved best — a ray of sun came, which, swaying to and fro, became a brush that painted a scene for her, always the same, yet clearer with each day.

One day the scene was completed. Slowly the smoky air was lifted up — upon light — the light of a spring afternoon, so uniform, so clear, that like golden pollen it seemed to rise from the earth, only its overflow gathering into the basin of the sun. Into the light came trees, their new leaves no more than a faint green down. And among the trees a crowd was walking — everyone was there, she with Tola, with Barbara and Alinka, those from Picrine and those from Trotyl, many coughing, all still in rags, but their faces cleansed by the great calm. Unhurriedly they walked on . . .

"Aurelia, do wake up, we must turn you!" someone — it was Alinka — shouted into her ear. "Leave me, let me be," she was about to cry, but it was too late: arms were lifting her, she was being turned, kneaded like a piece of dough, and turned again. Stiffened, her mouth pursed, Aurelia submitted. But in that moment her decision was made. She would not budge from the bunk, she would wait right here, until what she had seen came — the end, the end of the war.

Yet with each day more was demanded of her. "What, what is it?" she muttered, for typhus had stolen her hearing. Then, having caught the fugitive words, she did their bidding: she tried to sit up all by herself, nibbled on the bread that swelled to a ball of cobweb in her mouth, or gulped the valerian drops which Tola had got. "Tola, from Meister Grube," Barbara kept shouting into her ear — as if this source could sweeten their bitter taste.

No sooner were her chores done than Aurelia would lie still. As the sick everywhere and always wait for the visitor to come with gifts of books, of sweets, and above all of news, proving that beyond their hospital bed there is still a world, so she too was waiting.

"After the war" . . . and her visitor came in. She herself "after the war" was this visitor. "What shall I eat after the war?" she asked; and at once, cakes, bowls of broth or fruit were brought in. "How shall we dress after the war?" and the guest modeled a collection of conservative grays or browns, while clothes bolder in color were designed for Barbara, for Tola and Alinka; or again plans for the summer were made, for vacations by the sea or in the country.

"And what about the child?" This reminder did not take her by surprise. How could it, when even into typhus the child had pursued her with its cry? But everything in her rebelled against this belated motherhood. She merely answered, "The child is safe," as if speaking of a possession left in storage and not to be claimed yet. The least thought of the child, even a vague musing about the name the old couple might have given it, brought back the voice which through the crisis had insisted that a question had been left unasked. "I've been sick, I'm still weak," she said to this voice, just as to the faces. And like them the voice hurt her more each day.

What an exorbitant price had to be paid for those visits Aurelia soon came to understand. "Where shall we live after the war?" she had asked; and suddenly she found herself at her old address, in the loud dusty street, climbing the dank, ill-lit staircase, all the way to the door. A strange name stood on the door, a strange voice spoke inside. She turned, she was running back . . .

It was better to forgo those visits. She knew it, she fought against them like a temptation; yet without them the day grew interminable, the boards of the bunk cut into her flesh, and her heart seemed to be stumbling around as though it had lost its appointed place. She could not do without those visits. "Alinka, Tola, and I — where shall we live after the war?" she asked, careful to be most specific. There was no misunderstanding this time. Complete with droshkies, pigeons, and train, the little side street came to her. And here they stayed — Aurelia, Alinka, Tola, and the child, who was unobtrusively asleep behind a closed door.

With ease, as if the war had been only a prolonged vacation, Alinka fitted into her new life — into the schoolgirl's uniform, the schoolgirl's routine. In the afternoons — for Aurelia's habit of fretting about those she expected back had come intact through the war — Aurelia waited for her at the window; and here she was, the dark pleated skirt billowing in the wind, the starched blouse dazzling-white in the sun, and the briefcase swinging nonchalantly in the small yet strong hand. If the briefcase contained the school record, "Excellents" would line it in a long column, and remarks in red pedagogical ink would join with them in praise: "Mature!" they exclaimed, "Brilliant," "Left utterly unwarped by her past!"

With Tola it was different. Tola had no uniform to fit into; no husband expected her in a white manor house; nothing waited for her but her own face grown lovely after the war. After clothing had been found to bring out this loveliness to the full, Aurelia felt at a loss as to what should come next, as though she had been reading a book with too scant attention, so that the sequence was hard to follow. Nothing was clear; the camp and "after the war" getting confused, Tola came alone up to the bunk, alone she walked through the little street; and once it even seemed to Aurelia that here in the barracks Tola was wearing new clothes. "I must ask her about it," Aurelia decided.

"Tola, there was something . . . something I wanted to ask you," she began, but what it was she could not recall. Like her hearing, her memory was gone: each thought was like a needle — it pricked and slipped away, not to be found again. This time, too, a vague unrest was left, from which Aurelia took refuge, in the thought of Barbara's letters filled with tales of manor life.

Nothing was haphazard in her visions, everything had a function. If the letters, for all the magnificence they described, proved that the inevitable separation had taken place, in counterproof the train rolled by. "If they want to see you, they will come," its wheels rumbled. "We want to see you, we are coming," echoed Barbara's letters.

And suddenly it was winter; winter because Barbara's flushed face looked so beautiful in its frame of shiny fur; winter because, chilled by the weather, the guests could relish fully the warmth of their reception. The shining tile stove breathed warmth into the rooms, another warm breath wafted from jugs of coffee and tea. "Please, Barbara, please, do help yourself, Mr. Grünbaum." She passed around the trays of pastry. "Who did all the baking, Aurelia? You? No? . . . now really . . . I would have never thought . . ." If the Barbara from after the war retained her halting speech, she herself was endowed with a quickness of repartee. "Well, did you expect me to bake cakes out of rotten beets?" she laughed back.

Her laughter stopped. A faux pas had been committed, she knew it. For what if Barbara's husband resented the references to that past; what if he felt excluded, even ill at ease, the only man among four women.

The only man among four women . . . A chill was creeping into the warm rooms. Over the bookcase, over the music stand, a shadow trailed, stood distinct and black against the ever-closed door.

"Aurelia, you must try not to sleep all the time." This time she felt grateful to Alinka for calling her back. And when the girl announced it was high time for her to sit up for a spell in the barracks, Aurelia gave in. Shriveled and black, like a drenched crow, she sat on the bench by the stove.

"Are you comfortable?"

"How does it feel to be up?"

She looked at them, and suddenly those old apologies about being sick and weak lost their power. "Barbara," she cried, "Barbara, you look like — worse than a picriniac; and you, Alinka, you too have neglected yourself, and you — " "You Tola," she was about to say; the needle pricked again, and this time she held it fast.

"Why did you separate?" she asked in the loud voice of the deaf. "I told you not to leave Tola alone, I remember I did."

"Alinka was all worn out, and I," Barbara fumbled, "I wanted them to stay together but they wouldn't let me."

"This is a camp, in a camp one must never separate," mechanically as if it were a maxim, she recited, when all at once they were hustling her up onto the bunk, then sat with their backs joined, forming a dark screen. A chink opened in the screen; as though someone were walking on his hands, a pair of untanned boots swung in the air — it was an O.D. man holding them high up above his head because a woman was trying to snatch them away from him.

"Tell me, what day is it?" Aurelia asked to break the silence.

"Friday," said Barbara.

"Saturday," Alinka corrected her, her voice piping with anger.

How good Sunday was; they were together, all four of them. To show that the bunk was a home, safe against any excesses of weather, rain kept beating against the roof. Washed, combed and turned over, Aurelia lay looking from face to face. "What did you say? What?" she kept asking, and nodded anyhow, even when the answer escaped her.

In the afternoon a ray of sun reported the weather had changed. "Aurelia," Alinka said, "today you should walk outside for a while."

Outside behind the wires trees stood, their branches weighed down by the dark fleshy leaves. Aurelia looked, "What . . . day is it, what day?" she stammered out.

"Why can't you remember anything?" Alinka cried. "It's Sunday."

"No, I mean the date. I mean — how long have I been sick?" She had been sick for almost four weeks; it was something like the twentieth of May now.

"And the Russians, where are they?"

"The Russians have been stopped!" Barbara said so loud that Aurelia could understand at once.

"In Italy the Allies are moving on," Tola put in quickly. "They took Cassino and some other town."

"They are approaching Rome," Alinka said. "Think, Aurelia, Rome!"

"Italy." Aurelia nodded. "Italy. Tola, you should not have been left alone," apropos of nothing, she added.

"I was against it," Alinka cried, "and you, Aurelia, stop fussing. One more week and we'll all be together; you're going back to work in a week."

"Work — or off to Picrine you go," Foreman Vokunski seemed to shout as she woke up next morning. Shells jingled in her ear, "The Russians have stopped," whispers said. She had to run away. "After the war," she repeated, "after the war — "

Things were waiting for her after the war: a man's navy blue suit, the complete works of Goethe, and a music stand stored with some Poles years ago. After the war, would she claim those things back? And whatever her answer, it was wrong — wrong to leave them unclaimed, wrong to give them away, even to someone deserving; and to take them into her new home, to pass by them while talking, laughing, waiting for guests, this would be worst of all. Like a gray, long-nosed putti her husband's face rose before her.

No, this could not go on any longer, Aurelia decided. She sat up. As if munching on something her lips opened and closed. "Alinka," she brought out.

"Alinka has gone to work," Tola answered. "What is it you want, Aurelia?"

"I meant to ask her — no, nothing."

"Alinka, did I look? Then, in Radom, before we ran away, did I look at him?" was what she had meant to ask, what her husband had commissioned her to ask during crisis. For if she had not really looked — then it was still possible that he had got up.

"Try to remember, Alinka — you stumbled on me — you helped me up, and then — did we run away or did I look first? You cried something, Alinka, and then we started running. That much I can remember, but not what happened before — " She kept reworking her question, as though everything depended on the way it was asked.

Nothing depended on the question; everything lay in her own hands. "I did not look" — if she could admit this, if she could bear it, that like a child left alone in a strange dark place he had groped around trying to find her; and this too, that he had seen her leaving him, and tried to stop her, and waved and called until, grown still, he had watched her walk on farther and farther away — then, he had risen, then he still was somewhere.

He was alive. He must be — she knew this — she had never believed he had stayed behind.

"My husband is dead," she would say, and shame would come over her as though she were lying, as though to gain pity for herself she were dressing him in some grotesque, ill-fitting clothes. And when he came to her, when "I am dead, Aurelia," he said, then resentment would fill her, as on those evenings when she would sit and wait for him, now leaning out of the window, now reaching for the telephone, and all the time seeing him beaten and robbed, and all the time knowing where he was — in the Café Esplanade reading the evening papers; until anger would grip her, for the wasted fear, for the remorse lest the fear was not wasted this time, even for the joy, the great relieved joy, that rose in her when at last he came out of the dark.

After the war I'll look for him . . . for you, I'll look for you — and such weariness came over her that even to chase a fly off her face was too much.

Through the strange, uneasy half-dream images floated. She was walking somewhere, she was walking toward her old home, past the fire station, through a square beleaguered by traffic and noise. Sooty-faced children played in the littered grass; on the benches sat recruits staring at their purple fists; crowds moved on in the gritty dust. She could not leave this square. She paced up and down, looking at each passerby, each face, because it just could not be that so many, hundreds upon hundreds, should go by, and he, who for ten years had taken this way, should not come back.

He was back! The face she could not see, a newspaper was hiding it, but the hands that held the paper up could be only his, and the long balding head, and the black violin case like a patient dog lying at his feet. "Richard!" her mouth wanted to cry. "Don't do it," said her heart to warn her that such a sudden meeting was hard on any heart. She stalked on. She was almost there. She stood looking at him who still had not seen her, who went on reading, until suddenly the paper fell down. As though to halt her, he stretched out his arm —

"I knew it," clutching at him, she cried. "I knew it — always." They were walking on; in a room that had no walls, darkness fell upon them like rain. "Aurelia," he whispered, "Aurelia, do you think I should shave tomorrow?"

A spasm went through her. "I cannot think," she was telling someone, "I am so tired."

Sleep came at last, dreamless at first, as after a day of hard work. Then the Planty grew out of the dark; it was raining, balls splashed against the soggy ground, louder and louder, until "Stop it!" she cried, and woke up.

From outside the splashing was coming, loud, punctuated by hoarse shouts. Here in the barracks all was still; no crowds churned round the bunks; no line stood at the stove; only over a squashed potato flies were buzzing, iridescent in the sun. "Tola!" Aurelia cried, and suddenly, without knowing how, she found herself standing below her bunk.

A girl bent under a steep black sack tiptoed toward her; the sack was a hunch — this Aurelia did understand at last — though not why the girl kept hissing about gymnastics. "Gymnastics, watch out, gymnastics," the hiss rose from bunk after bunk, but Aurelia, pressing down the windblown shift, was walking on toward the open door.

In the mud the women lay sprawled — motionless bodies stretched out in a long jagged row. "Up!" The O.D. man swung his black truncheon, and they revived, they were hopping on all fours while she stood, shift flapping in the wind. At last she turned. Clutching at the bunks, the Hunchback's arms, the air, she staggered back to the bench. I looked, she thought, I did look, and she felt cold.

Mud hanging like blackberries down their faces, the women came in, and at once an outcry broke out against the Orphan, who had emptied the slops outside, who had brought the gymnastics upon them. Tola was the last to come in, shuffling heavily, because she wore big untanned boots.

"I know where you got those boots," Aurelia was about to cry. The bread Tola handed her silenced this cry, and the sight of the red points which the camphor injections had left on her own arms. "Let me stay here," she said softly, wiping the mud off Tola's face. "I — I'd rather not go back to the bunk. Please let me stay here." And for a long time after the nightshift had left, she sat staring at the exemption slip Tola had put into her hand.

Slowly her eyes began to move around the barracks. It had changed; unfamiliar faces looked from everywhere. On the bunk where the Rebbetzyn used to call upon God the hunchbacked girl sat, and across from her an old woman kept blubbering thickly, as though choked by wads of cotton wool. "Typhus!" Aurelia sighed. "Yes, typhus." Up on her bunk a ray of light spun through the dusk.

And watching it, Aurelia understood that the time for going back had come. I'm the oldest among them, she told herself, and found a peculiar comfort in this thought.

"I'm going back to work with you, tomorrow, or the day after at the latest," she announced as soon as Barbara and Alinka came in. At once they jumped on her; she should see herself, they shouted — all livid, not a drop of blood in her face. "Stop yelling at me, both of you!" Aurelia pushed them away and, though the bunk rocked like a boat, she climbed up all by herself.

"I'm going back because I feel better. And I want no special food anymore, do you understand? And no camphor," she said, forcing a mud-colored beet into her mouth. "As it is I've let things slide — " She faltered. "Look, I didn't mean to sound angry," she added more softly, "only I want us to be together, and Tola — Tola has been doing too much."

"We tried to help her, but no one wanted to give us anything for sale," Alinka said, and they were silent.

The light went out, and such a yearning filled Aurelia for the sound of their voices that "Let's talk," she whispered, "please let us talk."

"Foreman Vokunski has typhus," Alinka said.

"It was very warm today," said Barbara.

"And — what is the news?" Aurelia asked, not trying to sound indifferent.

"No news. I mean — I mean, the Allies are moving, in Italy they are," Barbara answered.

"Italy is of crucial importance," Aurelia began.

"Yes — perhaps," and already both of them were drifting away from her into sleep.

The quiet breath arched over her; the breath was a bridge joining those pressed against her worn-out body with those others from "after the war," now one by one rising before her. Somewhere a door opened, and for the first time the child appeared to her, lying — as small children always do — on its stomach, the blanket tossed aside, in trust that it would be covered at the first touch of cold.

"Ah, look how she sleeps," Barbara sighed.

"Hush, you may wake her up." This was Alinka.

"Someone should cover her; you, Tola, please, you do it," said she herself; and they all looked on while Tola bent down over the child.

Barbara would never have any children; Alinka had grown up motherless; Tola had no one left. Over each of them the unborn hovered, and the dead, their absence never to be grasped.

Slowly, like a fading light, the child drew away. But the other figures, though they grew smaller, each shone with a chiseled clarity — like medallions kept under her closing eyes.

Chapter 28

OVERNIGHT AURELIA had worked out her plan. Today and tomorrow she would exercise, would walk around the barracks and outside; and the day after it would be back to work for her. Hardly had the dayshift gone when she began getting dressed — slowly, because her hands, like newly hired servants, had to be reminded, now about a hook, now about the valerian drops to be put into her pocket. And just like such servants they begged for time off; they were tired, they needed rest.

Nor was it easy to get down off the bunk. Yesterday fear had helped her; before that, Barbara with Alinka or Tola. Now left unaided, she kept turning this way and that, until at last, arms wound round the post, she scrambled down, then settled for a moment of rest.

"Wa — wa — wa — ter," the old woman blubbered. The hunchbacked girl gave her some water. Then, bringing her long, acid face to Aurelia's ear, she explained that the old lady had suffered a stroke but was lucky, since her daughter — a doctor — was giving her physiotherapy. "This does marvels, just mar — " Half through the word the Hunchback vanished. From somewhere above, fingers reddened with trotyl pointed to the door.

This, Aurelia understood, was a warning. She must do something, must run, must hide. And she tried. Arms outstretched, she staggered to her bunk, to the door, to her bunk again. But everywhere she turned an O.D. man stood. The exemption slip she was showing them was snatched away by the wind. Suddenly fists struck her; she was sucked in by a jet of air, was carried past the overturned bucket, past the door and on.

Outside the crowd caught her like a net. Cries, arms tangled around her; prickly, like a pincushion, a shaved head pushed right into her mouth. The sun blazed. Behind the wires the too green trees swayed upward; as though perched on the scales' opposite side the crowd dove down, went up, and down again. I'm weak; even after the grippe one feels wobbly, Aurelia told herself. The swaying stopped, but her face felt numb, as though pressed to icy glass.

Muted by the glass, shouts reached her. The crowd swung. Something was happening; a column of fours was being formed — this was it. Gesturing because speaking hurt, she staggered along the column, begging to be taken in. But wherever she came the four was complete. "Move on," everyone cried, and fear seized her of being left out, to walk alone somewhere at the end. Then, faraway someone waved at her. "Mrs. Katz!" It was the Orphan calling. "Mrs. Katz!"

"Help me," Aurelia tried to say. "Help me!" cried the Orphan. They grappled with each other, they tottered, and would have fallen, when like a firm ledge the hump came between. "Lean on me," said the Hunchback, "both of you, lean hard." The Orphan wanted to grab all this support for herself, but Aurelia would not give in; she kept a firm grip on the hump. And so they moved on.

In the distance a balding long head caught the sun, vanished, reappeared there and there and there — wherever she looked countless Richard Katzes stood, only to flee from her. These are picriniacs — just picriniacs, she thought, and leaned harder.

Now everything was growing. First of all her body, loose like a wide cloak; she had stockings for legs, sleeves for arms. And around her the camp grew — the barracks, the streets, everything was drawing away. She must have walked miles, and the Appellplatz was nowhere in sight. At last the odor of chlorine burst from the washroom, the cloying steam, that was the coffee kitchen; but where the lake had come from, she could not figure out.

It was not a lake; it was the Appellplatz mud glistening in the sun. Splashes of glare leapt into her eyes, the sunrays drilled into her head, and most of all the Orphan's shrieks hurt. "Mrs. Katz," she kept shrieking, "Mrs. Katz!"

Aurelia could not answer, she could only look. The Orphan seemed to be wearing pendular earrings shining a pale green. "Mrs. Katz," the Orphan shook her head and the earrings — they were drops of pus — dropped down, "they are going to kill us, Mrs. Katz."

"Why?" Aurelia managed to ask.

In a sweeping gesture the Orphan pointed at the shaved heads, the tatters, and the legs slipping on the mud. "Why not?" she said. "Look! Why not?"

"You should be ashamed to spread panic," Aurelia wanted to say, but like an endless thread the answer twisted itself round her tongue. The Hunchback cried something about work. Far away the gate opened, its screech cutting into her like a sharp-toothed saw.

In the forest it was easier. Here green shade descended on her, here a breeze came to wipe the sweat off. "You — panic!" Aurelia turned to the Orphan, and took heart. Because like this answer, so the road ahead could be shortened; she would just divide it, would walk first to the white bush, then on to the clump of birches. Once the bush was reached she allowed herself to stop. She did nothing, just took a deep breath, when suddenly the air seemed to harden; pincers clutched at her throat, the tree against which she staggered felt like sponge under her back. Feet passed her, feet in sabots, in papers, in rags; O.D. men's boots stamped by, someone was hobbling on crutches made of sticks. Then no one came.

"Don't leave me alone," she tried to cry, but could not. From far away the Orphan's voice came: "Don't leave me," it begged. And here was the Hunchback. The Hunchback had left the Orphan to come to her.

Gratitude filled her, a great, soothing tenderness for this stranger, for the sound of her voice, though what this voice was saying she could hardly make out. "Water," it repeated, "I — water." The girl wanted to give her water, but she . . . she had something better, the valerian drops Tola had bought.

Cautiously with her chin, Aurelia pointed to her pocket, and now the valerian bottle was growing. Like a bronze lantern it swung before her, and behind this lantern the Hunchback's mouth gaped in a dark funnel. Understanding this sign, Aurelia tore her mouth open. Bitterness filled her mouth; she lurched forward, shattering glass fell around her. Then silence. When a shout cut through it she started, she tried to run away from the O.D. man who might hit her, might make her do gymnastics. But he stood very still, his eyes looking at her mildly — just as the Hunchback's were.

He is not shouting; I could lie down — the thought was dazzling, like a revelation. And hardly had it come when the earth reached up to her with a clump of soft moss. Now she was lying down, now nothing hurt anymore, only she longed to hold on to the Hunchback's hands. But they, as though suspended on a swiftly growing tree, rose higher and higher. From nearby, ferns bent down to her. She clutched at them — when of themselves the ferns leapt up, tore her hands upward, her arm, her shoulder. Slowly, the fern roots swayed and scattered over her face the moist crumbs of earth.

Chapter 29

WHEN THE FAINT SMELL of valerian drifted to her from the roadside, Tola, remembering that quite a few women had got hold of those drops, just walked on. But the stares halted her; they knew something. "Don't you know yet?" they asked, pushing her back, long before an arm pointed toward the bush.

From behind it a faint rustle came, then stopped. The branch Tola pulled at broke, and the white petals shed into her hands, onto the mossy ground, and onto another hand lying among squashed ferns.

Strangely dilated, Aurelia's eyes looked far above her; when wind came, when strands of hair crossed out those eyes, they just went on staring. Someone was moving nearby — an O.D. man walking toward her. He stopped. "Dead," he said.

A stone had been flung at her. It had missed but before more stones came she must make a big step across the broken branch, then another across the glass, and then she must run, back to the column.

And at once she wanted to run the other way, away from those stares asking something of her — something that she could not give. Elbows jutting, she pushed her way to the front, where the Kaelanki marched. Here no one knew her, here nothing was asked of her. When she stumbled the girls helped her up. "Leave me," she said, and they let her be. And a peculiar numb calm came over her: she had seen nothing, nothing had happened yet, only she must keep walking, past the gate, across the Appellplatz, then on.

Before the barracks she stopped, put her ear to the door, and listened — for what she could not tell — then, very cautiously she sneaked in. On her bunk lay a dark shape, a dark arm swayed to and fro: a sleeve — the sleeve of Aurelia's coat.

And now she was running, back to the gate.

Group after group marched in, the air grew bitter, the air glowed red with trotyl, and from each group Barbara and Alinka were running toward her. She must call, must give them a sign — when all at once they vanished, and only strangers were walking by. But they would come, they must. And then she would cry.

For a long while no one came in. Then dust rose; with a loud rattle a cart rolled through the gate. It was only a dark sack that was lying on the cart, she knew it, she had looked, yet her legs gave way under her. The rattle passed by, it was gone, and out of the silence came whistling. A guard was whistling as he closed the gate, because no one would come in anymore.

She could not bear to be alone, she wanted to feel someone close to her — anyone, even the picriniac with bandages instead of a face, even the old woman pressing a piece of kindling against her chest. But they, though she looked at them, walked on. Clasping her own body only hurt, and her mouth was clogged with a lump of dust.

Had they, unnoticed by her, come back? Was it Barbara touching her arm? An O.D. man was standing in front of her, the one she had met in the woods, she was almost sure. He had come to take back what he had said, he would lead her to Aurelia. And for a long while she could not understand why he kept pointing at her feet.

"Boots," he was saying. He wanted his money, or his boots back, the untanned ones; what was the matter with her, why was she gaping like a fool?

Without a word she handed him her bag, and watched how he licked his finger, how, baring his stubby teeth, he counted the money with a moist hiss.

"Anything to sell, anything?" with just such a hiss she seemed to whisper. The day was not fearful anymore. She could do it, now, right away; she could start walking through the barracks, she would buy and sell and haggle. "Anything to sell? I pay good prices." This is how Barbara would find her.

Suddenly she was running.

People stopped her. Was there any coffee in the kitchen? they asked. Was the washroom open? Was it true what someone had said about Mrs. Katz? "I don't know," she said; she said, "Yes, it's true."

The mouth that spoke felt like paper, the voice came from some-where far off. Who had spoken to her, why her face was crusted with mud she did not know, but she must have been walking for a long time, because as she sat down on a bench, noon had come, and barrels of soup were being rolled into the barracks.

A woman, molting after typhus like a bird, brought her some soup. As long as the bald head was bending over her she ate. Left alone at last, she gave the soup to a picriniac and walked on.

There was no quicklime on the crate; it glistened darkly in the sun. And from everywhere, from the moldering lid, from the wires, from the trees, the eyes crossed out by a strand of hair were looking at her. "Let me stay here," the tired voice was saying. "I'd rather not go back to the bunk."

"No!" everything in her cried. Those eyes were gone, but within her something was breaking open, something like the crate, and from it her other dead came tumbling out, each with eyes that looked crossed out, each staring. "No!" And she walked on.

Elbows pressed to her sides, knees dug into her chest, she sat on a bench. When someone sat down next to her she moved to the next bench, then to the next, each time careful to arrange herself — the elbows first, next the knees, and at last the eyes that must look only at the porous mud. There was, she knew, something to be pre-pared for, but the day was still long.

What had happened to the time? "Out, all without exemptions out!" came calls, and she, who was quite unprepared, was waiting for the O.D. men to chase her out of the barracks. But no one had noticed her hiding in a corner; the nightshift was gone; and the woman next to her, shaking the last drops out of the bucket — was just one of the sick.

When the woman went back to her bunk, Tola felt prepared. Someone must have told them. They would come in crying, Alinka forcing her sobs back, and Barbara — She could not imagine Bar-bara's cry. She plugged her ears against this cry.

They had not been told. "Aurelia," they were calling. They were climbing up onto the bunk, were climbing down, were running to the door. She stepped forward.

"Tola." Alinka was the one to speak up. "Tola, why are you here?"

"Here . . . I . . ." she could not go on. The hunchbacked girl wedged her hump between them.

"No exemption — O.D. man — they chased everyone out to work," the strangely shallow voice was saying, while she stared only at Barbara's shoes.

"Then she died," said the Hunchback, and Tola was waiting for the cry that now must come.

A knocking sound came from nearby. It was Alinka's fist, nailing one finger down to her mouth. Barbara's mouth, too, was white and gaping without sound.

"Barbara!" Tola cried. "Barbara!" But it was Alinka whom her arms clasped.

One by one they climbed up the bunk.

"Torn," Alinka said, "anyhow . . . it's torn," and lifting the coat with two bent fingers, she carried it out, then came back to take a place in the line waiting for bread.

"Eat!" she forced the bread upon them, "you've got to eat."

Obediently Barbara pushed the chunk into her mouth. Suddenly a choked cough spattered the crumbs around her, but her eyes were dry so that she seemed to be laughing.

Part Six

Chapter 30

No MOAN ever broke forth from her, no word of complaint, nothing but this cough — choked, too puny for her. Because it was as though she were growing, sprouting forth as adolescents do, suddenly and at random, each limb feeding at another's cost, each limb ill suited to the others, and she even slouched as they do, uncertain how to bear the weight of such growth. But what made people stare, what made them whisper "Is that she, the Pole?" was her face: gaunt, between cracked lips the teeth a too dazzling white, the eyes sunken under the heavy lids. And slowly those lids would rise . . .

Then her eyes did more than just look. Then like the eyes of an inexperienced traveler, constantly checking and rechecking to see that his belongings were together, still there, they kept darting from Tola to Alinka; or, again, they would widen, would grow still, as though she were waiting for someone looming in the distance to draw near.

Because at first she was waiting all the time. At first it was with her as with those who, when news of disaster comes, grant that such things might happen in the newspapers, or to someone else, but to themselves never. They wait, drawing comfort from this very waiting — trusting that their hope, which transforms each passerby into a messenger, each ring of the doorbell into a telegram about to deny that first unthinkable news, cannot be in vain; then, with the passerby gone, the ring an unwanted guest, they go on waiting, reassured by the fidelity of things: the bed still wearing an inviting look, the marker showing where the book must reopen.

Barbara was to herself such a thing: if what lay so utterly beyond her grasp had really happened, then surely something would have happened to her too, as to a glass that must crash to the ground when the hand that holds it is wrenched away. But not enough had happened to her. True, at night, when she saw mothers everywhere

— the one enjoined by that gooselike honk not to die, the paralyzed
mother using her daughter's arms for crutches — then she had to
bolt herself, like a house against burglars, against the least memory.
True, in the morning Alinka had to pummel her, in such dread
of the day that she refused to get up. And all through the day Barbara was like a patient who, a novice to his pain, keeps tossing in
the hope of finding a place of rest. Standing in the Appellplatz she
could not wait to march on; marching, she could not wait to sit
down in the hall; no sooner did she sit down than she was up again,
pacing to and fro.

"Sit down, Barbara," and she went back to her place. "Work,
Barbara," and she began to work. But then a woman would get up
— her glance, darting as though it were a busy thoroughfare she was
about to cross, her hopping steps, her hands — everything right
about her, only a gesture needed to be adjusted, only the smile's
shape. No adjustment was possible. Just a stranger had passed by.
And yet, if this woman so worn out, so old, was still here, how could
that other one — the name Barbara shunned, the name was forbidden — be gone?

If . . . if only . . . So her calculations of error began. If only
the O.D. men had respected the exemption; if Goldberg had still
been there; or if she herself had stayed in the camp. And had not
something forewarned her — on the way out, at the gate she had
still wanted to run back. There had been a mistake, an oversight
so slight that it could be corrected yet.

"You'll respect her exemption!" with this cry, had she stayed, she
would have pushed the O.D. men away; would have warmed the
ever cold hands, would have whispered, "Ah, thank God it's over.
Thank God."

Suddenly, a certainty: she *had* stayed, *had* offered thanks. The
evil fancy kept hold of her, but would be dispelled by one
word from Alinka or Tola.

"Work!" they cried. And within her a wall was crumbling stone
by stone; within her, dread arose for herself and for those two she
still had left. And it was then that she looked at them with those
anxious traveler's eyes.

How heavily they were weighing on her; she could not bear this weight — she wanted them to be gone. She could not do without them — "Wait, together," she ran after them. Until it seemed to her this much at least she deserved — that they should exist in duplicate copies, one always with her, the other stored safe from all harm.

She lived in fear of some harm. Sliding like an outsized cap down to the eyes, her hand would touch Alinka's forehead, checking whether typhus had come. Tola was not threatened by typhus; Tola seemed calm, and looked well, but at times a strange glance would make Barbara start. "What is it?" she asked. "What's the matter with you?"

"Nothing," Tola said, "absolutely nothing," and Barbara breathed a sigh of relief.

As the days went by, as she waited with ever fainter hope, to this relief a craving was joined — the craving for a task so exacting that it would free her from those calculations of error, from those nearly perfect likenesses, those nights, and from what oppressed her more and more, the sense of omission, as though an errand were being put off.

Grief was this errand. Grief was like gifts from home sent to the one who somewhere in the frozen dark was still struggling on, but growing smaller, more shadowy with each step. And Tola and Alinka, did they grieve? She watched them with shame, yet wistfully, begrudging Alinka even her fingers gnawed down to red stumps, but above all, pleadingly, as an older sister might watch the younger ones, begging them to keep well and leave all the mourning to her. For Barbara would mourn as soon as what had happened could somehow be grasped.

It was grasped; the waiting came to an end. But just before it ended, for the last time hope had leapt up in her, the hope that he, the little Pole running across the sunny meadow toward the column, was a messenger with news for her. He was coming closer, was shouting something — about France — about the Allies — that they had landed in France. And her gaze grew blank, as though to ask "Is that all?"

For the others, the women, the O.D. men, the picriniacs shining in the sun, that was enough. "A few more days and the war will be over!" They embraced one another, they laughed, while she stood on the side like a child not permitted to join in the game. She wanted this permission; for just one moment she longed to be like the others, to laugh, to wave like them.

"A . . . a few more days . . ." and she broke into her too small cough. Because now, when the war was to end in days, what had happened to her grew clear: only the three of them would leave the camp; to the manor, to Stefan, only three would come. Again a cough, and she grew stiff, as though with all her strength barring a door within her. But it opened. Like a model presenting clothes for all occasions, Aurelia stepped forth: now the bandages pressing the distended belly in; now the sweat-darkened shirt, and the inflamed face, now the drenched-crow look. Stealthily her hand groped for a moldy crumb. This hand was clutching at the bunk, was forced away; and the face, once again startled, because all, birth, and hunger, and typhus, had been in vain.

She could not bear to see this face, she pummeled and pushed till it vanished behind the slamming door. But through the chink those eyes stared, asking, "Won't you give me even that much?" She would give what they demanded, she would cry — right now!

"Allons enfants de la patrie," a chorus sang. Barbara felt hungry and a voice irked her, it was singing much too loudly. Tola was singing. When Barbara looked at her she broke off, then suddenly looked back with such derision that Barbara shrank back.

"What is it, Tola?" she stammered. "What's wrong with you?"

"Nothing, really, nothing." But Barbara could not believe this anymore.

Had her grief been more perfect, had the sign of stifled sobs helped her to distinguish between sacrifice and temptation, she might have given herself fully to her worry about Tola. Without such a sign — and with the past thrusting at her the memories of those bungling mourners who, between niggardly sniffles, checked to see if they looked well in black — what else could she do but divide herself between her new worry and her longing for grief.

At times it seemed that her longing would be fulfilled. Profound pity for herself brought tears to her eyes; soon she would get up; hurriedly, lest she break down right there in the hall, she would run to the latrine, would wait till everyone had left. And then she would cry. She did get up, she went to the latrine, and waited till everyone was gone. Then, sure that no one was looking, she bit into the rotten beets, and drank water till it oozed down her chin.

She was hungry as never before. A beggar seemed to have got into her. "Give me to eat," he whined loudest when she was about to cry. For, the moment she had turned from pitying herself to the one who had made her so pitiable, it all started again — the stiffening, the barring of doors; and at once a void gaped within her, at once in this void the beggar wailed for a spoonful of soup. But when soup was dealt out she ate gingerly, as though forcing herself.

So without her knowing how or when, a ritual of grief had evolved — a perfunctory way of eating, a wooden "Oh, I see" when gossip was repeated, or news. And when Alinka would scold that Barbara must take care of herself, must wash and mend her dress, she answered "I cannot. Not yet."

"How she grieves," the women whispered. "Oh, she's ruining herself with such grief." Like coveted praise those words were to her. And if she looked at Tola and Alinka it was not out of any apprehension — for her ruined body seemed to her like mourning weeds that could be cast off at will — but only to explain that, had she been able to face what had happened, then such praise would have been deserved.

Of the resigned whisper, of the wooden voice in the evening no trace was left. Slouched forward, the straggly hair falling on her face, she hurried to the work the doctor had found for her — cleaning the floor in the "sick barracks." There the last typhus cases and the other sick, whom the hospital could not contain, had been gathered.

"Come on, get everyone out of the way." Brandishing a broom Barbara yelled at the girl with the honking voice who had turned orderly to nurse her mother. Water splashed; her knees thudding against the floor, her arms moving in powerful strokes, she began scrubbing the floor. And this was the one vision of joy she permitted herself: a floor stretching in a vast plain, above it chunks of bread suspended, enough of them to build a barricade against hunger.

The chunk of bread that was her pay clasped fast for protection against thieves as well as against herself who yearned to gulp it, she hurried on to see if there was money for her or news. "No, no money for you, no letter," the O.D. men said. And to the hatred she felt against them a bitterness was added against the child, the embezzler gone with the capital of her hope to feed upon the old couple from whom no message ever came. If the money came she would buy a whole loaf of bread; if the money came she would forbid Tola to peddle once and for all.

"Tola back?" So she would burst into the barracks. No, Tola was never back. No, Alinka never felt like coming along to look for her; and Barbara, still hoping that a talk between the two of them might make clear what made Tola so strange, did not insist much.

"Stay here," she would order and was off to search for Tola in barracks after barracks.

"The peddler has just been here," the women called to her. She glowered; but it was the peddler whom she would find at last — screechy-voiced and with quick, sneaky eyes.

"Enough!" Barbara muttered. "You'll stop this peddling at once."

"I don't mind peddling," Tola answered much too gently.

"You should mind. This is doing something to you, Tolenka." Barbara tried to force down her anger. "Listen to me. You've done enough for us, you have."

"I'm not peddling just for you. I would have done it anyhow, for my own sake."

"Anyhow . . . anyhow," Barbara grumbled with some personal hatred against this word. Clutching at Tola so as not to lose her in the crowd she went from barracks to barracks, lost her, called, ran on, then, while Tola was looking over some rags, stood morosely on the side. A hint from someone that Tola was cheating, and Barbara flared up, 'How dare you? Do you know to whom you are speaking?!"

The women smirked. "Please don't make a scene," Tola would say. "Please go back. Alinka shouldn't be left so much by herself."

"Good, let's go back together." But she always had to go back alone.

Evening after evening was luminous and very still. Into the odor of urine and rotten beets came winds smelling of freshly cut grass; frogs sang somewhere in the dusk. And when the crowds dispersed, when window after window caught the last sun, then, more than ever, the camp looked like a village coming to rest after a long summer day. But all Barbara could see was Tola with those darting peddler's eyes. Should she go back to Tola? Should she talk to Alinka about her? Like someone afraid of a doctor's diagnosis, she kept putting the consultation off.

"Alinka, I've got to talk to you," she blurted out at last.

It was evening; the two of them were sitting on the bunk, Barbara naked under her coat since the girl had insisted on mending her clothes — yes, the underwear too, and not later but now. Wind came in, blew back the coat from Barbara's breasts that now, with none present to mourn their ruin, struck her as alien, almost fearful.

"It's about Tola." Barbara pulled her coat tighter. "She looks well; she seems — I mean, at first she seemed calm, but now she isn't herself anymore. She says less and less, she looks at me so oddly. Perhaps I'm just imagining things, still, today — " She broke off.

They had been standing in front of the soup barrels today, and as the sun fell upon the scrawny necks, upon the heads typhus had left half bald, Tola, thin but with her strong neck, her tanned face, looked so well by contrast that Barbara could not restrain herself. "You do look well," she exclaimed, "really."

"Of course, why shouldn't I?" Tola smiled a half-dreamy, half-mocking smile that Barbara could not bear to remember.

"I'm worried about her." Barbara whispered. "I'm so worried," she repeated, hoping that the girl would pounce on her for exaggerating as always. But Alinka went on sewing silently.

"Yesterday in London," came from the bunk below. Just a few bombs had fallen on London, Tola had said yesterday. Now the women spoke of many bombs — bombs that flew by themselves, like giant kites.

"Fools! How can you believe this propaganda!" Alinka cried. "Fools — propaganda — " Barbara was repeating when suddenly she saw Stefan lying, as in the summertime on the grass, on the pavement, plaster from the bombed-out house flaking down onto his gray face. As if he were a hypochondriac, come to plague her with an imaginary illness, so furiously she pushed him away. "Alinka!" she muttered. "Can't you answer when I speak to you?"

"I've nothing to answer. You spend every evening with Tola, you talk to her, so you should know what's going on. I only know that something is wrong with her. And you, you could . . ."

"What could I do? What?"

"You could take yourself in hand."

"Is that so?" Barbara gasped. "And who follows Tola around like a dog? Who scrubs floors, who brings bread every day? Take myself in hand! How? What more should I do? Should I start dancing for joy?"

"God forbid." Alinka spoke very mildly. "God forbid I should ask you to dance for joy, as we, as Tola and I do. But this I'll ask of you: go, get a mirror and look. Just for once look at yourself!"

And Barbara did look at herself, outside, in the windows tinged blue with the dust. At first, they just gave her hints, reflecting the spindly arm here, there the sunken cheeks, until in the last window, red with sunset, she saw herself fully and shrank back. Once before she had seen herself look like this, barefoot and in rags after the Strafappell, when the camp had appeared to her like a giant slug, drawing, sucking her in. "What vitality," Aurelia had said then. "To such as you nothing will ever happen."

A single cough shook her. And she stood motionless, her whole being sending a message to the one who had gone — the message that all gifts of grief must from now on be canceled.

I must stop eating beets, they give me diarrhea — she talked to herself all through the night — I will wash more; I will cut my hair. But at the thought of herself, not like a woman anymore, with cropped hair and drawn-out breasts, a shudder went through her. She sat up.

"Tola," she turned abruptly, "Tola, why aren't you asleep?"

"Stop watching me," Tola cried. "Stop it, leave me alone. I — " Tola broke off, touched Barbara's shoulder, and quickly drew away.

"Nothing," Tola said, "nothing is wrong with me." She would speak indulgently, with just a touch of annoyance, as one answers those given to fretting about some great misery, some profound yet hidden hurt; and she would draw herself up, as though to add "Look at me, do I seem unhappy?" Because she was not unhappy, because there was no misery, no hidden hurt, because she felt so calm, it seemed to her that were this bunk, this last home of hers, to grow empty before her very eyes, then, too, she would go on, just as each time before.

Only in those first days, when Barbara started at the least noise, when Alinka had a scar instead of a mouth, only then did she feel something — a sense of precariousness, as though perched on a steep slope she was waiting to be pushed down. This too was over. Since then she had been divided into three parts: one, able to carry on with such calm; another, the observer diligently collecting data about her; and the third receiving these data without the least surprise — for had not all this happened once before?

But the nights were hateful. At night she lay wedged between Alinka, curled into a tight bundle, and Barbara, sprawled out like a large tired beast, between the clicking of fingernails, on which the girl kept gnawing, and the choked cough.

"Hundred — hundred and twenty — I'll get the price down to a hundred, I'll sell for a hundred and twenty." Shoes, coats floated before her; she kept counting, kept haggling. Suddenly the counting stopped.

Even the dead too had to stand in line — the one who had just joined them forced to await her turn, those who had waited much too long now coming near. Her parents came. They looked — as once they had looked at her cousins, those children so much more considerate than herself — at the cough-cramped shoulders, the gnawed-up nails. They sighed, they turned toward her . . .

"Hundred — hundred and twenty — " They vanished, the cough stopped and the gnawing teeth. Careful not to waken them, she would rise, would look. She did not want to look. Yet something — was it the need to see what she dreaded, or the hope for a sudden change — forced her up. No change; gaunt, eyes sunken so deep that the sockets seemed empty, Barbara's face rose from the bluish dusk.

"Speak to her. To you she'll listen," Alinka insisted. How should she speak, about what? Should she recommend a special diet of foods nourishing yet light? Or a trip to the country? Or a long rest? Or, best of all, should she hold herself up as the shining example? There was nothing to be said. But breathing the odor of sickly flesh, she had to clench her fists so as not to grab Barbara and shake and shake her, till from the gaunt body that other Barbara whom she had dragged here from Werk A would step forth.

A rich "cousin" would have taken care of Barbara in Werk A. In Werk A they would have still been gaping at her — the "big Pole" who looked "as though she had just come from the Freedom." Here too they called her "the Pole." "Come on, I don't want to march next to the Pole," the women — again afraid of being taken to Picrine — hissed, tactfully behind Barbara's back. The fat Kaelanka who had taken Aurelia's place at Schmitz had no use for such tact. "Let me be," she cried when asked to march in their four. "If anything happens on the way, she'll drag me down." It was Barbara whom all shunned for fear she might "drag them down," while Tola herself was sought after. She thrived here. Why not? Quite a few managed to thrive in this place.

For the first time, Tola felt, she saw the camp clearly. Everything was exposed. How could one best get a new outfit here? By going with an O.D. man to the clothing depot, and into bed, the same bed over which, once, long ago, she had kept watch. Why had so many been sent to Picrine right after the typhus? Because they could not afford the ransom the O.D. men split with the Polish foreman. And the bread for sale, where did it come from? From the hospital, where like peppercorns dead flies dropped upon tangled bodies, while outside the orderly was sunning himself, — he, the wholesale dealer in their bread, their clothes, and their shoes.

In the barracks it was a free-for-all: the old accusing the young of being greedier than harpies, the young screaming "You old hag, haven't you lived long enough?" This — the soured odor of suspicion, as if even the air were rationed so strictly you robbed the others by taking an extra breath — was the only legacy of typhus.

One third of the Cracow women had vanished in the epidemic without leaving a trace. At Schmitz, where the shifts had been merged, not a seat was empty. In the barracks, where the women had made themselves comfortable, every bunk was filled. Friends lived on each bunk, friends, arm in arm, strolled through the streets.

And from above on the towers the guards watched. To her they were heralds proclaiming that all was well in this place where love was a children's game, the game at playing house with whichever partner came along; because the friends watched over so anxiously were replacements for those typhus had swept away, each found with the usual camp speed, in the usual camp way, by glimpsing a free place on a bunk, by asking "Are you, too, alone?"

Still, it was in these barracks that she felt at ease. While with Alinka and Barbara she had to watch out: against the bodies lying in the thicket beside the road which she tried to hide from Barbara by walking faster, by pointing at something in the opposite direction; or against that wistful look of Alinka's that she tried to dispel by talking about anything at all; and against herself, against that spite in herself urging her, each time Barbara gave her that bewildered look, to exclaim how lighthearted she felt, how calm — urging her to sing out, or to ask "Barbara, should I wear my hair in curls?"

When alone and peddling she could rest. True, with the market so glutted by typhus that lockets and gold teeth went for a crust of bread, she earned hardly a pittance, cheat though she did. But when she pounded her chest, when she screamed "Let me drop dead on the spot if I'm trying to cheat you," then a feeling of liberation came over her, as though this sparse body of hers were a cocoon out of which her true self was emerging, foul-mouthed and with fleshy legs — the spitting image of those vendors rumored to feast on the whitest of bread. No one seemed surprised. The barracks received her like a familiar neighborhood which, knowing all there was to know about her, could not have expected anything else.

Only Barbara and Alinka kept expecting something else from her. For them she still was the one "who had done more than enough" — the tender soul for whom peddling was bad. And if she told them that peddling was a sport for her, that what had established her reputation — her asking the soldier to save the child — had been done mostly out of vanity? Then Alinka would give her an injured look, and Barbara, "How dare you," Barbara would bellow at her as she did at those who dared to suggest that she was a cheat.

The reluctant way of eating, the wooden voice, even what was most stylized about Barbara's grief, Tola could forgive for the sake of that bewildered stare that made her long to sing. But this she could not forgive: those shouts, hardly more than a month ago offered to another and already passed on to her like clothing that must not go to waste. She did not want those clothes; they cramped her, they did not fit. And if anyone deserved to inherit them it was Alinka, not she.

Had it not been for her, Alinka would not have been left so much to herself. Had it not been for her, such tact would not have been needed, the bitter tact of the perfect lodger, a role the girl had taken upon herself: mending, cleaning, keeping an eye on Barbara with a show of indifference meant to prove she was not wooing them, oh no; just paying her rent. In the evening when Tola came back to the bunk, Alinka would move away promptly — the tactful lodger leaving the family alone.

Each evening Tola came back later. Each evening she walked aimlessly from barracks to barracks. Suddenly she would stop. Hidden in a corner she would watch those who had refused any re-placement — the mothers left with no daughters to shout their "you always" at. They were alike, inconspicuous, only some-what remote, like foreigners unfamiliar with the local language and customs; when spoken to they answered with a swift birdlike flut-ter, and one had to call many times before they fetched their ration of bread. Often a piece of stale bread or a spoon would fall off a bunk where one of them lived. At once Tola would tiptoe there, would lift up whatever it might be, then having drawn aside, imag-ine how she would lead the woman, left all alone, to their bunk — a guest soon to grow so dear that no one would care if she herself went away.

She wanted to go away. She waited for an event to set her free — for money from the old man that would make her unnecessary; for something unnamed that would tear her away; and above all for the shout. "You, how can you be like this?" Barbara would shout. "I can," she would say. "You see, I can." And then she would go her way.

"Sit down, get some rest at last," Barbara said when she came back; Alinka tactfully drew away. And now, after the cough had stopped, Barbara's stare kept her awake. "Stop watching me," she had cried finally. This was after the little Pole from Trotyl had spoken to her.

"Na, has Miss brought me anything but lousy rags?" he would begin whenever she dashed toward him into the clearing. This time he just gaped at her. The inspection must have pleased him, for he perked up. "Miss doesn't look too bad," he announced. "A bit skinny, one might say, a bit pinched, but not too bad. Things may start happening here soon, but with such looks Miss shouldn't be too afraid."

It was not fear she felt, only a greed demanding that whatever was to happen should happen at once. Yet the clearing was quiet, shadows of birds flitted across the shiny grass. The Pole spoke up and suddenly fear came, as numbing as though she had never before heard of such trains, such camps. The camp of which the Pole told her lay nearer to the front line than Skarzysko. That camp too belonged to Hasag. And since yesterday not a living soul was left there; some of the people shot, others, those whom it still paid to keep alive, taken somewhere in cattle trains.

"So it looks like they'll keep dragging you from camp to camp"; the Pole sighed. He looked at the trees, the grass, and at the trees again. Then, unable to help himself, he glanced at her bundle.

"Just lousy rags." She even managed a smile. "Still, you'd better look at them. We're gone and it's Schluss — no clothes anymore, not even such rags."

The Pole reached out for her bundle, but thought better of it and, shaking his head, was off.

"Tola!" First Barbara and then Alinka called for her from the window. She turned around, then in the doorway she stopped. Within the dense foliage shots of sun darted like fish trapped in a green net; and those other camps too were like nets, each letting fewer escape, until for the last time the net was cast — and no one was left.

"Why did it take so long? Oh, we were just talking," she answered Barbara. Latrine, laundry, washroom, silently to herself she listed the places where they could hide. No, the latrine was no good, or the washroom or the laundry; those other barracks around the Appellplatz were a possibility; they were raised above the ground on stilts. She must go and see if one could hide between the ground and the floor.

A stench of stale urine and of rot rose from under the barracks. Like scum of black milk, matted dirt swung from the rafters. Tola got up. Yes, one could hide under this barracks. But only two would hide there. She had had enough — of hiding, of choking in the stench, of boots stamping right above her head. She, who looked not too bad — a bit pinched, a bit skinny, but not too bad — would stand in the Appellplatz, among those thriving like herself.

The taste of rot was still in her mouth. She spat, then walked on, watching the clouds of dust swept up by the wind. And in the dust she saw them — flattened under the boards, Barbara's mouth opening to cry out, Barbara's mouth gagged by Alinka's fists. She saw herself too, wedged between them, her arms around them, holding them on and on till they were safe.

"I asked for warm water and they threw me out of the laundry," the Hunchback cried into her ear. The Hunchback would have to hide. No matter how afraid the Hunchback was, she had to stay with those threatened most. A shadow steep like a hillock trailed upon the ground. Tola watched. She envied the Hunchback her inescapable loyalty; she coveted her hump.

Next day the news that the Pole had brought spread all over the camp. Tola, for whom this new fear had already become habit, felt almost surprised by the silent groups, by the messengers darting to and fro as though those at the next corner, in the next street, had some comfort to give. In her barracks the women stood round the unlit stove. No one stirred. Only the Orphan kept stroking the black pipe, as if it were the arched back of a cat. "Pretty soon they'll finish us off," she said matter of factly. "They — " She bit her lips. "They'll shoot us," she whispered. "They will shoot us, they will," she repeated, begging someone to speak, to argue with her. No one spoke. A shirt rustled on a frayed rope.

"Tola!" ducking under the shirt Barbara cried, "Tola, have you heard?"

"Yes — just now."

"And . . ." Barbara stammered.

"And what?" Alinka turned upon her. "We were taken to this camp, we may be taken to some other camp soon. That's all there is to it. And if there is a selection then we — then one must hide."

"Yes, one must hide," Barbara said, her voice brisk like Alinka's. And Tola hated her — for this borrowed voice, for her eyes, and for those hands, groping over her hair and face. The hands clenched. "Stay here!" Barbara ordered in her own booming voice. "Stay, both of you, I'll be back soon."

Barbara came back, her hair cropped close to the skin and smeared with kerosene against the lice so that it clung like black silk to her head. She looked younger, yet more wasted, more conspicuous still.

"I look better." Barbara was clearly pleased.

"Yes, much better," Alinka exclaimed. "Don't you think so Tola, don't you?" They both turned.

"Yes — much — much better," Tola managed to say. But Barbara was not listening anymore. Cautiously, with just two fingers, Barbara was touching Alinka's forehead.

Alinka had typhus. As last time, the doctor came; as last time, Barbara watched him anxiously while Tola stood on the side. Only unlike last time they had to put their patient in the barracks for the sick — side by side with the Hunchback, whom some obscure ailment had laid up.

Later in the evening the doctor came once again. He glanced at Alinka's flushed face, he mumbled that on the whole the last typhus cases were not so severe, then sat watching the orderly fuss over her mother, who neither ate nor spoke anymore.

"A matter of days." Though the orderly was within earshot the doctor hardly lowered his voice. "So, if you want to take care of the girl, one of you can soon stay here in the orderly's place. Well, young lady, which of your friends would you like to stay?" He lapsed into the tone of a grown-up asking the child was it Papa or Mama it preferred.

Alinka preferred no one. "I can manage very well by myself," she cried. "I want no one to stay, I —" She glanced at Barbara, at the kerosene-smeared head. "I've changed my mind, I want . . . I think Barbara should stay," Alinka chose exactly as Tola had expected. Then with frantic haste she sent Barbara to fetch water for her; no, not from the pail, but fresh water, from the washroom.

"Tola, I wanted you to stay," she whispered when Barbara had gone. "Only it's safer for Barbara to be an orderly, but it was you I wanted, you," she insisted; and the blush typhus had brought deepened with shame for presuming that her preferences could matter much.

Chapter 31

THE MOUSE — and old woman who together with her consumptive daughter sat at Tola's table — saw him first. Ribs showing through her sweater, gray like everything about her, she had stood at the window watching the rain which was at last bringing relief from the heat. She turned back. "He . . ." she gasped, "he . . . Rost!" And ducking so low that her arms almost touched the floor, she scurried back to her seat.

Dust swept off the tables whirled through the hall. Bags, cans, anything that might displease him was being shoved under the tables. As though hoping to find a place where she could hide her mother like such a bag or can, the consumptive girl glanced under the table, behind the crates, then with shaking fingers began to tuck her mother's gray strands into the half-unraveled knot.

"Work! This is no time for smooching!" the fat Kaelanka rasped. And it was she who welcomed Rost, leaping up, shouting "Achtung!" in a hoarse, breathless voice.

"Achtung!" And with small rapid steps Rost came into the hall.

Tola watched him with the sense of disappointment felt when a stranger comes instead of the long awaited guest. For not the Rost remembered from the Strafappell had come in but a small parsimonious-looking man, his thinning hair combed carefully over the balding spot, his voice more high-pitched than she recalled.

"Work," this voice rose above the silence, "faster!"

It was the petrified silence that made him grow. It seemed that only he knew how to move freely, only he had the gift of speech, while the others — the hundred women bent over their tables — were just parts of a huge machine: screwing the tops on the shells, packing the shells into crates, lifting the crates up onto the cart that seemed to be moving of itself, so tightly did the transport men press against its load.

"Work!" and the machine moved into a more rapid gear. "Hurry!" and the cart rattled with redoubled speed.

Then a rustle. A bag, not hidden safely enough, had rolled onto the floor. Rost stepped closer, he looked at what had spilled out — a gnawed-up beet, a shred of paper with a single thread wound round it. Slipping on the floor as on ice, gnarled fingers picked up the beet. But the paper escaped them and drifted behind Rost as he walked on toward the glass door closing off what had once been the office of the foreman whom typhus had swept away. There he stayed watching — whom, Tola seated with her back to him, could not tell — but his shadow, now darting out, now drawing back, showed her that he kept leaning forward to look around.

Like someone embarrassed by his poor table manners, the Mouse furtively brushed the crumbled chalk onto the floor; the fat white arms shook in their hurry. Only Barbara, though Rost stood a few paces behind her, kept turning to the window, as if hoping to see all the way to Alinka's bunk.

The rain fell harder. Feet shuffled behind the clearing, then a voice called out. But this was far away, where people still knew how to move and speak. Here nothing but silence had ever been known; here the silence would stay on and on, until he would step forward, would give an order . . . What order, what would happen then — of this Tola refused to think. He had come suddenly; she could do nothing. Nothing . . . nothing . . . And she looked away from Barbara, who was gropingly touching her face.

Nothing . . . Tola started. Someone was walking through the corridor, the Meister perhaps, back from inspecting the shed. "Herr Meister, you know what a good worker my friend is — "; or "an excellent worker" would be better; but what "excellent" was in German she could not remember. Anyhow, it was not the Meister who was coming. He did not shuffle so heavily, he would not have come to such an abrupt halt.

"Open." Rost pointed at the door to the corridor.

The transport men both together pushed the door open. The corridor seemed empty, only in the far corner stood something gray, something squat and immobile like a sack. Rost glanced through the door and the sack moved. It was the paralyzed woman from Tola's barracks. She stood flattened against the wall, her one eye covered by the drooping lid, the other slowly turning toward him.

"Come here," Rost beckoned. "Come here," for the first time he raised his voice.

But the woman just stood there, one hand sliding down the wall, the other dangling limp like a glove. Like a glove, like an empty sleeve she tucked her hand, her withered arm behind her back; so, part of her packed away, she staggered toward him, first bringing the still live leg forward, next pausing to regain her balance, next bringing the other leg up, and all the time jauntily swinging her other arm — to show that this gait was simply a peculiarity of hers.

She stopped. The threshold had stopped her, it was too high, she could not cross it by herself. On their tiptoes, the transport men stole toward her. With a flick of his finger Rost ordered them away, and drew closer to watch the old woman. She was gathering impetus — drawing back and forward and back again, until she hoisted half of herself into the hall, gasped, tried to hoist in the other half but swayed and would have fallen had not the transport men caught her.

They were pushed away — by her this time. She seemed to have decided something, she seemed in a hurry. A shrug, and she unpacked everything — her hand, her arm like an empty sleeve. She dangled them, and gasped so that Rost would see what she was, old, and of no use with half of her already dead. But without granting her another glance he walked back to the glass door. The old woman staggered to her place and sat staring at the chair usually occupied by her daughter, by Doctorka, gone for the day to work in the shed.

Rost was coming toward them, Tola knew it from the sound of his steps. He was right next to her, his hand, on which a wedding ring glittered, leaning against the table. And if she grabbed this hand, if she pressed it, hard, so that the ring would cut into the pale smooth skin . . . Now he was raising his arm, was pointing at — no, not at Barbara but at the blond girl behind her. Clutching at the table, the girl got up and followed Rost to the door.

The Mouse was moving her jaw in and out. The consumptive glowered. And Barbara was doing something odd, Barbara was scribbling in the chalky dust: an "S" then a "P." "S" meant "Selection?" "P," "Picrine?" There was no selection, no choosing for Picrine. Rost was simply asking the blonde whether she spoke German well enough to be a work supervisor, an Anweiserin.

"Nix verstehen," said the blonde, "nix."

As though to welcome him again, the fat Kaelanka jumped up in her seat, her stare, her gaping mouth reminding him who it was that knew German, who had screamed "Achtung!" in welcome. The fat one wanted to be an Anweiserin — why not, such offices often went by weight. "Work!" she would scream. "This is no time for smooching!"

And with this scream it began: a premonition first, then a certainty that a transformation Tola had always hoped for could be hers. Only she must do something, she must get up so that Rost could get a look at her.

Tola rose. Squeezing past Barbara she tiptoed to the crate next to the table, put a few shells in, then looked up. Silence lay over the hall; yet to her it seemed that a race was going on — the fat Kaelanka, and another, and another yet, all vying for Rost's glance, all running to him and leaping up to snatch the prize that he, imperturbable and still, was dangling higher and higher up. She too was in this race; wherever he glanced her eyes followed; "Take me," they begged, "I speak German, take me!"

He looked at her, and she bent down to hide her face. He looked away and she felt limp with the sense of loss. She had lost: it was at someone in the back of the hall that he was looking. Now he was turning, was glancing at her. Of itself her hand jerked, stopped, jerked again, until her arm shot upward and "I, Herr Doktor!" the scream broke out of her. "I speak German, I!"

Was he smiling as he beckoned for her? She was almost sure he was. Yet this smile did not matter, nothing mattered but his look, transforming her into something so void of will, so light that she seemed to be floating — down and down like a withered leaf. Only this floating ended much too soon, only the Meister's return detracted from her newly won lightness.

"Do you speak German?" Rost asked.

"Jawohl, Herr Doktor."

"Do you speak German well enough to be an Anweiserin?"

"Jawohl, Herr Doktor."

"Responsible, you're responsible," the high-pitched voice was saying. Why she was responsible, for what, Tola did not quite hear. She just stared at his small, finely shaped lips. "Responsible" again; then, "Repeat my orders."

She had not understood his orders, she could not repeat them.

"Hurry."

Her mouth opened, the words rolled out like objects out of a drawer: "The quota has been raised; if it is not filled, I am responsible. The nightshift will be resumed; for anyone caught asleep I am responsible. Groups of no more than four are allowed to go to the latrine; if — " she broke off.

And for the second time she wanted to grasp his hand, to cling to him, because what had been promised her — the transformation irrevocable and complete — had not been accomplished yet. And already he was leaving, was standing in the doorway, while she, grown heavy again, had to see how Barbara turned to her with a dumb, noncomprehending look.

"Wait, not yet," Tola whispered, and hastily bypassing Barbara, walked on to her new place — to the chair the old transport man had put out for her at the door. Rost was still in the corridor, talking with the Meister, Barbara mustn't come to her yet — not yet — not yet. Or perhaps Barbara wouldn't come at all; perhaps Barbara was pleased to have an Anweiserin for a friend. The huge noncomprehending eyes were still looking at her. Tola flinched. "Leave me alone," she could hear herself rasp, like the fat Kaelanka. "Leave me! You'll drag me down!" She must not utter those words — never, no matter what might happen. But as she sat listening to Rost's voice, it occurred to her that what must never be said was, in the last analysis, true.

"She's an Anweiserin," after Barbara had whispered to those around, after she had nudged and poked them, the Mouse had answered. An Anweiserin was like an O.D. man, only less; Tola had become an Anweiserin — this much Barbara understood, but what she had understood did not explain that scream which had broken out of Tola, that flushed face, those eyes like glass.

Barbara got up, and with "No! Don't move! He's still here" the Mouse forced her down. Barbara looked at Tola, and at once Tola looked away.

"No . . . what's going on?" Barbara stuttered. No one answered.

"In the camp . . . did you hear? In the camp," came from the table behind her.

Everyone, the Mouse, her daughter, the fat Kaelanka, tried to hold Barbara back, but she tore herself away and dashed over. "What has happened in the camp?" she gasped. "Tell me. What?"

"Nothing has happened. An O.D. man just passed by and waved that all's quiet there," within an instant came the answer. But in that instant Barbara saw it all: the empty bunk, the coat — Alinka's coat — flapping in the draft; and herself too she saw, pacing up and down with that "If — if only — " ringing in her head.

"Quiet, all's quiet, thank God," she repeated; but this "if only — " would not stop. She paused. And again she looked at Alinka's empty seat, at Tola, then on to the clearing where Rost's car stood. Rost's coming meant that something might soon happen in the camp. The sick wouldn't be safe if something happened. Tola knew this; Tola, just as she did, feared for Alinka.

"Perhaps — yes," Barbara spoke louder and louder. "Yes, Tola must have done it for her, for Alinka's sake."

"For Alinka, yes," the Mouse agreed, too eagerly somehow. The others went on working. Yet each of them when reaching for a shell stole a quick glance at Barbara — at her face, her bony hands.

Barbara winced. "For — for me too; Tola did it for both of us," she said hoarsely. They looked up: and she saw herself through their eyes — scrawny, with an old leathery face, and afraid, so afraid she could do even this, could make Tola serve Rost.

"I won't let her do it," she said hastily. "I won't, because . . . because somewhere one must draw the line!" A formula from long ago came to her aid. The line took shape. The line was a barrier to be held fast. She tried to hold it, by turning away from her scraggy shadow and the empty seat, by breathing — like breathing the familiar smells of home — the odor of worn-out bodies, then by looking at the Mouse and her daughter, who, though threatened no less than she, went on calmly about their work.

The barrier was clasped firmly. "You won't do it, Tolenka, you've done enough for us," she would say; she would lift this new burden that, as once the peddler's pack, Tola had taken upon herself.

"The quota has been raised. Please work!" The scream — Barbara had all but forgotten about it — was back. It had nothing to do with Alinka and typhus, this scream. It was a symptom of that other illness which, suspected by her all along, had now broken out.

What should she do now? She didn't know; she must ask someone, must get help! There was no one to ask — at the table where once the four of them had sat, only she was left. And already, like some horrible cackly hens, fear after fear was breaking out. O.D. men might again drag the sick away; but she would soon be staying with Alinka, would watch over her. Tola would be left alone if she stayed with Alinka, Tola was almost like an O.D. man now, Tola might have to do something terrible. No, Tola could never do it! Never? And just as Barbara was chasing after her fears, catching one only to let another slip away, from across the table a small hand began moving toward her.

It was, Barbara knew, the mousy woman's hand, but the way the fingers were sneaking toward the crumb of bread was so faithful, so right that it seemed as if a keepsake — a kerchief or a shawl — had suddenly come her way.

Only when the doctor praised Alinka for typhus mild as the grippe would a bewilderment seize her, as though reassuring news should be sent to the one gone without leaving her address. But the hankering for grief was over. Now longing came, and changed to a call, so insistent, so pleading, that it seemed to her that she, overhasty, she, never patient enough, had done it all wrong; but now if she just kept waiting, kept calling, the answer might be granted yet.

She would look up — and there Aurelia would stand in the blouse made out of a shiny coat lining, in the skirt clinging to her bony hips. A smile, the gesture of checking, from the never-outgrown habit, that no bandage was showing, and she would trot on in small, hopping steps till, next to Tola, she would stop, her swollen legs shaking, her voice ringing and firm . . .

Someone had been here, had slipped away. If only she could break through the air that felt like a wall, if only she could follow. If — if only —

"There, do you see?" The Mouse nudged her, pointing at the clearing.

There a guard stood, a new kind of a guard, huge, his black SS coat shining with rain. He ran toward Rost, opened the car door for him. Hardly had the car moved on, when all over the hall the women began to turn, staring at her, Barbara realized; yes, right at her. And there at the door Tola was staring, her narrowed eyes asking, "Do you want me to do this, Barbara? Are you so afraid?"

It was decided, once and for all. Pressing a half-ripped patch back into place, Barbara marched through the hall. "You won't do it, I won't let you," she rehearsed with each step.

"For us? Tola, have you done it for us?" was what she mumbled with an abject remnant of hope.

"And if," Tola spoke up at last, "and if it was you?"

"No, you mustn't do it, not even for us."

"I was just wondering, Barbara. Because I did it only for myself. Why do you look so nonplussed? What is it? Anything done for someone else is a sacrifice, a noble deed; but try to do the same thing for yourself and the sacrifice becomes a disgrace. Why? I too am someone; I've no contract for survival, I too am afraid."

A hierarchy was tumbling down, Barbara's hierarchy of fears, assigning typhus to Alinka, the ruined body to herself, and to Tola only that toneless "nothing." Tola too was not safe, Tola was afraid just like her.

"But . . ." she groped.

"Go," Tola cut her short. "They're coming."

The women were coming. "Only four at a time!" Stiff as a ramp Tola's arm barred the doorway. "Dr. Rost's order — only four."

And Barbara, who had stuttered and fumbled, now felt at no loss for words: "Miss Anweiserin, may I go?" she would whine like those forbidden to pee. "Dr. Rost's orders? Oh, I forgot how you love Dr. Rost!" No, she must not do it. Had not her fury done harm enough?

Stepping aside, Barbara waited till the women came back from the latrine. Another group dashed out, then another, until at last no one went out anymore.

"Come with me." She gripped Tola's shoulder. "Why? Because I say so, that's why."

"I forbid you to do it," pulling Tola into the latrine, she muttered. "I forbid it," she repeated over and over again to blot out that moment when Tola's being an Anweiserin had seemed possible.

"We'll go to the Meister, we'll tell him that you can't go through with it. He's a decent German, he won't force you."

"And then?"

"What do you mean?"

"What will he do then?"

"He'll choose someone else."

"If someone else will do it anyhow, then why shouldn't it be me? I don't mind."

"You don't? The women are just up after typhus, they can't hold back, and you won't mind forbidding them to go to the latrine?"

"Someone else will do it if I don't."

"Sure. Suit yourself, be a slave driver, squeeze the quota out of them."

"Someone else will do it if I don't."

"Someone else — anyhow — someone else" — on and on, while Barbara searched for an argument no "someone else" could answer. "An Anweiserin may be ordered to do something terrible," she would say this, she must. "An — an — " Barbara could not go on.

"Someone else will do it if I don't," once again Tola would say, and then only one threat was left to her: "You stay an Anweiserin, and I'm through with you!" The suspicion that was sneaking upon her was a calumny, a shameless lie — Barbara felt certain of it and yet she did not dare to utter her threat.

They grew still. "We'd better go back," Tola said at last.

"No, not yet." With a vague anxiety Barbara watched the rain falling in through the broken windowpane. "Alinka!" she exclaimed, "the roof leaks above her bunk. It must be raining right on her." And for the first time Tola looked at her.

Alinka was the argument no "someone else" could answer. "What will you say to her?" Barbara clung to this argument. "What? You see, you can't answer me, you know what she's like. She won't put up with your 'someone else.' 'An Anweiserin may have to do something terrible,' she'll say. And if you don't give in she'll be through with you — with us, I mean — with both of us."

"Alinka won't find out," Tola said very softly. "Only a few women from Schmitz come to her barracks. They won't blab, I'll see to that. So unless you tell her, unless you want her to worry, now when she's sick, when she still has the crisis ahead of her, she won't find out."

And Barbara, remembering how bad worrying was for those who had typhus, said nothing, only watched Tola walk to the door.

There she stopped. "Barbara," her voice shook, "come, speak up, Barbara, tell me that I made a repulsive spectacle of myself, that the blonde too — and she knows German, of course she does — has no contract for survival. You — all of a sudden, you've become so gentle with me. Why? What's the use, when I know exactly what you think. 'How could she do it?' you're thinking; and I could, you saw I could. 'How can she be Rost's flunky?' I can, easily; I don't mind it a bit. I — "

"A flunky? You? You couldn't be a flunky, not if you tried. That's why you mustn't do it, because you can't, because this isn't like you, because you . . . you're good."

"Don't! Don't say such things," Tola whispered, and was gone.

No one was working when Barbara came back. Everyone was watching the Orphan hastily running through the hall. Before Tola she stopped, her hand jerked once, then again, until her arm shot upward, her mouth gaped like a livid hole. But no scream came, not the least sound. And just because unuttered, that screechy "I speak German! I — " seemed to resound louder and louder and the applause too, the giggles, the bravos, just because they were silent seemed to go on and on, while Barbara looked on not knowing at whom to pounce first: at those gapers, at the Orphan, or at Tola, smiling as once before — as when told that she was looking well.

Upon both at once she pounced. "You will not mock!" She pushed the Orphan away. "Oh, what shall I do with you?" she whispered to Tola, then turned to face the women again gaping at her, as she knew they would.

"Transport!" the fat Kaelanka yelled.

Barbara dashed to her table, lifted the heavy crate; then, her head tilted, her jaws clenched to prevent even one gasp from escaping, she carried it through the hall, all the way to the cart at the door.

The door opened. Her grizzled mane drenched with rain, Doctorka burst in, and stopped to ask something of the old transport man. He sighed in answer, but Doctorka looked pleased. She nodded, she even smiled.

"Well, Mama," taking her seat she said. "Well, how about another of your latrine trips? Go on — go and rot there!" The old woman blubbered something; Doctorka shrugged, and they turned away from each other, one staring at the window, the other at her own clenched fist. Then, slowly, the old woman reached out, her fingers nuzzled the tensed fist. Doctorka kept staring at her fist, Doctorka would not even budge. Suddenly, her arm swooped down, and it gripped the old woman hard, as though she, slumped to a heap, were about to break into a wild, unrestrained flight.

It was raining when the women were ordered to stop at the gate of the camp, raining so hard that at first Tola could not see toward whom the O.D. men were pointing, toward whom the SS guard was marching, huge in his black shiny coat.

Then a cry. Doctorka was crying. Doctorka was running after her mother, was trying to pull her away from the guard. An O.D. man dragged her away, but she broke loose; the gun swung at her, but she ran on.

Again the cry. Silence. Then a shot and the column marched into the Appellplatz. Along the wires Doctorka was running to and fro, to and fro. Until she stopped. From her fists pushed against her mouth, rain dripped in large, grimy drops.

All through the evening two chunks of unclaimed bread lay on the barracks table. Late, shortly before Lagerschluss, Doctorka came in, passed by the bread, and sat down on her bunk. Someone spoke to her, someone pointed to the table. Then a tiny white-haired woman, in a much too long black coat, put the bread before her and nodded, as though to show that in the sisterhood Doctorka had just joined to eat of the clay bread was not against the rules.

Was Doctorka eating? Tola could not see, for a girl with her cheek swollen to a purple lump was blocking her view. The girl was in pain from an infected tooth, the girl could not bear to work with such pain.

"Without a medical exemption no one can be released from work, no one!" Tola cried, and at once a window of opaque glass seemed to close upon this petitioner, guilty of transgressing the rules. Another woman came and the window closed tighter. Only when Barbara walked in did it open. Slowly, as though the white Anweiserin band on Tola's arm made her uncertain that this was the right place, Barbara was approaching their bunk.

Chapter 32

BETWEEN TOLA and the petitioners the window kept closing — pulled down swiftly and tight to shut out the boils, the festering sores, those bribes which the petitioners were trying to smuggle through the least chink, and which Tola neither could nor would accept.

"Without an exemption no one can be excused from work!" she screamed, with this scream hoping to crash through what appeared like another sheet of glass, dividing her from the paragon still out of her reach — that true Anweiserin able to give orders easily, with no dread of ridicule. That she, hectically flushed and shrill, was ridiculous, Tola knew, thanks to that other part of her, thanks to the observer, and to the women's leers.

Neither those leers nor the name of "cold fish" the women had given her bothered her much. And if she hated them with the impersonal hatred that one hurrying to his destination feels for the mob blocking his way, it was only for what they might do to her — and would, unless she took care.

Against her they stood six. "Work!" they warned. "She's coming!" Someone else might come, though: Rost, against whom one could not stand watch. Since his last visit blackout sheets screened the clearing from the hall: each sound from outside became ambiguous now; footsteps could mean O.D. men or guards, a rustle the wind, or the car bringing Rost in. He would come, would peek through a hole in the black sheet — a small hole, yet large enough to let him glimpse the snoring mouths.

"Anweiserin," he would beckon for her, "do you remember who is responsible for anyone caught asleep?" Then, as once the paralyzed woman, she in her turn would be snatched away by the huge SS man; then, as once Doctorka after her mother, Barbara would run after her, crying "I begged you not to do this, I begged you!"

"Work!" Tola would scream, imagining this cry, would scurry around, poking and shaking those dozing off, while there in the back of the hall Barbara sat — now a "keep out!" look on her face, now blinking as though something sharp had fallen into her eyes.

"Why do you stare at me, Barbara?" Tola was giving speeches now, imaginary speeches all the time. "I don't have a sensitive soul, I'm not like you." This she said, and more and more, till the words merged together, till only a formless shout was left, leading up to what must never be uttered, to the rasping "Leave me alone. You'll drag me down!"

Nights were spent in struggling with the women and this shout; the days, on the visits to Alinka. Each noon Barbara led Tola to the barracks of the sick. In the doorway the half-crazed orderly honked that the visiting hours had not begun yet. Outside the expectant crowd stood, Barbara always in the front, her outstretched arm like a messenger sent ahead to explain that she, detained through no fault of hers, was coming as fast as she could.

Yes, Barbara managed to transform even this typhus into a victory. Alinka was the victor. Washed and combed, her freckled face all smiles, she was the winner of the contest for the most proficient patient.

"Alinka, cover yourself! Alinka, don't sit in the draft!" Barbara grumbled from the doorway; and more grumbling for not sleeping, not drinking enough, and for Alinka's refusing to keep all for herself the bread they had brought. This bread was Anweiserin's pay, but Alinka was told that the Meister had sent it to her.

"He said it was for you, only for you, didn't he, Tola?" Barbara would wink.

"Yes, that's what he said."

Barbara nodded, Barbara beamed with each morsel Alinka took. Now Barbara was grumbling again; now they were smiling at each other while Tola sat on the side hoping to be forgotten so completely that she could slip away without being missed.

Alinka never forgot, not she! All the tact of the perfect lodger had been transferred to her new role — the role of the hostess solicitous even of the most cumbersome guest. "Yes — I see — " The more Barbara talked, the curter her answers became; "I see," then no answer, then a clipped "Barbara, keep quiet!" A crestfallen silence, and "Tola," the feverish whisper would say, "tell me, what's new with you?"

"Nothing much," Tola said. She smiled. Mispronouncing the names of French towns so that Alinka could correct her, she reported the news, and knew how forced her talk was, and how longingly Alinka glanced at Barbara, who had got down to scrub the floor.

"Well, time to run along," Tola would say the moment Barbara was back.

"Still peddling?" Alinka would snap. Tola was not peddling any longer. She had lost all desire for it, and besides, since her promotion the women would not entrust her with so much as a pair of torn socks.

"I . . . I'd better go, because . . ." Having found some excuse she would run off, then walk on and on, till it was time to start work.

"Nightshift get ready! All out!" She chased the women out into the Appellplatz. There, always among the first in the forming column, was Barbara, looking at the wires, at the sky, as if she did not notice who was rounding up the women like a vicious cur. But once, as Tola was leading one of those mothers without daughters to the column, Barbara quickly looked around summoning all to admire this act of kindness.

"Stop advertising my virtues. Stop defending me," Tola whispered.

For a long while Barbara looked at her. "I'm not defending you," she blurted out at last. "I cannot."

She wanted to defend Tola, she could not. Caught between two fears — the fear that such a defense might be mistaken for approval and that ever-stronger fear of failing Tola again — she resigned herself to a compromise, to hiding under that "keep out!" look, yet watching, always watching for a chance to speak of the true Tola in whom she still believed. A special mechanism had been perfected in her: "Not yet," it ticked when the women gossiped or joked. The talk would turn to typhus or hunger and "Now!" this mechanism prompted, "Speak up — now."

"Tola," she would break in, "without Tola we'd have starved long ago. Tola used to get camphor, and not once or twice but for days at a stretch." Even the child of the dead woman had been put to use: "Ah," she sighed, "ah, much more will come to light about her when the world is a world again." So with phrases borrowed from their speech, with secretive sighs she tried to convert the women to her faith. But they only stared blankly.

Still, Barbara felt comforted. Those words, though spoken in anger at their being needed at all, were to her like a rough sketch. And if the hall was quiet, if from the Anweiserin's place no screams came, then she began to fill in this sketch. Colors came: the red of fire glowing on those nights when, while she had slept, Tola had cooked soup for sale; the green of the shells loaded the day when they had asked the soldier's help; then the gold of kogel-mogel prepared for the one who, in these reveries, seemed transmuted into light that had once softened Tola's face; and the fading of this light, that was typhus and Tola's eyes as cautious as if even a glance could hurt. Distilled, purified, Tola rose before her. Nothing had gone wrong, nothing ever could.

"Work, please! Wake up, please!" Like a jagged line the scream crossed out this sketch.

Then Barbara would wince. "If you knew how resentful you look, how full of hate," she wanted to shout. And this too she wanted to say, that someone who had been wrong, even terribly wrong long ago, could now be right again. "Someone," not "I." Never! Because to say "I" would have been a travesty of truth; because it was not she who had once done wrong to Tola, only an intruder, a brazen creature with whom Barbara could feel no kinship, no bond.

Tola — and this was what silenced Barbara — was trying to re-establish this bond. With each shriek Tola was becoming so fully what this intruder — and she only in her worst moments — had seen in her, that Barbara felt Tola kept tugging at her, saying, "I'm playing my old part. And you, have you forgotten what your part used to be?"

Barbara tried to forget, she could not. A word would force itself upon her, a gesture, an unuttered thought — strokes with which the intruder had been composing that other disfiguring sketch, line by line, till it was ready for the night of birth. What had been said

then, Barbara could not bear to recall. "It was long ago," she argued to comfort herself, "long, long ago . . ."

The intruder belonged to "long ago," but not the Tola of those
days. Her thin frozen figure pursued Barbara — always bent under
the peddler's pack, always alone and poring over the disfiguring
sketch with the smile that said "Yes, this is what I am, exactly this!"

And already Barbara wanted it all to be happening over again,
now, so that she could run to Tola, could free her from her burden
and tear to shreds that sketch — composed why, or for what, she
did not know. And what good was there in knowing now, when
nothing could be done any more?

What should be done next, this she must decide. Time was running out; the orderly's mother was failing so fast that soon Barbara
would take over the job in the sick barracks and have to leave Tola
alone here. Should she plead with Tola to take it over for her? No,
Tola would never agree to this. Should she stay with Tola in the
hall? She could not. She had had enough of waiting for the O.D.
men, of asking "Is everything quiet in the camp?" and of going
through that endless moment till the answer came. But of something else too, Barbara knew, she had had enough: of those silences
between herself and Tola, those glassy eyes, those screams.

"Only four at a time are allowed to the latrine. Dr. Rost's orders."

"Please don't sleep, Dr. Rost's orders."

"Dr. Rost here, Dr. Rost there," Barbara finally flared up. "What
is he, our benefactor, our patron saint?"

"And how else would you keep the women in order?" Tola answered.

She would show Tola how else. Like a wriggling pup she would
carry Tola back to her old seat, would take over the Anweiserin's
place. Not that she would treat the women with kid gloves, oh no.
"Work!" she too would yell, "work, don't sleep." But after each
order, each shout, this she would say: "For whom are you working?
For that devil Rost? For me? Or for your own sake so that nothing
terrible will be done to you, so that you will get out of here and live
in decency one day." And she would not sit glued to her place, but
together with the women; and she would make everyone with a full
stomach work for two so that those half starved could rest. "See,
this is how I would keep them in order," she would say.

"Oh, you want me to be an Anweiserin after all?" Tola would answer, the narrowed eyes adding, "Are you so afraid, Barbara?"

To be an Anweiserin, even the right kind of Anweiserin, was wrong; wasn't it terrible enough that they had to make ammunition against their own people? Yet, that this work, done only so that someday they could breathe freely, could eat their fill, might bring harm to anyone, this Barbara could not really believe.

"All quiet in the camp?" her mouth at the hole in the latrine window, Barbara kept calling on that Saturday night.

"It's quiet there," the answer came from the dark. In the clearing outside Schmitz it was not quiet. There O.D. men shouted and iron clanged as, armed with pickaxes and spades, the men were being led to some new work — what kind of work no one seemed to know.

Late, long past midnight, soup was brought in. The line was still forming when the Orphan stuck her shaggy head into the barrel. She turned. "Women!" she wailed. "Women, the barrels are half empty!"

"Half empty!" And they who could hardly ever finish this soup that shook them with soured belches now swooped upon the barrels, and cursed and squealed, while on the side, having uttered a single "Quiet!" Tola stood, her stare asking, "Well Barbara, do you see what they're like?"

Like pigs they were, like pigs let out to the trough. "Give it to me!" Barbara snatched the ladle from Tola. Pummeling at the women she pushed her way to the barrels, and "You!" she swung the ladle over the screaming horde, "you, have you turned to beasts? Will you leap at each other's throats to get at this swill?"

A few women stepped aside. And those still clawing at one another she whacked, harder and harder, till one by one they shrank away and stood back, their faces soup-smeared and dazed.

"You've lost all shame," Barbara muttered. And she too felt ashamed for the ease with which she had subdued them, for her bellowing voice, her height, that made Tola appear smaller and more cramped even.

"Here, Tolenka, deal out the soup." She handed Tola the ladle and hastily walked out into the corridor. It was quiet there. Through the door open to the clearing wind blew in. And somehow with the warm gust autumn came to her — the vast empty skies, the empty fields, only here and there, bright red like clumps of poppies, fires rising into the clear air, and above the cornstalks soon to feed the flames, above the leafless bush and tree, smoke trailing in an ever-fainter smudge.

Here too the air was smelling of smoke overly sweet, as though leaves not quite withered were being burned.

Behind the glass door to his office, the dark silhouette of the Meister got up; a window opened in there, then slammed abruptly. Barbara waited. When the Meister sat down again she stole outside.

Huddled in a tattered cluster the transport men stood in the dark. One stepped forward, he reached out his arm, and farther away a flashlight beam slanted across the trees, then pointed at something — at a band of smoke unwinding above the black ridge of the woods.

"What is it?" Barbara called. "What's happening?"

"Graves are being opened. The Germans are removing all traces."

"Graves are being opened. The Germans are removing all traces," she rapped out, coming into the hall.

The clinking of spoons stopped.

"So," the Mouse bit her gray lips, "so . . . if they're getting rid of the traces then something will happen here . . . soon!"

"Something," Barbara could hardly breathe, "something . . ." And that specter haunting her during the endless waiting for the O.D. men's answer was back. Only now instead of the empty bunk she saw Alinka dragged off by O.D. men and guards, and herself too she saw, running — toward the girl and toward the guns aimed at both of them. She shuddered, looked at Tola, then away. No, Tola must not stay an Anweiserin; this had been decided once and for all.

Nothing seemed to have been decided, not in the morning, when the sweetish smell trailed over the woods, and over a body lying among the cluster of ferns. "Do it!" once again Barbara longed to cry — to save the three of them and to bring back Tola, who, walking alone at the side of the column, seemed like someone going away, faster and faster with every step.

Chapter 33

"So you did not know," said the Hunchback, bringing closer her long nun's face. "You didn't know — you didn't." The words twanged in Alinka's head.

Ever since morning she had been saddled with this head — huge, and still growing till it felt like a net stretching with each noise it trapped: with the clatter at the stove, the moans, the thumps. The hump was thumping. *Bump,* it hit against the bunk, *bump.*

"Stop tossing like someone possessed," a whine came from the bunk below. A pause, then *bump* again, and somewhere the orderly honked like a horn that had got stuck.

But later on, exactly when Alinka was not sure for time had turned topsy-turvy — it was afternoon, then morning again — she had discovered something that made her forget the head like a net, the honking, the thumps. It was the window. Dirt lay thick upon it, but high up where a piece of glass was missing shone the sky, citron-colored like — like lemonade.

Lemonade. The word lent itself to all sorts of variations: said quickly, it felt like a deep thirsty gulp; divided, spoken bit by bit, it was sips taken slowly from a tall crystal glass. The glass shone on a white-covered table; the table stood in a room, cool with shade.

"Do you know," she heard herself say, "during the war, when I had typhus — "

"Oh," her interlocutor exclaimed — he kept changing from Barbara's husband to Alinka's aunts now safely stowed in New York and Siberia. "Oh, so you had to go through that too!" She shrugged. "Anyhow," she said, "when I had typhus the one thing I really hankered for was — "

A sudden bang. An O.D. man was pounding at the window, the glass rattled, shouts broke out. What was it, was something about to happen? No, it was only about the spilled slops that he was shouting, louder and louder as he strutted around. Right next to Alinka's bunk he stopped — a repulsive little man, with his black cowlick, with the rotund blob of his belly reminding her of someone, of — she knew of whom.

He had a truncheon, he might hit her. Heavy steps, no doubt Barbara's, were coming from outside. If she dared to poke fun at an O.D. man how Barbara would laugh!

"Na — na — " The door opened. "Napoleon," she cried, "my dear Napoleon, you'll see what a saintly Helena we'll get you after the war."

It was a picriniac who had come in, it was the O.D. man who laughed — at her. "Freckles!" he sputtered, "you mangy, freckled brat." And now he was saying something else, something about the peddler, that the peddler . . . had turned Anweiserin because she had fawned on Rost . . .

He had left. Far up in the window shone the sky the color of citron. Like the lemonade, like the shaded room, Napoleon too had been a typhus dream. And just as Alinka had convinced herself that he had never existed, the Hunchback had brought closer her long nun's face. "Didn't you know?" she twanged. "Tola volunteered to be an Anweiserin — it happened a week ago."

"Shut up, you!" Alinka was about to cry, but checked herself just in time. "Of course I knew," she raised her eyebrows, "of course. What else?"

" 'Of course I knew,' Alinka said to me," the Hunchback would surely whisper at each bunk. "But when Tola and Barbara came, her first word to them made it clear that she had been told nothing." And "Oh, the poor child," the women would sigh; "Oh" and "Ah" and "Why such secrecy? Perhaps Barbara and Tola don't want her to know how much bread they are now getting. Perhaps — they want to be rid of her?" And the Hunchback, to add fuel to the fire, would tattle how each day "the poor child" was waiting for them as for the Messiah.

She must do something, at once. She would tell the Hunchback to go away. " 'Of course I knew,' Alinka told me, but as she was in such hurry to have me gone, it's clear — "

Alinka closed her eyes. After a proper pause, she began to breathe deeply, as though fast asleep, but aiming each breath at the Hunchback's neck. One more gasp, one more. At last *bump* and the whiny "Stop it, for God's sake!"

"What is it?" Alinka started as though just waking up. "What are you doing now?"

"It's you — you keep blowing, keep puffing at me."

"I? I was fast asleep. Look here, you're not doing it on purpose, but you jump and toss till my head splits. Do me a favor; go and lie down somewhere else, just for a short while till my head stops aching."

"You want me to go?"

"Just till I feel better, just for a while." And at last the Hunchback scrambled down.

Was it Barbara and Tola who came in? No, it wasn't they yet; but soon they would come, with their solicitude, their warnings against the draft, and with the bread that the Meister was sending out of his love for her.

"I don't want your handouts," so she would thank them for this bread. Or, better still, "Thank you. Collaborator's bread is not my favorite fare."

"Thank you — not my favorite fare" each time the door opened, "thank you — thank you." Outside the dusk fell, outside the crowds thickened as everyone was coming back from work. Most likely they too were back; a new friend, an O.D. man, had joined them on their bunk. "Come on, that pipsqueak can wait," he was smirking, and they agreed. "She can wait," they said. "After all, she doesn't even know we're back." She would disrupt this idyll, she would go to them, as soon as she found her shoes.

Fine . . . now they were here, smiling as though nothing was the matter. She might have been lying here for weeks, turning blue like the orderly's mother, she might have died of typhus without suspecting the least thing. Now she would pay them back, not because they had not asked her advice — why should they, they were not married to her, far from it; she was their inheritance, the millstone round their necks — but for this bread she would pay them back, for those lies, and for the way in which she had found them out, like a cuckold the last to learn what is going on behind his back.

"Thank you — not my favorite fare." Alinka waited, then glanced at their hands.

"Alinka, today's Sunday," Barbara said lamely.

Great news that it was Sunday. No, Sunday did mean something — that they had not gone to Schmitz, Sunday meant that they had brought no bread.

Some other opening had to be found.

"You . . . I . . . you . . ."

"How could you do this to me?" she longed to cry, but this was self-pitying, just hideous. "You . . . you," Alinka repeated, softer and softer, for hardly had Barbara bent over her when all that had happened seemed like a dream again. Dreamlike too the blurred figures floating round the stove, and the picriniac sucking on a beet. The sucking turned to thuds in her head. Perhaps if she closed her eyes some new idea would come to her.

A rustle came. Over the barracks a tree had grown, white petals shone among the dark leaves; they fell, they brushed softly against her face. How she wished that crying would stop.

"Barbara, it's raining on her!" Tola was crying. "We must move her — here, to the other side of the bunk.

Alinka did not want to be moved, she made herself heavy and stiff, but already she was lifted up, was put down again. The bunk creaked. "Someone's peeing on me!" came from the bunk below. Was it she who had peed when, dozing off, she had dreamt of the tree? No, water had been spilled. Barbara had done it. Barbara had upset the can put under the leaky roof.

"Hands of clay," Alinka hissed. And Barbara said nothing, just gaped abjectly.

With satisfaction, with glee, Alinka watched this abject face. It released her. A moment ago not one thought had come to her. Now they came rushing — words, whole phrases, each so perfect she could not decide where to begin.

"Do you know?" She tried to smile though her mouth felt coated with bark. "Do you know . . . I feel . . ."

"What do you feel Alinka? What?"

"Just . . . a little disappointed. I'm sick — of course, not so sick that you should worry about me, that anyone should worry, any-one," she insisted to blot out that repulsive, self-pitying snivel. "Anyhow — when one is sick, one waits for something pleasant to happen. And here, you could have given me so much pleasure — yet you didn't tell me a word about . . . about Tola's great success!"

That they did not want to share their bread with her, that they were trying to get rid of her, was not, could not be true. Yet now she could not bear even to glance at them, for fear that by winking, by secretly looking at each other, they were agreeing upon the same lie.

At last she raised her eyes. Both of them were looking only at her. "We didn't want to worry you," both of them cried.

And Alinka, shamed by her suspicion, Alinka, grateful for this shame, might have let things rest at this were it not for Barbara, that abject stare of hens.

"Stop it!" Alinka spluttered. "Stop looking like a whipped dog. After all — " She groped for another of the perfect phrases. "Yes, after all, an honor has been bestowed on us, a great honor! Oh, people will remember this honor long after the war. 'Here comes our Dziedziczka, so fascinating, so full of life' — this is what they used to say about you, isn't it? But no one will say it anymore. 'Here comes the Anweiserin's friend,' everyone will say, 'the Anweiserin from Schmitz — the one who used to chase dying women out to work!"

"Don't!" Barbara cried. "Don't — Tola only has orders to supervise the women."

"Only?" in premonition of some new hurt Alinka whispered. "Only!" Oh, poor Barbara — having a mere supervisor for a friend when she had hoped to be chums with the right hand of Rost! "Rost . . ." she stammered, "Rost." When Rost had come, Barbara had looked like a whipped dog; Barbara had quaked with fear then, Barbara—

"Did you do it?" Alinka brought out. "Did you push Tola into it?"

"No!" Tola cried. "Barbara begged me not to do it, Barbara forbade me."

"I did," Barbara broke in, "even though you're sick, even though — "

"What? Even though what?" An icy lump seemed to block Alinka's throat. "Even though I'm sick I could get up, I could stand in the Appellplatz, I could kneel, I could march for hours, if something happened here."

"Alinka, nothing is about to happen, I swear." As always, Tola was the first to understand, Alinka thought with a sudden remorse. How she had come to this remorse was no longer clear. I was afraid something might happen, she retraced her steps, I was afraid Barbara pushed Tola into being an Anweiserin . . . Tola was an Anweiserin . . . Tola . . . She could not think anymore; she must rest, keeping her eyes open so as not to doze off again.

On the next bunk she saw the orderly stare like a baffled child at the drops oozing from her mother's loose mouth. As if someone had fallen into a puddle, a reflected figure lay in the pail of dark water. She must not think of that puddle, she must not look at the loose mouth. Hardly had she turned away when it seemed as though someone were calling for her. Barbara was calling "I can do nothing" she was saying, silently, just with her hands. The hands pointed, and "You," they insisted, "you can do anything." "Only you," said the eyes, the nod, the smile.

Now when it was almost too late, Barbara was coming to her; now! Alinka did not even know where bitterness left off and where joy began — the joy that thanks to her all would soon be well, only the right gesture must be found, the one right word. And as the joy grew so did the apprehension; because that word kept escaping her into the noise; because again both Barbara and Tola were doing it — were kneading her into someone she was not. One sigh, showing how deeply Barbara felt everything, and she hardened; one glance from Tola, and she shrank into being a helpless child.

"Don't," Alinka panted. "Don't look at me as if I had just turned five. I'm not five. I know what hobnobbing with the Germans may mean. You . . . you may have to do such things — " Alinka broke off; she had said those very words before, but then she had just been reciting one of her perfect phrases, without understanding what Tola had done.

Now she was doing her utmost to understand. Looking away from Tola's worn-out face, she put a shout into her mouth, a stick into her fist. But right off the shout and the stick slipped away — accessories to a costume that would never fit.

"I don't understand," Alinka cried, "I can't. You an Anweiserin, you? The O.D. man — or was it the Hunchback — I don't remember who — said you volunteered. Did you?"

"Yes."

"You went to Rost and said, 'I want to do it'?"

"Yes."

"And not because something is about to happen, because I'm sick?"

"No."

Yes — no, yes, as in the game of twenty questions in which you have to guess the person others have agreed upon. And she was guessing, she was, much too fast.

"You chase the women out of the barracks?"

"Yes."

"And at Schmitz you drive them on to work?"

"Yes," then "Yes," again.

And "No" Alinka was crying. "No, this isn't like you. I know it! Barbara, stop gaping. Tell me what she's like, as an Anweiserin I mean — tell me!"

"I don't beat anyone, if that's what you mean," Tola answered, and everything had been guessed: Tola did not beat, Tola just spoke to the women in this icy voice; Tola looked at them, as once at the clothes for sale — carefully, her glance pointing out each flaw, till what had been a dress or skirt that could still be changed into bread, turned into a dirty rag.

"I won't let you do it, I won't," Alinka whispered, while chasing after some other thought about clothes. The coat — there it was. "After they had taken Aurelia," she would say, "I carried her coat out, I did it for you Tola, I didn't want you to carry it out, I didn't want you to be like a hired help, first doing the nursing then the cleaning up. And I didn't know what to do with it, I just walked and walked, then I threw it — on the beets, behind the kitchen, on the rotten beets."

"I . . . the coat . . . I carried . . ." No, she couldn't go through with it. "Stay with me," she whispered instead, "I know you've done enough, still, do this one more thing. Stay with me. The doctor may arrange it so that both of you can stay. But it's you I want, you." She clung to what was a lie, a complete lie — because it was so hard to bear with that news from France, those forced smiles, that each day she hoped more and more Barbara would come alone.

"You I want," she repeated hoarsely. To screen her eyes from the glare, she made a visor out of her damp hands, then lay very still.

Not since those days in the Cracow camp when there had been only two of them, she and the one whose coat had been thrown onto the rotten beets, had anyone looked at her as Tola did now. She looked back and Tola turned away.

"Tola," she called softly, "Tola." The noise was gone and the glaring light; they were alone, Tola and she. They stood in a darkening field, far from each other, and she, though longing to run to Tola, to bring her back, only beckoned, only called for her as for a creature once tame, now gone back to the wild. A voice — Barbara's — spoke up, then a parched whisper that was her own. What it was saying didn't matter, she must just lie very still, must wait until Tola looked up.

Now Tola was raising her head, was drawing closer. "I'll stay with you," Tola would say, and all would be well.

"I can't do it — And now I must go, I'm supervising work in the kitchen. It's late, I must go."

"Go?" Alinka hardly understood at first. "Go? Oh, I'm not holding you back. Go — hurry up — No, don't go — wait. I've got to show you something. Wait," and Alinka groped in her pockets, in her shoes. In the shoe; here it was. "Here." She moved the crumpled slip into Tola's face. "My exemption slip, in case I lose it, in case you come to drag us out. Here! and now go! Both of you!"

"Lagerschluss!" the shout broke out.

"Go!" Alinka cried; she pushed them with her feet. But they were still there, Barbara saying something about fever — that someone must stay with her because of fever.

"If you don't go, then I will, I'll put my coat on and leave — I will!" And at last they were climbing down.

Had both of them left? Tola was still there near the pile of kindling. Tola was tugging at a twig caught in her skirt. A withered leaf brushed against the stovepipe, turned to a black shred, then to smoke.

"Go!" — and she was alone. She would pull the coat over her eyes, she would fall asleep as soon as that clanking stopped. It would not stop, it kept growing louder; a charred stick pried the lid from the stove, flames burst out, the water in the pail turned red, and the faces, and the hump hoisting itself up the bunk. Boards creaked. The net that was her head could not contain this creak; it was bursting, noise after noise was spilling out — a grinding, a clatter, a rattle as of rolling lids, and she, stunned, she, knowing nothing anymore, was pushing through this tumult to get at a word that must be caught.

"Crisis" was this word. "Crisis — I'm afraid!"

From under the hump a hand crawled out. It was not this hand she wanted; it felt clammy, this hand, felt cold; she wanted the door to close, the wind not to smell of burning leaves. The door swung wider; an O.D. man came in looking for someone — for those trying to hide from work. Her fist sealing her lips, she waited for him to be gone. He was going, was standing in the door —

"O.D. man!" it broke from under her fist. "O.D. man, please come here . . . Mr. O.D. man. It's important, please Mr. O.D. man . . . I . . . I'm the Anweiserin's friend." And at last he came closer.

"Tell her," by now she could hardly speak, "tell Barbara, the big one, you know her, you must, tell her to come, and Tola the Anweiserin, too. Both must come," she cried after him.

"Both, I said," she whispered as Barbara came in.

Barbara said something about work, about Tola and work, the Hunchback moaned, and this voice that she had never heard before, that she must never hear again, was her own. "Barbara," it was screeching, "Barbara, this will poison us, because I want her to do it, because I'm afraid. I am afraid — " she gasped and darkness fell in a sudden splash.

All through the night, all through the night they were swarming around her — pallid and smooth at first, like white balloons afloat in the dark. They descended, they sprouted noses and lips and eyes. "You can't be here," she said to them, "you were shot in Radom." "Ah, won't they get you, too, in the end?" their stare leered. She pushed, she butted against them till they floated up into the dark.

And against Barbara's face, too, she wanted to butt, she wanted to pinch, to hurt it, so that Barbara would do something about the gag choking her mouth, about the crust encasing her body, now burning with heat, now cold. And the cold, this was rain; and the rain, this was Radom; this the figure sprawled in a puddle and the faces approaching with a harsh, rattling sound.

This rattle grew harsher. "She is dying," someone said. But it was not she who was dying; she could hear everything — the rattle, the sudden silence, the howl; she could see how someone with long arms and no head was stumbling across a beam of light.

Tola had come with this light, Tola was going again. "Stay with me!" Alinka tried to cry and could only hoot like an owl.

Yet the faces came no more. Instead of the gag, something cool touched her lips. Drink, she thought, and water filled her mouth; Rest, and the darkness felt soft as down. Shavings of light flitted through the dark; they blurred, and footsteps came, as she had always known they would.

That all three of them would come arm in arm, like girls fond of walking together, like girls who sing as they walk — this she could never have known. She would run away from them, she wouldn't answer when Aurelia called. But it was not Barbara and Tola who came with her, just two old women with buns of hair white and tiny like balls of cotton wool. The women vanished. Aurelia was smiling a foolish smile that showed she was up to no good.

"Aurelia," she snapped, "what are you up to now?"

"I'm going . . . I'm going to a special camp," and off she went with small trotting steps. It did not matter that Aurelia was gone; if it was possible for them to meet once, they would meet again and again.

But the darkness she did not want to lose. She clung to it by closing her eyes tight, by hiding them under her clasped hands. Yet already it was fading to an impure dusk. Voices spoke in the dusk — Barbara's voice calling for Tola, Tola's asking where Barbara had gone; they kept looking for each other, like passengers at a railway station, each fearful of losing the other.

The voices came no more. Had they found each other, had they gone off arm in arm, like girls who sing as they walk? She did not know, she did not care to know. All she wanted was the darkness because it felt soft as down and because in it anything was still possible.

Chapter 34

THEY HAD NOT FOUND each other. Silently they stood in the gray morning light, and when they spoke it was as those who after a long parting clutch at the bond of their last common friend: Alinka, they said, Alinka was worn out by the crisis. Alinka would need time to gain strength.

"Yes, she will need time . . ."

"Yes, she seems very weak . . ." Again a pause.

"Water!" a whisper came through the open barracks door; stiffly, the orderly marched past the empty bunk; she stumbled. "Give me water!" the whisper changed to a cry.

Slowly Tola turned toward the barracks. "You're taking her place as of today," she told Barbara, pointing at the orderly. "Everything is arranged, I've already reported you're staying here."

Barbara knew she was staying, Barbara knew what it would be like as of today: perfunctory visits, forced words, forced smiles, and the helplessness weighing her down just as now, and already turning to such fury that "We're through!" she longed to cry, "do it, and we're through forever."

She reached out to touch Tola's shoulder. And when Tola shrank back, it seemed to her as if all was over, as if she had uttered her threat and "I don't mind if we're through" Tola had answered; Tola seemed so much like someone about to go away that nothing mattered, only to follow, to bring her back — even in that one way Barbara still had left.

Something terrible — Tola might have to do something terrible, Barbara repeated, to put obstacles in her way. But even that obstacle could not stop her now; it seemed so far off, she would bypass it when the time came.

No, once again she tried to stop herself, No, this will poison us. And that was her last try.

Because suddenly, "Barbara, I'm so afraid!" Alinka seemed to cry, because the stretcher was being dragged past her feet, and behind the stretcher the orderly, erect, her eyes wide open and dry.

Far away the lid of the crate banged. And "Tell me!" it broke out of her, "do you want to be an Anweiserin? Answer me, yes or no!"

"Yes."

"Then go ahead and do it," Barbara exclaimed, loud with relief that her secret was out. "I won't stand in your way, I want you to be an Anweiserin, yes, I do. Why are you staring at me so? I used to say one thing, now I say another, that's all. I have the right to change my mind, don't I? No!" she corrected herself, "nothing has changed. From the beginning — I mean almost from the beginning — I mean — " The hectic flush, the shriek, those symptoms of illness had been in the beginning, but even that must not be thought of now. She must go on now that Tola was listening, was looking at her at last.

" 'Do it, be an Anweiserin.' Right after it all had happened I wanted to say this to you. Why didn't I? Because of my vanity, that's why. 'Will Barbara agree even to this? Is she so afraid?' Everyone was saying it, and you too, not out loud to be sure, but your stares were clear enough. And do you know what?" Barbara broke off to relish her triumph, for were she to leave now, Tola wouldn't let her, Tola would run after her to find out what she had to say.

"Yes, I agree even to this. Yes, I'm so afraid!" was what she had to say. "I'm afraid, not of hunger, not of Picrine — all that wouldn't matter, not a whit, as long as I knew I'd come out alive. But when I think that I won't survive — that they might kill me — that I might die — " Her tongue shrank away from those words, yet now, once uttered, they seemed to speak of an event to be endured just as any other. Only for an instant, when she grasped that this event would not, could not be endured, her lips turned to ice.

"Listen," Barbara could hardly speak, "listen, is it the same with you? Because I — when I think that I might not live, I — I can't believe it. I know I should, but I cannot. And when for a moment I force myself to believe it, then something happens to me. I can't breathe, I'm numb like a stone. So afraid I am, so terribly afraid!

"And what of it? Should I hang my head in shame? Should I

plead guilty that I want to live? I want to live, I want to get out of here, and not alone, but with you and with Alinka." She paused; and gradually that old smile — the smile of the simpleminded amazed by their sudden cunning — spread over her face. "And you," the smile widened. "For whose sake have you become an Anweiserin?"

"For my own sake."

"Are you sure?"

"Absolutely sure."

"Absolutely, ab-solutely." Barbara was almost singing. "And if — God forbid!" she interposed hastily, "God forbid, but if you came to this barracks to Alinka's bunk and found it empty; and if you knew that somehow you could still bring her back, would it be only for your sake that you did this, would it?"

No answer.

"You see? You see?" Barbara repeated, and was still.

That obstacle, once lying so far off suddenly stood before her. She did not know how to bypass it. "An Anweiserin . . . may have to do something terrible . . ." She fumbled, looking to Tola for help.

"Someone else will do it if I don't," the blank look answered.

And Barbara, knowing that everything was at stake, Barbara utterly at a loss, made herself into that someone else: she was bursting into the barracks; she saw those sick and dying clutch onto their bunks; she, with her own hands was pushing them down.

"I . . . I can't, no, I could never do it. But if I myself was threatened — I don't know what I would do then, I just don't." Again Barbara was still. She was looking, first through the open barracks door at Alinka's arm hanging limply from the bunk; then at the bench where an old woman sat with her face uplifted to the sun; and at last at her own, mud-caked feet. "I don't believe something so terrible could ever happen, I don't," she cried, putting her faith in the innocence of her demand — to survive together with those two still left to her. "But if it happens, then . . . perhaps one could warn those in danger, perhaps one could hide. Somehow one would know what to do then, one must know. And right now," her voice hardened, "we mustn't think about it. Alinka is sick. We're starving. We have no one to help us. And you, what evil are you doing now? True, you must keep the women in order, you must make them work. Order must be kept, not for Rost — he is nothing to us — but for them, for their own sake. They must behave like women, not like pigs. They must work, not for him, but for themselves, each for herself, because if they don't, something terrible might be done to them, because they want to live. Oh, whack them, yell, do anything, but tell them, all the time tell them, why they must work, for whom. 'Dr. Rost's orders,' this is what you tell them. You do it all wrong. 'Tola will poison us,' Alinka said. But it's yourself you're poisoning, only yourself. Why? What has happened to you?"

Barbara fell silent, because Tola was smiling, her half-mocking, half-dreamy smile.

"Don't worry, I won't be poisoning you much longer," Tola said very softly. "And you, you haven't changed, Barbara, not at all."

It was happening, now Tola was talking as never before, with no pause, no thought, till it seemed someone else was shaping into words that cry which had broken forth at last.

"You can't change, Barbara. You never will. 'I am afraid,' you say; no, you proclaim it, just as once you proclaimed, 'I came here of my own free will.' And you did come here, you did! To be the queen of the ball — that's why you came; always taking the lead, always the first — first in self-sacrifice, first in grief, first in courage, first in fear. What happened didn't really matter as long as you could be the first. Now it's the same: others do Rost's dirty work, but you, you would have embarked on a mission. Others become flunkies, you would have been a leader, the leader of the people! You missed this mission. Never mind, you'll still get your glory — by proxy — through me! 'Ah!' everyone will marvel. 'Ah, look what Barbara managed to make of that peddler, that cold fish!' But there's no glory to be got out of me, not a shred. I'm not like you, I must be an Anweiserin in my own way. Why should I tell them that they want to live, when it's easier for me to threaten with Rost? Much easier! And you should understand this. After all, you were the first to discover everything that could be 'easy' for me." Another cry was already rising in her, but she must wait till Barbara uncovered her face.

"It was so long ago," Barbara whispered. "How can you still remember, when it was so long ago?" But now, drawing away from

the door so that Alinka would not hear them, Barbara did remember: then, too, with her whole body she had pushed Tola on;
then, too, they had grown still; only it had been dark then; only
she had been fleeing then, not from Alinka but from Aurelia,
whose eyes seemed to be asking, "Could you say this Barbara,
could you?"

She did not know what to tell those eyes. She would go away,
would think, would find the answer. No answer could be found —
she knew it — and panic struck her as though she had been trapped
in an airless dark.

Somewhere far away lay the release from this dark. Barbara
groped for it, running from that night long ago back to this morning, recounting each gesture, each word. "You're staying here as of
today," she remembered; then the haste with which Tola had shrunk
away, then the soft "I won't be poisoning you much longer." Tola
wanted to leave them — this was the release; and what once had
seemed a calumny, a lie, now meant simply that she would be freed
from having to find the answer.

Timidly, still with disbelief, Barbara looked up: and it seemed
that not Tola whom she had longed to bring back stood before
her but a stranger — a thin-lipped shrew.

Fool that she had been, worrying her heart out, fretting, chasing,
and after whom? After someone who, having said such things to
her, was now glancing around for fear of being late for those morning shrieks; who, while she herself felt bewildered and dazed, was
most calmly scraping a spot off her blouse; and who before, knowing Alinka was just past the crisis, had been polishing her shoes —
carefully, with spittle and saltpeter paper, a piece of it still stuck
to the toe.

"How elegant one can be, even in the camp," Barbara longed to
shout. She should be cautious, though; she should keep quiet and
wait. Now these thin lips quavered, they parted, but closed again.

"Yes, I said it that night," Barbara was circling, slowly, cautiously
circling round the one withholding her release. "I did, I admit it.
Of course Alinka had nothing to do with it. Of course you'll go on
taking care of her, you — "

"I . . ."

"Yes?" Barbara gave an encouraging nod.

"I . . . I want to be alone."

"I see. And why do you want to be alone? Why? For what reason?" On her rights Barbara was insisting, on the receipt proving that they were even; more yet, that there had been no debt; because if she had guessed Tola's true reasons — and she had, she had — then what she had said to Tola on that night was just as true.

"Why? Do tell me why!" With each "why" Barbara was drawing closer, putting her bare mud-caked feet next to those freshly polished shoes, her torn dress next to the clean blouse. She even bent forward till her cropped head was touching Tola's carefully combed hair.

"Why?" she whispered. "Answer me. Why?"

"Because . . ."

"Yes?"

"Because . . . you'll drag me down!"

"What did you say? I didn't quite hear you, I didn't," Barbara insisted so that Tola would repeat those words, so that Alinka would hear them and that other one too — the one who had stared with such disbelieving eyes.

The thread of gold between the scabby lips, the eyes sunken under the withered lids, clearer than ever before the dead woman rose before her. And next to Aurelia, as though they were inseparable, as though one could not exist without the other, Tola — moistening those lips, putting a compress on the fevered head. "Like this," Tola seemed to whisper. "See, Barbara, you do it like this."

"You heard me, Barbara!" Tola was shouting now.

"I did." Barbara reached out. "I did, and I won't believe you, no matter what you say, no matter what you do, I won't believe it, I won't, ever!"

Tola looked at her, Tola was ducking under her arm — and now she was gone.

Barbara ran after her, through the barracks, through the crowded streets and on into the Appellplatz.

"Form fours!" Tola was calling. "Form fours or you'll get it!" Her voice rose to a shriek.

And Barbara drew away. There was nothing more she could do. As long as she followed Tola, this shriek would burst forth — to prove that what she would never believe was true.

"Forward, march!" Column after column moved on, the gate slammed, and all was quiet. A bird called out in the sunny woods. Another answered and another . . . Then a shout, then stamping of boots. Picriniacs who had hidden from work were being chased out; Barbara knew it, yet could not breathe, could not run fast enough.

"Alinka!" she cried from the doorway, "Alinka," she repeated, bending over the girl.

The long lashes quivered. "Leave me," the toneless whisper answered, "leave me alone."

Barbara said nothing; she pressed a moist rag to Alinka's lips, brushed off a strand of damp hair, then sat chasing the flies away.

"Water!" came from the next bunk.

"Orderly, water," a chorus of moans broke out. She climbed down, filled the rusty cans, then stood looking around. Dead flies floated in the puddle at the door, ashes lay around the stove and from the bunk right above her an old woman was dropping potato peels onto the floor.

"Is this a pigsty?" Barbara bellowed. "Is it?" She swept up the peels, knelt down, and began to scrub the floor.

Part Seven

Chapter 35

Now TOLA HAD what she wanted — a place in the Kaelanki barracks, a bunk all to herself. Now she was alone at last. And it
seemed to her as though she had been out on a visit — an uneasy,
awkward guest, straining hard to please until she could not take it
anymore, until an obscene grimace had broken through her Sun-
day-best face. But now it was over; here on the bunk next to Rozalia the vendor she could relax, could rest.

Only at first there had been no rest, at first a sense of something
unfinished was preying on her, as if a message had not been delivered and those for whom it was intended were still waiting, still
looking for her. She too was waiting, peeking through the chink in
the door to see if anyone was standing by her bunk, starting at each
rustle, each step. And at night dialogues that dreams had begun
went on and on, each word soon like a memory, till she felt that
what was happening to her would never end: those two had come,
the message was delivered again, but again they had not understood, again they called for her, and she wanted to hide, under a
barracks, by the crate, anywhere at all until they, having understood,
would no longer look for her.

Had she hidden, she might still be lying there waiting for the
search to start. Because no one was looking for her, no one called.
She was not indispensable, that was it. And why should she be?
Was having the Anweiserin for a friend such a great joy? Yes, with
her gone, they were doing better, so much so that it seemed she had
been dragging them down. Perhaps. And perhaps she would tell
them this, if ever they came; or at least "Aren't you better off with
your new protector?" she might say.

The doctor was the new protector.

"Ah, Miss Ohrenstein, what a woman! Ah, I simply have no words
to describe her," he exclaimed each time Tola went to the dispen-

sary to get the exemption list. And each time there was something
else: "The sick are getting some rest at last," he would say; or, "The
air feels better there, much purer — you know — and the floor, not
a speck on it"; and again, "She washes every patient from head to
toe. What do you say to that?"

She said nothing. Had he not been told? she wondered; or, on the
contrary, had he been told to report how little she was missed?

"Please, Miss Ohrenstein," he said one day, "could you give them
this piece of bread and sugar? It's not much, still — "

"I cannot, Doctor. I don't go there anymore."

"You mean today — you will not be going today?"

"Altogether. I mean altogether."

And now he really did lack words. "So," he muttered. "Ah — so —
very well," he brought out at last. "But let me tell you, I've been
places, I have. In Majdanek, in the Warsaw ghetto. And there —
there," he managed to go on, "I saw those dignitaries, those An-
weiserins, those — God knows what, go under when something
happened, like this!" His fingers snapped with a dry crack.

That being a "dignitary" was no blessing she knew without him.
But this talk about something happening took her aback. Had he
heard some news? Yet, how could he have, when all the O.D. men
said that nothing would happen for a long time; remains had been
burned before, they said, and that other camp had been deported
only because the work done there was not indispensable as it was
here.

A piece of grease-stained paper — who, without taking bribes,
could afford well-buttered bread? — floated down to the floor. She
picked it up. "Well," she pointed at the greasy spot, "well, Doctor,
don't we all try to survive, each in his own way?"

He winced. "In!" he yelled. And clutching as if at valuables that
thieves might grab, at their boils, at their cough-racked chests, the
sick burst in.

The waiting stopped. And soon it was as though she had been
left behind by those two who had moved on to a place of rest and
of purer air.

There was a sense of absolute timing in her. In their sameness
her days were a place passed through, then entered again, each least
event so certain to recur at the expected point that whatever came

too soon or too late seemed a thing imagined or remembered from before. The slow, uneven steps and the freckled face, the voice — her own — saying "Go, I may poison you," and the regret at not having said "I'll drag you down" instead, seemed, having come too late, just a memory of some imaginary scene recalled as the sun woke her up.

Whether the late morning sun wakened her, or the glare in the hall, was never clear at first. Sent out scouting, her hand groped through the heat until it found proof that the nightshift was over: the sheets, her due as an Anweiserin, spread smoothly over the bunk. Silence lay over the barracks. It was early, this silence said; she must have slept just a couple of hours, and tired, yet pleased with the gain of such peace, she lay quiet, only now and then moving away from the sun. When the sun usurped the whole bunk it was time to get up.

Behind the curtains of prayer shawls satiated lovers lay. To her right, her face like a crumpled paper bag pressed into a heap of straw, Rozalia snored, her curtain pulled as tight as if the bag with bread were a lover to be hidden from curious eyes.

"In-telligenzia," Rozalia called her. "In-telligenzia has caught a cousin, but of the invisible sort!" Rozalia would sneer if she screened off her bunk. Without such a screen and with men everywhere, she had to dress cautiously; cautiously too, stopping each time the stovepipe clanked, she would walk through the barracks. But invariably the straw would rustle. "Ver is dus, who is it, who?" Rozalia hooted in bilingual fear.

"Her again — she always prowls — " the drowsy mutters followed her out into the blazing sun. Though hotter each day, the sun was an ally sending her shadows as warnings. When one flitted toward her she would turn away and fumble with her shoe; it drew closer and she would walk into the nearest door. She did not want to talk. Even to say "No news" or "Hot!" meant dressing up, slipping on a makeshift face over what she felt was her true face now — something immobile and smooth, the lips' seam drawn tight.

And in the washroom, when she looked into the broken mirror perched up on the pipe, the too-red mouth it reflected, the large tired eyes struck her always as something arbitrary, no longer hers.

But the body was her own: flat, with no breasts, its strength invested in what paid off — rubbery muscles on arms and calves. She took the paper curlers out of her hair, washed slowly, then walked on to what had become her second room, a strip of grass so close to the wires and towers that no one ever dared come near.

Holding down her skirt in protection against the wind, she lay fitted into the conical shadows that the towers cast. Behind the wires, trees swayed in the wind, a twig or leaf would brush her face, and the green spots — sun sneaked them under her lids — turned to petals, then to faces of long ago. Each day they came, always of their own accord, always in patterns of their own choice — arranged by addresses or by trades, shopkeepers, teachers, beggars, neighbors from childhood, from ghettos or bunks, and invariably, as if they had lived at each address, had practiced each trade, her parents, and lagging behind them the child, afraid of being called "the Frog."

None of them, not even the child, had ever existed. Each was just an actor in a play seen long ago, each while performing his role, while proselytizing for crystal or singing the Psalms, knew what the final scene, the final line must be. Only sometimes, when fear that it was at her the guard was laughing echoed with childhood fear, or a distant voice echoed with the bagel vendor's cry, when just one, be it child or beggar, became real, then within her an insurrection took place, then all protested that they really had existed, all pushed forward to tell what had been done to them, there in the last line of the last scene. She sat up. Here were the towers, here the white stove, and the steps that were her clock.

"Early — still early," infrequent steps ticked. "Getting later, getting late," the loud clatter signaled as she lay waiting for the alarm to go off. With a crowd stampeding to the stove, with splashing water and snapping kindling wood, so it went off each day. She rose, made sure her skirt was not tucked up, and walked back.

Smoke churned in the barracks. Like bees from a hive, flies swarmed from the next bunk. There Rozalia sat, smiting her blanket-draped chest and swearing she was selling her goods for a pittance, for nothing at all. "Robber!" her clientele shouted back. And the scampering, the whispers: these were the Schmitz women scurrying lest their Anweiserin, seeing what they had bought, should demand higher bribes for not sending them to load shells.

Just two or three each day, the bribe-givers came, some brazen, some uneasy, like people uncertain whether the proprietor should get a tip. She was no proprietor, she took the tips. The money saved up for some dark hour went into the purse sewn into her skirt, the potato or slice of bread into the bag at the other end of the bunk. And now she wanted curtains, many, to screen her off on all sides. For around her everyone was having a feast: Rozalia sucked on bread as on mushy fruit, blobs of beet-marmalade oozed down smacking lips, even the picriniacs gulped their beggar's soup with relish, as if those slops turned sweet in their yellowed throats.

Eyelids, closed tight, served her as a screen. Withdrawn behind them she sat on the bunk, thinking but one thought — that the night was still far off, that it was only around one o'clock, around two. When buttocks bounced down on her bunk, she said, "Please don't block my air." When steps drew near she identified them without looking up: the heavy tread was just picriniacs carrying their exhaustion like bulk; light footsteps, a young girl trading her bread for soup. She could not bear to eat the soup; she was hungry; still, what was in the bag must be saved for the night.

But when night drew near and she ran down to the Appellplatz, then, always at the same spot, at the O.D. men's barracks, she would stop and, looking away from them — who were like traveling salesmen in a smoker, laughing at greasy jokes, playing with greasy cards — she would reach into the bag and stuff potatoes, bread, everything she had into her mouth, and gulp the unchewed chunks fast, ever faster, just to do something, just to forget that she must go back into the hall, and to those women whom she had come to hate.

Not because of their talk though, oh no. "And you?" she could say to them as they tattled about how she had run out on "the Pole." "Yes, you, have you forgotten?" She forgot nothing: this woman here, given half a chance, would have abandoned any friend to get out of the quarantine barracks; that one there and that and that would have done the same, or more, to stay in Werk A. Even without such details she had no lack of data. That they were here, and alone, or with partner X in the row, were her data, her proof, that those who had taken such good care of themselves could have been neither too self-sacrificing nor too brave — just average, like her.

Like the bunk all to herself, like the identical quiet days, so being average was a place, newly won, indisputably hers. And out of this place they kept ousting her, doggedly, all the time. They would fall silent, would look at her, and at once those injured eyes branded her the black sheep, the exploiter grown fat on their misery. But when a brawl broke out as in a marketplace — the screams about how the best had died while such carrion lived on proving to her what they were willing to barter for gaining the last word — then it was impossible to believe she had ever thought herself like them; and just then, by forcing her to bring them back to order, to silence those screaming mouths, they pulled her down to their level, and lower still. Because their screams were gratuitous; hers were paid for with German bread.

What they were did not matter to her as long as she knew them for what they were, as long as — the rare exceptions excluded — she could fix them within a few clear-cut words. Yet just as she had them firmly fixed they escaped her, as on that first night when selecting for shell-loading had begun.

Had it not been for those exceptions she might not have even bothered to select them. Seen from across the road where she stood, the column looked like a strip of discolored cloth stretched against the brick wall, the gaps between each four like the marks on a measuring stick. To select fifteen women, as the Meister had ordered, she would count off the marks, then from afar, with a single word, would cut off the right length of cloth. Instead, remembering the exceptions who must not load shells, she stepped closer.

"Why did Moses wander for forty years through the wilderness with his Jews?" "Because he was ashamed to show himself in such company on the main road!" On the way to work, while they shoved and cursed, this old joke had come to her. Now Moses would have been proud; now a finishing school could not have been more mannerly than they, so quiet they were, their innocent look asking if she would do what none of them could do, oh never!

And perhaps it was true. Perhaps if someone else had led them, someone who would now call out that here was a chance to show their solidarity, their pluck, they would have responded to this call at once.

"Women!" she knotted her clammy hands, "this week, beginning with tonight, fifteen women will be going to load shells. It is impossible for me to know who has had typhus recently or who has fully recovered. But each of you can gauge her own strength. If those volunteer who are strong enough — and there must be quite a few of you — the work of loading will be rotated and the weak will be spared. So, who will volunteer?" she asked hoarsely, and turned away.

Now let them volunteer, let them show the Meister — most likely he was watching through the curtain of his office window — how they would stick together. First the Kaelanki and the young girls would step forward, the older women right behind, each running after her friends and calling "If you go, I go too!"

"You go!" a morose voice honked. "You stuff yourself with German bread."

She turned back. How she wished for a camera to take a picture of them: for anyone claiming that the women only needed a reminder of how much they wanted to survive; for herself, too, for the time when they would try to dupe her with those innocent looks; and above all for them, so that each could see herself in her most characteristic pose. The Kaelanki, too highly connected ever to be touched, stood quite unconcerned; the others pushed, backed away, here simian shapes sneaking behind the crowd, there someone squatting down to hide; and farther away, among a tangle of wrestling arms, the tiny woman in black turned around, her bewildered stare asking what was going on.

> "All the ladies we let through,
> Only one we're choosing — you!"

The incongruous childhood rhyme buzzed in her ears. "Quiet!" she cried, "be quiet." She broke off because in the window the curtain stirred, because she, screaming till her throat hurt, was also in the picture — the zealous Anweiserin all afire to send her people to load shells. "Quiet, please be quiet," she pleaded, running to and fro. "Quiet, for heaven's sake, or I'll do something, I — " She stopped. "Automatically," she said softly, "whoever even moves will load shells, automatically!" As though a whip had struck they stood stock-still. "I'll pay," a whisper broke the silence, "miss, I'll pay."

She got a sample on top of the promised pay: the fleshy arms, the eyes saying, "Take that one, take anyone, just not me." This was her sample of those to be selected. It matched, and "Step forward," she said. "Step forward at once or you go to load shells now and tomorrow too." "Tomorrow — morgen auch," she was saying to the Yekie, when from the row behind, the Orphan — Yekie's companion since her twin had died — leapt out, her lips tightened as though they must hold something in. But the cry would not be held in: "Together!" it broke loose, and with this cry from the Orphan, bilious and greedy as she was, the picture collapsed, as if in each one of them this cry was stored, as if each might have uttered it had the one for whom it was saved up been there.

"I'll pay," again, then, "No — together." A mob pushed into the hall; and quiet fell, as one by one the women settled down to work.

Each night this was the hour for resolutions, for putting her thoughts in order. The Meister was just an underling who knew nothing. Rost was another underling interested only in squeezing the most out of them. And if she kept busy the night would quickly pass.

To stock up with fresh air for later she would lean out of the window. Outside heat was being rolled into the crimson pack of the sun; the trees shone; birds dissolved into the smooth white sky. And behind her laughter was passed from table to table; skipping her, it moved on to the next row. Isolated phrases about mirrors, about gilded frames rolled toward her, like pieces of a puzzle being busily put together.

"Before the war" was being pieced together. The Kaelanki, they whose neighing laugh was a shipping label saying "slum born and bred," had once dwelled among such mirrors, such gold, while the Cracow women, being of more sophisticated taste, enlarged windows, removed walls, till their homes rose near-ephemeral, just air and flowers and sun. And through this past, so refurbished, they themselves moved, whispered of reverently like the dead; generous — no beggar left their door empty-handed — and patient, ah, so patient none of them had ever known how to say a harsh word. She came by and there was silence.

They, each of them, loved themselves. Each, had she become an

Anweiserin, would have done so in the service of an idea, in a self-sacrificial act. Such self-love she did not feel. She wanted safety and the bread that would come later at night.

Gradually, as trees darkened and the sky, night was drawing near. Under the cover of first dusk, the voices coarsened. "Light," they cried. "Hey, give us light!" She ordered light, but as the transport men fumbled with the blackout sheets she clung to the hope that something had gone wrong, that no light would come and she could go back to her bunk. It flashed on. And at once it was as though she had never been away from the heavy air, from the mealy dust settling upon the black piles of crates, and from those faces which seemed to swell with the glare.

She shunned those faces. She looked only at the hands; hands ordered to work faster, hands sticking out from under the tables, pulled at to waken those asleep, uplifted hands of those asking to go to the latrine, counted again and again.

One — two — three, like a tune that, its text ended, just would not stop, numbers echoed in her head. And so, to make time pass, she went on counting: the crates, the cracks in the cement floor, the steps both large and small which it took to cross the hall. When there was nothing more to count, she played a game with the clock. Let us see, she said, if I go up to the Meister's office and stand outside for a while, will five minutes pass or ten? "Five," said the clock as she came back. If she won, if more than the hoped-for minutes had passed, then the same joy filled her as when she found unexpected crumbs in her bag.

The clock was the first to tire of this game. The hands barely moved, the minutes refused to pass. She walked up and down, stopped to scratch a speck on her blouse, or went to the latrine, where women squatted like nursing mothers with their dresses torn open, the better to get at the lice. "Report us for taking a rest, go on, report us," they scowled, when ordered to leave at once. "I won't report you, I'll just send you to the shells." She spoke softly, like one trying to conceal ugly family squabbles from a fastidious guest.

The Meister was this guest. For him she curled her hair and kept her clothes clean; for him she prepared phrases and nods and smiles. Unlike the women, the Meister was fixed firmly, consisting, like a box, of bottom and lid, of two well-fitting parts. The Meister was cowardly and good. Being a coward, he did nothing to help, he merely looked on; being good — or, rather, constrained by his very cowardice to be good — he felt guilty and groped for an excuse. They, his charges, were his excuses. Not that he could ever believe in that Nazi claptrap about Jews; still, by sheer chance, his Jews were such a low, ruthless lot that, though most eager to help those truly deserving, for those ready to step over corpses to survive, he could not, he had no right to take any risks — just because he was good, and good men, being scarce, must be preserved. To find the deserving one would be an affliction for him; to learn that everyone he came to know was of the ruthless kind, a boon, a birthday gift.

The women, by egging Tola on to report them, hoped to make her into this gift. "Herr Meister, I must report," she would say, and at once, as though she were not shaping those words but they her, her mouth, she felt, would turn into the fat Kaelanka's snout, thus giving the Meister what he hankered after. Sorry, she could oblige neither the women nor him. She needed him too much, for that far-off time when something would happen in the camp. For then he must speak up for her to Rost.

The Mouse was the only one insisting that something would happen soon. "First this burning of remains, and now this sudden hurry to get the shells loaded," the Mouse had whispered on the first night the Schmitz women were sent to that work. "Miss Anweiserin, Miss Ohrenstein," she stretched her gray lips into a smile of refined supplication, "Miss Tola, my daughter is in the sick barracks with typhus. Please ask the Meister what's going to happen here."

"And if you knew, what then? Would you write to Rost that you are not going to any other camp, because you don't feel like it, because the climate won't agree with you?" she wanted to snap back. That the Meister was an underling who knew nothing was what she said. She had added that if by chance he knew something he would certainly not publicize it. But every night, the moment she rose from her chair to go to the Meister, the Mouse too rose, and sent her that refined pleading smile which, not to be shaken off, somehow joined with the smile the Meister kept in readiness for her.

The good part of him was smiling; the cowardly part glanced around as if spies were hiding in the green walls, or under the pa-

pers on his desk, while — this being the compromise he had hit upon
— he addressed her with the labored courtesy reserved for cripples
and the poor.

"How much of the quota has been filled, Fräulein?"

"About one half, Herr Meister."

"With quite a few women working elsewhere, is there any difficulty in getting the quota filled?"

"No difficulty, Herr Meister." A pause; the draft ruffled a newspaper page, where crosses marked the names of those fallen für
Führer and Vaterland. "And how are your friends?" he asked
next, or, to vary the meager fare of their conversation, "How is the
little girl, and the big woman — die grosse Frau?"

"They are well, thank you. Of course, it requires a great deal of
work to keep a barracks with sixty sick women utterly spotless," she
answered, feeling as though she were speaking of someone she
had never known; or, "It isn't easy to get sixty women washed with
just one basin and no soap."

From under the green lampshade light fell softly on his large
clumsy hands; a chair in the corner swayed, as though inviting her
to sit down. She longed to sit down, she longed to touch his hand,
and beg him to let her rest here for a while, because for years she
had not rested in a real room, because her eyes burned, because
there in the hall something she feared was waiting for her. But already he was reaching for the parcel of bread. She wouldn't take
the bread, she would say something to him. Wasn't it sad he was
guarding a bunch of Jews instead of fighting for the Führer, she
would say, or would ask if no one had yet reported to him that she
had no friends.

"Thank you," she said, and walked out, arms tight against her
body as though something might spill within her.

It did spill, every night. The Meister is an underling, Rost wants
only work — so, pressed against the radiator, she re-established order. "Nothing new," she said in the hall and counted again, the
women this time, lest one had escaped while she was gone. There
was one too many, she must count again; one was missing, she
ducked under tables, looked behind the piles of crates. Now it
came out right; now she would eat. All stared, all traced her every
move, while she ate slowly, holding the bread in her fingers, between

her lips and against her gums as if each part of her suffered a separate hunger that touch alone might still. "No more," the empty
palm said. "More," hunger clamored, promising that if it got a bite,
just a crumb more, then it would stop. Denied this crumb it stayed,
and it grew when barrels of soup she could not bear to touch were
rolled in, when in the faces not to be shunned any longer, the eyes
seemed like fingers, snatching a chance for thicker soup, for a better place in the line, the mouths too like fingers, poking her with
loud "Don't you give me just water!" "Fill it up, you!"

"Mr. O.D. man, is everything quiet in the camp, is it?" The
Mouse tried to make herself heard above the noise.

It was always quiet in the camp; there cool air came through the
opened door, there one could rest. Here the screams rose ever
louder, the women shoving forward, rushing at the barrels in a mob
— as much in need of that reminder of wanting to survive as is the
crew of a life raft tearing off the grip of those abandoned to drown.

And those in need of such a reminder, the exceptions, whom one
by one she had to lead to the barrels: Doctorka, the tiny woman in
black, and the few others; had she asked them "Don't you want to
survive?" they would have looked at her as though to ask "But what
for? Why?" The Old Meyerova, whose head, dangling like a coco-
nut with brown wisps, bobbed over the second table, would not
even dream of asking such questions.

Don't! You must not think about her! But to warn "You must
not think," meant that she was already thinking: of the Orphan
first, shouting "You old hag, you've lived long enough!" at Meyerova, who had spilled her soup, then of the answer Meyerova gave
her. "You'll rot deep underground, you! And I'll survive," came loud
in the sudden hush. She stepped closer to Meyerova; she gave her a
prolonged look. Yes, Meyerova might survive, why not? She knew
how to take care of herself, she had managed to survive her entire
family — her husband, his workshop had not been far from the
Ohrenstein store, her mild-looking son, and herself of that time,
holding on to a baby carriage with one hand, trumpeting "Ohoo,
hoohoo" into the other; then, as windows opened upon curious
friends, Meyerova's mouth turned into a veritable zoo — such crow-
ing came from it, such mooing and barks — until at last the reward

was granted, a smile from her grandchild, whom she had survived equally well.

Some new smell seemed to join the odor of beet-soup: the smell of diligent and aimless preservation, of medicine and mothballs which marks the rooms rented to those left alone. Having survived to be all alone, the Meyer woman sat in such a room. She tidied up, she counted her change. Footsteps, a telephone ringing, and she would listen, would run to the door, because perhaps the telephone had rung for her, perhaps the landlady was coming to ask her to tea; the ringing stopped, the footsteps passed by. She tidied up, she counted her change.

"What is it?" Meyerova snapped. "I am working, so why do you stare at me so?"

"Of course you're working, of course." And if she had said what it was — ? Would Meyerova have crumpled up like a toadstool that, stepped upon, shrivels into a flat rind and a puff of sooty dust?

That was how it had begun, this game with future and past. Let's see; if I go up — forty large steps, sixty small — She tried to forestall it, but everything conspired against her, even the black crates, piled up like luggage, even the rattle of shells, rhythmic as a train. The hall was a train; in a mob the passengers had burst in; then, seats and possessions secured, they became civil, each telling the others where she had come from. Soon enough all civility had been cast off, soon each mutter, each stare showed from where they had really come. Nothing was new, everything was a keepsake from the past: those stares envying an extra slice of bread; those nods saying, as once of jewels or furs, that everyone knew how such luxuries were come by; that snatching of latrine trips as once of bargains grabbed whether needed or not; the listless shuffles, the gossips, the smirks; and those eyes gaping from everywhere, those vacant fishlike eyes. All this had been brought from the past, all this Tola collected, out of all this she made one woman — called "They." "They" was the common denominator subsuming everybody — the young still aspiring to become like her, and the old, or the nearly old, who, having been like her once, would always look at that time as the crown and apex of their lives.

"They" appeared to her most clearly in curlers and a dressing gown, while "their" child was a mere outline, and soon to be sent off to school. In the room, where like gnawed apple cores, remnants of yesterday lay in full ashtrays and in films of dust, the mirror suggested that something had been misplaced: a face, their own — for it was clear that this puffy blotch could not be theirs. A dab of powder, a speck of rouge, the face was put back on. "They" felt cheerful and looked forward to the busy day.

A little cautiously at first, checking in every mirror they passed to see if they held together, they went on their errands. Another store, another bargain sale. Something must be exchanged, something was lost but found at last. Packages filling their arms, boxes dangling on tightly looped strings, they ran after a streetcar, scrambled in, and when a young man offered them a seat, blushed, and knew it, and felt pleased.

Too soon the stop next to home was here. In front of the store window with the thought that this or that was overpriced, with the memory of how a month ago or two — or even a year before, here in this very spot — they had thought this very thought, the suspicion came that time, like closed-in air, was always the same, nothing changing but their face, now so much like that puffy blotch that why the young man had risen so fast was not clear at all.

But something would happen — a letter, a special call. "The weather . . . the child . . . thank God!" the letter said. "Nothing new," said the husband on the telephone. And the child, when asked what was new at school, drew back as abruptly as if it had discovered an unseemly secret about them.

It was so early still; it was suddenly so late.

Dust gathered on the cupboard, ashtray after ashtray was filled. Something must be decided before the day was out. It was decided. They would go away alone to the country, into the mountains. And the mountains were beautiful, and the waterfalls. Yet, a pane of glass seemed to enclose this beauty like goods too costly ever to be reached. Thoughts dashed off to that dress, that hat. Nor was help to be had from their fellow happiness-seekers whose "How majestic!" came ever a trifle too loud, a trifle too late.

Even so, it was good to have gone away; on the train they knew that it was good. Because, just as it pulled into the station fear struck them for the child, lest something had happened to it, an accident, an illness beyond cure, and running through the crowd, and holding it tightly, they knew that here was a part of them, here one for whom they would give their all — if the time ever came and the need.

And the time had come, and the need.

Tola never looked up at this point. She waited for someone to come, for something to happen, so that the women crying "together!", those clinging to each other would once and for all prove her wrong. Nothing happened. And as she looked at them, identical, like a hundred Meyerovas with crunching jaws, like worms that, a part of them cut off, keep gnawing the dirt, then it was certain that on such a night Rost must come. Or perhaps he had already come, perhaps this very moment he was looking through the chink in the black sheet, was laughing and pointing out to the Meister the sight that must not be missed.

She herself was the sight. On her Rost was having his joke, his little practical joke. How to control those harpies without becoming like them — that was his joke. And she tried; she moved gingerly, she spoke softly, and at once saw herself for what she was — a simpering upstart trying to disclaim her own. "It is for yourselves you must work, to survive," she tried again, and knew her voice and eyes showed that it could not matter less whether such as they went on gnawing or not; and when, to display her one gift — the gift of knowing her betters — she looked to the exceptions, to Doctorka, and to the woman in black, even they turned against her, they, who in the next selection would be the first to go.

> "All the ladies we let through
> Only one we're choosing — you!"

The refrain would not stop.

No, she would never have to select; the Meister would help her. "She is different," the Meister would say. "We'll see." Rost would smile. No, by then the Meister could not help her. She must do something now, before it was too late, now, this minute, she must beg the Meister to release her. But Rost wouldn't forget her, Rost would find out if she was too squeamish to carry out his orders.

There was nothing she could do, nothing! And she hated herself; for being so clever, yet not clever enough to have known who would call her a flunky and at what price; hated Barbara, too, who had understood nothing; and above all she hated those harpies, that horde sliding under the tables, snoring, sneaking out, till she had had enough, till nothing mattered anymore, only this: to leap upon them with such a scream that the Meister, that anyone who might be near, would rush in, and then as they looked on, to beat and beat and beat!

"Work!" she cried. "If I have to die it won't be for you!" She might as well have said "I could have made a better match." And always at this thought she dashed outside.

How peaceful the night was. In dark towers, dark domes, trees rose against the starry sky; nothing stirred, only far away a blue stem of smoke swayed above the ramparts of woods. And the silence that cleansed her face like water carried her on across the shadows upon the pale ground, into the thicket where grass was tall and damp. From the thicket a rustle came. When it swelled into a noise, almost like the swishing of branches pushed by a car, she went back, always slowly, always stopping at the wall to soak in the chilly damp.

"Work!" someone was crying, someone was darting through the mealy dust, but it was not she — she had legs of cardboard and a cardboard face; only the eyes were alive still, light prying into them like a lancet. For one moment, just one, she would close her eyes; chunks of bread, faces swarmed into the dark; crushed as under a hard heel by the tightening lids they broke into smithereens and were gone at last. Now she was resting, not dozing off, just resting, so that she could hear each sound, so that she did not have to look up yet. "Not yet — not yet — " The sounds withdrew, the chair rocked to and fro.

Was it the glaring sun that had startled her; was she back on her bunk? Its weight pulling all of her down, the limp arm groped around, the fingers touched something porous and shrank back. It was the cement floor she had touched; it was night still, since she had dozed off barely a minute had passed.

Knowing the minutes would never add up to a night, she no longer watched the clock. Should I do something — shouldn't I? To chase a moth or a fly away was a decision that demanded thought. Should she — shouldn't she, when soup was about to spill, or a crate of shells. Sometimes a mumble rolled off her stiff tongue, sometimes she just stared, while figures, small, as though seen through the wrong end of field glasses, hopped around crying something about danger, danger of explosion, of being killed.

But just as the suspension of day was both natural and certain, here on the black pile of crates a bundle of rags stirred; the old transport man luxuriously stretched himself; he leapt down. "Ah, what do you say to this, ladies, what do you say, my girls?" he beamed as if announcing some great news. "It's almost four, soon we'll have air — fine fresh air" was his news. Even for the air she kept them waiting: "Not yet," she ordered. "Wait, not yet — " At last small gray points dotted the blackout sheets. "Now," she cried. The sheets rose, wind smelling of damp earth broke in, and as it swept the stale air out, as the shells glistened in the rising sun, light began to return into the lifeless faces.

"How good the air feels," the women said. Here laughter would break out, there a snatch of song, and those finished with their work helped others to get their quota done.

When heat was being unrolled from the red pack of the sun, those who had been sent to load shells came back in and sat sucking at their bruised hands. Tola counted them, she counted all of her women — twice, once in the hall, once outside after the column had formed. "Abmarsch!" she cried, and leaning upon one another the women staggered on.

Someone always slept on her bunk while she was away, someone littered it with hair and crumbs. She shook the sheets out and, plugging her ears, she lay down. "Love," she repeated, as bodies heaved and bunks swung, "now I live surrounded by love." Then sleep, free from dreams, then the glare — of the sun at last.

Not sun but rain woke her that morning. Rain obliterated the warnings of shadows, rain kept her away from her second room — from the strip of grass near the wires. When it had last rained she had not yet moved to this bunk. It must have been about a month or three weeks ago. Two weeks ago, she remembered, and drew deeper into her bunk.

As though put off by the weather no bribe-givers came; stopping before the O.D. men's barracks, she found only a beet in the bag.

She bit into it, and holding a piece in her mouth like a candy, ran on to the Appellplatz. The column just would not form. Splashing through the puddles the women chased after windblown sheets that picriniacs had shed, made canopies and capes out of them, but the blast tore the sheets away, and on they dashed with shrill cries. "Keep still!" she shouted. "Keep still, you cattle."

"Tola," someone was calling through the rain. It was the blue-eyed girl, once her neighbor from the lower bunk. "Tola, it's Sunday, the shifts have changed." And Tola waited, for the laughter, for the leering: "Look at our eager Anweiserin! Look, our volunteer for overtime!" But the women just cowered in the rain. From behind, a faint jingling came: a tall guard was standing behind her, the rifle twitching on his back.

She went into the washroom, put the piece of mirror on the pipe. "Cattle," she cried soundlessly, then, with as much care as if her face were a shawl whose folds must not be disarrayed, she bent toward the mirror: the beet-smeared mouth gaped in a red circle, the tongue curled like a whitish slug. Not very beautiful, she thought, but at least she had nothing to fear; she would never be shot like that girl in Brzesko, for being too beautiful to be a Jewess.

Back in the barracks she made two holes in a sheet, hung it on the nails in the bunk posts, and sat behind it, as behind a white cataract letting in nothing but dusk.

Chapter 36

"ALINKA!" Barbara had cried during her first days in the sick barracks, "Alinka!" pleadingly, sternly, with anger, with all the voices she knew, with all nuances of tone, trying to call back the one who had brought her here, the one of whom she — never at rest, climbing up onto the bunks, climbing down, fetching water, emptying slops, she, for whom "Orderly! Pole! Barbara! You!" the sick wailed till she hardly knew her own name — stood in greater need than ever.

But the contender passing all tests with flying colors was gone; a child had taken her place, a dreadful, morose child, staring blankly, knowing no other word but "no": no to bread, no to soup, no to washing, no to being combed, until at the end of her wits "Tell me, what is the matter with her?" Barbara appealed, as to a tribunal, to the other sick.

The tribunal invoked precedents. "Always," they said, "after crisis they get to be like this, always."

Always? To verify the verdict Barbara recalled that other, that first typhus case. Yes, then it had been so. No, that first case did not apply — there was no previous illness this time, no heart in need of camphor. "I don't know," she sighed, "I just do not know," and she waited for the doctor to come.

He came, most punctually each day, came to bask in the light of her anxious gaze. For that instinct of flattery which had sprouted in her during the first case of typhus had by now reached its peak. With her hushed "Alinka, the doctor," her hand meanwhile smoothing out the paper sheets, she transformed the bunk into a sickroom where the patient rests among flowers and lace, and the doctor into the great Warsaw specialist whose every word would be obeyed like an oracle's.

And already he was growing into his role. "Good morning," he boomed, flicking a speck off the threadbare corduroy. "Good morning, and how is our young lady today?"

Half dead, half bald, the young lady lay there, lips tightened to a string, fingers clutching so hard at the coat covering her that with a shocked "Alinka, the doctor!" Barbara had to tear it away. "Hmm," he cleared his throat, "hmm," and the examination began.

Yellowed, like an old pillow with gray tufts sticking from it, his head rested against the tiny breasts; his fingers galloped up and down the scabby back; he looked up, he gave a nod. "Like bellows," so he always began, "lungs sound like bellows."

"Like bellows. And the heart? Ah, also in order. Yes?" Barbara beamed. "Did you hear, Alinka, did you?" Then she walked him to the door and there, in a whisper, as though inquiring about another patient whose prognosis might not be so good, she asked about the camp. All was quiet, the doctor assured her; by the time anything happened the girl would be out of the woods. "She — she is doing well, Doctor, isn't she?"

"Iron," he answered, "this child has a constitution of iron." He repeated.

"Orderly! Grünbaum! You!" the clamor rose, while she, hearing none of it, contemplated what he had given her. Iron constitution meant not just the overcoming of typhus, not just her own rescue from ultimate abandonment: it was a link, a chain of unbending loyalty. Here lay this child, so wasted, so frail that no touch could be cautious enough. Typhus gone, the camp diarrhea had come, along with boils and a scabby itch. Yet the child endured, she went on, loyal to what she must still become, and what Barbara perceived but dimly — as a shape, glimmering and pure.

To carry such a chain, strength was needed; to gain strength, food, and that she must provide. A day in the sick barracks and Barbara had taken a census of the local rich, knew to whom the vendors came, who had sold, who had bought what. To those she went. "My dear" — since names slipped through her head as through a sieve this was her form of address — "my dear, you've just bought some flour — some cornmeal — some beans — let me have oh, a couple of spoonfuls," she demanded matter-of-factly as though placing an order in a familiar grocery store.

A few, few indeed they were, filled those orders, having taken pity on her, cast off by the Anweiserin and saddled with that cranky child to boot. Most refused, but only at first. If refused, she smiled. "Suit yourself," she said, "of course, suit yourself. But I'll remember."

This she did — without mercy. A drink of water she might reach to them, but let them try sending her on errands. "You go yourself," she would bellow, "you've just had yourself a feast, you must be strong." And it was then that she looked at the door, hoping that at such a moment Tola would come to see who was doing dirty work and with what ease.

That Tola was not gone for good, that the true Alinka only had to return to bring Tola back, Barbara fully believed. And at times Alinka's return seemed near. The girl would start up, a questioning look would come into her eyes. Yet soon it faded away, as though "It's early," she had told herself, "I can still rest."

When the rest had ended, when Alinka in her usual sharp tone asked "Where's Tola?" then Barbara longed for the dreadful child to be back, for the moans to call her away, for anything that would put off the answer. What was there to answer? To repeat what Tola had said would be now, as ever, a calumny, a lie, and what to her — still convinced that the Anweiserin, the cold fish, was not really Tola — seemed much nearer the truth, some story about Tola having had to leave, suddenly, on an urgent trip, of this the camp deprived her. And so she sat with her hands big and helpless in her lap.

"What — no, wait," Alinka checked herself. "How long have I been lying here like this?"

Long, it seemed so long that Barbara had to calculate hastily with the help of food — there had been a cornmeal day, a bean day, then a day of nothing but soup. "A week," she said with a start, "just one week."

"A whole week! And for a whole week Tola has not been here? Is she all right? Yes? Then where is she, what's happened?"

"What?" In a sudden fury Barbara blew up. "Don't ask me what's happened. I don't know, I don't understand anything. I really don't know," she repeated softly; then, looking away, "Tola has moved to the Kaelanki barracks right across from where we used to live."

It was morning, chores had to be done in the morning. Her face turned away so as not to breathe in the vile smell, her arms clasping the bespattered barrel, Barbara rolled the slops out to the latrine. Next, to let the wind cleanse her from the stench, she sat outside for a spell, then slowly walked back into the barracks.

Alinka was gone. Only the Hunchback lay on the bunk.

Barbara waited; she ran to the corner; she dashed forward at each sound, at each shadow darkening the sunlit earth. At last, small and dark, a figure appeared far away, stopped to lean against the barracks, then clutching the wall, moved on in slower and slower steps.

"God, how you fuss," Alinka gasped out as Barbara came running to her. "You just fuss and fuss!" the girl repeated while being lifted up onto the bunk. Then for a long while they sat looking away from each other, until "Why?" Alinka cried. "Why did you say it to her? You — you — " The girl paused.

And in this pause Barbara saw it all — Alinka carefully collecting her belongings, the coat, the can, the bag; Alinka, without one word, one glance, leaving her, leaving the one who on that night of birth could have said to Tola so terrible a thing. She would deny everything, she would say Tola had lied, she would.

" 'Go, I might poison you!' Tola said to me. Why can't you ever keep your mouth shut, Barbara? Why do you always have to blab? Why? And why do you look like this, so filthy, and in rags? When did you wash last, when did you mend your dress?"

The child was gone; the true Alinka was back.

More tyrannical than ever, she perched on the bunk as on a lookout. "Women, let Barbara be!" one could hear her cry all day long. "She has only two hands. She isn't made out of iron." But when her nose turned white, when she clenched her fists and cried "Stop beating!" — it was Barbara she meant.

And Barbara, who since Alinka's return had been living like a victim of blackmail, Barbara, so afraid some malicious gossip would make Alinka pack up and go that a displeased glance made her wince, in those moments would not give in.

"I'll beat them," she muttered, "I will — and how!"

She could not help herself: she had to beat. That something in

her welcomed every chance for dealing out blows, that she was paying the women back for granting her this chance, for leaving her
uncertain whether even without this chance, hunger, weariness,
and this latest hurt might not have driven her to the same fury — all
this she knew very well.

Yet she beat, without scruple, without remorse.

"Pigs! Are you?" This was her warning; and if it went unheeded,
if for a crumb of bread, for an inch of space at the stove, or for no
reason at all they pounced at one another and shrieked and clawed
till their bodies merged into one throbbing mass, their faces into
one mouth spouting spittle and screams, then she would grab whatever was handy, a piece of kindling, a board, or a broom, and whack
with all her might.

Not only at them did she aim those whacks, but at a presence to
be chased off once and for all. Yet the presence returned, grown
clearer each time: a rumormonger, a tempter darting on swift
soundless feet, giving a push here, a nudge there, spreading the rumor into all too willing ears that they were pigs anyhow, that they
might as well let themselves go, why not? And when they gave in—
no scream too loud for them, no insult too vile — then, with a satisfied nod he would return to her, changing his tactics, now asking
with great concern why she did not take what was her due — a
share of their bread, a rest in the sun, and let those pigs wallow in
their own filth.

"Quiet!" and the broom swung until at last the solid mass broke up
into women, the one gaping mouth into faces startled as though they
had wakened from an evil dream.

"When you turn into pigs, I have to beat," Barbara would announce calmly. This, that one must not turn into a pig, became the
dogma she embraced with the ardor of a neophyte. Slovenly not
by nature but on principle, since order smacked of pedantry, and
pedantry of concern with small things, she now conceived a passion
for hygiene. Just one peel had to fall to the floor, and at once she
glowered, at once silence fell over the barracks, that fearful, de-
licious classroom silence — somebody else about to get it for a
change — while she, having made sure that no high fever excused
the misdeed, sneaked up in gleeful hope of taking the culprit by

surprise. "Pick it up!" her bellow burst into the silence. "If you have the strength to litter, you must have the strength to clean up!" And she aired and swept and forced others to air and sweep.

Came morning and everyone had to wash. "Everyone, everyone!" she yelled, passing around the only basin. "Aha, afraid of getting wet, like the devil of being sprinkled with holy water!" Or standing soot-smeared at the stove she would scowl at the procrastinators, then between grumbles go back to puffing at the fire so that the water for the very sick would get warm at last. These sick she washed herself — awkwardly, her glances asking of Alinka "Am I doing it right — like this?" while the others had to shift for themselves.

Which was exactly as far as her justice went. "You play favorites, Barbara, I swear," Alinka complained. "I, never!" she protested, though without conviction. She could not help herself. She was just like those novice teachers, the quick, the willing pupil their delight, but with no patience to spare for the dullard, his dumb stares exposing all their efforts as futile.

These she favored: the young girls who watched over each other; the healthy checking whether the sick had slept, had washed; and the sick whether the healthy had been fooling around, whether the O.D. man had left the bunk on time; and the old ladies of such unimpeachable propriety that though covered by the same coat and fed by the same spoon they would not dream of addressing each other by first names; and the remnant of the remnant, the mothers, still hissing their "You always" — these she favored above all.

But there were others; terrible crabby women, by day hibernating with food stored under their sticky buttocks — "Will it hatch," she leered at them, "will it?" — but with the dark reviving; with the dark gnawing on and on as though they had attacked the very boards, not from hunger — often they were the rich — but from a greed that could not bear to leave anything in sight undevoured.

"Rodents, scavengers," she growled at them.

One of them died, and Barbara feared that there had been something in this woman which she in her disgust had missed. Another one just like her joined the sick — and it was "Rodents, scavengers!" again.

The two O.D. men in charge, these she hated most; not for

grabbing whatever the lonely dead had left behind — one had to live, and were it not for her horror of the O.D. men, she might have done the same — but for those inspection visits to the very sick, for those stocktaking glances, for that "Orderly, when she dies not a button must be missing!" shouted right across those who lay clutching at coat or dress to prove these rags were theirs still. "Come, I have to tell you something, come, come," she beckoned to lure the O.D. men away.

Death too was a rumor: subtly, with more cunning by far than the one who spoke of the women being pigs, a tempter spread it around, whispering that it was not worth struggling so hard, that anyhow it was all in vain; and if she agreed just in her thoughts, just for an instant, then the one so tempted sensed it and gave her a satiated, much too calm look.

With the stiff paper strips bandaging bedsores that opened like windows upon bare bones, with soup forced into mouths reddened by consumptive foam, she tried to fight this rumor. "You'll get well," she promised, "you will, you must." But then, hour upon hour, their stares followed her, pleading for one token of this promise, for one proof; and when the plea was not granted, when fever, when cough came instead, then that other look was back — calmer, more satiated still. Therefore she learned to forgo this promise. When ministering to such sick she balanced, as on a steep pinnacle, on the present moment, trying to think only of the wound to be dressed, the foam to be wiped off — and she failed, and slipped, and could not wait to get away. But they held on to her with hands like leaves, leaves turned limp in the rain, leaves dried out by too much sun.

All clung to her; not out of fondness, for this she was too oppressive, too harsh, but out of a need felt by patients anywhere, the need to prove by tales of riches left behind — the adoring husband, the exceptional child — that it was they and not the one in the adjacent bed who deserved the most devoted care. Their riches, though, were all of the past. After the names of husband and child came "of blessed memory" — the inevitable epithet that for her somehow had merged with the title once her own, "lady of the manor" — and memory seemed an estate where those remembered had chosen to dwell.

"Of blessed memory — of blessed memory," the phrase echoed

throughout the barracks; while "poor" one said of the local dead, "poor," just that, with a condescending pity as for the inept whom ill luck pursues.

The number of those poor kept growing. A sense of unrest would spread over the barracks, an impatience as though death, like someone long overdue, should hurry up and come. "Do something, move her away" the plea would come next, this "her" uttered uneasily, as though the one to be moved had acquired an uncertain status between a person and a thing. Until at last the O.D. men came, and behind them the picriniacs bringing in the stretcher.

Never was death so far from Barbara as at those moments. To some of her sick it simply had to happen that they would one day wear that stern, censorious look; that the yellowed arms would throw them on the stretcher, sagging, light though such a burden always was. But this was forbidden: to think of the place where the stretcher was going and to ask herself if they had thought of that place before becoming so stern.

The door closed. And already she was pushing them away, as recklessly as she pushed away those begging her for the exemption slips that would keep them from returning to work and that were not in her power to grant.

So it was if they who died had been alone. If they had not been alone, if a sister or a friend was still to be told, then she kept starting up, kept looking at the door. They came; they were told by the other sick, even by Alinka, for she herself could not bear to be messenger of such news. She only watched them; she waited to see whether without a word, clutching the inherited bread, they would run out— Could I have been like this? something would nag at her then, Was I? — or if the silence would go on and on, so unbearable that "Move, cry, do anything!" all eyes pleaded of the one bereft, until at last the sobs broke out, to which she listened with shame, with envy, and with remorse that, like so much else, must not be thought of.

She might be scrubbing, or kindling the fire, when suddenly Tola would appear to her — running through the dark, her hand passing over her cheek. After she had done something terrible, Tola would run so; what Tola might have done Barbara did not try to imagine. All she knew was that afterward Tola would look very calm, would even smile to show that anything was easy for her — anything at all, her smile would announce throughout the long hours at work, throughout the march back to the camp — and only when no one was looking would she run on and on, hand pressed to the white face.

She did see Tola once, early in the afternoon — a time always reserved for Alinka. How Barbara waited for this moment when they would sit outside, undisturbed, just the two of them. It came and an unaccountable shyness seized her; by contrast to this diminutive girl she felt so awkward, so huge, that "Hot!" was all she could find to say, "Oh, isn't it hot!"

Alinka took over, asking questions about life in the manor: who her guests had been, who the friends; and had they gone horseback riding, had they danced at the harvest feast? Uneasily she answered, as the old do when drawn out about the exploits of their youth — distant, theirs no more. Then, "Wait!" for here was an exploit still hers. "I remember," she laughed, "oh, I do. We were dancing, the village elder and I, and 'Dziedziczka,' he said, 'when Dziedziczka steps on my foot it feels like a ton of bricks!'" Warned by the dismayed glance that this just would not do, she broke off. "Certainly they still wanted to dance with me," she hastened to agree. "Why not? I was no eyesore after all."

So, Alinka leading, Barbara now stumbling, now catching the proper rhythm, they moved through the estate; then on to Warsaw, on to Italy, where she remembered only a lizard asleep in the Forum, and how her shoes had pinched. But at once with an "Ah, Italy is wonderful!" she recovered herself and the tour proceeded, through Spain, through France, and back to the manor; now Alinka doing the honors of the house, leading Barbara to all that would await her there — dances, soirees, stately feasts, and on to the children she would bear Stefan, then . . . after the war.

"After the war — " Abruptly Alinka broke off, stared at the ground, at the barracks, the shining tar roofs, and on into the next street. There was Tola, arms clasped behind her back, her feet in high-heeled shoes stepping hard, as if walking meant forcing something into the ground.

"After . . . after the war," Alinka began anew. Again she stopped, because at the corner a group was forming, then another and yet another, all hushed as on that day when news had come of the other camp. "Alinka!" Barbara cried, "Alinka, something is happening, come, come with me. No, you stay right here — no, come!" She clutched at Alinka and behind them came the Hunchback, tottering on reedy legs.

"Trucks!" as they walked into the next barracks everyone was saying, trucks, loaded so full that the canvas bulged, had passed through the woods. The hump shook, the freckled nose turned white. "Trucks — what about the trucks?" Barbara was about to ask, when from behind whispers came telling of prisons that were being emptied, of politicals — bodies of politicals that were being brought to be burned in the woods. If prisons were being emptied so would the camps, she understood at last. Once again she stiffened; once again with her whole body, her whole strength, she was holding a door shut to keep out what might happen to her, to the one who had just passed by, and to the girl whom she was clutching tight.

Later on the doctor came in. "You have nothing to fear," he said. "As soon as I can, I'll list the girl as an orderly. And as orderlies you are both safe — absolutely safe," he repeated, and in her once more the door slammed shut — upon the sick who would not be safe if anything happened in the camp.

All through the evening whispers of the trucks went on. But by the next day it seemed one had always known that they would come, that stronger than ever the smell would clog the hot air. "Hot," Barbara sighed as they sat down outside the barracks. "Oh how hot!" she repeated, waiting for the Hunchback to be off.

The Hunchback stayed; the Hunchback had latched on to them for good: morose and sallow-faced, she perched on the bench, casting the shadow of her hump upon the white manor, upon Italy and France — the shadow of an injustice that, incomprehensible, not to be redressed, would be carried from before into after the war.

Nights, without the girl's guidance, Barbara ventured into "after the war." At night everything was growing: sleep into rooms where the women had gone to rest; bunks into houses rising row upon row, street upon street; and the barracks into the city lying vast and quiet in the warm summer night. In the distance other cities lay, populous, so many of them. That they could all be wiped away, this could never be . . .

The day would come when the boundaries of barbed wire would be razed to the ground. Then all of them would walk out and on, first to a transit place, no longer of war, not yet of peace, a place where no one shouted "Orderly!", where lights shone muted, and food, mild as in childhood, was brought in. At times Stefan came just to prove he was safe, just for a brief visit — as if to him, too, she had to grow accustomed, as to richer food, as to more brilliant light.

Years sped on, always toward the same day, which, cliché though it was, having been gleaned out of family tales and the cheap romances she had loved to read on the sly, held her in an ever greater spell. White and red was this day, white of jasmine, red of first roses, red of wine, white of damask cloth. At the tables so adorned, guests were taking their seats — a motley crowd that she, touched by the foreboding of a depopulated world, gathered as best she could — the relatives returned from the four corners of the earth next to the bulky peasants, the Kaelanki next to the dziedziczki, swathed in musty silks. So in order of importance the guests were coming: Marta, her huge breasts squeezed under a too tight dress; Antoni, uncomfortable-looking as always when his shoes were new and the guests many; next, reaching its final metamorphosis, Aurelia's child, just a bow, white socks and banged-up knees; then she — then Tola, who must, who would be there.

A whisper and all rose, all looked at her in whose honor they had gathered here, Alinka. Led by Stefan she was coming in, white and airy in bridal lace. Only *him*, indispensable though he was for this day, she could not imagine at all: fashioned in the image of men she used to fancy, he seemed unreliable, as such gallants tend to be; subdued, he lacked élan, he seemed mousy, until, modified to a neutral shadow, he was the first to absent himself.

One by one in order of their arrival the guests took their leave. Alone the white figure stood in the silenced room, a glass of wine caught the last light, a petal drifted into the dusk.

Moonlight lit up the barracks. Then, blurred by sleep, a voice would call a name of long ago, another called, then another. She listened: from the estates of blessed memory the dead were coming into the night.

Chapter 37

Now ALL WAS STILL. Only far away a hinge screeched, and here across the whitewashed stove a shadow was jerking up and down, as though hooked on a protruding edge. The shadow swung; it broke loose. And suddenly what had started Tola from an uneasy dream was back — the shout, faint, still distant, but already drawing closer, already caught up by other voices, more of them and more, till it seemed that all, the screaming women, the men breaking into hoarse shouts, were chasing one another out, faster and faster, as doors slammed, as feet raced down to the Appellplatz.

"Wait for me — wait!" someone called; someone shuffled with slow heavy steps. They stopped. And now silence, as though the camp were empty, as though only she, still lying on the strip of grass, were left, alone, with the guards high above her. Boots pounded; in thin dark lines, shadows of rifles fell from the towers. Tola got up, and shielding her back with her arms ran on.

The streets were deserted. A splash, that was slops dripping down the latrine steps; a rustle, the stretcher left lying by the crate. Farther down the doors swung upon empty barracks, upon floors littered with sabots, with cans and rags lost in the crush.

Only the hospital was not empty yet. A filthy lump of a bandaged arm stuck out through the door; the lump swayed, and above the moans, low like the buzz of flies, a rasp called out. "Killed!" it said. "Killed!"

Would they, the sick, be killed, or she for coming too late? And it was late; the whole camp had gathered in the Appellplatz, not in columns as usual, but in a crowd, silent, heads uplifted, as though watching something in the hazy sky.

It was an O.D. man standing high up on a cart. The O.D. man was announcing something — what, she could not hear yet; a sudden clatter was drowning his voice. Everyone in the crowd turned toward her. And as she shrank back from those stares, from those arms ordering her away, the clatter went on louder with her every step. A can caught under her heel was clattering. She kicked it off, then stiffly, trying not to run, walked into the nearest doorway.

It was dark inside. From the blackened laundry kettles boils of linen swelled into the stinking steam, but what at first seemed like another boil was a head — a girl's shaved head, bobbing up and down in the wooden trough. One of the hospital sick — when discharged they were always bathed in water left from the O.D. men's wash — was trying to get out of the trough. The girl kept clutching at the rim and slipping back with a thin startled cry.

"They left — Come — come here." The girl's hand reached out of the steam.

Though sickened by this flat sallow body, Tola came closer, and reached out for the hands: instead the wet arms clasped her neck, clung harder, and as the girl weighed heavier and heavier upon her "Is it true?" the feverish whisper asked, "is it?"

"What?" she gasped, putting the girl down on the bench. "Is what true?"

"That he — Hitler — was killed, that the war — is over." Brown like bedbugs, drops oozed down the spindly legs. "Over — is it?" the girl repeated.

Over — the war is over, Tola thought, and could not understand what this meant, as though for her, unable to see herself anywhere but here in this camp, there was no war. If the war is over there will be no work tonight; the trucks won't come again if it is over; the smell will lift. And now when she began to understand, panic gripped her; she must run, must find a place to be alone, at once, before everyone burst into a jubilant shout.

But it was very still outside; here the girl shook with a dry cough. "Go," between the coughs she cried, "go, find out — and come back. You will come back, won't you?"

There was nothing to find out; before the guards bellowed and the clubs flailed, Tola knew it — from the eyes, the wide extinguished eyes of those who, having traveled from afar to see a most rare sight, find the place abandoned, the door locked.

"No — Hitler wasn't touched. The revolt is squashed," whispers rose over the shuffle of feet, hurrying, breaking into a trot as the O.D. men swung their clubs. Suddenly she too flailed with her fist. "Move on, move!" she was shouting; but already Barbara and Alinka, who had turned to look at her, were running on, and when they stopped it was to wait for the Hunchback tottering behind them like a black pack on stilts.

"Move — move on!" There was no one left to shout at. Only in the corner a Picrine woman stood, muttering against that nitwit of an O.D. man who wouldn't wait to hear the news until the end, who instead had come screaming that Hitler had been killed. "And — and if he had been killed — " The woman started and stood staring at her arm spotted with sores like moist purplish mouths.

Silence spread over the camp, the strained, obligatory silence that comes after disaster has struck someone who, having left so long ago that it seemed he had already died a discreet death, now repeats it to extract his due of grief. From the barracks hardly a sound came. Outside, lines were forming quietly in front of the barrels, and here, where the shout had first reached Tola, the crowd usually stampeding at the stove gathered in a hushed circle, those about to put their pots on careful to adjust the required look which says "Yes, after all, life must go on." A head shaved to the skin brushed against her. The girl! she remembered; perhaps the girl was still there waiting to find out. She turned back. Halfway to the laundry she shrugged and went to her barracks.

To show that nothing had changed, guards were marching through the woods. At Picrine, at the Trotyl plant the Meisters flashed triumphant smiles. And when the women walked into the hall — immediately, for the work at loading had stopped — in the clearing where Meister Grube stood, news was being broadcast, this too a proof that nothing had changed. But he, the old transport man, would not give up hope. "Shh, be quiet," he whispered, leaning out of the window. "Quiet, quiet!" though no one spoke. "Can't hear, the wind is too loud — I can't. Miss Anweiserin, you go to him; go, he won't mind, he'll tell you what's happening."

"So, this will never end" was what the Meister had to tell her. Jawohl Herr Meister, Thank you Herr Meister, the habitual answers ran through her head; and because they would not do, because to face him dumb, her arms dangling, was too much, "And what about us?" she said, "Herr Meister, how will it end for us?"

She had asked. I know nothing, he would say; he knows nothing, she would tell the women, and shut them up for good.

"Nichts, nothing," he began; then, preferring a comfortable lie, "You have nothing to fear." And she smiled, remembering how once the little Pole from Trotyl had reassured her with those very words. Would the Meister, like him, compliment her next on her looks — a bit skinny, a bit pinched, but not so bad?

"I'm sorry," he broke in. For her friends he was sorry, he had tried to help them, he had failed. "I tried," he repeated, then went on about "die Unentbehrlichen," the indispensable ones who would stay on; about "die Arbeitsfähigen," those able to work, who could not stay. He went on and on, while she stared at his rapidly moving lips.

He stopped. "No," she said. "No, I don't understand. I — "

"The O.D. men and their aides," he went on, "will stay here to take inventory, then will go to the camp in Czestochowa. It's a good camp, I've been there and I know." He nodded, and the comforting smile that stretched his lips stayed on even while he spoke of those who could not stay, who would be sent away sooner, but only "die Arbeitsfähigen," only they. "Still, in this respect, Fräulein, your friends have nothing to fear," he concluded, the forgotten smile removed at last.

She understood what this meant, she understood everything, yet it seemed to her that only a minor complication had set in, to be cleared up as soon as he left, as soon as she could move. Only before he left she must still ask him something. "When?" she asked. "No, that's not what I meant," she was about to say when he interrupted her. "The front is still faraway." His voice was deep and too relaxed. Till the front moved closer nothing would change here, and of course, before anything was to change, he would let her know, of course — he —

"No, but where will they go. Where?"

"To Germany."

Auschwitz was in Poland, not in Germany; no, Auschwitz was

Germany now. Still, just a moment ago he had said something proving it could not be Auschwitz; he had said that only those "arbeitsfähig" would go to Germany. This meant all not arbeitsfähig
would be selected. A selection proved it wouldn't be Auschwitz;
there was never any selection before Auschwitz.

"Where in Germany?" she asked hoarsely.

"I don't know; they don't tell me much." Then, motioning incongruously as though having opened the door, he invited her to go before him. She moved on. Right behind her his shadow trailed, the
shoulders shrugging at each step. "Of course," this shrug said, "she
will abandon her friends, just as I thought."

"Of course, Herr Meister, I'll stay with my friends," she said, and
hurried on for fear he should see through her, should know that she
would not stay with them, because . . . nothing . . . because anyhow she could do nothing.

Nothing — nothing, pressing against the peeling wall she repeated; then outside, pressing against the broad tree trunk, Nothing
— nothing again to the rhythm of rattling carts. Picriniacs, two
O.D. men right behind, were pushing the carts. The picriniacs
won't go to Germany, they wouldn't be welcome, they cough too
hard. The O.D. men would be welcome anywhere, the O.D. men
were indispensable — and how much so! Who but they could salute
that elegantly, necks craning toward the Meister's window, boots
leaping up in the dust.

"Good evening, gentlemen," she waved, "good evening to you."
They looked at her; one tapped his forehead. She was cuckoo, he
was saying. She was not cuckoo, far from it; she was clever, so
clever she even knew why it would be Czestochowa for them, why
such tender loving care. Because they were indispensable, that was
why, indispensable for that great final joke, for the remnant to be
sent out with the label "This is what you fought for" after the war.

After the war . . . after the war . . . After the war, at a station
crowds would gather, enormous, very still; would shudder as the
train rolled in, would shrink in awe as the doors opened. And now
they were coming, the tragic victims, the mourners bent under the
weight of bundles of shoes and clothing that the last inventory had
supplied; arguing out a poker game, laughing at a dirty jest, they
pushed on through the crowd, while on the side, feeling quite safe

— for which of them, to tangle with him, would risk missing a bargain — Rost stood smiling at the success of his joke. It had come off perfectly, ja, just perfectly; it was even better than that other joke planned in case of victory, better than the "circus of the indispensables," open to the public free of charge, so that none would miss the spectacle, so that all could watch the chosen few mate, cheat, denounce, and above all select one another, on and on, till just a handful was left, just two, just one — and he in his last moment still leaping up, his limbs wriggling as though one arm were selecting the other arm, one hand the other hand.

She smiled, rubbed her frozen hands, then slowly walked back to the hall. In the doorway she stopped: all at once the women rose, their faces lit by the last sun, and leaning forward, like that other crowd gathered at the station, they too waiting — for those who they had never been, those who they would never become, for themselves from before the war.

A chair scraped. Brown wisps flapping over her eyes, Meyerova was strutting toward her. She stepped closer to the old woman. "Well," looking into the bleary eyes, she said, "well, why such hurry? Who will be waiting for you after the war?"

Meyerova blubbered something, then tottered back, heavily and stumbling like someone else before — like Doctorka's mother, whom the SS guard had shot. Again a chair scraped; brushing back her grizzled mane Doctorka got up. "Beast," she said under her breath, "you nasty little beast!" And at the next table Meyerova sat, her mouth open as if those bent over her were feeding her, crumb by crumb. Hope was being fed to her — the false, the unshakable hope that somewhere in another camp someone would survive to wait for her after the war.

"After the war — " whispers rose from everywhere. "After the war — "

She would eat after the war, she would stuff herself till she burst. Or, why wait so long? Tomorrow, first thing in the morning she would buy bread from Rozalia, lots of bread, with all the money she had saved up.

"Here, eighty zlotys, Rozalia," she said in the morning, pulling away the prayer shawl. "Give me a cup of cornmeal and a loaf of bread."

"Not selling." The copper head shook. "My goy says great hunger is coming. I'm not selling, Intelligenzia, scram!" Rozalia screamed, drawing the curtain so abruptly that the darkly striped folds brushed against Tola's face.

Chapter 38

It was as though in that moment when the cry had broken upon the camp, everywhere, on all continents and in all lands, peace, till then no more than a slogan, had become an address, a place that would be reached with one last attempt. And the attempt was being made: each day brought the fall of a city, on each front the offensive moved on. And here at Schmitz the noon break was no longer time for soup. As though pampered, as though they had been nibbling on sweets all morning, with such indifference the women passed by the barrels and formed a wide circle round the oak. On one side of the circle stood Tola, on the other the Meister, staring at the loudspeaker box. Once again a trumpet blared, a drum rolled its last beat. Silence, then a rasp as of one uneasily clearing his throat. And at last the news.

In a planned strategic maneuver Lublin had been abandoned; to shorten the front line the German armies had withdrawn from Baranow, from Lvov. The women nodded, the women turned to look at the Meister, then with hardly a sound they lined up before the barrels of soup.

No one pushed anymore, no one complained about old hags; like tourists who long before a trip practice the foreign idiom and manners, they, even the bilious Orphan, even the ex-orderly with the honking voice, practiced the patient, soft-spoken ways recalled from before the war. The trust in masculine guidance had been restored to them too — its recipient, Ziegelman, the wizened transport man.

"So, Mr. Ziegelman, what do you think, Mr. Ziegelman?" They flocked toward him.

"Well, when I was a sergeant in Kaiser Franz Joseph's army," in a clipped voice he would begin, would talk of "pincers" and of "supply lines"; then while his fingers whirled like airplanes, while they charged and crept like tanks, a new note sneaked into his voice, and "if they have taken Zamosc then they must get to Sandomierz soon," he sang in a Talmudist's dreamy chant.

To Tola, still standing to one side, this old man was telling no more than rumors: each city that fell seemed faraway, the armies that advanced never drew nearer to the camp. The Meister held them at bay; until he gave the sign no change could come.

And whatever signaled a change seemed, like the heat, like the sweetish smell, always to have been there. Knowing it was unsafe to be sick, those barely recovered had always swarmed back to work; rumors that the sick barracks would close had been heard before; even the new SS guards had always been here; and the trains loaded with machinery had always left from Werk A.

Only what was happening to her body was new. Dysentery plagued it; dysentery wrung her harder each day. She tried to find remedies: since a jolt or a sudden breath set off the wringing, she carried herself on stiffened legs, she breathed slowly and with caution. The remedies helped little. Each day she sat longer in the latrine, cramped, staring at the initials blunt nails had scratched; beneath them, like a fresco from another era, an arrow-pierced heart.

She had one fear now: that suddenly, without warning, she would be wrung out, would stand amid jeers in the Appellplatz, in the hall, or right under Grube's eyes. When "Ja Herr Meister, Jawohl Herr Meister" she had to say, she breathed carefully, she even counted to calm herself down. But sweat broke out all over her as she reached for her bread. Her legs could hardly move, the room grew larger with each step — the glass door, the corridor and at last the latrine.

In the hall she was not indispensable anymore. The women worked, went out, came back in such perfect order that the seam of her mouth never needed to be opened. She, who lived from bread to bread, counted the hours to ration time, or she watched the others speaking, moving with such ease that they seemed like some different species living far away behind the haze of sun and of chalky dust.

But at times some noise outside would bring them closer. "Mr. Ziegelman," her bloodless lips quivering, the Mouse would be calling, "Mr. Ziegel —" she never needed to finish, for already he was at his post, climbing up the crates at the window. When "Ah, nothing, calm down," he assured them — it was only the wind rustling the leaves. When he shrank to a flat black heap, guards, the helmeted SS men, were marching by. But when "Hush!" he breathed, hanging out of the window, the O.D. men were coming with some news. Everyone would get up. "Yes?" they whispered, their alarmed eyes, Tola felt, tugging at her. "Yes, have they come for us? The trains, have they come?"

"God forbid," Ziegelman answered. "Wait, let me talk to them." "God forbid," he repeated, turning back. "Russian planes have been seen, the O.D. men say. A village was burned in reprisal for helping partisans. The news is good."

"And the machinery?" the Mouse would ask.

"Trains are still coming for it. But, but — " Now peremptorily, now with a humble plea, he argued that the Germans could not drag them out, because they needed every train for themselves, because the Russians would bomb the tracks — because — because —

"Perhaps. Anyhow what can we do?" Soon those resigned sighs made them as far away as the very old who must know what would soon come to them, yet whose calm seems to prove they can handle it with expert ease.

The bread dealt out in camp had been always corroded with mold. "We are just as hungry as you," the Kaelanki had always cried at the picriniacs. For the hunger Rozalia's goy had prophesied did come; with the Poles from Trotyl now hoarding food nothing was smuggled into the camp. But Rozalia was kept in style by her goy, Rozalia ate; first the green ration bread, next her own fresh bread, next potatoes, and later, for a nightcap, she drank the potato water, her lips smacking loud in the dark.

Lagerschluss was not observed at all; long after it had been announced figures flitted past the windows, couple after couple, like night animals roaming in pairs. When the figures vanished, when the gleam of the O.D. men's flashlight only rarely hit the cracked pane, then Tola would step outside.

As though new camps had sprouted up all around, countless searchlights moved across the sky, illuminating the band of smoke above the distant woods. Men from Werk A had been digging graves in those woods; trucks, not with bodies but with Polish prisoners, had been going there. Tola hardly ever glanced at the smoke. Freed by the empty dark from her fear of being jeered at, she walked on past the towers, past the wires cutting like a denuded hedge into the sky, then on past that barracks where fevered voices cried for something to drink. When her body felt like glass spun so fine it could be crushed by the slightest touch, she went back to her bunk.

"Ver is dus, who?" Rozalia cried in terror of thieves. From the bunk above, dust shed onto Tola's face while she lay there looking at that bag filled with bread. Not of bread she dreamt, though, but of the Mouse: the gray face quivered under her clenched fists, it winced, it fled into the dark — and having struck that face she ran until a beam of light picked her up, like a long finger a speck of dust. Hunger would start her from this dream; hunger changed to a sense of expectation; something, she knew, must still happen to her, something unnamed that must come not a moment too soon or too late, but exactly at the appointed time.

But the next day was so much like the day before that time seemed not to move, and she could hardly believe Friday, the day she did her wash, was here again. In the laundry, where she went for hot water, two white coats hung, one large, the other small as for a child. "For the orderlies." The woman in charge pointed at the coats with a flat paddle.

"Why?"

"So they'll look official. The sick barracks has been closed, I mean the sick are still there, about nine of them, not more, but they're listed in the hospital. And the orderlies too are listed on the hospital — what do you call it?"

"Staff," she said, "hospital staff," and watched the paddle strike the boils of linen so hard that they collapsed into the kettle with a thin hissing sound.

Chapter 39

"You heard him, I know nothing." Then a pause, then a cautious breath, and again, "You heard him, you did." Because they had ears just as she did, because the Meister had spoken to them, just as to her: the shipment of copper wire had not been delivered; even so, as long as any wire was left, the work must go on. This announcement had been made often before, parts for shells had been late before, but now all of them kept running to her, one more, and still one more, then, pulling her daughter along, came the Mouse for the second, no, for the third time.

"Please." Tola's lips felt stiff from so much talking. "Please, go back at once." But they both kept staring with their identical moist eyes. "Please!" They were gone; the others too left her alone, and at last the morning moved on quietly, just as always.

Only the weather was not as always. The heat had broken; the downpour of last night had washed the oversweet smell away, and the air felt as spacious, as pure as in an invalid's room when the illness ends and the windows reopen all at once. At times, a twig the storm had snapped would fall to the ground, or a cluster of leaves scattered raindrops as it flitted by. And at each rustle the women would start, would turn to the piles of crates where Ziegelman kept watch. "Oh, just a branch," he calmed them. "Just wind."

"Just —" He broke off. Over the hall such silence fell that the boots seemed to be stamping right inside; it was not guards, just soldiers marching by. The last one — small, and squashed smaller still by his pack — peeked in, then ran on, his helmet wobbling like a lampshade all askew. Slowly Ziegelman slid down the crates. He tiptoed to the door, then out.

A shell rolled jingling on the floor, a chair creaked, and the thud of something falling — that came from outside. Ziegelman had fallen down. Ziegelman was lying on the ground, pressing his head here, there, and everywhere, as though someone was calling to him from under the shiny grass. He rose; his mouth gaped on pallid gums.

"It moved," he said softly. "The earth, it did. I felt it, like a shudder from a cannonade, from bombs. I felt it, and then — nothing — then I could feel it no longer."

"I could feel nothing — nothing," he kept reporting. And while the coils of wire grew thinner, while hands moved slower and slower, Tola watched the clock, counting the time left until the Meister's bread: three quarters of an hour still . . . half an hour. "Transport," someone called and stopped short when the Mouse pointed to Ziegelman, still listening to the ground. So as not to disturb him the women were carrying the finished crates out themselves, each one coming back cautiously, like a stranger not sure what might await him inside. And when the last crate was gone, when of the wire not a piece was left, a forlorn look came into their faces, as though they were lost in an unknown place.

"Let us," the Mouse began, "let's — yes, let's clean up." Brooms scraped, paper, rags swished, brushing the chalky dust away. Once more the brooms swayed, once more white puffs drifted up, and they all sat still, looking at Tola, who squeezed deeper into her chair.

Three of them came to her. "Speak to him," they said. "Speak to the Meister, he must know something, he will tell you — "

"Nothing," even as she was getting up she foresaw her answer, "he told me nothing." "He has gone," she had to say instead. "He . . . he must have just stepped out to see about the wire. He . . . " She fell silent, listening to the footsteps outside. It was just O.D. men coming with the soup, an hour earlier than on any other day.

Why so early — the O.D. men did not know. "We've just been ordered to bring in the soup right now," they said, and the crowd moved away to the loudspeaker under which Ziegelman stood. Not a sound came from it.

"It's a sign," he whispered. "Ah, it's a sign."

"Why, Mr. Ziegelman, of what, Mr. Ziegelman?"

"Of fear, of course, what else? The Russians must be almost here, just a few hours, a few miles away. But they don't want us to know it, that's why the radio is mum." The women nodded, then turned; and to Tola it seemed as if a single look from them would make her slink away just as the Meister always did. But they, without even glancing at her, lined up before the barrels.

The Orphan, leading the Yekie by the hand, was the first in line. She sniffed the soup; "Pigs' swill," she declared, and the rotten beets splashed back into the barrel. It was as though now, with no audience present, a demonstration was taking place: one by one the women stepped to the barrels, sniffed, then as carefully as if the rain-washed grass were a tablecloth no spot must mar, they poured the soup back. The line dispersed. But at once another line was formed facing the road through the woods. A group of picriniacs passed by, a cart rattled, and shouting could be heard. The O.D. men were calling from afar that Schmitz had been ordered back.

"Some new work has come up," they said. "Yes, urgent work that must be done today." And while the column was forming, while the Mouse whispered that something was brewing, and Ziegelman that this was a sign, Tola waited for the Meister to come with her bread. But the bang was only an O.D. man shutting all doors, the steps a guard marching round the hall.

The woods were quiet. At Trotyl, where the machines had never stopped before, leaves now rustled in the wind. Bolted up, the windows coated with yellow scum, Picrine looked like a ruin the woods had claimed with lichen and moss. And when no one came to announce "All quiet in the camp," it seemed as though a signpost had been torn down.

If it were quiet, she would get coffee and bread, and then she would sleep; Tola enumerated these errands, bending her fingers to mark each item on the list. It was quiet in the camp, yet one by one her fingers opened, crossing off items not to be had: there was no water, no coffee, the bread was so moldy she spat it out, and even sleep could not be had anymore. Silence kept her awake, silence magnified each sound — the screak of bunks where lovers huddled together, the footsteps of those who, still waiting for their men, paced from window to door, and the whispers from all over the barracks. "Trains," they repeated, "the trains won't come." "The trains — I heard a Pole say the trains don't run anymore."

"A Pole, what can such a goy know — " a picriniac muttered, stopping by her bunk; told not to block her air, he moved on. And just as he stopped, to gape as at something never seen before — at his arm bright ocher in the sun — "Coming!" the Hunchback cried outside; then a hush, as though no one was left in the streets.

But they were all there: those men in jackets with the sheen of tar, those women in blankets or tattered coats, all fully prepared, all with their luggage of cans and of greasy bags. They drew together, they moved apart to let a guard pass, then an O.D. man, and a girl looking for someone who had had to wander off even in such a moment, as always — just as always.

Around the hospital the crowd stood, all looking at the doctor; he, silent as they, kept stretching out his hands, the fingers sallow and loose. A woman asked him for something; the doctor shook his head. It was for the sick they were asking, because if something happened no one in the hospital would be safe. It was the sick he had to deny them: he had his orders, and anyhow, what could be done with them, too weak to take even one step. He paused. From the hospital barracks someone cried for a drink of water.

She too felt thirsty, her throat burned. But neither in the washroom nor in the kitchen was there any water; only Rozalia was drinking, sip by sip. "Nu," water oozed from the crumpled mouth; "Why are you staring at me, Intelligenzia?" And Tola did stare, straight at the bag between Rozalia's knees. Here was a larder, here bread was waiting for her. She could take the bread, could eat; only a sign was needed to show that the time was right.

"Scram," Rozalia snorted, and from above a boot fell down right next to the bag. Tola picked it up, stroked the cracked leather. Why do you look so worried? she would say to the O.D. man. You'll find another cousin in Czestochowa, soon, the very first night. Had she spoken without knowing it? Because his arm swung at her, but it swerved and pointed at the window — glowing red as though the sun were setting, shortly after noon.

The barracks became empty; the window grew black with the crowd; the window glowed red again. A clatter, a heavy thump. Then, from the Appellplatz, from barracks, from the streets, "Out!" the shout came, "all out at once!'

Tola walked to the door, came back inside the barracks to fetch a pin for the loosened Anweiserin band, back once more for the flashlight an O.D. man had ordered her to take along, then walked on so slowly that by the time she came to the Appellplatz a column had already formed.

The column retreated; shining green trucks rolled into the road; a cordon of guards moved in upon the column, and somewhere nearby two voices called — one a throaty bellow, the other still childlike and high.

An O.D. man leapt from a truck; smiting his chest like Rozalia swearing that her price was fair, he swore that they were only going to work.

Tola did not want to work; she must get out of here, and must hide. But already the column was carrying her on, past the gate, past a heap of leaves, then on to the truck. There was no air in the truck, only flesh, blinding her, clogging her lungs. She butted with her head, elbows, and knees and dug her way through until a wisp of air brushed her face; it spread out and turned into wind. From behind, the heaving mass pressed upon her, the edge of the steel wall cut into her belly, but here in the back of the truck she had air at last, and light, tinged red by fire.

Darkness, then sunlight, then darkness again, like a succession of hurried days and nights. Until at last the darkness settled. It smelled of swamp and of damp wood, and behind her the Yekie kept mumbling about the Meister — no, about the Wachmeister, the guard who might say where they were going — where? Wohin?

"Herr — Herr Wachmeister, wohin fahren wir?"

"Graben," said the guard.

"Gra — ben?"

"Graben is trenches, you fool."

"Schützengraben, Herr Wachmeister, Schützengraben, ja?"

"Ja, Schützengraben."

Something glittered silver through the trees. It was railroad tracks. But this was not the place where once Tola had loaded the shells. Here no embankments ran along the tracks, here the broad meadow was dotted with birches; and what from afar looked like a heap of gravel was a grass-covered mound.

The trucks stopped. "Trenches?" as they tumbled out everyone cried. "Tren-ches?"

"Yes!" it was Ziegelman calling. "Yes" and "yes" again. Perched

on a boulder he was pointing to the road behind, was gathering his
evidence — the horse carts, the cars, the trucks crowded with them,
with Germans who would never be allowed to see anything — and
"Anything terrible," he faltered, as "Trenches?" the shout broke out
from the approaching trucks.

"Yes, trenches!" Above those shouts, dipping low at the question,
rising up at the answer, "Maria!" a woman in a flowered kerchief
cried, "Ma-ria!" and as though this were a masquerade, as though
this Maria of hers might be disguised as a picriniac, an O.D. man,
or one of the sooty-faced women from Werk A, she kept stopping,
kept looking at each of them, even at the old guard repeating
something with a toothless hiss.

"Shot," he was saying; if the ditch was not finished by midnight,
twenty would be shot right there.

"Maria!" the woman cried in Tola's ear.

That those two whom the doctor watched over could be here was
not possible. Still, Tola would check after the column had formed,
after the spades had been picked up. The spades glinted in the
sun, and she was running the length of the column, faster and
faster, because already, down a grassy mound between the meadow
and the grove, guards were sliding toward them, already they were
pushing her out of the way. But she was done, she had made certain
that neither of them was there.

Heads down, the guards drove into the column. With rifles and
slashing arms they split it in two, flattened the double rows into single lines that stretched across half of the meadow — from the
mound to the mouth of the woods. A whistle. The lines bent and a
dark gash cut through the tall grass.

Wheelbarrows rattled, spades gritted. "Los!" the guards shouted.
"Los, faster!" echoed the O.D. men darting through the dust.
And the dust was everywhere. Like steam from huge spoons it
rose from spades into the sweaty faces; mingled with leaves, with
grass and roots, it churned above the ditch, above the barrows,
above the ridges of dugout soil rising higher and higher alongside
the grove of birches and the tracks.

Water glittered behind the tracks; to drink the water was forbidden. "Shot," a guard yelled as Tola turned toward it, "anyone caught
behind the tracks will be shot at once."

Those threats meant nothing to her by now. It was the dust she could not bear, the clamor, and the coughs pounding at her till she did not know what part of herself to protect first — her ears, her eyes, or her belly still racked with cramps. And now a new noise: the screech of saws cutting the birch saplings down. It stopped; shedding yellow dust, a saw swung toward the road; there, above hoofbeats, above the rumble of trucks, a woman was crying — something about die Züge, about trains. A horse whinnied. "Soldaten — in Worten — in Taten," snatches of song drifted through the haze; then a loud shout. "Ja!" said the shout. "Die Züge gehen wie immer."

"Did you hear?" fumbling with a rusty hairpin the Mouse gasped. The hairpin slipped from her fingers; gray strands fluttered down her back dotted with burs. A volley of coughs broke out, and a thistle flower floated past, then like a pompon of red silk settled on the bare foot. "The trains are going," the consumptive daughter stammered between her coughs. "Did you hear?"

Tola did not answer. Stumbling on the spilled dirt, she walked on, along the ditch, along the ridge, to and fro, up and down, until her legs were numb. Soon the screeching and coughing merged to one blurred noise. Her cramps too stopped; only her mouth hurt, parched with thirst.

She would drink; let the guard watching the tracks turn away, and she would dash across, and drink her fill. Now — the guard was sliding down the ridge, was running toward the road. In no time he was back. From the cigarette hurriedly stamped out, smoke curled round his boot.

A growl of motorcycles came from the road. It broke off, and all motion was arrested. In the sudden silence Tola could hear how one by one pebbles fell from a shaking spade. A spot of bright red flitted through the grove. "Achtung!" Spades swung, all eyes stared down at the dust. But to Tola it seemed she had always known that just after the spade had shaken and the pebbles fallen, Rost would come, and behind him the SS. Everything was as expected — the yells, the haste with which Rost ran up the mound, even the whip a helmeted SS man swung like a lasso round an O.D. man's neck.

But that Rost would stay on the mound so far away from her she had not expected, nor those stares dogging her steps. No one else dared to move from his place; that was why they stared. In two rows guards lined the ridges. Down below the O.D. men stood like black posts. Tola bent, squeezing between the spades, between barrows and saws, sneaked on till she stood across from the mound.

There the arm with the red band rose; the black posts swayed and "Los!" a raucous chorus started up. "Los! Work faster. Los!"

A spade that spindly arms could barely lift pelted her with earth; she turned away and muddy spittle spattered into her face. She jerked back; just like the O.D. men she planted her legs wide apart, wrenched her mouth open just as they. But no cry came. On the mound next to Rost the Meister stood looking right at her.

Each time her lips parted he seemed to be staring at her face; each time, to escape his eyes, she tried to move on, an O.D. man's fist pushed her back toward that shaking spade, toward these shoulders racked with coughs. Around her the black posts swung, mouths gaped, as though to drink in greedy draughts, and a club thudded on a gaunt back. "Los!" the chorus grew louder, the clubs gleamed reddish in the setting sun. And fear seized her — of the cry stuck like a pit in her throat, and of time moving much too fast.

The sun sank behind the woods. Between the glow of sunset and of flames dusk hung like a bridge between two fires. It deepened; the arched backs merged into a shadowy wave. As the dusk darkened, as color after color went out, only white was left of the fallen birches, of the grove; and up on the mound the disk within the swastika armband glinted like an eye.

"Licht!" Lights flashed; beams tangling to a net closed around the ditch. When the net rose, an arm seemed to be pulled along out of the dark, a shaven head, then another head, no — a stone that a picriniac was hoisting out of the ditch. His muddied hand nudged her. "He's coming," the picriniac whispered, "he's coming. Ask!"

The Meister was coming, was standing right behind her. "It will be tomorrow," he said without being asked. "I'll be back here tonight."

"What did he say, what?" whispers sneaked toward her.

"That he will come back."

"And —"

"Nothing else. Nothing." Nothing, she repeated to herself, nothing — nothing. He was going at last, only this mattered. The tall slouched figure vanished into the dark. "Los!" her screams pierced the sudden hush. "Lo-o-os! Work!" like a hemorrhage it poured out of her, with another "Work!" another "Los!" louder, more piercing yet as darkness fell over the mound, as the white eye began moving away. Rost was leaving, all of them were. "Los" once more; the eye stopped. He had heard her, he was pointing her out to the guards. And the beam caught round her foot was the leash that would drag her to him.

With the clang of metal, light hit the ground. Spades were clanging, spades were falling down, runaway wheelbarrows veered toward her, and from behind the grove no noise came, as though the road had been razed, as though it had never been.

"N-no," a moan broke out, "nn-not trenches, no!" Rifles in hand, guards were bearing down upon the dark welt of the crowd. A voice cried out, an arm pointed to the sky, and a pale shape — a man stripped to his waist — leapt into the ditch, the others right behind, the others following with such haste that the ditch grew full at once. A few figures still rose from the dark; they hit the ground, and now only she was left alone at the edge of the ditch. "Down," a guard shouted. "Down or you'll be shot." Her eyes closed, she fell.

The staccato rattle came from machine guns firing somewhere faraway; the clammy touch was fingers gripping her wrist. She did not want to be touched, she pummeled and struck till they were gone. But the whispers would not be gone. "Look — up there — look," they forced her to open her eyes.

In black streaks earth gushed from the fallen barrows. At the foot of the ridge lay the guards, their rifles aimed at the ditch paved with heads. The heads turned up toward the sky.

Planes were coming — that was all. Louder, closer by, machine guns began to rattle, searchlights tinged orange by the fire shot across the sky, but the planes rose, dove into the clouds, into a bank of smoke, then reappeared, swooping down so low that the darkness shook with the grinding noise.

The whispers were back, saying something about the camp. "What about the camp?" she started.

"They must know we're from the camp, they won't bomb us."

Must they know? she wondered, looking at the ditch. There arms shot up, as though to bring closer the white cloud moving from the planes down into the dark.

"Look . . ." someone stammered. "Pa-ratroopers."

"Trash," said she, "just leaflets, just trash." In the road motorcycles started. Rost was leaving, and the huge SS men.

Someone was clutching at her and would not let go, someone was sniveling about trains and Rost. But past her, easily, like skaters sliding across ice, O.D. man after O.D. man dashed by. A part of her, a part that was truly herself, was running like them, only swifter, with even greater ease; she must catch up with that part, she would, if only those hands would let her go — if only the light would stop blinding her eyes.

"You," the O.D. man flashed his light again, "don't you know what has happened?"

"What happened?"

He answered, and "Oh," she said, "oh," with relief but above all with scorn for him, in such a frenzy just because of orders from Rost. If the ditch was not finished on time ten O.D. men would be shot, Rost had ordered. "This means you too," the O.D. man panted. "You too may be shot."

"Of course," she answered. "Of course I may be shot." Then as he turned to dash off she, seized by a premonition of some gain, grasped his arm. "We'll be shot there at the ridge," she repeated, trying, by mimicking his panting, his twisted mouth, to understand what for her was no more than a refrain running through this night: shot for not finishing the ditch, shot for not falling down, and for something else too, one could get shot — for water, for drinking water behind the tracks.

"Water! Hey, give me some!" she cried, because there behind the uprooted bush someone was drinking, just as Rozalia had before, with the same sucking gulps. The man was only sucking his bruised hand. Even so, the refrain became clear: she would be shot; like a stone that boots trampled she would lie in the dirt, but Rozalia would go on, drinking, eating, stuffing herself, and those others who had gorged while she had starved, they too would go on — the fat Kaelanka and this one and that and that. Scraping off the dirt that made all alike, she picked them out of the dark, and bread instead of earth she stuffed into their mouths, and weighed the flesh on each still-supple arm. Like a nip of fat on broth a vaccination scar shone on the pudgy arm. She reached out to the bush. Sap oozing down her palms, she twisted a branch off, then stole on.

"Work!" The branch struck, the fat squelched like pale sticky mud.

It had happened, she had caught up. First the beam of her flashlight shot forward, then she. "Stop! Stop blinding me!" a cracked voice would whisper; the stick swished, the dust turned sweetish in her mouth. And at once her light sneaked on, from under the barrows, from piles of earth, from the ditch, flushing out those whom she must force back to work. Only when Rozalia darted from some muddy hole Tola stopped, looked at Rozalia's bag with the bread in it, then went on with her hunt.

This was what it was: a hunt, a fair and equal hunt. Even though she was armed with a light and a stick, she was only one. Those who would do her in were many. If she did not mind driving them on — they who had gorged, who had called her "peddler" and "cold fish" — not one of them, none, would mind seeing her shot at the ridge.

Rifles cutting through the dark, and the crumbling earth; cramps wringling her out, and guffaws that went on even as shots rang out — this was the outline of her death. She studied this outline, she learned it by heart. Soon it was no longer needed. The eyes on which earth rained, the mouths choked by earth were drawings which, by switching off the light, she could erase from the blackboard of the dark. What she never erased, what her light brought into full relief, were those backs, those arms that did not move — or that moved, yet not fast enough, that must move faster yet. Now racing with the O.D. men, now swerving to feel their hot breath, she ran where her light led. Her stick struck, she was sated; and already the blow had dropped into the dark, already she was dashing on to the next blow, always like the first because she felt empty as at first.

Someone who had fallen barred her way but she just leapt across him. Something, a reminder of those two who could not possibly be here, loomed out of the dark but vanished behind the ditch, grown wide like a riverbed.

Was the ditch finished, were they going back? No, only a single truck had come, only a few O.D. men had been brought in the truck. They stood in a dark cluster, then trudged on.

And those others, those once agile like skaters, now kept slouching around, then scrambled heavily up the ridge. "Help me," she ordered and they pulled her up, "Move," and they made space for her, but when "Los!" she cried to spur them on, they scowled and turned to look at the road. A child was crying there, a dog barked. Then a loud report. "A blowout," an O.D. man cried. "It's nothing, just a tire," the others echoed, sliding down.

She stayed. Far, far below, the dark mass shook like a machine of many blades; at her feet lank grass hung from lumps of earth, thistles shone a moist purple, and each time a barrow spilled its load, the ridge heaved like the flanks of a huge soft-fleshed beast. Astride this beast she kept the machine in motion. With light slashing across eyes, with shouts, she made the machine move and with earth, lumps of earth hurled so that they spattered against the clotted mass. A fist shook at her; struck by a clod of turf it opened into yellow fingers. And the beams of light that guards flashed at her were fingers, lifting for inspection her arm, her gaping mouth.

"Los!" once more. Here at her side the spades were moving in perfect rhythm, but across the ditch they were slackening, were not moving at all. Arms spread out, she slid down the ridge, through the crowd, down the walls of the ditch, on and on till she fell on something hairy and soft — roots, just a ball of roots. Her flashlight, her stick had slipped from her. She groped around. And just as she found the flashlight, silence fell behind the ditch — not an O.D. man stirred, not a guard. Only from the road came the sound of trudging feet, then a shout, then more hard, even reports. Tires . . . only tires again, she repeated to herself. Work! she tried to cry. Instead she stood still, the stick dangling.

Something had happened to her, something had hit her like a stone. She would not find out what it was, she would hurry on. Yet everything around was holding her back: these faces, the glistening eyes, and the whispers rasping one and the same word, "Selection — a terrible selection."

"Se-se-selection?" she brought out at last. "Who was taken in the selection? Answer me. Who?"

"How can we know? They had barely a moment to speak with the O.D. men."

"Which O.D. men? Who spoke to them?"

"They — the O.D. men brought by the last truck. From the trucks they could only manage a few words with the people from the other camp."

Oh, it was just in some other camp that there had been a selection! It was only people from some other camp who had been marched by on their way to trains. And the shots she had heard had been fired at them too.

Spades gritted. "Trains — for us, too, trains will come," the people whispered. Anyhow, Tola answered silently, I'll probably be killed before you. "Hunchback," she cried, dashing forward, "Hunchback, wait!" The hump, that reminder of those two who could not be here, had vanished somewhere in the dark. And her "Anyhow, I'll be killed" was denied by the ditch, which had grown so wide that it must be finished on time. If the ditch was finished no one would be shot here. This meant something: this meant that there was no need to find out who else might have come with the Hunchback. She ran on. "Work!" she could even shout, then stopped short.

The rifles, the crumbling earth — everything was back with this cry, only instead of the Hunchback those two, who might after all be here, stood at the ridge. Even with the ditch finished something could happen here. Rost could have given an order for shooting: he would, to lull all suspicions, to show that there would be no more selecting in the camp. She must find out who had come with the Hunchback, at once.

"Don't — you're blinding me," the cracked voices cried, but she, to find some distinguishing marks in those faces mud made alike, had to blind them with the flashlight, had to squeeze between the arched backs, between arms scabby with dirt. Again the light flashed, again a cry. And she would no sooner have finished searching a stretch than someone very tall loomed behind her, or someone thin and tiny like a child; and at once, a boulder or a stump picked out to mark how far the search had gone, she would run back to look at a stranger's face, then back to search again, now for the mark that spilled earth had erased. Until a new fear seized her — that she would be looking for them on and on through the night.

This could not go on. She would ask, simply ask for them. But old Meyerova would not tell her a thing, nor Doctorka, nor the Orphan, mumbling as she passed by. The Yekie might answer, the Yekie had spoken to her at times. "Listen," she wiped the grit off her tongue, "have you seen them, the orderlies or the Hunchback?"

"Die Hunchback nicht." The Yekie too wiped her tongue. "But die Orderly ist here, dort neben Stumpf." "Next to the birch stump," the unexpectedly helpful Orphan said. "See, first comes a broken barrow, then a bush, then the stump. There she is, I've just spoken to her."

Tola too must speak to her, "When . . . if . . . if it looks as if something might happen . . ." No, by then it would be too late. "As soon" — that was it: "As soon as the column has formed let me know where you are so that I can speak up for you to the guards."

"Fräulein Anweiserin!" the guards would laugh, "Oh, Fräulein has been treating her own people so well; let her show us now how she treats her friends; show us — bring your friends here to the ridge." The O.D. men would plead for them. No, the O.D. men could do nothing; the O.D. men were no better than herself. Someone else must help her — the Meister. He had promised to come back.

She hid her stick behind the stump, turned back to pick it up again, then walked on. "Work, Orderly!" "Force yourself, Orderly!" came from the dark, until to her, seeing only strangers around, it seemed that everyone knew the one whom she could not recognize anymore.

"Come, I will help you. Push, Orderly, now!" an old man called.

"I cannot. I cannot anymore," a honking moan answered. The girl with the honking voice was still called "Orderly"! "And the other orderlies," Tola called, running to and fro, "are they here?"

"Who can tell in such darkness, such crowds?" And her light flashed again.

The light was a path taking her back to a time long ago. For here they all were: Cantorova, the barracks elder from the Cracow camp, and the mother of Tadzio, who had been left in the ghetto; the old woman and the girl from the bunk below. They all followed her. "Six," they said, "someone must stand six," and the gaunt man in glasses took her flashlight with an approving nod as though she had kept a promise once given to him. He knelt down, from his cupped hands light fell upon the crumpled white scrap.

" 'The victorious armies of the USSR,' " he read; then something about the cruel invader, about partisans and a heroic fight. "And about us? What do they say about us?" Tadzio's mother exclaimed, as though asking "Any regards for me?"

"Why should they worry about us, about you for example? Oh, I know — because you took such good care of Tadzio, of course, that's why," she could say this, she could say anything at all, but what for, when she had said such things before? And an apprehension that in spite of all precautions something had been ill-timed joined the fear of looking for those two on and on throughout the night.

It had grown harder to look by now; with the ditch widening, the ridge had moved so close that the spades kept pushing her into the dirt, the dirt back at the spades, to and fro, like a ball tossed, falling, then tossed again, against a sharp boulder, against someone vaguely familiar, then against a head that looked covered with rust.

A whiny blubber throbbed into her ear. "Work, or I'll do such things to you," a hard voice threatened. It was Rubinfeldova whose voice had grown so hard, it was Seidmanka who blubbered and whined. And farther on the tiny woman in black was being pulled along by her sliding barrow; leaves and moss clung to the bag stuck between Rozalia's legs, and the stone sticking out from the ridge, there it was — the hump.

"Hunchback!" Tola leapt up the ridge. "Why — what are you doing here?"

"Catching," panted the Hunchback, "I'm just catching my breath."

"No, I mean altogether, how did you come here? And they, are they here?"

"Barbara?" loud and clear the Hunchback said. "Barbara and Alinka are with the doctor in the dispensary. I went to pee and got nabbed."

So! It was for the Hunchback they had called when the trucks had come; and the Hunchback had been having fun, oh yes, had been playing hide and seek with her. Now what was it she said, who had got lost?

Doctorka was lost. "We lay together in the ditch," the Hunchback wailed, "we climbed out together, and then, suddenly she was gone. Have you seen her?"

Tola did not answer. She watched how the dark lumps rolled down the hump as though it were crumbling away. Pushing another lump down, her foot edged forward; now with the heel, now with the toe it nudged the crooked shoulder, was about to step on it; then "Go!" she screamed, "get out of my way!" The Hunchback scurried on, while she stood there trying to remember what it was she still had to do.

She remembered. And now she was running, faster and faster, lest what must be still hers be lost. Nothing was lost; there in the bag wedged between Rozalia's legs was her bread.

"Rozalia," softly, very gently she called. "Rozalia, sell me some bread! I'll pay you, I'll pay you well."

The pink rabbit-eyes blinked. "Sell it?" Rozalia crooned. "Sell — and why should I sell it, Intelligenzia? I — I — I'll give it to you, for the asking, gratis! Here, potatoes, almost two pounds, take them, Intelligenzia, they're all yours. Here's cornmeal, just watch, my dear, the side of the bag got a bit ripped. Nu, why are you staring, Intelligenzia? Help yourself, eat — eat in good health. You will have plenty of time to eat in Czestochowa, I'll have no time in Auschwitz."

"Au — Ausch — " The blubbering throbbed nearby. "Not Auschwitz, the guard didn't say we'd go to Auschwitz," Rubinfeldova cried. And "Bread," she was shouting, "Rozalia, give me your bread!"

Rozalia was hiding. Behind the noncomprehending eyes, behind the mouth that quivered, Rozalia was hiding, behind the innocent face that Tola could not, would not ever strike. "Nu," the blackened mouth sneered, and a regret seized her, as though a chance always longed for had been missed. But she recovered this chance, she brandished her stick, till that other, that innocent face, was back. Now the mouth was quivering. Now, with her fist — hard at that mouth! She struck. Phlegm, spittle squirted over her fist, and within her a boil seemed to have burst, something was rising within her, something gargling and thick. She would strike once more and be full, once more so that the squeal would stop, and once more to hear it again, and once more on the eyes, on the mouth, on the eyes — now, once again — for the last time — Her fist slid, her fist found nothing to strike. From below, from the ditch now the squeal came. She must leap down, must strike once more.

The squeal had stopped, the ditch was empty. Round her foot trapped by the bag, arms were crawling toward the small, gnawed-at chunk of bread. "Mine!" Tola clutched the bread. "Mine, mine," she stamped on those arms. They fled; scattering potatoes and meal, the bag fell into the ditch. Her body too was a bag filled — though not quite — with the gargly mush. Cautiously, not to impair this fullness, she hoisted her body up the ridge, stopped, and looked for a place to sit down. Here, on the pile of birches was a good place. First she would stretch her legs, then she would wipe the mud off her hands and her mouth. And then she would eat.

She had eaten, her hand was empty. And down below, barrows rolled toward the meadow beyond the ditch, whistles shrilled down there, O.D. men shouted about trucks — that they would be coming any moment. She would press herself against the wall of the truck, she would press against the bunk, she would walk, would get water to drink. Or better still, she would drink now, from the water behind the tracks.

Somewhere nearby hobnailed boots hammered against the tracks, glass was breaking nearby. But to her only the water was startling — so fresh it felt, so cool in her burning mouth. She sprawled out; knees and elbows dug into the soggy ground, she drank on and on, till the water came up her throat, till she was inflated like a rubber tube. Again the whistles shrilled. She rose and very slowly walked to the meadow beyond the ditch.

The quadrangle bristling with spades — this was the column waiting for the trucks; the red spark — a guard, cigarette in mouth walking toward it. He spoke, the spades swayed; instead of being laid down, they tangled, they clashed, and "No!" a moan broke out of the column, "no! We can't go on."

"We can't," the O.D. men were crying.

"No, I cannot," Tola moaned.

Heads down, guards dashed at the column, with rifles and slashing arms split it in two, flattened the double rows into single lines. "Los!" The spades screeched. "Vierzig!" a guard muttered — if the ditch was not done by the morning, forty would be shot.

"Erschossen — vierzig — " The words merged to a droning buzz. Spades, ditch, barrows, everything was turning with this buzz. She too was turning — she would walk, would hunt, would grow full, then empty, as now, round and round, on and on, till the very end. Somewhere, she knew, there was a way of hastening those turnings, of cramming them all into one scream, one leap. Yet how to do it she did not know; she felt dazed and her eyes hurt.

At least everything was being speeded up. Already the noise of motorcycles was here, already the helmeted SS, and the glare forming a luminous puddle around some figures propped against the slope of the mound. The guards leapt down; in two long shafts the glare went back and forth along each side of the ditch; whenever the shafts rose the black silhouette of an O.D. man was plucked along; they swooped down and the silhouette swung as though pounding something into the ground. Those who could not go on were being pounded: she knew this, but the shouts, the moans, the thuds — all was sucked into the constant, the ever louder buzz. She too was being sucked in, she was a numb speck whirling in the dust. Only her mouth refused to grow numb; self-contained and firm it felt each touch of wind, of leaves and grass.

Bright green leaves shone in the glare; gray strands fluttered; over a wheelbarrow that would not budge backs strained till they seemed to crack. The glare swerved, it hit fingers, dangling like lips torn loose in front of a gaping mouth, then a scrawny neck, then a fist, her own fist, still clutching a stick. She would rest, after the light had plucked her, after it hurled her down at the Mouse, then she would rest.

"Licht, light out." Metal clanged in the dark, spades were falling, were pushing her into those groping arms that clasped her, that held her fast. She tried to break loose, she could not. And all the time while planes ground the dark, she lay pinned between these two bodies, one burning with fever, one like ice, one shaken by coughs, the other by a worn-out, stuttering heart.

"Licht!" Light flashed. Light prized her loose, but now something was happening to her head, it was like an eye that would not close, an eye that had no lid, against it faces pressing, faces with eyes earth made blind, with mouths choked by cough, by dust and mud, and when she ducked, when her arms covered her eyes, the blubbers came, the thuds, and the voices crying "We can't . . . we can't go on." She too could not go on, she would sit somewhere — there by the water behind the tracks.

Guards stood by the water, guards lined the tracks. But there, propped against the mound, the dim figures sat undisturbed and still.

So that she would feel no touch she stiffened, made her skin numb; then she moved through the crowd of diggers, and on into the ditch. Again no touch must be felt. The ridge now, it wasn't too high. What loomed in the narrow passage was just motorcycles; one more step now, one more — and at last the mound.

Three women sat propped against the mound. They shifted slightly, they slid toward her. They might talk, those women, they might want something of her; if they talked she would not answer, she would not even move, no matter what happened she would not move. And now at last she could rest.

The three women glided down yet did not speak, guards passed by yet did not draw near; only a distant cry still hurt her, piercing like a needle through her head. But soon from the ground a chill rose, it thickened, it closed around her like glass. At times steps came from behind the glass: "Four," someone was counting, "three before, now four." Then from above, from under boots, pebbles rolled down upon gleaming spots, upon eyeglasses crumbling with a fine tinkling sound. And the woman pelted with pebbles just lay there, the smithereens falling into her fixed white eyes.

The woman was dead; all of them were. The bespectacled one reminded her of Kohn, the others with their sharp noses of the Rebbetzyn who used to light candles on the Sabbath. Kohn was dead, Rebbetzyn was dead. Beyond the glass a dark crowd stirred, it grew, it drew closer. But she held them at bay; she, to even all accounts, was collecting everything to pay her debts: the hunger, the earth in her mouth, and above all what once had given those coming such power over her — that last scene, that last dread, which, she had learned, was no more than a moment, no more than a falling to the ground.

Now she and they were even, now they were coming, all together, the dead of the war and those of long before — Grandmother, and Grandfather who had died young without any war, her mother with Aurelia Katz, her father stripped naked and alone, Goldberg, the Chinaman and Richard Katz. It was a reunion, a roll call of the dead. To each name, "Dead," a voice answered; "Dead," said the nameless faces, "Dead," the voices that had no face; and more were coming, were winding around her — she was the spool, they the thread; she the pit, they the enormous fruit.

Even between her and those two in white accounts had been settled. Were they to call for her, as they had yesterday at the gate, were they to lift her up, she who could no longer move would have dragged them down. Free from such burden, they moved into the glowing night, slowly at first, then faster as though taking flight.

Leaves, sticks, everything was fleeing out of the wheels' way. The dead women too were in the way, the dead women twitched and lay still. She, like them, would lie still; she would just close her eyes.

Light tore her eyes open, light shattered the wall of glass. "Move, do something, move!" someone seemed to be calling — it was she herself, she still refusing to die, still waiting, still thirsting for what was to come. It was too late. They would shoot her if she moved, they were coming. Helmets shone, wheels gritted against the ground, hit a stone, screeched, swerved aside. And the black lines — those were whips, checking who was dead and who would still cry out.

She like the dead must make no cry; no cry — as the whips hissed, no cry — as they singed her mouth, her lids, her eyes; no cry — not yet, they might still hear her — not yet — Now silence fell. Now — and now she was crying, with terror, with pain, and with thirst for this cry, for this proof that it had not happened, that she was still there, still holding on to a stone and a jagged branch.

It had not happened — like a message she had left for herself, the thought awaited her when she came to. Why it had almost happened, why such blindness, such pain, she did not know, nor why her head had grown so huge that it weighed her down, that it would not move. Her hands could still move. Slowly, with effort, they groped on, touched something damp, something crumbly and cold. And whatever the hands touched were syllables which she made out and put together into words: grass was her first word, then earth, then stone; and what felt like a damp stone, what her fingers refused to touch, was an arm.

Whose arm she would find out later, now something else must be found — a sound, a sign she had not been left alone. This was not the sign, this was just gravel falling, just trees rustling, just the wind . . . Now she was hearing something — a shout blurred by the wind: "Los," it said, and her hands ran to her face. They faltered and shrank away but she drove them on, to the swollen mouth, across the crust of blood on to the welts that were her eyes. Teeth clenched, she was forcing those welts open; they were opening, only by the pain did she know it, because the darkness would not lift.

She must wait, she must lie still and wait. Gradually the darkness faded, a shape drew near, then another, and yet another. And to her it was as though someone had come, someone cautious and mild was feeding her the world again — a tree, a torn root, and a star, the David star upon the crumpled white band. The whiteness spread; mist came, wound around her like a cooling bandage. Only what trickled down her hand felt warm.

For her face was too numb to feel those tears she was crying, for what had been done to her and for what she had done to those two with whom she would soon be together. Someday she might speak to them, might try to explain; "I'm coming with you," was all she would say now, and they would wash the blood off her face, if there still was time.

Now time was running short; whistles blew, feet padded in the rising mist. She must get up, it did not matter that she had fallen, she must try again and again. And at last she was rising; like an acrobat lifting a heavy weight, she was hoisting the burden of her head; she reeled and stood still.

The ditch was done. Where once had been a meadow, ramparts of clay earth shone in the rising sun. Far away a pile of spades caught the light, and behind her, in the grove, the people were crouching in long silent rows. They started as she staggered by, they cried out, loudest the Hunchback running toward her. "It's nothing," she tried to say, and only a stutter came from her bruised lips.

But she must speak to him, to the Meister. Head turned away, arms paddling to ward off those reaching out to him, he was rushing up and down the grove. An O.D. man stopped him, and pointed to the mound. She had been shot, he must have said, because the Meister flinched.

"Herr — Herr Meister," she called him with lips that would not meet. "Herr Meister," the Hunchback helped her. And at last he heard them, he was coming slower and slower with each step, until he stopped, flinched, then drew closer again. "Hide," he spoke up at last. "They may do something to you at the selection, hide!"

"Se — se — lection?"

"Picrine will be taken, and the old. The others go to Leipzig — " Seeing a guard come near, he broke off, then in a rapid whisper said something about time, about counting and time. They wouldn't be counted at the selection, he had meant, there would not be time for it. He was gone. In his place a young picriniac stood, she remembered him from the shell-loading.

"Hide," leaning upon the hump, she stammered. "Hide," the Hunchback cried. The boy was her example of those who must be warned; whenever she came upon one young like him she stopped. "Hide!" she said. "Hide!" the Hunchback echoed, and they moved on.

From a low stump one who did not match this example got up. He did not speak, he just stared with eyes like yellowed leaves, and at once others old like him rose one by one, as if to line up for this chance, as for a ration of soup or bread. She had nothing to give them. She must keep this chance for the young, for the handful that could hide without being found. Using the hump as her crutch, she hurried on, past the young who could not be warned because of those others still watching her, past the old Meyerova, and the tiny woman in black, and on to the edge of the grove, where trees hid her from those still watching.

"Hide!" her fingers bent to keep count of those warned. "Hide!" to the young yellowed with picrine. "Hide!" to the old whom she could not bear to leave unwarned: to Rubinfeldova, to Ziegelman, to the Mouse. "Hide!" the Hunchback cried at Doctorka, who kept staring at a crushed twig.

"They'll take you," the Hunchback pleaded, "you look terrible, they will." The spinsterly lips tightened; Doctorka shrugged, when of themselves her eyes turned to the earth crumbling down into the ditch. She winced. Then like one defeated, one put to shame, she drew her shaggy head between her shoulders, so that she looked misshapen like the Hunchback, who was pointing at the trucks coming up the road.

The trucks must turn around before going back. To be first in the camp they must be last on the trucks. At the last truck an O.D. man was shouting something, that it was no longer quiet in the camp, he was shouting, that the huge SS men had come.

"And . . . in the dispensary?" the Hunchback whispered.

An SS man had gone to the dispensary. The SS man had demanded that everyone still listed as sick last week should be reported at once.

"No!" the Hunchback cried. Tola stood still. She was watching to see that they who must be the first back would be the last on the truck.

Why the doctor had been ordered away, why he, helmeted and huge, was ranting so, Barbara could not understand; she just kept looking at Alinka, at her face that had gone all white. When "Nix verstehen" the girl had said, "Nix!" Barbara cried; when the girl was silent, so was she. Later, after they had been brought back to the sick barracks, she began to understand; from Alinka first, from her stare, fixed as though it were forbidden to look at bunks, at faces, on the pipe of the stove; then from him too, from his hands in the dark shiny gloves. Those hands rose, they came toward her face, but did not strike; they stopped, the fingers outstretched, all but one.

Nine fingers he was holding up. "Neun," an old guard said as he came in. It was nine women he wanted — nine of her women, of the sick who were left in here.

"Nix," said Alinka.

"Nix," said she.

In bluish wisps ashes drifted from the pipe. "Alle," he in the helmet said, and when his arm swayed, as though to sweep the barracks clean, she understood: "Alle" meant that if he didn't get the nine he would take them all.

It was still in the barracks, so still that the rustle of straw seemed loud, as though something was being crushed. A hand was rustling the straw, a denouncer's hand. It rose, pointed to the bunk above; the guard approached, and it was gone.

Boots stepped onto the splintery edge, arms reached into the bunk, and pulled and tugged, as though to drag down a large unwieldy thing. And it was not a woman they pulled down, not the one whom only yesterday Barbara had combed, had taught how to walk, but a thing, a heap of rags shedding dust and spittle and straw, shaking as fists, as boots hit out, and when that heap fell to the floor, from under a tucked-up skirt a brown strip of paper unrolled — the bandage with which she had dressed the bedsore the night before.

"Don't you dare move!" she cried to Alinka, "nix," and she pushed the helmeted one aside. "Nix," and she ran to the woman, she lifted her up, and smoothed out the coat.

"Alle," the guard said. Somewhere straw rustled again. Barbara looked at the denouncer, then very slowly walked to the bunk she was pointing at.

Who was cowering on this bunk she must not know, she must not recognize the face. But whatever she looked at was a face: the feet dug into straw, the neck, in which breath was stuck, and the hands, clutching at the posts, all were like faces fear had struck. She touched those hands, she stood still when fingers clasped her wrists. Only when they groped for the bag with spoon and comb and the unfinished beet did she shrink away. But at once she drew closer and closer still, until everything — the huge SS man, the rifles, the rumble of a truck outside — was gone, until only this woman was left whom she must help to get down.

A withered cheek pressed against her cheek, arms clung to her neck, and even when she had put her down the woman still clung on, holding to the skirts of her coat. All of them, those who kept staring into her face, and those who turned away, those who whispered and those who were mute, all clung to her till she could barely turn to look at Alinka. Alinka never looked back at her. Alinka was staring at the SS man, at his still upraised hand.

Sabots slipping off trembling feet, fingers reaching for a piece of bread — one more bunk, one more, until the nine women stood around her. There across the barracks the gloved hand was still uplifted — one finger up. "Not ten, neun, nur neun!" Alinka was crying. The old guard spoke up, and the women clung harder as he in the helmet came near.

Barbara would not let him have them yet . . . she would bring them to the door, to the truck. She would lift them into the truck, they must not be thrown into a heap like those already inside, like the hospital sick.

This time, when lifting them she kept her eyes closed, tight and tighter still, but her hands were like eyes, her hands knew by heart each one they were touching, each feature, each face. Linen, she was touching now, smooth linen, and curly hair. She turned; with balled fists, with her whole body she thrust Alinka away. "No," she was crying, "no!" and hardly knew it when she herself was pulled by gloved hands back and up onto the truck.

The truck moved, the truck was not moving fast enough. There right behind it the little white figure was running, breaking away from the doctor's, from an O.D. man's arms, was coming, was coming closer. Barbara grabbed whatever she could, a bag, a can, a chunk of bread, and hurled them at Alinka's head — missed and missed again. "Hold her," she cried, "somebody hold her."

"Anweiserin," someone was shouting. It was Tola, Tola was coming, Tola was holding Alinka. "Hold her, do you hear me? Hold — " on and on until the camp gate slammed, until the two clasped figures vanished in the sun.

She shuddered, she drew back; and already from the sudden dusk, groping figures moved toward her, more and more till her arms were full, till her hands could no longer reach her enormous, her still disbelieving eyes.

Epilogue

Epilogue

THE FLAME FLICKERED. The old man put a match to the wick of the oil lamp, but just as the flame flared he blew it out, replaced the glass, and walked slowly to the window. Outside, asters matted by September rain caught the last light; a patch of fresh straw shone in the lichen-covered thatch. Over the low whitewashed room dusk was spreading swiftly; the outlines of scant furnishing were blurring, the gleam of crockery faded, only a white envelope glimmered on the table, and behind the door opening into the next room the icon lamp cast a circle of ruby-red light. There was a thud and a thin cry.

"Marta!" the old man shouted, "Marta, keep her quiet, can't you!" Skirts swished, a woman's voice cooed and sang till the cry grew softer, till it changed to laughter.

"'Keep her quiet'!" the old woman grumbled, coming in. "Can't the child make so much as a peep? Should she go dumb to please you, should she? Oh—" She noticed the envelope. "Oh, I see. Who is it from?"

"Haven't read it."

The old woman said nothing. From the niche in the whitewashed stove she took a newspaper sheet, and cleaned the glass of the lamp. Again the flame flickered. "When people write," she began, turning the flame up, "it is not to have their letters left lying around. To have them read, that's why they write."

"Is that so?" He gave his long mustache a tug. "Is that really so? Now let me tell you; I did not ask them to keep writing to me. That first letter from London, that was fine with me, and that other from Miss Alinka, fine too, very fine. But all the rest, from the doctor and the doctor woman, from—" He broke off, and watched his wife cut the envelope open. "Here," she put the letter on the table, and he, without another word, began to read.

By now he knew those letters by heart, even their shape — a few lines at the beginning, a single line at the end, and between them two columns, one short and one long, which made him think of a cripple's uneven legs. Stuff and nonsense, apologies which he did not want, explanations which he did not need, stood in those first lines: that the undersigned had got his address while visiting Miss Alinka in a convalescent home near Leipzig; that according to Miss Alinka he had a contact, a man regularly traveling between Poland and Germany; and since the mail between Germany and Poland had not been fully re-established yet, the undersigned, after many apologies, took the liberty of asking him to forward the enclosed lists of the survivors and the dead to the Jewish committee in Cracow so that relatives — if any were left — could be informed; then in case such relatives were found, to forward their addresses to the undersigned who, having once more apologized and thanked, remained most respectfully his.

And he did what was wanted of him; he copied those lists name by name. He did it and hated everyone and everything: the one who had given him this task, his scratchy pen, his own old shaky hand, and those whose names he was writing, each of them; those from the short list for returning, for being here, those from the long for remaining just names to him — alien always, vaguely unpleasant Jewish names, a litany of Rosenbaums, of Grünbergs and Kohns that went on and on, until she who would never return, she who was no more, was sucked in by them — until, to protect her, "She!" he used to say of her, just "She!" in a hard wrathful voice; but soon he said nothing, soon she became for him just a flashing eye, a smile, and the pain that shot through him, choked his breath, then slowly died away.

This letter — Malvina Rubinfeld was the undersigned — was just like all the others; among the names in the longer list some like Ohrenstein and Seidman were already familiar. Only at the end, where not just one but a few lines stood, a word that did not seem to fit caught his eye.

Adjusting his spectacles, he raised the letter to the light, when from below a child's hand reached for the lamp. "No! for God's sake!" He clutched the child. "Don't you ever touch it! and you," he turned upon his wife, "you know how to coo and trill, it's tsatsa-

tsa and tralalal from morning till night. But 'Watch her, woman!'
I say, and you don't listen. She might have been burned alive . . .
she . . ."

"God forbid." The old woman took the child from him. "Hush,
Antoni. God forbid," she murmured while he bent over the letter.

He finished it, and put it on the table.

"So what did it say?" the old woman asked. And he who once
had dreaded her voice, her eyes hanging hopefully on his lips, now
shrank from the way she asked this question — calmly, as though
saying "What did they say in the paper today?"

"Just the usual thing, and then about the oats."

"About what?"

"Oats, how she died, because of oats."

The old woman started. "Oats?" she whispered. "No. I don't
understand. The letters from London and from Miss Alinka . . .
said . . ."

"Fool. I was talking about that other one, about that Miss Ohrenstein."

"Oh! but why oats? Miss Alinka wrote that it was because of food
that — then almost at the end of the war — after they had dragged
them out of the camp she tried to get some food — "

"Sure it was food, sure. When people march for weeks with
nothing to eat but nettles, then even oats are food. But otherwise it
was just like Miss Alinka wrote. They were starving; that other
one, that Miss Ohrenstein, could barely drag herself, so the girl
dashed into a field to get her some oats," he read a phrase from the
letter. "A guard pulled his gun, that Miss Ohrenstein saw it, ran
forward, to warn the girl, I figure, to drag her back, and she got
hit."

"I see," rocking the child the old woman said. "I — and where
are you off to?" she asked seeing him take a coat off the peg.

"I want to get some air."

"Now? Soon it'll be dark. It's not safe to walk about in the dark."

"I want to get some air," he repeated, slamming the door.

Like yellow beads, lights of oil lamps and of tallow candles were
strung through the dark. Somewhere a crane screeched. "Let His
name be praised," a woman's voice greeted him from the warmth of a
cow barn.

"For ever and ever amen," he answered, then hastily, so as not to be stopped again, he walked through the village and on to the road over which poplars were shedding their last crinkled leaves.

Where the road bent, there he sat down. Across from him dried-out cornstalks rustled harshly like tinsel. Farther away beyond a flat pasture, a chimney, all that was left of a ruined farmhouse, loomed black against the windswept clouds.

The clouds parted. Through a crevice a shaft of light fell upon the still-green earth. And for an instant they all, they who were just names — like the girl killed for a handful of oats — and she who was his sorrow, his pain, rose before him like foals let out upon the green of the early spring and already hidden by the swiftly falling dark.

Slowly the light faded. From a leafless tree a bird swooped down, picked a wisp of straw, then vanished somewhere beyond the ruined house. The old man got up and, holding his collar up against the wind, began walking home.

Afterword

I

Recommending a novel about the Holocaust to a general public is a risky business. There are people who won't read books about concentration camps, and there are people who seek out books about concentration camps, as if it were a choice of mysteries over science fiction. This makes a kind of sense for that body of nonserious Holocaust literature which at one end of the spectrum is sentimental and at the other end pornographic, that is, books that are meant to induce an enjoyment of victimization. But if the Holocaust was a significant event of our century and not a gruesome fluke, then thoughtful books about it are not a literary subgenre, not a kind of historical Gothic.

For a long time after the war a discussion of the camps in any but the most general terms was virtually taboo. It was considered bad taste in America to approach this subject with some patience and in detail and with that differentiation that evokes empathy rather than condescension or revulsion. In recent years we have had the opposite phenomenon: an intense and widespread preoccupation with the Holocaust and perhaps merely the flip side of the earlier attitude. It is a little worrisome to observe the popularization and even commercialization of past mass murder. Moreover, I suspect that even now there is a lingering tendency to drop a curtain, a metaphoric barbed-wire curtain, between ourselves and the memory of the Nazi crimes. Whatever is on the other side of that barbed wire of the mind appears to us as undifferentiated horror, starvation, torture, and we see the prisoners of the camps as either martyred saints or snarling animals whom the instinct of self-preservation had driven below the threshold of humanity.

Ilona Karmel's book is the best antidote against such simplification, but by the same token the complex of prejudices and preconceptions I have mentioned may have prevented *An Estate of Memory* from gaining the readership it deserves. Even more than her first novel *Stephania*, *An Estate of Memory* was received not only favorably but enthusiastically when it was first published by Houghton Mifflin in 1969. Yet it has fallen into semioblivion and is now unknown to the general reading public, though a group of *cognoscenti* has continued to treasure it as one of the few great realistic novels about the Nazi camps. Sidra Ezrahi, in an authoritative study of Holocaust literature, considers it to be one of the most "convincing realistic interpretation[s] . . . of the possibilities of life under the Swastika."[1]

Karmel's first novel, *Stephania*, published in 1953 and written under the guidance of Archibald MacLeish while Karmel was a student at Radcliffe, deals with another type of enforced community, a group of women patients in a Swedish hospital for the handicapped. It can be seen as a prelude to the second and more important work. In both books the author explores basic deprivations and their psychological and moral consequences. Putting it this way will perhaps allow us to see that the uniqueness of a Holocaust setting does not exclude a potential for themes to which the reader can relate without a special stance of pity or piety. *An Estate of Memory* stands in the tradition of the great modern prison books that, to my mind, begins with Fyodor Dostoevsky's *The House of the Dead* and includes Aleksandr Solzhenitsyn's *One Day in the Life of Ivan Denisovich* and Jacobo Timerman's *Prisoner Without a Name, Cell Without a Number*. Like them, Karmel's novel draws us into the daily rounds of work and the details of eating and sleeping and enduring physical stress under conditions that are unnatural for human beings. But she has not written a documentary novel, even though the documentary value of her book is considerable. Good prison books are always about freedom, which they define by its absence. Karmel's characters survive (as long as they do survive) by holding themselves suspended between past and future, memory and hope.

Her protagonists are people who cling to relationships that stand out more sharply in a life where selfishness would seem to be identical with self-preservation. A basic assumption of *An Estate of Memory*, however, is that human beings live by bonding and not in isolation. While Karmel does describe hardship and terror with uncompromising severity, the book is largely about friendship, about women bonding. The word "together" dominates from the beginning. Almost every prisoner is part of a team, sometimes of relatives, sometimes of friends. Lest this be thought to be an exercise in wishful thinking, a careful reading of memoirs from the camps and ghettoes will bear witness to the prevalence of such bonds. To name two of the best-known ones, there is the father/son relationship in Elie Wiesel's *Night* and the friendship between Primo Levi and Alberto in Levi's *If This Is a Man* (or *Survival in Auschwitz*). These relationships are not only altruistic, although they are of course related to a person's moral self-definition. They arise, first of all, out of the psychological need not to be alone and the willingness to make great physical sacrifices for the sake of warding off isolation. In simpler terms, this book raises the question how and why we love. It is a question that can be tested better at the limits of endurance than in typical situations. German has the useful term *Grenzsituation*, which is often translated as "life under extreme conditions," but means literally "a border or fringe situation." For our time the Holocaust is perhaps the most recognizable *Grenzsituation*.

The kinds of concerns I have suggested require a dual perspective. They require both empathy and judgment for the prisoners must be our sisters, yet we must not forget that we are free. This is obvious enough when the book asks us to recreate the prisoners' ways of coping and at the same time remain objective observers. Food, for example, is so graphically presented that we have a clear perception of the unhygienic and unhealthy slop that the prisoners are fed; but even more insistently Karmel describes what chronic hunger is like and the greed with which the women crave the stuff that revolts us in the description. Similarly, while they are largely unaware of their gradual physical deterioration, the women once in a while catch a glimpse of themselves in a surface that serves as a mirror or they see themselves through the eyes of others. They are alternately intimates and strangers to the reader, depending on whether our point of view is theirs or that of an outsider. We "normalize" their experience as they do, only to be brought up short by a sudden distancing device.

But there are more complicated situations, calling for closer attention, that aim at the same effect. *An Estate of Memory* is not an easy book to read. For not only does it take place within a foreign, a borderline, territory where we have to orient ourselves as we go along, but as a psychological novel it asks us to follow shifts of perception and misperception in circumstances we ourselves have not fully grasped. A careless reader is likely to lose her place in the story as well as in the characters' thought processes. For example, there is a scene that describes a *Strafappell,* a punitive roll call, where the prisoners have to endure several hours of standing, kneeling, and exposure to cold. The point of view is that of Barbara, a woman who does not understand German. At first Barbara does not know what is happening, and throughout the *Appell* she remains unaware why the group is being punished. Out of her ignorance she assumes that she herself may be the cause of this misery, and consequently she is terrified. The reader shares her confusion and becomes involved in her fear of the unknown, which culminates in a kind of self-recognition about the limitations of courage. At the same time the spectacle of the abuse of prisoners unfolds. The interrelatedness of these two levels, the facts and their partially incorrect perception, makes for an extraordinarily dense and complex texture. It is somewhat like the filtering of a battle through an inexperienced mind in Stephen Crane's *The Red Badge of Courage,* another book about a *Grenzsituation* told in psychological terms. But in Karmel's book we are exposed to an overwhelming assault on the ego, without the sheltering framework of a war whose rationale and outcome we know and presumably approve.

II

The book focuses on Jewish women who were forced laborers in Poland during the war years. Male prisoners live in the same camps but are only tangentially connected with the four main characters. Two of these four, Barbara and Tola, are our guides and have "transparent minds," to use Dorrit Cohn's phrase. Barbara Grünbaum at first denies her Jewishness and lives as a Pole under an assumed non-Jewish name, but cannot bear the dissimulation and separation from her people and joins them. The theme of individual Jews who voluntarily take on themselves the fate of the rest of Jewry is common in Holocaust literature. It illuminates the problem of individual morality in a world that malfunctions morally, or, put differently, of saving one's soul while in hell. The outstanding example is Ernie Levy in André Schwarz-Bart's *The Last of the Just.* Ernie finds that he has descended to the level of an animal, that he almost literally leads a dog's life, as he wanders as a vagrant across the French countryside, concealing his Jewishness. He returns to the condemned, and as one of the Just Men of legend he boards the train to Auschwitz. His last act is to comfort the children who are about to be murdered. Ernie is cast as a saint who overcomes temptation. Schwarz-Bart writes within the implied framework of a theodicy and tries to place the Holocaust within Jewish history.

Karmel's book is secular: it does not raise religious questions. Yet her Barbara, who is obsessed by the idea of sacrifice, can be mistaken for a saint. Barbara sees herself as an infinitely giving, generous person, but like the others she finds her limitations in the camp. More than once she chooses to live and work under harder conditions than she has to, yet her altruism is subject to analysis as well as admiration, and it often fails. Her author is tougher than she is and has sketched her as merely a romantic, though with saintly impulses. There is a sentimental strain in her, and she has a dream life that is partly inspired by the cheap romances she used to read. During a delousing session Barbara is revolted by the proximity and stench of bodies and instinctively rejects the communality she has sought. Nor can she ultimately sustain her friendship with Tola, and toward the end, as a hospital orderly, she beats her patients in the interest of a dubious principle of order and cleanliness. She has become oppressive and harsh.

Her counterpart and friend is Tola Ohrenstein, who begins and ends a loner. Tola is the last survivor of a large, wealthy, and respected family who were killed before the book opens. As fearless as any of the women and often as generous, she is hard and unflinchingly rational from the start. Tola's forte is jokes rather than dreams. Through her we are first made to confront the tension between self-preservation and altruism that pervades the book. When the other inmates assert that no one has the right to try to escape from the camp, since an escape may bring punishment on those who are left behind, Tola is convinced that, on the contrary, anyone who has an opportunity to save his or her life ought to do so. During a selection she hides under a mattress, while the other women expect her to share the danger. Once she tries to flee and pass for an Aryan, thus moving in the opposite direction from Barbara, who has successfully passed as an Aryan and returned to the Jews. Tola's analytical, uncompromising view of the camps drives her into further and further isolation. At first she is "standing six," that is, standing guard for the others against the authorities, but toward the end she has become an *Anweiserin*, an overseer who drives the others to work. In this position, the moral equivalent of hiding under a mattress, she separates herself from her community, abandons her friends, and is finally left alone, which is what part of her has wanted all along. But to be left alone in this case requires collaborating with the Germans.

The other two main characters are Alinka, an apparently hard-boiled and often hostile adolescent, who accidentally survived a mass execution and is deeply attached to Aurelia Katz, a woman who crawled out of the mass grave together with her. Aurelia is pregnant and thus provides the novel with its central episode, the commitment of the other three to see her through childbirth and to smuggle the newborn out of the camp. Although this episode is the story about a successful and altruistic cooperation, it is shot through with tensions, disappointments, human failure, and the deterioration of a friendship. Karmel is at pains to show that heroic efforts cannot be sustained and that they may even be destructive of other relationships. The baby is saved but the war is not over, and the four women still have to continue their struggle for survival and are more and more worn out by their efforts. When Aurelia dies of disease, Barbara and Tola become estranged. In the end Barbara dies with her patients and Tola while protecting the fifteen-year-old Alinka. Thus both Barbara's romantic self-image and Tola's bleak rationality are ultimately justified and redeemed, but only after they are put to some tests that they fail.

An Estate of Memory is a book that describes life among women who can expect nothing from men. It locates the central experience of a forced society in a clandestine birth in which four women participate in varying degrees, and it places the human dilemma of identity and a shared existence in a female context. The commitments and daily decisions of these women are not of the melodramatic kind that Styron imposes on his Sophie, when a Nazi officer forces her to choose between her two children. Rather, with Karmel, decisions are integrated into the "normal" routine of camp life, involving such questions as whether to hide during a selection, to share or not to share extra food. The most dramatic decisions concern the concealment of the pregnancy and birth. Another glance at *Sophie's Choice* may prove revealing. Styron's heroine lives in the shadow of several men. Her prewar and her postwar life are defined by what men do for her and what they demand of her (for example, various forms of subservience and betrayal). Her relation to her children, important as it is to the story, is not explored. Styron uses it merely to serve his plot and to make a rather abstract point about dilemmas. After she has lost her daughter, Sophie's failure to save her son in Auschwitz appears as a failure to deal with the camp commandant. Male/female relationships dominate to an implausible extent. Karmel, on the other hand, uses motherhood to tell of women whose common cause is to protect a nascent life and whose community of purpose is quite impenetrable by men. Where men enter into their plans, they are peripheral. The women pay them, persuade them, use them in whatever way will work, but they shape their own goals and define their own responsibilities. In a broad and nonpolemical sense, this is a profoundly feminist book.

The peripheral male characters are often more helpless than the women, and when they do have a measure of power, like the Jewish police, the O.D. men, they exhibit a mediocrity of character, a kind of uncomplicated heartlessness that is much rarer in Karmel's female characters. Even the men in the flashbacks who had power in a patriarchal world fall short of their women. Tola's father, the wealthy Mr. Ohrenstein, appears in a scene where Nazis humiliate him. Aurelia's husband, knowing that he must die the next day, asks her helplessly and incongruously whether he should shave in the morning. In answer and out of pity she makes love to him for the last time and conceives the child she will deliver in the camp. This child, referred to as "he" throughout the pregnancy, not coincidentally turns out to be a girl. Barbara, who is a big, motherly woman and longed for children, was married to a much loved husband who flunked his academic courses and later turned out to be sterile, thus a failure in two ways. The German soldier who helps save the child is a bumbling creature who clings to his Nazi beliefs in the face of atrocity and can be manipulated by the women who are his superiors in intelligence. In one of her compensatory dreams about the postwar world, Barbara imagines Alinka's wedding. All the details are there, only the bridegroom is without substance: "he seemed unreliable . . . subdued, he lacked élan, he seemed mousy, until modified to a neutral shadow, he was the first to absent himself." Even in their dreams, the women in these pages cannot reestablish a patriarchy gone haywire that has betrayed and abandoned them.

III

Ilona Karmel was born in Cracow in 1925 and came to the United States in 1948. She is a senior lecturer at the Massachusetts Institute of

Technology, where she has been teaching creative writing for the past eight years. She is married to an applied physicist. She has written both her novels in English. Foreign-born writers, even when they have Joseph Conrad's stature, are often and easily accused of making mistakes in their adopted language. But to hunt for foreignisms may be less productive than to ask what they convey, for good writers often build them into their prose for a purpose. The background of this book is obviously not "Anglo," and the English language may be none the worse for lacking an indigenous vocabulary that does justice to life in concentration camps. An unidiomatic phrase will often give us a better sense of what is meant than "pure" English. In connection with human rights violations in Latin America, we have learned to use the word "to disappear" transitively and to make a noun of "disappeared," borrowing from Spanish a terminology that is more effective than ours. Some deliberately un-English phrases increase in significance in the course of Karmel's story. She uses a phrase like "in the freedom" to assign a spatial dimension to what is otherwise an abstraction, a concept. The prisoners who think back remember freedom as a place, even as memory is an estate.

Like all human attributes, language has its limitations in the camp. The events surpass the ability of the victims to narrate them. Aurelia tries to give an account of the mass execution that she and Alinka survived. But Aurelia has no literary talent. She has irritating mannerisms, and her telling of this tale is also irritating. She uses clichés and journalistic phrases. Her style and vocabulary are no match for what she has lived through. She speaks of "the atrocities," "the bestial Nazis," "the helpless victims," and her voice is a "mechanical drone." Hers is an extreme case of the problem of Holocaust literature, the matching of words to a reality for which the words are too common. The *Grenzsituation* of this average woman as witness to mass murder and her subsequent inarticulateness bear on the more general question of the relationship of life and language.

So does a revealing conversation between Alinka and a young Nazi soldier. The soldier is new and he is appalled at what he sees in the camp. He asks Alinka where her parents are. Now Alinka's parents happen not to be victims of the Holocaust, for her mother died before the war and her father is in Russia. But since this is her opportunity to tell the soldier about the fate of the Jews, she "lies" by informing him that her parents were shot. It is a detail that forces us to think about the nature of truth and fiction, for Alinka is telling a fiction and not a lie. The real story of her parents is uninteresting within the context in which she and the soldier meet, whereas what she tells him is meaningful and eminently "true."

An Estate of Memory lives out of such paradoxes and ironies. Generosity and meanness of spirit are inseparable; infernal experiences evoke a banal vocabulary; but just as we dismiss Aurelia as a woman without a soul and no expressiveness, we learn that she has a good singing voice and that her child was conceived as a couple's way of sharing the last hours of life. At the same time Aurelia "peddles" her story, that is, she uses it to her advantage. To the others she seems at first affected and phony, and her horrendous brush with death does not make her more lovable. Nor does it make her larger than life. The women in the camp instinctively react defensively, with a sense of "We all have suffered" and are alternately drawn to her and repelled by her. She brings on herself a complexity of reactions that is not unrelated to the reader's own tendency to reject the suffering of others when we cannot help it or sublimate it, reactions that are related to the mixed feelings that the postwar public has had toward the Holocaust.

Aurelia's pregnancy is shown to us in mercilessly repellent physical terms. Aurelia spending her nights on the latrine eating soup, Aurelia wishing for the death of the fetus, Aurelia bandaging her body to hide the pregnancy—none of these scenes is designed to evoke spontaneous sympathy. Tola unfairly and incorrectly assumes that Aurelia got pregnant by being too lethargic to reject the advances of a stranger, and we, as readers, find Tola's hypothesis plausible. Yet these women help her in spite of her uninspiring character traits, stake their faith in the future on her child, and choose to give meaning to their own wretched lives by making its safe birth and survival a joint project.

Alinka's German soldier, who ultimately helps in saving the baby, is a fat convinced Nazi who tries to reconcile his ideology and instinctive humanity by persuading himself that the Führer did not mean to hurt Jewish children but only Jewish capitalists. In his helplessness and anxiety the soldier gives the starved girl the preposterous present of a bagful of peppermints. The reader who may think that the gift is useless is brought up short when Alinka exchanges it for good bread. Similarly, the women manage to incorporate the young man's concern with children into their plans when they persuade him to take the baby to a safe destination. But we also see this soldier in a state of frustration beating the prisoners. He is a Nazi who in every phase upsets our expectations and who is yet wholly plausible. At no point does Karmel indulge our desire to despise or to admire him. From start to finish he is unprepossessing, he does not redeem our faith in the goodness of man, yet he is probably a better than average human being, and his action would seem heroic if only he had the character of a hero.

IV

Ilona came from Boston to visit me one afternoon last spring. She filled my house with flowers, suggested a walk, and refused to be interviewed. Forget her life, she said, she had written a book, wasn't that enough? It was neither a feminist nor a Holocaust novel, I was wrong on both counts, it was simply the best she could do, given her understanding of the world. She had used her experience, which happened to be with women and of a certain kind. She resists classification and hopes that her novel does, too.

But she knew that I would only partially agree. I had first met her some years earlier, after asking a common friend to introduce us. Like her, I am a survivor of the camps and I had wanted to meet her because of what she had written about our common past, about my childhood. Having taught Holocaust literature for several years, I am sure that women have a somewhat different knowledge of those years than men and that Ilona's book is a storehouse of such knowledge. I also know that Holocaust literature at its best is not self-enclosed but opens in all directions where the hard questions wait.

But I understand her reluctance to speak of her background. As a Jew in Nazi-occupied Poland, she must have experienced hairbreadth's escapes like all survivors, and these make for bad fiction. People ask, "How did you escape?" and in response one either tells pathetic-sounding tales that invite a sentimental, condescending reaction, or one tells adventure stories of a cruder kind. In the second case the texture with which the novelist indicates a lived life and which is a debt that the survivor owes to her past, becomes lost in the story of her escape. Karmel, after all, is not the only serious novelist who dislikes mentioning her own life.

So we walked across the Princeton campus with its fine lawns and old trees, on a brilliant day when the weather seemed to contribute to the

air of peace and privilege, a place untouched by catastrophe, so contrary and somehow incongruous with what was on our minds, two
middle-aged women speaking of a desperate time in a language that is
neither of our mother tongues and in which she has written her novels.
I wanted to tell her something about what the book meant to me, how I
see in it a validation of the past, mostly our past, but perhaps the past of
anyone who is at home in this century. I wanted to say how the book's
most pervasive paradox is suggested by its title. The women depend on
what they used to be, no matter how absorbing the details of physical
existence have become. Hope feeds on memory. Unhinged from the
world we know, our past lives are all we own, the only thing from which
we can rebuild our identities. All else can be taken from us. And
whatever can be taken, will be taken: there is no safety.

Instead I told her how I brought virtually no peacetime memories
into the camps. Like a film with a blurred beginning, my memory
starts to focus with the Hitler period. I was simply too young to have
had a past. As a result, I depended on the past of others. I felt
admiration tinged with envy for those whose minds stretched back
beyond Hitler. It was they who made me feel truly impoverished,
while I couldn't get enough of their stories. They were nostalgic,
humdrum stories about dances and dinners and swimming lessons in
the municipal pool, about Socialist and Zionist meetings, house pets,
and easy conversations with brothers and fathers. Items that I had
never used occurred in them, such as bicycles and telephones. For
these women the camps were an intermediary stage that had interposed itself between a controllable past and an imaginable future. I had
to make up my own future from *their* memories or from pure fantasies.
And all the time I suspected that I could face the present better than
they because I couldn't skip it in my imagination, since I had virtually
no comparisons. There was a tinge of contempt in my envy when it
occurred to me that they didn't always understand where they were.

The same ambivalence informs the function of future and past in
Karmel's book. Memories are a sustaining framework. Her women
recall superfluity—of food, of space in which to live, of privacy and of a
love that is not as costly in the exercise as it was in the camps.
Especially Barbara has the ability to leap from the past to the future so
that remembrance and hope collapse and become one. With that
bittersweet irony that is a hallmark of her style, Karmel describes a

figment of Barbara's imagination, an Alinka of the future, who is a brilliant schoolgirl and completely unaffected by her previous imprisonment, which has become the future perfect of that projection. Is this transcendence or escapism? The question remains suspended, but its authenticity goes beyond mere realism.

The title of the novel refers to the actual estate that Barbara owned "in the freedom," before she came to the camp, and that plays a considerable role in the flashbacks. In addition, each prisoner has an "estate." Barbara's patients, when she is an orderly, tell her of their husbands and children, "tales of riches left behind." Since the women know that their families are dead, they add "of blessed memory," so that "memory seemed an estate where those remembered had chosen to dwell." Asleep, the women call out for those whom they have lost: "Moonlight lit up the barracks. Then, blurred by sleep, a voice would call a name of long ago, another called, then another. She listened: from the estates of blessed memory the dead were coming into the night." And Tola, shortly before her death, feels herself surrounded by the dead of her family, who envelop her as if she were the spool of their thread or the pit of which they are the fruit.

It is in these rare lyrical passages that the novel reveals its final secret. For the title ultimately refers, I think, to the substance of the book. What it commemorates in the telling is after all not a gift of life and freedom, and not even hope, but merely those who held hopes that were sometimes indistinguishable from wishful thinking. The book ends with an old Polish couple picking over their mail. We learn that Alinka, the baby, and some minor characters are alive. The postwar period has begun.

The affirmations of the ending are real enough, but they are guarded, as they must be. The great catastrophe has taken place, and nothing can balance it. If freedom is a place, then we have switched places: the estate of memory is now the ditches and camps where we left the dead, blessed or not. For this is the unresolved ambiguity of this tale of two estates, that the legacy of *our* past is a history that is as hard to digest as the camp food we have been reading about. *An Estate of Memory* registers a strong and convincing "nevertheless" by allowing the redemptive qualities of its characters to be effective beyond the chaos and into the future. And that must be enough. With its seesaw between recollection and hope, its precise experimentation with the nature of friendship and human love in a borderland between life and death, *An Estate of Memory* is a novel for our time, as we look back on the century that is drawing to a close.

Ruth K. Angress
University of California, Irvine

NOTES

1. Sidra deKoven Ezrahi, *By Words Alone: The Holocaust Novel in Literature* (Chicago: The University of Chicago Press, 1980), p. 119.

The Feminist Press at The City University of New York offers alternatives in education and in literature. Founded in 1970, this nonprofit, tax-exempt educational and publishing organization works to eliminate sexual stereotypes in books and schools and to provide literature with a broad vision of human potential. The publishing program includes reprints of important works by women, feminist biographies of women, and nonsexist children's books. Curricular materials, bibliographies, directories, and two quarterly journals provide information and support for students and teachers of women's studies. In-service projects help to transform teaching methods and curricula. Through publications and projects, The Feminist Press contributes to the rediscovery of the history of women and the emergence of a more humane society.

FICTION CLASSICS FROM THE FEMINIST PRESS

Mother to Daughter, Daughter to Mother: A Daybook and Reader, selected and shaped by Tillie Olsen. $9.95 paper.

The Other Woman: Stories of Two Women and a Man. Edited by Susan Koppelman. $9.95 paper.

The Parish and the Hill, a novel by Mary Doyle Curran. Afterword by Anne Halley. $8.95 paper.

Reena and Other Stories, selected short stories by Paule Marshall. $8.95 paper.

Ripening: Selected Work, 1927–1980, 2nd edition, by Meridel Le Sueur. Edited with an introduction by Elaine Hedges. Afterword by Meridel Le Sueur. $9.95 paper.

Rope of Gold, a novel of the thirties, by Josephine Herbst. Introduction by Alice Kessler-Harris and Paul Lauter and afterword by Elinor Langer. $9.95 paper.

The Silent Partner, a novel by Elizabeth Stuart Phelps. Afterword by Mari Jo Buhle and Florence Howe. $8.95 paper.

Swastika Night, a novel by Katharine Burdekin. Introduction by Daphne Patai. $8.95 paper.

This Child's Gonna Live, a novel by Sarah E. Wright. Afterword by John Oliver Killens. $9.95 paper.

The Unpossessed, a novel of the thirties, by Tess Slesinger. Introduction by Alice Kessler-Harris and Paul Lauter and afterword by Janet Sharistanian. $9.95 paper.

Weeds, a novel by Edith Summers Kelley. Afterword by Charlotte Goodman. $8.95 paper.

The Wide, Wide World, a novel by Susan Warner. Afterword by Jane Tompkins. $29.95 cloth, $11.95 paper.

With Wings: An Anthology of Literature by and about Women with Disabilities. Edited by Marsha Saxton and Florence Howe. $29.95 cloth, $12.95 paper.

A Woman of Genius, a novel by Mary Austin. Afterword by Nancy Porter. $9.95 paper.

Women and Appletrees, a novel by Moa Martinson. Translated from the Swedish and with an afterword by Margaret S. Lacy. $8.95 paper.

The Yellow Wallpaper, by Charlotte Perkins Gilman. Afterword by Elaine Hedges. $4.50 paper.

For a free catalog, write to The Feminist Press at The City University of New York, 311 East 94 Street, New York, NY 10128. Send individual book orders to The Feminist Press, P.O. Box 1654, Hagerstown, MD 21741. Include $1.75 postage and handling for one book and 75¢ for each additional book. To order using MasterCard or Visa, call: (800) 638–3030.